Alex swung down from his horse and stalked toward her.

"Do you have any idea how close you just came to death?" he demanded softly.

"MacDunn, I—"

He grabbed her by her slim, bare shoulders, needing to touch her, to be sure she was still whole and well.

Gwendolyn stood paralyzed as MacDunn's mouth covered hers. She had never been kissed before, for no one in her clan would have dared dally with the girl marked from childhood as a witch. But even in her innocence she could feel his unleashed passion. A flame burst to life in the pit of her stomach, and her blood quickened, making her feel flushed and strange.

She leaned into his muscular frame and locked her arms around his neck, clinging to him as she urgently returned his kiss. Power seemed to emanate from him as his hands roamed her body. Pleasure washed through her as she pressed against him, and a soft cry escaped her throat.

Alex began to explore the narrow path of her back, the satin skin of her shoulders, the delicate cage of her ribs. He wanted to take this witch now, here, in the forest, to lay her down on a bed of fragrant pine and lose himself to her softness and heat. . . .

ALSO BY KARYN MONK

Surrender to a Stranger

The Rebel and the Redcoat

Once a Warrior

THE
WITCH
AND THE
WARRIOR

Karyn Monk

Bantam Books

New York Toronto

London Sydney Auckland

THE WITCH AND THE WARRIOR
A Bantam Book / May 1998

All rights reserved.

Copyright © 1998 by Karyn Monk.
Cover art copyright © 1998 by Franco Accornera.
No part of this book may be reproduced or transmitted in any form or by
any means, electronic or mechanical, including photocopying, recording, or
by any information storage and retrieval system, without permission in
writing from the publisher. For information address: Bantam Books.

If you purchased this book without a cover you should be aware that this
book is stolen property. It was reported as "unsold and destroyed" to the
publisher and neither the author nor the publisher has received any
payment for this "stripped book."

ISBN 0-553-55760-3

Published simultaneously in the United States and Canada

Bantam Books are published by Bantam Books, a division of Bantam
Doubleday Dell Publishing Group, Inc. Its trademark, consisting of the words
"Bantam Books" and the portrayal of a rooster, is Registered in U.S. Patent
and Trademark Office and in other countries. Marca Registrada. Bantam
Books, 1540 Broadway, New York, New York 10036.

PRINTED IN THE UNITED STATES OF AMERICA

OPM   10 9 8 7 6 5

FOR MY BROTHER DAVID,
WITH MUCH LOVE

THE WITCH AND THE WARRIOR

CHAPTER 1

The Highlands of Scotland
Summer 1209

Her back ached from leaning against the frigid wall, forcing her to rise with slow dignity.

Squinting against the thin veil of light spitting from a torch, she made out the beefy figure of her jailer, Sim. Two others loomed behind him, their faces nearly obscured by the darkness. She studied them a moment, then eased her grip on the small, sharply edged stone she held in her hand.

Robert was not with them.

"They're ready for ye," announced Sim. "An' a fine evenin' for it, too," he added, the black cave of his rotting mouth twisting with malevolent pleasure. "The wind is just right."

Battling the desire to smash her fist into his face, Gwendolyn stepped forward.

"Give me yer hands," he ordered, brandishing a rough length of rope.

Her fingers clenched into fists, hiding her pitiful weapon as the cord bit into her wrists. She could not imagine what Robert feared she might do as she was escorted to her death by these burly warriors. When her bonds were painfully secure, the two men grabbed her by the arms and shoved her into the dim corridor. The stench of unwashed flesh, rotting food, and human excrement filled her lungs. She moved swiftly along the slime-coated passage, her feet splashing in murky pools of water. A clump of fur scurried across her path. She stopped with a gasp.

The warriors laughed.

"A witch afraid of a wee rat!" snorted one. "Don't ye bite their heads off afore ye bleed them into yer potions?"

"Why don't ye just cast a spell on him, like ye did yer poor father?" taunted the other.

"I'm saving my powers for the spell I plan to cast over you," Gwendolyn replied, deriving bitter enjoyment from his sudden fear.

They climbed the staircase to the main level of the castle. Here the terrible stench of the dungeons gave way to the heavy redolence of spilled ale and roasting meat. A magnificent feast was being prepared to celebrate her death, and all the clan had been invited to join Laird MacSween and his family on this glorious occasion. The greasy reek of charred animal flesh churned her stomach. She hurried past the smirking guards at the door and stepped out into the warm evening air.

"There she is!" someone shrieked hysterically.

"Witch!" hissed a wild-eyed girl, clutching her baby against her breast. "Ye've given my wee babe the fever!"

"Evil murderess!" snarled a skinny youth who didn't look to be more than thirteen. "It was you who killed my mother last month, wasn't it?"

"And ye caused my poor son to crush his leg beneath that tree," cried an agonized woman with graying hair, "leavin' him a cripple, ye whore of Satan!"

Everyone in the crowd began hurling awful names and accusations at her, their faces contorted with hatred, their bodies braced for violence. Gwendolyn stopped, afraid.

"Come on, witch," growled one of the guards. "Move." He gave her a push, and she stumbled.

The crowd instantly surged forward, clawing at her hair, her face, her gown.

"Devil's bitch!"

"Spawn of Satan!"

"Filthy harlot!"

Gwendolyn was terrified. She raised her bound arms in a vain attempt to shield her face as her clan rained blows on her back and shoulders. When she could bear no more, she fell to her knees.

"Enough!" roared an enraged voice from somewhere beyond the fray. "Cease, or I'll tear out your hearts!"

Her attackers hesitated, uncertain who had spoken. They looked questioningly toward the scarlet-and-gold-draped dais on which Laird MacSween reposed with his wife, his young son, and his brother, Robert.

"It seems our guest, Laird MacDunn, has little stomach for justice," observed Robert dryly. He sighed. "Never mind. It is going to be a spectacular fire. Allow the witch to proceed to the stake."

"Yes," added Laird MacSween, not wanting it to appear his brother was giving an order without his consensus. "Let the witch pass."

Her ring of tormentors eroded, and Gwendolyn was roughly hauled to her feet. She did not spare a glance toward the dais, where she knew Robert would be watching her triumphantly. Instead she fixed her gaze on the crudely constructed platform ahead of her, on which a slender stake had been erected.

The structure was high, to allow everyone in the clan a good view of her death, and had been strategically positioned at the end of the courtyard near the outer wall, as far from the castle as possible. This, Robert had informed her, was because Laird MacSween's wife and daughter had complained that if the stake was placed in the middle of the courtyard, the stench of Gwendolyn's burning flesh would waft into the windows and offend their delicate senses for days. Robert had been equally solicitous about the time of day for her execution. Early evening, he decided, would be best, so the flames could burn brilliantly against the advancing darkness, yet her lovely face would not be veiled by the shadows of night.

As she walked through the pearly, fading light, Gwendolyn felt a warm breath of wind caress her skin. Her jailer had been right, she realized dispassionately.

It was a fine evening.

Dry branches and peat had been heaped on the platform and below it, needing only a spark to burst into flame. Gwendolyn slowly mounted the steps, trying not to contemplate the heat of such a fire. It wasn't her death that she feared, but the method of it. Drowning would have been preferable, or even having her throat slashed. But burning was the execution decreed for those condemned of witchcraft.

Robert had hoped her fear of such a hideous death would break her will and she would finally reveal to him the hiding place of the jewel.

But he had miscalculated her desire to live.

She took her place on the platform and raised her wrists so the guard could slash open the rope. Her arms were wrenched behind her around the stake and bound again, and another cord secured her body to the pike. In the process of burning, the stake would hold her upright and keep her from falling in a crumpled heap into the flames. She found the thought comforting. Somehow, it seemed more dignified to die standing.

After her escorts left her, the abundantly nourished Father Thomas haltingly ascended the platform steps.

"Well, Gwendolyn, are you ready to finally confess your sins and beg God's forgiveness for the evil path you have chosen?" he demanded loudly, so his audience would be certain to hear.

She turned her head away from his ale-soured breath. "I have committed no sins, Father."

Father Thomas frowned. "Come, now, lass, you will soon be facing God. He will send you straight to hell, where you will burn for all eternity, unless you plead for forgiveness now."

"Not even a priest can help you, evil bitch!" a man shouted furiously.

"Nor the devil!" added another.

Gwendolyn eyed Father Thomas steadily. "And if I do confess, will I find mercy here, amongst my own people?"

"You are guilty of murder and witchcraft," he pointed out, shaking his head. He turned toward his audience, raised his arms, and finished grandly, "No woman guilty of such vile crimes shall escape the everlasting torment of hell—for *'the Lord will swallow them up in his wrath; and fire will consume them'*!"

The crowd cheered.

She considered this for a moment. "If I have no hope of avoiding death, then I see no reason why I should refrain from confiding in you, Father."

He looked startled, but quickly composed himself. He nodded sagely and folded his hands on the great swell of his belly. "God is listening, Gwendolyn," he assured her.

"I am innocent. Consider that as you sit at the laird's table tonight dressed in your finest robes, and gorge yourself on enough meat and ale to feed a child for a month. Reflect on the fact that you murdered me, Father, and pray that you don't choke."

His round face grew crimson with fury. "How dare you speak so to a man of God!"

"If you really were a man of God, you would have tried to protect me instead of destroy me."

"This is the devil talking. You were just a child when your mother was burned, but evidently you were old enough for her to pass her wicked ways on to her daughter."

"My mother was no more guilty of witchcraft than I."

"You will burn, Gwendolyn MacSween, so that your black soul can be sent straight to hell, where it belongs." He quickly made the sign of the cross, then began his labored descent down the stairs.

"God will know I have done nothing wrong," she countered, "and when He realizes I was murdered, it is *you* who will be going to hell."

"Burn her!" screamed someone from the crowd. "Before she works more of her deviltry on us!"

The crowd rumbled with agreement and began to chant, "Burn her—burn her—burn her!"

Laird Cedric MacSween rose from his seat and carefully unraveled a scroll. "Gwendolyn MacSween, you have been found guilty of the charges of witchcraft and murder. According to witnesses, evidence of your evil powers first became apparent some twelve years ago, when several children in your presence saw you cast a spell over a rock, causing it to fly through the air, until it eventually transformed into a bird. That was the same summer four beloved members of our clan died of causes that have since been attributed to your foul sorcery. . . ."

Robert was watching Gwendolyn from his place beside his brother, his expression resigned, his fingers drumming impatiently on the arm of his ornately carved chair. They both knew it was too late for him to stop this travesty of justice. He had condemned her in a moment of panic, and by doing so, he had lost all hope of acquiring the one thing he so desperately wanted. With her death, the power of the jewel would elude him forever. She tossed him a derisive smile filled with triumph, as if she were the victor in this battle. Then she jerked her gaze away, unable to stomach the sight of him a moment longer.

If, by some miracle, she did have a spiritual existence after this world, she vowed to spend it tormenting Robert to his grave.

Her attention shifted to someone she did not recognize, an imposing stranger mounted on a gray charger, positioned in a place of honor near the laird's dais. This must be Mad MacDunn, she decided. When Robert visited her for a final time early this morning, he had told her Mad Alex MacDunn had just arrived in search of her. On learning she was sentenced to death, he had offered to buy her. Of course his offer was not accepted. But because Laird MacDunn and his men had journeyed far, Laird MacSween graciously invited them to stay and witness her burning, and enjoy the glorious feast afterward. This was the man, then, who had ordered her clan to stop beating her. Perhaps he'd been impatient to get on with the burning.

He was a startling figure of a man, tall and broadly cut, with a wide chest, enormous shoulders, and muscled arms that could easily wield the heavy broadsword glinting at his side. His shoulder-length hair was the palest of gold and of a thickness and shimmer that would make any woman envious, which seemed incongruous with the rest of his ruggedly masculine physique. She could not see his face, because in that terrible moment, as she was about to be burned alive, he was incomprehensibly absorbed with the task of rearranging the already meticulous folds of his plaid.

Unaware of being watched, MacDunn carefully adjusted the deep green and yellow fabric of his plaid and straightened his leather belt. When his outfit was finally fitted to his liking, he glanced at the silver brooch tacking his mantle to his shoulder, frowned, and began to fastidiously polish the already gleaming piece with his sleeve. This action caused him to raise his head, revealing a handsomely sculpted face with a wide, firm jaw, a deeply grooved chin, and well-defined cheekbones. He seemed determined to elicit more shine from his jewelry and rubbed away at it with great concentration.

Only when a serving boy approached him with a tray of refreshments did he reluctantly permit himself to be distracted from his task. He studied the platter of fruit and drink, then withdrew a heavily jeweled dirk from his belt and delicately speared a large red apple. He examined it and, evidently finding some flaw, returned the offending fruit to the tray and chose another. He buffed it well against his plaid before nibbling at it. In that moment, perhaps sensing that he was being watched, he suddenly raised his head and looked at her. His expression was infuriatingly insouciant—the look of a man who had few cares in his life and did not intend to let something as insignificant as her death detract him from either his attire or his hunger.

". . . And because of these *unholy* activities, the fact that you bear the unmistakable mark of the devil on your person, and finally, the *vile* murder of your *own father,* a crime so *fiendish,* it could only be work of a filthy *whore* who lies with the *devil* . . ." ranted Laird MacSween, emphasizing as many words as possible for dramatic effect.

MacDunn studied her a moment, idly twirling his apple on his sparkling dirk, no doubt wondering if she was really capable of committing all the dreadful deeds of which she stood accused. She glared back at him, wondering for what base purpose he had sought to purchase her. His expression remained bland, but there was an intensity to his gaze that was strangely incompatible with his fatuous, lean-witted manner. His scrutiny was unnerving. It made her feel as if he were penetrating the protective shield of her anger, searching for the real woman beneath. A ripple of heat coursed through her, rendering her oddly breathless. MacDunn regarded her another few seconds, then suddenly dropped his gaze to his apple and resumed pecking at it, as if she no longer merited his attention.

Shaken and humiliated, Gwendolyn looked away.

Laird MacSween continued to read the list of charges against her. The MacSweens listened with rowdy enjoyment, regularly interrupting to hurl some crude insult at her. It seemed everyone in her clan was crammed into the courtyard to witness her death, from the tiniest of infants to the frailest of elders. Judging by their fiercely righteous expressions, it was clear they believed they were merely carrying out God's will on this day. She scanned the crush of faces, vainly searching for a scrap of pity or compassion. But the MacSweens had feared and ostracized her for as long as she could remember, and there was no one she could call a friend, who might feel empathy for her. She did, however, notice another stranger, whom she assumed was a warrior of Mad MacDunn's, as he sported the same dark green and yellow plaid. He was a huge bear of a man, with long, fiery red hair and a thick red beard. His considerable bulk had enabled him to force his way through the crowd and he now stood just below the platform, swaying drunkenly as he lifted a bucket of ale to his mouth. The dark brew sloshed down his face and chest, soaking his shirt and plaid before it dripped onto the ground. Finally, when it appeared his enormous body could absorb no more, he lowered the bucket, wiped his mouth with his arm, and expelled the most resounding belch Gwendolyn had ever heard.

The crowd roared with laughter, causing Laird MacSween to pause and regard them in confusion.

"Your pardon, MacSween," apologized the warrior thickly. " 'Tis an exceptionally spirited ale." With that he raised the bucket and began to drink once more.

Disgusted, she shifted her gaze, only to notice another MacDunn warrior perched in the second-floor opening of a window, his slim legs dangling against the castle wall. This slight fellow was almost elfin compared to his burly clansmen, and only the light brown growth upon his cheek assured Gwendolyn he was actually a man and not a boy. Though he had managed to procure a most enviable seat, he appeared uninterested in the drama playing before him in the courtyard and was absorbed, instead, in whittling a stick.

Another MacDunn warrior with dark hair and a neatly trimmed beard leaned casually against the outer wall, shamelessly flirting with Laird MacSween's daughter, Isabella. Clearly he held Isabella enchanted. He leaned inappropriately close to her, his lips nearly grazing her hair as he whispered something into her ear. She raised her hand to her throat in feigned shock and giggled prettily. Gwendolyn watched her with irritation. As Laird MacSween's only daughter, Isabella did not have a worry in life beyond what gown she was going to wear that day and which of her many suitors she might ultimately decide to wed.

Meanwhile, while Mad MacDunn and his boorish warriors were engaged in coy seduction, crafting toys, or getting blinding drunk, Gwendolyn awaited her death by burning at the stake.

". . . therefore the *devil* within her *must* be sent back to the fires of *hell,* so she can no longer unleash *death* and *destruction* on this clan," finished Laird MacSween.

"Burn the bloody bitch!"

"Quickly, before she casts more of her evil upon us!"

"Burn her, burn her, burn her . . ." The chant rose like a prayer, until the entire clan was demanding her death.

As Gwendolyn stared at their snarling faces, she understood the utter despair her mother must have endured on the day she was executed. But her mother had suffered more, for she had died leaving an anguished husband and a tiny daughter. At least Gwendolyn left no one behind. Her father was dead and was therefore spared the horror of watching his child die as her mother had died before her. There was some solace in that, she assured herself, fighting the tears that stung her eyes.

"Light the fire," commanded Laird MacSween, striving to be heard above the chanting crowd.

The clan raised their arms in the air and cheered.

Two men stepped forward bearing torches. Gwendolyn's breathing grew shallow. She braced herself against the stake.

Please God, let me faint before the flames begin to devour my flesh.

She hurled one last, hate-filled look at Robert. He lounged back in his chair and regarded her with something akin to triumph, but she knew his victory was hollow.

You'll never have the jewel now, you bastard.

The first torch began its descent. Terror gripped her, but she willed herself not to whimper.

One guard smiled as his torch hovered just above the dried grasses and branches. "Away with you, witch," he snarled. "To the fires of—"

She waited for him to say *hell,* but all that came out was a stifled groan. Gwendolyn watched in confusion as his eyes widened, then rolled upward. With a sigh, he collapsed heavily onto the ground, the jeweled hilt of a dirk protruding from his back, his fallen torch abandoned in the branches.

The other torchbearer stared at his dead partner in shock. Then he tossed his torch onto the arid nest at her feet.

The red-haired, drunken warrior at her left heaved his bucket of ale over it, extinguishing the flames. Then he slammed the pail hard onto the guard's head, spun him around, and gave him a solid kick to his backside, sending him flying into the crowd of astonished MacSweens.

"What's happening?" demanded Laird MacSween, straining to see through the crowd. "Is that red-haired fellow truly so drunk—"

"*Stop him!*" roared Robert as Mad MacDunn began to gallop toward the stake. He sprang to his feet, knocking over his chair. "*Stop MacDunn!*"

The flames from the first torch had spread hungrily through the branches untouched by ale and were now lapping at the hem of Gwendolyn's gown. The bear warrior leaped onto the platform and hacked at the ropes binding her to the stake as Mad MacDunn thundered forward on his horse, his great broadsword raised high in warning to anyone foolish enough to get in his way. The astonished MacSweens obligingly parted, realizing he truly was mad, or perhaps thinking this was some terrible feat of magic Gwendolyn was working. As MacDunn reached the burning platform, Gwendolyn felt the last rope give way. She started to fall, but the enormous warrior easily lifted her off her limp legs and threw her onto MacDunn's horse.

"Hold on to me!" commanded MacDunn. He jerked her arm forward around his waist.

One of Robert's men was racing toward them, his sword aimed at the chest of MacDunn's horse. "You'll not get away so easy, MacDunn," he swore, drawing back his blade.

An arrow sliced through the air and neatly punctured the warrior's back. Gwendolyn glanced up to see the elflike warrior in the window positioning another sharply carved arrow against the string of his bow.

"Surround them!" shouted Robert, jumping from the dais and running toward his own horse. "Don't let them escape!"

MacDunn began to thrash mercilessly with his sword at the advancing crowd, forcing them to part as he urged his horse toward the gate. Gwendolyn clung to him, her arms wrapped around his waist, aware of the power emanating from him as his muscles shifted and flexed beneath her hands. His plaid was soft against her skin, but the body it covered was rock-hard, and she leaned closer, drawing courage from his strength.

Someone grabbed her leg and began to drag her off the charger.

"MacDunn!" she cried.

MacDunn turned and drove his sword into the man, then swiftly pulled the dripping blade out and speared another MacSween who had been about to hack his ribs open with an ax. The man crashed heavily against MacDunn's horse, causing the animal to rear. Gwendolyn began to slide backward. MacDunn's hand clamped painfully onto her arm and held her fast as he continued to use his other arm to hack at anyone daring to come near them.

"Hold on!" he commanded furiously.

In that instant Gwendolyn saw another of Robert's warriors taking aim at MacDunn with his bow and arrow. Suddenly remembering the sharp stone hidden in her hand, she hurled it through the air. The warrior howled and dropped his weapon, then raised his fingers tentatively to the ugly cut leaking blood just below his eye.

"Jesus Christ," muttered MacDunn.

Gwendolyn sensed he was impressed, but he wasted no time thanking her, for they had nearly reached the gate.

"The gate!" bellowed Robert, who by now had mounted his own horse and was thundering toward them. "*Close the bloody gate!*"

The MacSweens surged toward the gate, each one clamoring to get there first. This resulted in a great deal of tripping, cursing, and ultimately wrestling among themselves. From the corner of her eye, Gwendolyn could see both the bear warrior and the elf were now mounted and racing toward the break in the curtain wall.

She leaned into MacDunn and pressed her face into the warmth of his plaid.

Thank you, God.

The wooden portcullis crashed to the ground.

Having reached the end of the courtyard, MacDunn was forced to abruptly halt his horse. The snorting animal reared once more.

"You really must be mad, MacDunn," Robert called out scornfully as he rode up to them, "to attempt such a ridiculous abduction."

It was over, Gwendolyn realized. For some reason these men had risked their lives to save her, but they had failed. Now they would all be killed.

"I am sorry," she said to MacDunn, her voice ragged. "You shouldn't have tried. Now you will all die." She eased her grip on his waist, preparing to slide off his charger and meet her fate.

His hand clamped firmly over her wrist, holding her to him.

"I really think you should open the gate and let us pass, MacSween," said MacDunn pleasantly, ignoring Robert.

Laird MacSween, who had not ventured from his honored seat on the dais, looked uncertainly at Robert.

"I don't believe you quite understand your situation, Laird MacDunn," drawled Robert, his tone heavily mocking. "Permit me to enlighten you. You are surrounded by my warriors."

MacDunn lifted a brow in surprise. "Forgive me. I was under the impression that your brother was laird."

"He is," Robert conceded stiffly, "but *I* lead the Mac-Sween army. And by my estimation, there are but three of you against hundreds," he added, gesturing to his clan.

"You are right," agreed MacDunn, not sounding overly concerned. "But if you do not permit us to leave, I am afraid we will have no choice but to kill her."

Gwendolyn gasped and tried to wrench her hand away. MacDunn tightened his grip, holding her fast.

Robert regarded him in disbelief. And then he threw back his head and laughed. "This is your threat to me?" he sputtered. "By God, it seems you really are light in the head. Kill her, then, MacDunn, if it pleases you. You will merely be saving me the trouble."

"Really?" said MacDunn. He appeared genuinely perplexed. "I would have thought you were fonder of her than that."

Robert's amusement increased. "I care nothing for her," he assured MacDunn. "Do what you will."

MacDunn contemplated this a moment, then shrugged his shoulders. "Very well, then. Kill her, Brodick."

Gwendolyn squirmed to get down, but MacDunn did not release his iron grip.

"*Papa!*"

Everyone turned and gasped. Isabella was seated on a horse in front of the same MacDunn warrior who moments earlier had been making her breathless with desire. Her need for air seemed even greater now, but that obviously had something to do with the dagger he was pressing to her throat.

Laird MacSween's wife stood, screamed, then fainted dead away.

"Are you sure you want her dead, MacDunn?" asked Brodick. "She's rather comely."

"I don't want her dead at all," MacDunn assured him. "Robert does. He doesn't care for her."

"Release her!" snarled Robert.

"Really, Robert, I wish you would make up your mind," said MacDunn. "You just finished telling me I should kill her."

"You know bloody well I wasn't talking about Isabella!"

"Then who would you like me to kill?" asked MacDunn, trying to be patient.

"Papa, do something!" pleaded Isabella.

Laird MacSween opened his mouth to speak but was instantly cut off by his brother.

"What can you possibly want with this witch?" Robert's expression was reserved, but Gwendolyn knew he feared MacDunn had somehow learned of the stone. Affecting a more persuasive tone, he added, "Surely you must realize that by stealing one of our clan, you risk war."

"I am mad," replied MacDunn, shrugging. "Mad men do mad things. Besides"—he tilted his head toward the blaze now raging around the stake—"I thought you were finished with her."

"She is evil," Robert persisted gravely. "And a murderess. You cannot take her, MacDunn. She must be killed or she will destroy you and your people."

MacDunn smiled. "Thank you, Robert, for your concern. I am deeply touched. Now raise the portcullis or Brodick will slit fair Isabella's throat."

Robert hesitated.

"Papa, make them open the gate!" squealed Isabella.

Laird MacSween finally rose from his chair. "Surely you are not so heartless, Laird MacDunn, that you would kill a helpless young woman."

MacDunn studied the anguished father a moment. Then he sighed. "You're right, MacSween," he conceded. "I'm not."

Robert smiled, realizing his adversary was now trapped.

"But Brodick is," MacDunn assured him pleasantly. "Aren't you, Brodick?"

"Aye," replied Brodick, giving Isabella a little squeeze.

Isabella whimpered.

"Raise the portcullis," ordered Laird MacSween, "and let them go."

Gwendolyn watched as Robert battled his frustration. Reluctantly, he lowered his sword.

"Now, that is the decision of a rational man," commented MacDunn appreciatively. "I'm impressed. Your entire clan will fall back, Laird MacSween, permitting us to ride through the gate. If anyone attempts to harm us as we leave, or if any of your fine warriors come after us tonight, Brodick will cut your charming daughter's throat. If, however, you exercise patience and restraint, then fair Isabella will be released unharmed tomorrow morning. I am certain with their considerable abilities, Robert and his men will have no trouble finding her and returning her safely to you."

"I will have your word, MacDunn," said Laird MacSween, "that she will not be harmed."

MacDunn regarded him seriously. "You have my word."

Satisfied, and having no other choice, Laird MacSween signaled for the portcullis to rise.

"His word is nothing!" protested Robert, enraged. "He is a madman!"

"So they say," agreed MacDunn cheerfully, adjusting his plaid as his warriors rode through the open gate.

"You know, you were absolutely right, Robert," he reflected, tossing a final glance at the burning stake. "It really is a spectacular fire."

He winked at him, then turned and thundered into the advancing darkness, leaving the MacSweens staring in bewilderment.

CHAPTER 2

She was a prisoner again.

MacDunn and his warriors had ridden hard for several hours, not speaking once during the journey. Gwendolyn had found the pace exhausting, but her weariness was nothing compared to her exhilaration at finally being free. She had turned her face into the wind and felt it blow softly against her, washing away the stench of smoke and death and hatred, cleansing her senses of even the foulness of the castle dungeons, until she was aware only of the warm summer night and the freedom that loomed for miles around her. She had leaned close and tightened her hold on MacDunn, vowing to somehow repay this mad, magnificent laird who had risked everything so she could live.

That was before he hauled her off his horse, bound her aching wrists, and tied her to a tree, along with Isabella.

"You cannot treat me this way!" wailed Isabella loudly,

struggling against her bonds. "I am the daughter of Laird MacSween! You cannot leave me here tied to this evil witch!"

"For God's sake, Brodick, can't you get her to be quiet?" grumbled MacDunn.

Brodick withdrew an oatcake from his saddle bag and sauntered over to his captive. "You must be tired, m'lady," he remarked sympathetically. "And hungry, too, I'd wager."

"How dare you speak to me, you savage brute!" Isabella flared. "I hate you!"

"Bella, you wound me," replied Brodick, looking injured. "I never meant you any harm."

"Liar," she hissed. "One word from your mad laird, and you would have savagely hacked open my throat."

"Never," he protested, his tone soothing. "Your throat is far too lovely to mar. Here, I've brought you something to eat," he added, offering her the oatcake.

"I'd sooner swallow the blackest, foulest of poisons than accept something from a scurrilous knave like you," she assured him haughtily. "And when my father's men come, they will take great pleasure in slowly carving you open so you can watch your hot, bloody entrails fall out piece by dripping piece and steam upon the cold ground!"

"Such an inspiring image," Brodick marveled. "Have you ever actually seen them do that?"

"Dozens of times!" she snapped. "After which they will flay you, cut you into tiny pieces, and then feed you to the wolves!"

"Now, that doesn't make any sense, sweet Bella," he remarked, shaking his head. "Why would they go to the trouble of flaying me if they are just going to cut me up?"

"They will do it because *it will amuse me to watch*!" she screeched.

The noise was like an ax splitting Alex MacDunn's skull. "Brodick," he began tautly, "I cannot endure much more of this."

"Have some oatcake, m'lady," Brodick suggested, trying to tempt her with the biscuit. "You'll feel much better if you eat something."

"I already told you," Isabella raged, "I'd sooner swallow—"

"Poison," finished Brodick, shoving a large chunk of biscuit in her mouth, effectively gagging her.

"A pity we don't have some," muttered Alex.

"There, now," said Brodick, as Isabella struggled to chew the dry oatcake. "That should keep you occupied for a moment, at least. What about you, fair Gwendolyn?" he continued, moving to her side of the tree. "Would you care for some food?"

She glared at him.

"You should eat something," he persisted, raising a morsel to her lips. "It isn't much, but it is better than the hollow ache of hunger."

"Get away from me," she warned softly, "or I will cast a spell that will cause your most valued extremity to shrivel up and fall off."

Brodick's eyes widened with uncertainty. And then he hastily retreated to his place with MacDunn and the other warriors.

"By God, Brodick, I can't remember the last time you were rejected by a woman," laughed Cameron, the bear warrior, slapping his friend heartily on the shoulder. "But to see you rebuffed by two women in the same night, 'tis almost more than a man could hope for."

"Their bondage puts them in shrewish spirits," protested Brodick defensively. He glanced at MacDunn. "Really, Alex, is it necessary to—"

"They are prisoners," he interrupted firmly. "I'm not of a mind to be searching the woods for them tonight, should they decide to escape. They will remain as they are."

Brodick did not argue. It was clear that MacDunn's word was final.

The laird may have been mad, but it was obvious to Gwendolyn that his warriors trusted and respected him. Although her rescue had been daring to the point of folly, he had been successful. And during their retreat through the dark mountains and woods, he had never once faltered in his route, using the stars as his guide as he led them across the black terrain. He paced the horses well, riding them far beyond what Gwendolyn would have imagined were the limits of their endurance.

When MacDunn finally ordered the men to make camp, the night had grown cool and damp, but he rejected the comfort of a fire and hot food, for fear Robert and his warriors might see it, or even smell the scent of it on the wind. Instead the warriors ate a mean dinner of hard biscuits, washed down with tepid ale. Gwendolyn was starving, but fury and what little remained of her tattered pride prohibited her from nibbling from the hand of her jailer like some trapped animal.

"Cameron, you and Ned take the first watch," commanded Alex, removing his sword and lowering himself onto the ground. "Let's hope MacSween's fear for his daughter makes him heed my terms and not send his warriors out until morning."

"He will not wait," Gwendolyn assured him.

"No, he most certainly will not," agreed Isabella hotly, finally managing to swallow the last of the oatcake. "And when his warriors get here, they will strip your flesh from your bones, shred it into tiny bits, and stuff it into your own bowels, before roasting you over a fire."

"By God, you're a bloodthirsty woman!" roared Cameron, thoroughly amused. "How did such a milksop of a father sire a daughter with such a fiery tongue?"

"How dare you insult my father! He is laird of all the MacSweens—"

"Sweet Jesus, I shall count the seconds until we free that one," groaned Alex. "Once the MacSweens find her tomorrow, I doubt Robert will come after us. He's not likely to risk any more men for the sake of a witch who was meant to die anyway."

"Robert will come," Gwendolyn countered. "And when he does, he will not be satisfied by Isabella's safe return."

Alex regarded her curiously. "You think he will come after you?"

She said nothing.

"Why?" he persisted. "You were about to be burned. Why would he risk more of his men just to recapture you?"

"Robert is determined to see me destroyed," she replied, offering part of the truth. "He will not rest until it is done."

So MacDunn did not know about the stone, Gwendolyn realized, relieved. Whatever his motive for saving her, it was not because he sought its powers.

"She is a witch," Isabella added fearfully. "You have heard all the terrible things she has done to our clan. And she viciously murdered her own father."

"How?" asked Brodick.

"She cast a spell on him." Isabella's expression was grave.

"What kind of spell?" asked MacDunn, studying Gwendolyn. He appeared more intrigued than concerned that she might do the same to one of them.

"A death spell," Isabella clarified impatiently, as if the answer were obvious.

"That's it?" said Brodick. "No rotting flesh, or agonizing illness, or limbs dropping off for no apparent reason? Just 'a death spell'?" He sounded disappointed.

"His death was hideously painful," Isabella assured him, sensing that her story was not having the desired impact. "Robert said her father staggered around in agony, clutching his chest and begging his daughter to stop as she slowly drew his very soul from him."

"And how did Robert know this?" inquired MacDunn, his gaze never leaving Gwendolyn.

"He was there," Isabella explained. "And thank God he was, else we might never have been able to prove that she was responsible for the dark deed."

Gwendolyn fought to control her rage and despair at this spurious account of her father's death. She returned MacDunn's scrutiny with deliberate calm, neither confirming nor denying the horrible allegation. She did not know why he had stolen her, but her bondage made it clear Laird MacDunn had not been motivated by pity or gallantry. It was better he fear her, or at the very least be wary of her abilities.

Suddenly Ned, the elfin warrior, dropped down from the

tree above, whispered something into MacDunn's ear, then turned and pointed into the darkness. MacDunn quickly signaled Ned into the woods, while Cameron and Brodick withdrew their swords and disappeared into the shadows. MacDunn then hurried over to Gwendolyn and Isabella.

"It seems we have company," he declared softly, slicing the ropes binding them to the tree. "It could be the gallant MacSweens coming to rescue you, Isabella . . ."

Isabella brightened.

". . . or it could be drunken thieves who will rape you repeatedly before cutting your throats. As I'm not of a mind to permit either to happen," he continued, binding their tied wrists together, "you will hide beyond these trees and keep quiet until I tell you it is safe to return. If either of you get any foolish notions about trying to escape, be warned—if the wolves don't find you, I will." His tone suggested being mauled by wolves would be preferable.

Gwendolyn watched as he vanished into the darkness.

"We can't just stay here," protested Isabella nervously. "We must try to—"

A strangled groan pierced the night.

"By God, MacDunn," thundered Robert's furious voice, "show yourself and fight like a real warrior!"

"Robert!" squealed Isabella. "I'm over—"

"Squeak again and I'll turn you into a rat," hissed Gwendolyn. "Do you understand?"

Isabella whimpered and nodded.

Alex swiftly withdrew his sword from the belly of a MacSween, then spun around to deflect the blow of another. His attacker's blade forced him to leap back. The weapon's point sliced into his shirt, and he was vaguely aware of a stinging sensation in his chest. He raised his sword and buried it deep into his opponent's gut.

"Damn you, MacDunn," cursed the warrior, sinking to his knees, "you've got the devil on your side." He grunted, then fell onto his face.

Warm blood was seeping into Alex's shirt, but he ignored the pain. The ringing and scraping of steel told him Cameron and Brodick were well occupied. He cautiously moved forward, searching the veil of trees for more MacSweens.

Suddenly a huge brute of a man leaped out from behind a tree, his ax poised to split Alex's skull open. Before the weapon began its descent, the warrior gasped, took a faltering step, then collapsed. An arrow protruded from his back. Alex looked up to find Ned's small form perched on a branch, another arrow already taut against the string of his bow. Alex followed his aim and saw Robert moving toward him through the darkness, unaware that he was about to die.

Alex raised his hand, signaling for Ned to hold.

"Good evening, Robert," he called pleasantly. "I must confess, I wasn't expecting you quite so soon."

"I'm sure you weren't," Robert sneered. "I prefer to surprise my enemies."

"Enemies?" repeated Alex, sounding surprised. "But what a sad turn of events this is, when just hours ago you so graciously invited me to attend your marvelous witch burning. You know," he continued conversationally, planting the tip of his sword in the ground and leaning against it, "I was really looking forward to that feast."

"You should have kept out of it, MacDunn," Robert advised, moving closer. "You were a fool to think I wouldn't come after you."

"Oh, but I knew you were coming," Alex assured him. "Gwendolyn told me you would. Her powers of perception are quite extraordinary."

Concern flashed across Robert's face, but he was quick to master it. "What else did she tell you?" he demanded, closing the distance between them.

"Everything," Alex promptly lied. "In fact, we had quite a long talk." He idly adjusted the folds of his plaid. "She really is an intriguing creature, isn't she? I can understand why you want her back."

"I want her back so justice can be carried out," Robert replied shortly. "She is a witch and a murderess."

"Ah, yes, that nasty business about her father. Fortuitous that you were there to witness it, wasn't it, Robert?"

"Where is she?" demanded Robert, taking another step forward.

"Actually, I'm not sure," Alex replied, shrugging. "She is hiding somewhere out there," he added, gesturing vaguely with his hand. "I honestly don't believe she is anxious to see you."

"Bring her to me," commanded Robert, raising his sword, "or I will carve you into a dozen bloody pieces, MacDunn."

"You know, Robert, I do find it a bit puzzling that you have not yet inquired about your dear niece's welfare. A charming girl, that Isabella, despite her penchant for rather disagreeable threats. No doubt she gets that from you?" he suggested brightly, making it seem a compliment.

"Bring Gwendolyn to me, you mad fool!" snapped Robert. "Or I'll splay you wide like a fish and pull out your—"

"There, now," interrupted Alex, "you see what I mean?"

"By God, MacDunn, you've had your chance," snarled Robert, drawing back his sword.

"Now, that would not be prudent," observed Alex, his own weapon still comfortably acting as a crutch. "Would it, Ned?"

"No," agreed Ned, from his perch in the tree above him.

Startled, Robert looked up.

"You know, I really don't think you would enjoy having an arrow in your chest," Alex remarked.

"Or a sword in your belly," said Cameron, appearing through the trees.

"Or a dirk in your eye," added Brodick, standing beside him.

Robert hesitated. Realizing he had no choice, he threw his blade onto the ground.

"I believe I'd like your dirk also," said Alex. "I seem to have misplaced mine in the back of one of your warriors."

Robert scowled, then withdrew his dirk from his belt and tossed it beside his sword.

"Excellent. Now, as you have no weapons, and as we were forced to kill the warriors you brought with you—"

"You couldn't have killed them all," objected Robert.

"Well, I distinctly remember killing at least two," Alex said. "What about you, Brodick?"

"I killed two as well," Brodick replied.

"And I finished off three," added Cameron, moving behind Robert. "How many did you kill, Ned?"

"Three."

Alex counted on his fingers. "I believe that makes ten. How many warriors did you bring, Robert?" he asked curiously.

Robert's face was nearly crimson with rage. "Damn you, MacDunn! This means war!"

"Now, don't blame yourself," soothed Alex. "After all, there were eleven of you, and eleven against four does seem like good odds. Listen, you've had a difficult day, and it doesn't seem to be getting any better. Have a good night's rest, and things will seem far better in the morning."

"I've no intention of resting, you dull-witted clod!" Robert raved. "I may be your prisoner, but I intend to—"

Cameron slammed the hilt of his sword on Robert's head. Robert sighed and sank to the ground.

"He'll sleep like a babe," Cameron assured Alex.

"Good. Tie him to a tree, just in case he wakens early," instructed Alex, moving back toward the camp. "Maybe now we can finally get some sleep."

Gwendolyn searched the darkness, debating whether she should take her chances and try to escape with Isabella. The fighting seemed to have come to an end, but she wasn't sure who had emerged the victor. A tall figure appeared through the trees. Moonlight washed over him as he stepped into the clearing, leaving no doubt that it was MacDunn's enormous frame she beheld.

His shirt was soaked in blood.

"You're hurt," she gasped, emerging from her hiding place with Isabella in tow.

"I told you my father's men would carve you open," Isabella said with dark satisfaction. "I told you they would shred your flesh—"

"Brodick, cut Isabella loose and bring her here," ordered Alex brusquely.

"Why?" Isabella demanded, suddenly nervous.

"You are going to repair the damage your father's men have done to us," Alex informed her.

"I won't!" she protested as Brodick cut the ropes binding her to Gwendolyn.

"Forgive me, sweet Bella, but you would be wise to do as MacDunn says," Brodick advised, pulling Isabella across the clearing. "And after you've finished, I've a scratch to my arm that needs tending as well."

"And I've a split in my scalp," added Cameron.

"I won't help you!" she raged. "I hope each of you bleeds to death from your injuries, you vile, thieving, murdering scum!"

Alex stripped off his shirt, revealing a pulsing slash across his upper chest. "You will fix this," he commanded. "Now."

Isabella took one look at the blood dripping down his torso and promptly fainted.

Cameron roared with laughter. "It seems the lass's tongue is stronger than her stomach!"

"She is tired," protested Brodick, gently gathering Isabella's crumpled form in his arms. "She has had an exhausting day." He carried her across the clearing and lowered her onto a bed of moss.

Alex shook his head in disgust. "Very well, then, witch," he said, eyeing Gwendolyn. "Now is your chance to demonstrate your special healing powers."

Gwendolyn stepped forward, her mind racing. Where had MacDunn gotten the idea that she had healing powers? While her mother had been a skilled healer, Gwendolyn's father had forbidden Gwendolyn to practice the art, for fear it would draw attention to her, and give someone reason to accuse her of possessing unnatural abilities. Although she had understood her father's concern, Gwendolyn had secretly spent many hours studying her mother's carefully scribed notes. While she had found these studies fascinating, she had never actually practiced her mother's techniques on anyone. How on earth was she supposed to tend to a battle wound?

"If you walk any slower, I'll be dead before you get to me," MacDunn complained dryly, as he lowered himself to the ground.

"Forgive me," Gwendolyn said, hastening her step.

She knelt down beside him and bit her lip. A gash as long as the span of her hand sliced across the hard muscle of his upper chest. Blood was leaking profusely from the cut and seeping down his front, making it look as if he had been hacked wide open.

"I think it looks worse than it is," she murmured, more to reassure herself than him. She gingerly touched the raw edges of the wound, trying to establish its depth. Blood spurted from the opening. She jerked back her hand.

"It needs to be stitched," MacDunn told her.

She nodded.

He regarded her expectantly. "Go ahead."

Gwendolyn frantically tried to recall her mother's instructions on closing wounds. She herself had never stitched anything beyond garments, but surely the principle was the same. Except this, of course, would be messier.

"I will need more light," she decided, tentatively daubing the wound with MacDunn's discarded shirt. "Do you think it is safe to build a fire?"

"The warriors Robert brought with him are dead," MacDunn replied. "A fire will not matter now." He signaled to Ned, who promptly began to toss sticks into a pile.

"Is Robert also dead?"

Her voice was flat, but Alex could sense a flicker of desperation behind her inquiry. "No," he admitted, feeling oddly as if he had failed her. "He is not. But he cannot hurt you," he added, wanting to reassure her. "You belong to me now. I protect what is mine."

His expression was deadly serious. Gwendolyn stared at him a moment, contemplating the power emanating from him even as he lay there bleeding. She had no doubt he believed what he said. But the stench of flames still permeated her senses, reminding her of how close she had come to death that day. She could never be safe, she realized stonily. And though she might be MacDunn's prisoner, she was certainly not his possession.

"I belong to no one, MacDunn."

"You are wrong."

She lowered her gaze to her task. "I will require needle and thread, and some water," she said, changing the subject.

"See to it, Cameron," MacDunn ordered.

Gwendolyn folded MacDunn's shirt into layers and pressed it firmly against his wound, trying to stanch the flow of blood. Hot scarlet liquid soaked into the fabric and drenched her fingers. She was unnerved by all the blood, but she vaguely recalled her mother's notes mentioning that sometimes relatively insignificant wounds could bleed horribly at first. More pressure on the wound was apparently needed. She pressed down as hard as she could, causing MacDunn's firm muscles to leap beneath her palm.

"Sweet Jesus," he swore, grabbing her wrist with bruising strength. "What the hell are you trying to do?"

"F-forgive me," she stammered, startled by the pain she had caused him. "I did not mean to hurt you."

Alex regarded her in surprise. Her gray eyes were wide with concern, which seemed incomprehensible in a witch guilty of murder and all the other hideous crimes of which she stood accused. Her wrist was slim and fragile in his grip, and he was acutely aware of the velvety touch of her skin against his palm.

Abruptly, he released her.

"Here are the things you asked for," said Cameron, handing her a dripping leather pouch and a slim needle.

"Where is the thread?" asked Gwendolyn.

"I couldn't find any," Cameron replied. "Isn't there something else you could use?"

Gwendolyn thought for a moment. Her mother's notes had mentioned that hair could sometimes be substituted for thread, if no other fibers were available. She reached into her scalp and pulled out several long, dark strands. "This might work," she told MacDunn.

The bleeding had slowed, so she rinsed his wound with water and blotted it dry. Satisfied that the cut was clean enough for her to close, she carefully threaded her needle. Then she bent her head, swallowed hard—and froze.

"What's wrong?" MacDunn asked after a moment.

"I—I am merely planning how I am going to close it."

Realizing he found her hesitation peculiar, she summoned her courage and tentatively inserted the needle into MacDunn's skin, fully expecting him to writhe in agony.

He didn't flinch.

Marginally encouraged by that, she punctured the raw flesh on the opposite side of the gash, then stole a quick, apologetic glance at him. He was watching her with enormous calm, his blue gaze intense, as if he were evaluating her work. He certainly did not look like a man in unbearable pain. Satisfied that she was not causing him any great distress, she exhaled the breath she had been holding and continued her task.

Alex watched her slowly lace his wound closed. Firelight played upon her pale cheek as she worked, which was smooth and unmarked by illness or time. Her face was a study of somber beauty, with high, sculpted cheekbones, a narrow, delicate brow, and graceful, berry-stained lips that she bit as she concentrated. Her eyes were wide, gray, and utterly serious, and he found himself wondering what it would be like to see a little merriment reflected in them. Her hair was as black and glossy as a raven's breast; it fell like a heavy cloak around her, shrouding her. She was far from the ancient old hag he had believed he was seeking at the MacSween holding. He had known only that he sought the MacSween witch, and to his knowledge, all witches were hideous, shriveled crones with long, yellow teeth and horny, spotted hands. And yet, from the moment he first saw this pale slip of a girl being led to the stake, he had realized her beauty was not of this world. Her face was too perfect, her coloring too startling, and her slim, curved body too tantalizing to be anything but the work of the devil. She could kindle a man's desire with nothing but a glance, or the simple gesture of brushing a wavy strand of dark hair off her cheek. Even now, he was overwhelmed by the light touch of her cool hands against his torn, burning flesh, by the gentle cadence of her breath as she threaded her own hair in and out of him, by the tangy sweet scent of heather about her, mingled with the smoky aroma of her gown. It had been years since he had endured a woman's ministrations, for his health was infernally excellent, and he was rarely wounded in battle. Surely that was why she was having such a profound effect on him, flooding his senses with heat and fragrance and need, stirring his blood and quickening his desire until he wanted to sink his hand deep into that inky cape of hair and pull her atop him.

"There," Gwendolyn breathed, knotting the last stitch, "I believe that will hold if you are careful not to move too much. Now we need to bandage it."

"I have only my shirt," said Alex, vaguely disappointed that she had finished so quickly.

"That won't do," Gwendolyn decided, critically eyeing the discarded garment. "It is soaked with blood." She considered a moment, then grasped the fabric of her gown where it met her shoulder and yanked down, tearing off the sleeve. She quickly did the same with the other side.

"Did you sew that gown?" asked Alex as she reduced the sleeves to narrow strips of fabric and knotted them together.

"Yes—why?"

"I was just considering how easily the stitches gave way."

She glanced at him, uncertain whether or not he was teasing. His expression was contained, but she thought she detected a hint of amusement in his eyes.

"Your stitches will hold well enough if you are careful," she informed him defensively as she wrapped the bandage around his chest. "But I think you will have to refrain from wielding your sword for a few days."

"Then let us hope no one else comes after you for a while."

"Robert came for Isabella as well," Gwendolyn pointed out. "If you do not release her, Laird MacSween is certain to send more men to retrieve her. She is his only daughter."

"Isabella will be released unharmed," Alex replied. "I gave MacSween my word. Besides, she is of no use to me. Come here, Brodick," he called, before Gwendolyn could ask what possible use he thought she was going to be. "Let the witch close that arm of yours."

Brodick eyed her nervously. "It is fine, MacDunn. It can wait."

"If you leave it, it may fester," countered Alex. "Let her see to it."

"It is not nearly as bad as I thought," Brodick assured him, adjusting his sleeve to conceal the wound. "It does not bother me at all."

"By God, she's frightened him with that business about casting a spell on his manhood!" burst out Cameron, roaring with laughter.

Alex gave Gwendolyn a warning look. "You will do nothing but fix his arm, is that clear?"

She nodded.

"Get over here, Brodick," Alex commanded.

Reluctantly, Brodick approached Gwendolyn.

"Careful you don't make her angry," Cameron teased. "There'll be many a lass left sorely disappointed."

"You're next, Cameron," announced Alex. "That cut in your scalp is turning your hair even redder, if that's possible."

Cameron's face fell. " 'Tis barely a scratch, MacDunn. There's no need for the witch to—"

"Worried about disappointing your wife, Cameron?" Brodick drawled as Gwendolyn examined his arm.

Cameron scowled.

"Why don't you heal his wound with witchcraft?" Alex asked, watching as Gwendolyn carefully bathed Brodick's gash.

She raised her eyes in confusion.

"You have special powers," he reflected. "Let me see you use them."

His scrutiny was unsettling. There was a powerful emotion smoldering within the depths of his blue eyes, a sentiment he was struggling to mask, which she could not immediately identify.

"If it's all the same to you, MacDunn," began Brodick nervously, "I would prefer she not go to any trouble on my account."

"Do you have these powers or don't you?" Alex persisted.

There it was. That lightning flash of emotion, so fleeting she nearly missed it. Yet in that brief glimpse, there was no mistaking what it was.

Yearning.

So this was why MacDunn had rescued her. He did not know of the stone, but apparently he believed she was a witch with unnatural powers. When his attempt to buy her failed, he developed a plan to rescue her, so determined was he to have control of her and her abilities.

He was no better than Robert, she realized bitterly.

"Of course I have great powers," she lied. It was clear now that her very existence depended on this fabrication. If MacDunn believed she had no powers, he might well decide to either kill her himself, or send her back to her clan. "I am, after all, a witch."

He nodded with satisfaction. "Good. I would hate to think I had just killed over a dozen men and invited war with the MacSweens for a woman who is of no earthly use to me."

"The fact that I was about to be consumed by flames did not trouble you?"

"You were found guilty of serious crimes," he replied. "It is not my way to interfere with another clan's justice. To do so is to risk war over matters that do not concern me. I have the welfare of my own people to consider."

"That is most prudent of you," observed Gwendolyn. "I am surprised you took such enormous risks today."

"I plan to benefit from your powers," he assured her. "The rewards you will bring me will far exceed the risks."

Somehow she managed to refrain from striking him across the face. He intended to use her, just as Robert had hoped to do. No doubt he wanted her to bring him victory in war, render him invincible, and then fill his coffers with unimaginable riches. Why had she thought, even for an instant, that this mad warrior was beyond such selfish, shallow cravings?

"Can you use your powers to heal?" he demanded impatiently.

"I can, but only to a certain extent," she lied, realizing the need for caution as she wove her claims. "I cannot cast a spell to close these wounds, or else I would have done so already for you." She pulled several more strands of hair from her scalp and threaded her needle. "I can, however, call upon my powers to control the pain once the injuries are stitched."

"Really?" MacDunn was obviously intrigued.

"That won't be necessary," announced Brodick. "I don't believe I'll be feeling any pain. In fact," he continued, rising, "my arm is already much—"

"You will demonstrate this on my men," MacDunn interrupted, firmly pushing him down again.

"What about you?" asked Gwendolyn.

"I prefer to watch you cast your spell."

"It may not be possible," she warned, searching for a tangible excuse in case her "spell" failed. "There are many things I need, and I have brought nothing with me."

"Tell Ned what you require so he can fetch these things while you stitch Brodick and Cameron."

Gwendolyn considered a moment. "I will require five smooth, unblemished stones no larger than the palm of my hand," she began. "I will also need a single, perfect feather from the wing of a sparrow hawk, a fistful of fresh, very green moss, a strip of bark from a pine tree, twelve crushed pine needles, six drops of blood, a freshly caught fish, a scoop of earth—"

"For God's sake, it's the middle of the night," Alex complained. "How the hell is he supposed to catch a fish?"

"These are the things I require, MacDunn," she informed

him flatly. "If you cannot provide them, I cannot cast the spell." She calmly began to stitch Brodick's arm.

"Fine," he growled. "Is there anything else?"

"No," she replied. "That is all."

"See if you can find these things, Ned."

The small warrior looped his bow over his shoulder and disappeared into the woods.

Brodick's arm was far simpler to close than MacDunn's chest had been. By the time Gwendolyn was mending the tear in Cameron's scalp, she was feeling somewhat confident in her stitching abilities.

"There, now," she said, tying off the last of the thread. "Keep this clean, and it will heal very nicely."

"Thank you, m'lady," said Cameron, rising. "My wife would have been most upset to have me return with a gaping hole in my head. The lass is prone to rather unseemly fits of temper when it comes to my injuries." His voice was gruff, but Gwendolyn sensed the warrior's fondness for his wife.

"I don't think Ned is going to find everything I need for my spell tonight," she mused, relieved. "Perhaps we should just—"

At that moment Ned emerged through the trees. He went straight to Gwendolyn and deposited a knotted, squirming bundle at her feet.

"You'd better hurry," he advised. "That fish won't last much longer."

Reluctantly, Gwendolyn unknotted the bundle and unpacked the items. She examined each one carefully, searching for some flaw.

"What about the six drops of blood?" she demanded, seizing upon the missing item.

Ned held up his hand. "You will cut me when you need it."

"Actually, I don't believe I will need any blood for this spell," she quickly corrected, sickened by the idea of cutting Ned's hand for her little ruse. "I can manage without it."

She made a great show of arranging the five stones in a circle around the fire, occasionally staring at the moon and stars to give the impression that she was positioning the rocks in accordance with some complex celestial relationship. Once the stones were in place, she tore off a piece of moss and concealed it under each, then sprinkled a little earth over them. That done, she took her place by one of the stones, lay the now expired fish at her feet, and placed the feather and the strip of bark beside it in the shape of a cross.

"Now, each of you warriors must pick up exactly four pine needles and take your place by the remaining rocks," she instructed, her voice low and solemn.

Brodick, Cameron, and Ned glanced at each other uneasily.

"But I'm not wounded," Ned protested.

"Nevertheless, I need all of you to participate," Gwendolyn said. "Only MacDunn can watch."

The three warriors reluctantly took their positions.

"You have one rock too many," pointed out Brodick, stooping to pick it up.

"That one is left for the spirits," Gwendolyn quickly improvised. "Now slowly crush the needles between your thumb and forefinger to release the ancient essence of the woods, then raise them to your nostrils, close your eyes, and inhale deeply."

The three warriors regarded her skeptically.

"You must do as I say," Gwendolyn insisted, "or the spell won't work."

Feeling foolish, they followed her instructions.

"Good. Now we must wait," she said, closing her eyes and spreading her bare arms wide over the fire, "for the howling of the spirits."

At that precise moment, Isabella stirred from her swoon. She took one look at them and screamed so loud she sent a flock of bats screeching in a furious cloud over their heads. Then she collapsed in a dead faint once more.

"Christ!" swore Cameron, swatting at a bat, "what the hell is wrong with that lass?"

"The spirits have howled," Gwendolyn pronounced gravely, her eyes still closed. "They are with us."

Brodick cracked open an eye.

"Close your eyes, Brodick," Gwendolyn scolded.

He obeyed, uncertain how she had known, since her own eyes appeared tightly shut.

"Oh, great spirits of the darkness," Gwendolyn moaned, swaying her arms over the fire, "I call upon you to relieve the suffering of these weak, foolish, ignorant, puny mortals."

"Did the lass call us puny?" asked Cameron, baffled by her description.

"She must mean Ned," Brodick decided.

"What do you mean by that?" demanded Ned, opening his eyes.

"You can't think she is referring to me, Neddie," Cameron scoffed. "That's plain enough, I think."

"Or me," added Brodick.

"Maybe you're the foolish, ignorant mortals," Ned suggested testily.

Gwendolyn opened her eyes and planted her hands on her hips in exasperation. "Do you want me to cast this spell or don't you?"

The warriors exchanged sullen glances, then closed their eyes once more.

"Fine," she muttered. "Let's just hope the spirits didn't get annoyed with you and leave." She closed her eyes and slowly circled her hands over the fire. "Oh, great spirits, I ask that you drain the feeble bodies of these warriors of poisons, illness, and pain, and fill them with strength." Her voice began to crescendo as she continued. "Peel away the layers of their pathetic mortal suffering, that they may rest well tonight and feel better with the rising of the sun!"

A deafening crack of thunder shattered the stillness, immediately followed by a silvery streak of lightning. Dark, ominous clouds suddenly choked the clear cape of night, and a powerful wind blasted through the forest.

"By God, lassie," Cameron marveled, his red hair blowing crazily around him, "I think you woke those spirits up!"

Brodick warily eyed the roiling sky. "Do you think she's made them angry?"

"Maybe they always react like this," suggested Ned.

Another ribbon of lightning split the sky, followed by an explosion of thunder.

"Is this normal, lass?" Cameron shouted, his words muffled by the wind.

Gwendolyn regarded the sky in bewilderment. She had never witnessed such an abrupt change in the weather.

"Everything is fine," she assured them loudly. "The spirits have heard my plea."

They remained in their circle, watching the sky pitch and flash as a cool gale whipped their hair and clothes. And then, just as suddenly as it had burst upon them, the storm died. The wind gasped and was gone, and the clouds melted into the darkness, unveiling the silent, tranquil glow of the moon and stars once again.

"By God, that was something!" Cameron roared, slapping Brodick heartily on the back. "Have you ever seen such a thing?"

"Did you see that, Alex?" asked Brodick, looking uneasy.

"Aye," Alex said. "I saw."

Brodick raised his arm and cautiously flexed it at the elbow. "I think my arm feels better." He sounded more troubled than pleased.

"I *know* my head feels better!" Cameron said happily. "What about you, Neddie?"

"I have no wounds for the witch to heal." Ned frowned. "That's odd," he remarked, slowly turning his head from side to side. "My neck has been stiff and aching for a week, and suddenly it feels fine."

Gwendolyn folded her arms across her chest and regarded them triumphantly, masking her profound relief. Clearly just the suggestion that they would feel better had had an effect on them, which was what she had hoped would happen. Luckily, the weather had complemented her little performance.

"Can you cast that spell on anyone?" asked Cameron, still excited.

"Not everyone," she replied carefully. "And my spells don't always work."

"What do you mean?" demanded Alex.

"The success of a spell depends on many things," she replied evasively. Although it was essential MacDunn believe she had powers, she did not want him to think she could simply say a few words and fell an entire army. "My powers will not work on everyone."

"I don't give a damn if they work on everyone," he growled. "As long as they work on one person." His expression was harsh. "Cameron, take the first watch. The rest of you get some sleep. We ride at first light."

Brodick produced an extra plaid from his horse and carefully draped it over Isabella's unconscious form. Then he lay down just a few feet away from her, where he could watch over her during the night. Ned and MacDunn also stretched out upon the ground, arranging part of their plaids over their shoulders for warmth.

"Do you sleep standing up?" asked MacDunn irritably.

"No," replied Gwendolyn.

"Then lie down. We still have a long journey ahead."

She had assumed they were going to bind her to a tree. But with Cameron watching her, she would not get very far if she attempted to escape tonight. Obviously that was what MacDunn believed. Relieved that she would not be tied, she wearily lowered herself to the ground.

Tomorrow would be soon enough to find an opportunity for escape.

The little camp grew quiet, except for the occasional snap of the fire. Soon the rumble of snoring began to drift lazily through the air. Gwendolyn wondered how they had all managed to find sleep so quickly in such uncomfortable conditions. The fire had died and the ground was damp and cold, forcing her to curl into a tight ball and wrap her bare arms around herself. It didn't help. With every passing moment her flesh grew more chilled, until finally her entire body was shivering uncontrollably.

"Gwendolyn," called MacDunn in a low voice, "come here."

She sat up and peered at him through the darkness. "Why?"

"Because your chattering teeth are keeping me awake," he grumbled. "You will lie next to me and share my plaid."

She stared at him in horror. "I am fine, MacDunn," she hastily assured him. "You needn't concern yourself about—"

"Come here."

"No." She shook her head. "I may be your prisoner, but I will *not* share your bed."

She waited for him to argue. Instead he muttered something under his breath, adjusted his plaid more to his liking over his naked chest, and closed his eyes once again. Satisfied that she had won this small but critical battle, she vigorously rubbed her arms to warm them, then primly curled onto the ground.

Her teeth began to chatter so violently she had to bite down hard to try to control them.

"For God's sake—" swore MacDunn.

The next thing she knew, MacDunn was stretching out beside her and wrapping his plaid over both of them.

"Don't you dare touch me!" Gwendolyn hissed, rolling away.

MacDunn grabbed her waist and firmly drew her back, imprisoning her in the warm crook of his enormous, barely clad body.

"Be still!" he ordered impatiently.

"I will not be still, you foul, mad ravisher of women!" She kicked him as hard as she could in his shin.

"Jesus—" he swore, loosening his hold slightly.

Gwendolyn tried to scramble away from him, but he instantly tightened his grip. Realizing she was hopelessly trapped, she opened her mouth to scream.

His hand clamped down hard over her lips.

"Listen to me!" he commanded, somehow managing to keep his voice low. "I have no intention of bedding you, do you understand?"

Gwendolyn glared at him, her breasts rising and falling so rapidly they grazed his bandaged chest.

"I may be considered mad, but to my knowledge I have not yet earned a reputation as a ravager of unwilling women—do you understand?"

His blue eyes held hers. She tried to detect deceit in them, but could not. All she saw was anger, mingled with weariness.

"I have already risked far more than I have a right to, to save your life and take you home with me, Gwendolyn Mac-Sween," he continued. "I will *not* have it end by watching you fall deathly ill from the chill of the night."

He waited a moment, allowing his comments to penetrate her fear. Then, cautiously, he lifted his palm from her lips. "I will keep you warm, nothing more. You have my word."

She regarded him warily. "You swear you will not abuse me, MacDunn? On your honor?"

"I swear."

Reluctantly, she eased herself onto her side. MacDunn adjusted part of his plaid over her, then once again fitted himself around her. His arm circled her waist, drawing her into the warm, hard cradle of his body. Gwendolyn lay there rigidly for a long while, scarcely breathing, waiting for him to break his word.

Instead, he began to snore.

Heat seemed to radiate from him, slowly permeating her chilled flesh. It warmed even the soft wool of his plaid, she realized, snuggling farther into it. A deliciously masculine scent wafted around her, the scent of horse and leather and woods. Little by little, the feel of MacDunn's powerful body against hers became more comforting than threatening, especially as his snores grew louder.

Until that moment, she had had virtually no knowledge of physical contact. Her mother had died when she was very young, and her father, though loving, had never been at ease with open demonstrations of affection. The unfamiliar sensation of MacDunn's heat and strength wrapped protectively around her was unlike anything she had ever imagined. She was his prisoner, and he had saved her life only because he intended to greedily abuse the powers he erroneously believed she possessed. And yet, she felt impossibly safe.

You belong to me now, he had told her. *I protect what is mine.* She belonged to no one, she reflected drowsily, and no one could protect her from men like Robert, or from the ignorance and fear that was sure to fester in MacDunn's own clan the moment they saw her. She would escape him long before they reached his lands. Tomorrow she would break free from these warriors so she could retrieve the stone, return to her clan, and kill Robert. Above all else, Robert must die. She would make him pay for murdering her father and destroying her life.

But all this seemed distant and shadowy as she drifted into slumber, sheltered by this brave, mad warrior, feeling the steady beat of his heart pulsing against her back.

CHAPTER 3

Her father sat before the fire, smiling with pleasure as she read to him.

John MacSween was proud that he had taught his daughter to read, though he had to keep her ability a well-guarded secret. None of the other MacSween women were permitted to learn this skill. This was not done out of some nefarious desire to purposely deprive or control them. The MacSweens simply saw no need for women to read, since it was only men who drafted and received important messages, treaties, and agreements. Why would a young girl waste precious hours deciphering scratches on a page when she could be doing something useful, like gutting fish, combing wool, or plucking feathers? But Gwendolyn's father had originally come from a clan farther south, and their ways had not been as traditional as those of the MacSweens. He had taught his wife to read and write, and then he had passed the same skills on to his daughter. Gwendolyn had learned them clandestinely, at night, within the safety of their small cottage. Her father did not want to give the MacSweens yet another reason to fear and ostracize his beloved child.

"When I am gone, you will still have your friends in books and stories, my sweet Gwen," he told her.

Gwendolyn looked up from her book and frowned. "Wherever you go, Papa, I am going with you."

A sad smile shadowed her father's gentle face. And then he began to fade.

Cold seeped through Gwendolyn. She curled up even more and struggled to keep her father in his chair. But his image had vanished. Shivering, she inched backward, searching for the comforting wall of heat that had enveloped her all night.

It was gone.

Feeling lost, she opened her eyes. Her father was dead, she realized numbly. There would be no more nights of reading to him before a fire or listening to the glorious tales he loved to tell her.

MacDunn and his warriors were already up and preparing for the day's journey. Brodick was cooking a simple meal of fresh oakcakes and fish over a small fire, while MacDunn, Ned, and Cameron were tending to their horses. Gwendolyn sat up and rubbed her bare arms. Isabella, she noticed, was still comfortably ensconced beneath Brodick's extra plaid, sound asleep.

"Good morning, m'lady," Cameron called cheerfully. " 'Tis a fine day, is it not? I must confess, my head feels remarkably well this morning, thanks to your spirit friends."

"That is good," she murmured.

"Will you have some oatcake and fish this morning? The fish was just caught by Ned, and is sure to be sweet."

Gwendolyn shook her head. The pain of missing her father had destroyed her appetite. "I am not hungry."

"You will eat," MacDunn commanded, not looking at her as he adjusted the girth of his saddle.

"I am not hungry," Gwendolyn insisted stubbornly.

"Your body requires nourishment," he argued. "You ate nothing yesterday, and I'd wager that during your time in the dungeon, you ate little, if at all. You are thin and weak." He critically eyed her up and down.

"I am not weak," she protested. In truth, since the death of her father just four days ago, she had become a little thin.

"A better nourished woman would not have felt the cold so severely last night. You will be lucky if you are not burning with fever by midday, and dead by tomorrow morning."

Gwendolyn stared at him blankly. What was this bizarre preoccupation with her health? "I have no intention of getting a fever—"

"Your life now belongs to me," he interrupted. "And I have decided you will eat."

She was about to point out that her life most certainly did not belong to him or anyone else when Brodick cautiously approached her with some food.

"Do try some, m'lady," he invited. "Even if you are not hungry now, it will be several hours before we stop again to eat."

The aroma of the freshly grilled fish stirred the emptiness in her stomach. "Perhaps I will have just a little," she conceded. "But I am *not* doing it because you ordered me to, MacDunn."

MacDunn shrugged his enormous shoulders. "As long as you eat, I don't give a damn."

"I'm hungry," announced Isabella sleepily, stretching her arms over her head.

"Good morning, Bella," called Brodick. "Did you sleep well?"

"Certainly not," she informed him coldly. "I'm bruised all over from lying on the hard ground, and this filthy, coarse plaid has scratched my skin to pieces. I couldn't sleep at all."

"You appeared to be resting well enough last night after MacDunn showed you his wound," observed Cameron teasingly.

"Oh!" Isabella exclaimed. "That was absolutely horrid. However could you expect me to fix such a thing?"

MacDunn shrugged. "After all those grisly threats of yours, I would have thought you would have enjoyed plunging a needle in me."

"Don't think about it anymore," soothed Brodick, bringing her a cloth filled with food.

Isabella wrinkled her nose. "This smells burned."

"I am sorry," he apologized. "It is all there is."

On learning that, she greedily began to devour it. "You had best ride fast today," she said between mouthfuls. "Robert is certain to come after you again. He will not rest until I am safely returned to my father."

"At the moment, Robert is somewhat outnumbered," said MacDunn. "Unless your father makes a decision to send out more men, I do not think we will enjoy the pleasure of Robert's company today."

"Then tomorrow he will come," Isabella predicted. "And when he does, he will tie your limbs to two fine horses and send them galloping in opposite directions, tearing you apart and dragging your ragged, bloody remains across the Highlands."

Cameron laughed. "By God, I'm actually going to miss her threats."

"I'm not," Alex muttered, hoisting himself onto his horse. "It's time to go. Ned, you will take the witch behind you today. You're both light, so your mount should be able to keep a good speed."

It was a perfectly reasonable explanation, he assured himself, watching as Gwendolyn climbed up behind Ned. He thought she looked slightly surprised, but Ned gave no indication that he found this order peculiar. In truth, Alex could not bear another moment of feeling her soft, slim form pressing against him. He had lain awake the entire night, keeping her warm in the shelter of his body. He had thought the act would be nothing, that he would simply lie next to her and fall asleep. Instead he was acutely aware of every breath she drew, of every small turn and shift and sigh of her delicately feminine body, which was far too fine and fragile to withstand the harsh rigors of life in the Highlands. He had sensed her tension and so he had feigned sleep, knowing she did not trust him to keep his word not to ravish her. And long before light began to filter through the feathery spires of the pines above them, he had questioned his ability to honor his oath. Somehow, this pale wisp of a girl had managed to kindle a heat and need in him that he had never thought to experience again. His flesh had felt as if it were afire, and his loins had hardened until they ached.

And he was appalled.

"I'm not ready to leave yet," announced Isabella, untroubled by the fact that everyone was mounted and ready to go. "I haven't finished my breakfast, and after that I will need a few moments to wash in the stream." She began to nibble at a second oatcake.

Brodick urged his horse over to her. "Alas, sweet Bella, this is where I must bid you farewell." He bent down, scooped up his plaid from her shoulders, and folded it behind his saddle.

She regarded him in disbelief. "You're leaving me?"

"I gave your father my word that I would release you in the morning," Alex reminded her. "Although your father did not heed my conditions, I intend to keep my part of the bargain. You have ample food and water, and you should keep the fire burning. Robert has been released from his bonds, so when he wakens shortly in these woods he will find you. You can either ride home with him or wait until more of your father's men come to retrieve you."

"But I must go with you," she protested. "Since my father didn't honor your conditions, you must take me with you."

Brodick glanced questioningly at Alex.

"She is of no use to us," Alex said bluntly. "And I have done enough to incur the MacSweens' wrath without also permanently stealing their laird's daughter. She stays here." He turned his horse and began to ride away.

"No!" exclaimed Isabella, rising to stand before Brodick. "You cannot just abandon me here. You cannot!"

"Forgive me, m'lady," Brodick apologized. "It was not meant to be."

"You cannot leave me!"

"Farewell, sweet Bella," he crooned. "I'll not forget you." He tilted his head in a bow, then turned his mount and rode away, followed by Cameron and Ned.

"This isn't over!" Isabella raged. "I'll make sure my father's warriors hunt you down and crush every bone in your body, you vile abductor of helpless women! Then they'll carve out your eyes and mince them into paste . . ."

"Poor lass, I think you've gone and broken her heart," said Cameron as Isabella's gruesome ravings continued.

". . . *and grind your organs into mush* . . ."

"If that's what she's like when her heart is broken, I'd not want to see her angry," reflected Ned.

". . . *you scurvy, rotten, fulsome bastard!*"

"She'll get over it," Brodick assured them.

"Aye," agreed Cameron, laughing. "They always do."

The air was aromatic with the sun-washed scent of damp earth and the tangy fragrance of heather that burst in purple puffs around them. But Gwendolyn was far too absorbed in considering her situation as they galloped through the meadows and woods to derive pleasure from her surroundings. Every mile took her farther away from Robert and the stone, and so with every mile her resolve to escape grew.

She was certain MacDunn intended to use her to either strike an enemy or fatten his coffers, or perhaps both. Although she had been fortunate in proving her supernatural powers with her little "spell" last night, she had no hope of faking someone's death or making riches suddenly appear. The moment she failed to do so, MacDunn would realize he had been duped and his rage would be awesome. After he finished punishing her, he would give her back to Robert in order to prevent war. She would be imprisoned and burned, and Robert's treachery would go without retribution.

She could not allow that to happen.

"The horses need to rest," MacDunn suddenly announced. "We will stay here by this stream awhile."

Gwendolyn wearily let go of Ned. Although MacDunn had said no MacSweens would come after them today, he had led his warriors like a man possessed. It was clear he was most anxious to return home with his prize. Her arms were stiff and her backside aching as she slid off Ned's horse, only to collapse in a startled heap on the ground.

"Are you ill?" MacDunn asked, racing toward her. He dropped to one knee and laid his rough hand upon her brow. "Do you feel feverish?"

"I am fine, MacDunn. My legs are stiff from being on that horse too long, that is all. I am not accustomed to riding such a long distance."

His hand moved from her forehead to each cheek, as if he did not quite believe her. When he finally decided that her temperature was acceptable, he regarded her sternly. "You should have said something if you were finding the ride too difficult."

She did not know what to make of that. After all, she was his prisoner, and had assumed her comfort was irrelevant. "You are obviously in a great hurry and—"

"Your well-being is of paramount importance to me," MacDunn interrupted. "In the future, you will tell me when you are feeling ill or overly tired. Is that clear?"

She reminded herself that his anxiety sprang from greed rather than a genuine interest in her health. He had told her she was useless to him if she fell ill. Nevertheless, his touch was infinitely gentle as he wrapped his arms around her and helped her to her feet.

"You must walk a little, to get the blood moving in your legs," he instructed, leading her across the grass. "Better?"

"Y-yes," she stammered, unsettled by the feel of his hard body supporting her. "I'm fine now, MacDunn." She broke free from him to walk on her own.

He watched her a moment, as if to be sure. Then he turned and led his horse to the stream. Cameron and Ned followed with the other horses.

"Has he always been this preoccupied with illness?"

Gwendolyn asked, moving to where Brodick was laying out some food.

"No," he admitted. "But that was before he learned how formidable an enemy illness can be."

"Was he sick?" Gwendolyn was unable to imagine MacDunn weak from disease.

Brodick shook his head. "MacDunn has always enjoyed excellent health."

"Then who was sick?"

"It is not my place to tell you about MacDunn, Gwendolyn. Whatever he wants you to know, he will tell you."

She didn't care, she reminded herself. MacDunn's problems were of no interest to her. Her only concern was escaping. And with MacDunn, Cameron, and Ned down by the stream, this was probably her best opportunity. They had stopped at the edge of a thick forest. If she could lose herself in there, she would be able to find someplace to hide. She raised her arms in a casual stretch, sighed, then began to wander nonchalantly toward the woods.

"Where are you going?" Brodick demanded.

"I require a few minutes of privacy," Gwendolyn called over her shoulder.

"You must wait until MacDunn returns. He would not want you going off on your own."

"Unfortunately, I cannot wait," replied Gwendolyn, still walking. "Don't worry, Brodick, I won't go far." With that she slipped into the woods and quickly disappeared behind a tree.

She glanced back to see if Brodick would follow her. He stared in her direction a moment, as if debating whether or not to go after her. Then he lowered his head and continued to unpack food from his saddlebag.

Every second was precious. Gwendolyn gathered her skirts in her hands and began to swiftly thread her way deep into the woods. She tried to step lightly over the carpet of pine needles and twigs, conscious of each snap and rustle as she raced from her captors. It would be only moments before Brodick decided she had been gone too long. She needed to cover as much distance as possible before the warriors came after her. Her heart pounded and her breath was reduced to shallow, desperate gasps. Still she ran, heedless of the branches clawing at her face, farther and farther into the quiet green sanctuary of the woods. She was well ahead of them now. The forest was so dense and dark, surely they would not be able to find her here.

"Gwendolyn! Where are you?" Brodick called, not sounding nearly as far away as she would have liked.

She did not pause, though her chest felt as if it were being squeezed of air.

"Gwendolyn!" called MacDunn, his voice harsh, "come out here at once!"

Exhaustion forced her to pause a moment and lean against a tree, greedily gasping for breath. They would never find her now, for the woods were far too large, and they could not possibly know which direction she had taken. Still, there were four of them, which meant they could cover virtually every direction. The sound of branches breaking and twigs snapping told her they had begun their search. She glanced around wildly, looking for a place to hide. There was nothing but the endless, narrow columns of trees. She debated trying to climb one of them, but feared she lacked the strength and agility to get sufficiently high, and might only reveal her whereabouts in the process.

"Come, now, m'lady," called Cameron, affecting a reasonable tone. "You cannot be thinking of spending the night alone in these woods."

She picked up her skirts and began to run again, encouraged by the fact that his voice was muffled. Obviously they were going in the wrong direction. Her breathing grew labored once more, and her heart began to pound against her chest. Still she ran, focusing on her need to escape, to free herself from MacDunn and his selfish desires, and to find Robert and bury a dirk deep into his heart.

The ground began to rumble beneath her. She ran even faster, but now she could hear branches cracking, heralding the advance of a rider. Despair overwhelmed her. Realizing she had been caught, she stopped and turned.

MacDunn was thundering toward her, an arrow taut against the string of his bow. Rage had hardened his features into a terrible mask. Gwendolyn stared at him in horror, her heart frozen. Instead of lowering his weapon as he drew close, he aimed it straight at her.

In that moment, she realized he was truly mad.

She opened her mouth to scream as he released his arrow, but all that came out was a strangled whimper. A hideous shriek of pain shattered the air.

Confused, Gwendolyn looked behind her.

An enormous wild boar lay upon the ground with an arrow protruding from its side. Blood poured from its wound as the heavy creature struggled to get up. Another arrow sliced the air beside her and plunged cleanly into the poor beast, killing it. Gwendolyn stared at it in shock. The animal would have killed her, she realized numbly.

Slowly, she turned to face MacDunn.

He swung down from his horse and stalked toward her.

"Do you have any idea how close you just came to death?" he demanded softly.

"MacDunn, I—"

He grabbed her by her slim, bare shoulders, needing to touch her, to be sure she was still whole and well.

"You would have been killed," he bit out harshly. "That boar would have knocked you to the ground and trampled you until every bone in your body was crushed."

His grip was punishing, but she dared not complain. She did not want to provoke his rage even more than she already had.

"And I would have been powerless to save you, Gwendolyn," he continued fiercely. "Had I arrived but a moment later, there would have been nothing I could do."

This, perhaps, was what alarmed Alex the most. He had vowed to protect her, yet her own folly had placed her directly in death's path. And now she stood, trembling yet defiant. He wanted to shake her, he wanted to frighten her, he wanted to make her understand that she could not trifle with her life in this way.

And so he lowered his head and captured her lips in his.

Gwendolyn stood paralyzed as MacDunn's mouth slanted over hers. She had never been kissed before, for no one in her clan would have dared dally with the girl marked from childhood as a witch. But even in her innocence she could feel the unleashed fury in the way his lips ground against hers. A flame burst to life in the pit of her stomach, and her blood quickened, making her feel flushed and strange. MacDunn's tongue swept demandingly along the soft crease of her lips, and the sensation was so exquisite Gwendolyn opened her mouth slightly. He instantly plunged inside, hungrily exploring. Gwendolyn leaned into his muscular frame and locked her arms around his neck, clinging to him as she urgently returned his kiss. He growled and wrapped his arms around her, drawing her even closer, kissing her even harder, until there was nothing but the solid wall of MacDunn wrapped around her and the incredible fire that raged between them. Power seemed to emanate from him as his hands roamed down her back, cupping her hips and pulling her firmly into the hardness of his arousal. Pleasure washed through her as she pressed against him, and a soft little cry escaped her throat.

Alex continued to taste Gwendolyn as his hands began to explore the narrow path of her back, the satin skin of her shoulders, the delicate cage of her ribs. And then he laid his palm against the lush swell of her breast and groaned, for he could not remember ever touching anything so soft. It had been four years since he had felt the least flicker of desire, and the lust surging through him in that moment was beyond measure. He wanted to take this witch now, here in the forest, to lay her down on a bed of fragrant pine and bury himself deep inside her, to lose himself to her softness and heat, without even taking the time to remove her gown. His desire was staggering, it stripped him of his ability to think, until he was aware of nothing but the blaze devouring him, and the certainty that only this mysterious smoke- and heather-scented woman could slake his need. He could not remember a moment in which he had been so overwhelmingly possessed, not even with Flora, though there had been many a time when he had spread his plaid over a mattress of ferns and pleasured her in the golden warmth of sunlight. But that was a lifetime ago, when she had been fit and glowing with laughter and love, and he had laid his face against the creamy softness of her breasts and vowed with all his heart and soul that he would never love another.

Shame sliced through him, dousing his ardor. He released his hold on Gwendolyn and stepped back, appalled by his behavior.

"Forgive me," he murmured roughly, not certain whether he was asking for her forgiveness or Flora's.

Gwendolyn regarded him blankly, bewildered by his abrupt change in manner. A moment ago he had been powerful, aroused, a great laird who was thoroughly in control and who was using that control to spin the same veil of desire over her. Yet now he seemed distant, almost sad. The grim set of his mouth told her he was still angry. But she sensed his fury was no longer directed at her.

"MacDunn!" called Brodick from the distance. "Did you find her?"

"Aye." Alex didn't take his eyes off Gwendolyn. "We're over here. Tell Ned to come and fetch her."

Gwendolyn was staring at him in confusion. Ripples of sunlight and shadow were playing over her, glossing the tangled mass of her black hair. Her gray eyes were wide and pensive, her cheeks and lips flushed from the heat of his kiss. In that moment, standing amid the green and gold light of the forest, she seemed more mythical creature than flesh-and-blood woman.

"You will abandon this absurd notion of escape," he commanded tautly, resisting the impulse to lay his hand against her cheek and feel its softness. He turned and moved toward his horse, anxious to have distance between them. "Next time," he continued, hoisting himself into his saddle, "I may just leave you for either Robert or the wild boars to find."

With that he galloped away, leaving Gwendolyn alone with the slain boar.

• • •

I'm sorry.

He lay back and contemplated the sparkling cape of night, only vaguely aware that the ground was damp and the air unseasonably cold. The physical discomforts of the body had never bothered him much, and tonight he was far too preoccupied to give them any notice whatsoever. Flora's star was smaller this evening, and the light it cast was sad and flat. At first Alex had had trouble finding it amid all the others. He had wondered if she was so injured by his betrayal that she would not show herself to him at all. If so, he could not blame her. But long after the camp rumbled with the sounds of sleep, he finally found a pale glimmer in a distant corner of the sky. Of course he knew Flora's spirit did not actually dwell within that shimmering silver orb.

Her soul was all around him, watching over him as he tried his damnedest to live out the rest of his shattered existence without her.

The night his fragile wife finally died, Alex had stumbled blindly into the courtyard and raged at God, cursing him for stealing away the woman who meant more to him than life. He had bellowed at the top of his lungs, waking all of his clan as he vainly tried to purge himself of the pain tearing through him. And through his fury and despair he suddenly noticed a tiny, brilliant star that he was certain had not been there before. He had been so astounded, he went immediately to Morag, the clan seer, and demanded to know the meaning of it. And the wise old woman had assured him it was a sign that Flora was watching over him.

From that evening on, Alex never slept without first searching the sky for Flora's star.

Forgive me, my love. It meant nothing.

He laced his fingers behind his head and sighed. He had no doubt she believed him. His Flora was the most tender-hearted of women and would never imagine him capable of anything but honesty. Still, his confession did not ease his shame. He had betrayed his beloved wife, and he did not know how to cleanse himself of that unforgivable act.

Four years. It was not so long, really. Barely a drop in the ocean of time, and certainly not long enough to numb his suffering. At first he had been far too enraged with God to continue with his duties as a laird and father. What kind of God would bless him with unfailing strength and good health, while slowly leeching the life out of his innocent wife? Flora had been as lovely as a flower, and as delicate. When Alex met her at the MacLean holding, she had not known he was laird of the MacDunns. A lively, rosy girl with laughing eyes and hair the color of fire, she spurned his arrogant advances with her quick wit and saucy manner. And Alex, who was accustomed to women throwing themselves in his path, was completely enchanted. He courted Flora with a patience and determination he had not known he was capable of. And finally she gifted him with her love. He proudly brought her back to his clan as his bride, and a year later his son was born, making his life complete.

But after David's birth, Flora lost a child, and then another, each time losing a little more of her color and strength. She began to complain of internal pain and weakness, and could barely find the energy to rise from her bed. Overcome with worry, Alex sent for the finest healers in Scotland, who spared neither effort nor expense as they bled her and purged her and forced her to swallow all manner of foul potions. Poor Flora endured her suffering with courage, though Alex knew she often wept at night when she thought he was sleeping. At times he wondered if his love for her had made him cruel, for surely it was inhumane to make her bear such hideous ministrations. But he clung to the hope that her illness was but a fleeting blot on an otherwise perfect life. Eventually they would find the right treatment and one morning Flora would waken and smile, cured.

Instead his beautiful wife wasted away, until finally she was but a thin, pale wisp of the glowing girl he had so proudly presented to his people.

Her illness lasted for nearly a year. When she realized that she was going to die, her greatest worry was Alex's unhappiness. Over and over she pleaded with him not to grieve, but to promise her that he would marry again and get on with his life. *How can you ask such a thing of me?* he had demanded, pressing her slim, cold hand against his cheek. *I swear to you I will never love another.* He had sworn this oath as a way of binding her to him, of making her see she could not possibly desert him. But one night Flora was finally released from the torment of her treacherous body. Though he knew she was at peace, Alex had felt empty, abandoned. When Flora died, the light in his life was extinguished.

And now God was determined to take his son from him as well.

He could not imagine what terrible sin he had committed to make God want to punish him so viciously. His life had been far from pure, but whatever his sins, he did not think he deserved this additional, unbearable agony. He knew for certain David did not. The lad was scarcely ten and surely was entitled to live a much longer life than that. But David had been blessed with his mother's bonny features, and plagued with her frailty. Although Alex had done everything he could to shelter his son from the rigors of life in the Highlands, he had failed to protect the lad from the feebleness of his own body. That curse, it seemed, was beyond Alex's earthly control.

But not, perhaps, beyond the control of the darker forces.

He glanced over at Gwendolyn, who lay huddled on the ground shivering beneath Brodick's extra plaid. His last hope, faint as it was, was that this witch would be able to save his son. He nearly laughed at the absurdity of it. She was a condemned murderess, who looked as if a strong gust of wind might blow her away. Yet this was the woman he would entrust David's life to. He had brought in healers for the lad, who had solemnly purged and prodded and bled him, but David only grew weaker. Since neither God nor science seemed able to help him, Alex decided to turn to witchcraft. If Gwendolyn MacSween could not heal David with her sorcery, then he did not know what more to do.

The thought filled him with despair.

It was Morag who had convinced him to seek out Gwendolyn. There had been stories drifting through these mountains of the MacSween witch for years, bizarre tales of magic and devil worship, which had never particularly interested Alex. But suddenly David's condition deteriorated, and Alex feared he was dying. He went to Morag and begged her to tell him if anything more could be done for his son. And Morag had told him to find the MacSween witch and bring her to his castle.

At first he had thought he would simply offer to pay the witch for her services. But when he arrived to find she had murdered her father and was sentenced to death, he attempted to buy her, thinking that spineless fool, Laird MacSween, would be only too happy to make a profit from someone else's misery. What he had not anticipated was her clan's almost gleeful determination to see her burned. And so he resolved to rescue her, even though he had just four men to fight an entire clan of several hundred.

No wonder people thought he was mad.

He could not forget his shock when she first emerged from the bowels of the MacSween castle. How could this beautiful young woman be the murdering witch of whom her clan spoke with such dread? When they fell upon her with their battering fists, he had been ready to kill every bloody one of them. And then Gwendolyn rose and continued to walk toward her death with solemn, unwavering dignity. In that moment he had forgotten the crimes of which she stood accused, had forgotten even that she was his only hope of seeing his son well again. All he knew was, whatever the cost, he would not permit them to hurt her.

And he had felt the same powerful sensation today.

The terror that had gripped him when he saw that boar charging her was not so peculiar, he assured himself. After all, she was his last hope to cure his son. That was why he had barely been able to breathe as he thundered toward her on his horse. And surely it was blinding rage, not passion, that had caused him to crush her in his arms and kiss her. He had imprisoned her against him and roamed his hands over her delectable body because he wanted to punish her for trying to escape him. And more, he needed her to fear him. With fear, he would be able to control her.

"MacDunn."

He looked at her through the darkness, surprised that she was awake. She was shivering with cold, which concerned him. "Yes?" he replied, rising to build up the fire.

"How many more days' journey is it to your lands?"

"Why? Are you planning your next attempt to escape me?"

Gwendolyn shook her head. She had not relinquished the possibility of escape, but she knew MacDunn and his warriors would prevent any opportunity of that. She would have to wait awhile. "I was wondering how far your holding is from the MacSweens."

"Because you believe they will come after you again?"

She did not answer.

"Laird MacSween seems a reasonable man, Gwendolyn, and he knows I lead a formidable army," he pointed out, tossing some dry twigs onto the dying embers. "Once he has his precious daughter back, I doubt he will be foolish enough to sacrifice more warriors in a battle over a condemned witch, especially since she was stolen by a madman."

"You have insulted him," Gwendolyn argued. "And you have sullied the clan's honor."

Alex leaned low and blew onto the coals, coaxing a small flame to life. "I plan to send Laird MacSween a letter formally apologizing for my unseemly behavior while I was his guest, accompanied by a chest of gold. That should adequately restore his tarnished honor, and the gold will more than compensate him for any damages I have caused."

"Your offering might appease Laird MacSween," she acknowledged, "but Robert will not be so easily placated."

"He does seem inordinately anxious to get you back," observed Alex, tossing a few more sticks onto the fire. "Why is that?"

"I am a witch." She shrugged. "Robert believes I must be destroyed."

It was a reasonable answer, but something about it did not sound altogether sincere. Alex found himself recalling Robert's near obsession with Gwendolyn as he faced Alex in the woods, and his relative lack of interest in Isabella. For some reason Robert was desperate to have Gwendolyn back, and Alex sensed his motives had little to do with upholding justice or restoring his clan's honor.

"If Robert comes again, I will protect you," he stated flatly. "As will all the MacDunns."

"You cannot expect that your people will want to risk their lives for a witch," she countered.

"My people will do as I tell them," Alex told her, arranging two huge logs on the fire. A brilliant spire of flames began to lick hungrily at the well-seasoned wood. "Whether you are a witch or a murderess has no bearing on their loyalty to me. Now come here and warm yourself, before you are wracked with fever." He moved away from the fire and stretched out once more on the ground.

It was only then Gwendolyn realized he had been restoring the flames just for her. She rose and hurried toward the blaze, which was blasting a delicious aura of heat. After warming her bare hands and arms, she curled up beneath Brodick's extra plaid and wearily closed her eyes. MacDunn was only concerned with her welfare because he wanted to use her, she reminded herself fiercely.

The moment he learned she had no special powers, he would cease to care whether she was cold, or hungry, or dead.

CHAPTER 4

꒰ꕤ꒱

꒰꒱ "By God, there's no sweeter place in all of Scotland," Cameron remarked happily, inhaling a deep breath of air.

Alex stared vacantly at the whitewashed cottages tidily arranged on the green and purple mountain rising before them. The fields were crowded with shaggy, plump cows, fat geese, and apple-cheeked, bare-legged children who were squealing with excitement as they ran to greet their laird. He raised his gaze to the dark castle at the crest of the mountain. On the day he brought Flora home, he had proudly boasted to his new bride about the splendor of the enormous stone fortress—how it was a testament to simplicity, order, and the latest developments in military defense. Now, as he looked at it, he could think of only one thing.

This is where my son lies dying.

"MacDunn! MacDunn!" called the children, their voices bright. "You're back!"

"They seem happy," observed Brodick. "That's a good sign."

Alex nodded. If David had died during his absence, the clan would be in mourning, and dreading their laird's return. But his people were gathering together and waving at him, their faces lit with guarded optimism. Obviously they hoped he had found the witch and that she would be able to cure the lad.

"Come," he said, anxious to see his son. "Let's hurry."

Gwendolyn clung to Ned as they galloped past the waving MacDunns. The moment their eyes fell upon her, their smiles were erased by wariness and fear. It was a look she knew well. Ignoring their stares, she gazed at the enormous castle looming above her. It was a cold, forbidding structure, roughly chiseled from black stone, with four ominous towers and a massive curtain wall that stretched some sixty feet into the air. The stronghold had been built solely for the purpose of defending its occupants. It was so lacking in either warmth or grace that it seemed more a prison than a home. As she drew closer, she noticed that every window in the keep was tightly shut, which seemed peculiar, since the day was warm and bright.

MacDunn and his warriors clattered through the yawning iron jaws of the gate and entered the courtyard. Men and women were pouring out of the dark castle, hastily adjusting their plaids and gowns while rushing to greet their laird. On stepping into the bright sun, they squinted and shaded their eyes, as though they found its brilliance almost blinding. Several men were taking in long, greedy drafts of air, leading Gwendolyn to wonder about the purity of the air inside the castle.

"Welcome back, MacDunn," called a slender, brown-haired lad who ran up to catch hold of his horse.

"Thank you, Eric," said Alex, dismounting. "The horses require extra care today. They have been ridden long and hard."

"Aye, MacDunn," said the boy solemnly. "I will see to it."

He stole a curious glance at Gwendolyn, and then turned to carry out his order.

Gwendolyn slid down from Ned's horse, acutely aware of everyone's eyes upon her. Their expressions ranged from uncertainty to outright dread. The men had positioned themselves in front of the women, and the women in front of the children, each trying to shield the other from Gwendolyn's evil. She returned the MacDunns' wary stares with frigid calm, giving no hint of the emotions roiling within her. Long years of being treated as something vile and dangerous had not hardened her feelings, but those years had taught her how to conceal her own fear and humiliation. For a brief moment during her journey here, she had actually thought that the fact that the MacDunns were seeking a witch might mean they would treat her differently than her own clan had.

She had been mistaken.

MacDunn was striding purposefully toward the castle, apparently oblivious to the cold reception his people were giving her. On realizing Gwendolyn was not with him, he stopped and turned.

"Are you coming?" he demanded impatiently.

Gwendolyn tossed the MacDunns a dismissive look, then slowly began to walk toward their laird. The MacDunns instantly parted, giving her a wide path. Brodick and Cameron positioned themselves on either side of her, while Ned walked behind her. Evidently the warriors were trying to reassure their clan that she was their prisoner and therefore the MacDunns had naught to fear. Her head held high, her expression serene, she moved toward the castle with unhurried dignity, exuding what she hoped was a compelling aura of power. Above all, she must not let these people think she cared about what they thought of her. To do so revealed weakness, and weakness would only invite persecution and contempt.

She joined MacDunn in front of the massive oak door leading into the keep. The stone arch framing the door was festooned with a garland of rowan branches and berries, and a small, bulging sack had been tied with red wool and nailed to the scarred boards of the door.

"What is this?" Frowning, Alex tore the linen bag off the door. A foul stench instantly filled his nostrils, causing him to gag.

"Sweet Jesus," he swore, flinging the bag aside. "What is the meaning of this?" He turned to face his clan.

The MacDunns regarded each other uneasily. No one spoke.

"The mixture in that bag is meant to ward off evil spirits," offered Gwendolyn calmly. "The nail and the length of red wool are charms against witches, and the rowan garland is supposed to ward off curses or prevent anyone with an unholy purpose from entering."

Alex regarded her with surprise. "You have seen these things before?"

"Of course. The MacSweens were quite skilled at making items of this nature."

Her voice was flat and her expression contained, as if this attempt to drive her away was no more than she expected. But her hands gripped the gray fabric of her gown. It was this wholly unconscious gesture that stirred fury within Alex. Reaching up, he tore down the arch of rowan branches in one powerful motion, then cast it into the crowd.

"I ask that you welcome Gwendolyn, formerly of the Clan MacSween, to the MacDunn holding. During her stay, I expect her to be accorded the reverence due an honored guest. Is that understood?"

The MacDunns exchanged uncertain glances.

"Aye," called out a man reluctantly. "Welcome, m'lady."

A few unenthusiastic welcomes followed.

Marginally satisfied by their acquiescence, Alex threw open the door to his castle and went inside.

"*Bloody Christ!*"

A few choicer expressions came to mind, but he had to be content with that, for the noxious cloud of smoke he had stepped into had reduced him to a violent fit of coughing.

"That's it, laddie, get it out, get it out," advised a cheerful voice.

Gwendolyn entered hesitantly behind Alex and blinked

until her eyes became accustomed to the smoky interior. The chamber they had stepped into was dark, save for the sunlight fighting its way in through the open door behind them, and a number of oily torches spitting far more smoke than flame. A gust of fresh air was stirring the heavy veil that choked the room and as the haze thinned she was able to make out an enormous great hall. Two fires roared at opposite ends of the huge room, over which numerous cauldrons were placed, each spewing an acrid funnel of black. The heavy wooden tables around the room were crowded with pots, bowls, and jars of every size and description, all smoldering with a variety of pungent substances. The walls and ceiling of the room had been draped with drying herbs, elaborate amulets, and more rowan branches, giving it a strangely mythical appearance, and the stone floor was covered with a mass of rotting rushes. The resulting heat and stench and smoke made the air virtually intolerable, although the snowy-haired man who suddenly emerged through the fog seemed to be bearing it well enough.

"Don't worry, laddie, it just takes a minute to get used to," he said, whacking Alex on the back. "Come, now, take another breath—there—you see?"

"What in the name of God is going on here, Owen?" demanded Alex hoarsely.

"Why, we're preparing for the witch," Owen replied, as if the answer were obvious. "And a damned unpleasant task it's been, I must say. Bloody awful, if you must know. Oh, beg pardon, m'lady," he apologized, noticing Gwendolyn. "Sometimes an old warrior forgets to soften his language in front of a lady. Do forgive. Owen MacDunn, at your service." He tilted forward in a slow, creaking bow and pressed a gallant kiss against her hand. "She's very comely, MacDunn," he remarked, smiling as he eyed Gwendolyn up and down. "Is she Brodick's?"

"No," said Brodick, entering the hall with Cameron and Ned. "Jesus, Owen, what is that hideous stench?"

"Mind your language," scolded Owen, wagging a gnarled finger at him. "There is a lady present, and I would ask that you behave accordingly, you young scoundrel. High time you abandoned your rakish ways and settled down. Our Brodick has broken many a fair maiden's heart," he confided to Gwendolyn. "Too damn handsome for his own good, that's what. Well, now," he continued, stoking his white beard, "you can't be Cameron's, or Clarinda would have something to say about that. Yes, indeed, I'm sure she would." He chuckled, clearly amused by the idea. Then his blue eyes suddenly grew wide. "Good God," he gasped, stunned, "you're not . . ."

Gwendolyn stiffened.

". . . Ned's lady friend, are you? Because that would be just marvelous if you were," he exclaimed, "simply marvelous."

She glanced helplessly at Alex.

"She is not Ned's," Alex said, looking irritated. "Can we please get back to the subject of the hall?"

"Why, I told you, laddie," Owen reminded him. "We're preparing for the witch. Do forgive, my dear," he apologized, patting Gwendolyn's hand. "A frightful mess, I know, and the stench is absolutely abominable. But we have to make certain the old hag can't cast spells on the lot of us, now, don't we? We MacDunns must show her we will not be subject to her wicked mischief. Why, I remember when I was just a wee thing, there was a witch who came here and tried to turn our laird into a goat. The spell didn't quite take, but for years afterward poor old MacDunn had the most dreadful habit of gnawing on the table at mealtimes. Completely destroyed one perfectly fine table within a year. Do you remember that, MacDunn?"

"I wasn't born then."

Owen frowned, considering. "No, of course not." He swept his gaze appraisingly over the rest of them. "None of you were," he decided. "Oh, well. No matter."

"I've really got it, this time!"

Gwendolyn turned to see a thin, dour-faced little man enter the hall carrying a bubbling silver cup. He appeared to be very close in age to Owen, with thin scraggly white hair circling his virtually bald head, and a heavily creased face that seemed to be screwed into a permanent mask of disapproval.

"Here, now, MacDunn, we must get the witch to drink this at once," he instructed, indicating the dark green potion that was frothing grotesquely down the sides of the goblet.

"Why, Lachlan?" asked Alex.

Lachlan glanced suspiciously at Gwendolyn, wondering whether she could be trusted. Deciding she could, he lowered his voice and explained, "This elixir I made will prove whether or not the witch really is a witch. If she is, her evil powers will protect her from the effects of the poison. That is how we will know for sure!" he finished triumphantly.

"And what if she is not a witch?" Alex inquired.

Lachlan regarded him in bewilderment. "What do you mean?"

"I mean, what if you give that ghastly-looking concoction to someone who is not protected by evil powers?"

Lachlan scratched his bald head, baffled. "You said you were going to get a witch, MacDunn," he pointed out, sounding somewhat defensive. "You never said anything about getting someone who only *might* be a witch. Might being a witch and being a witch are two entirely different things."

"He's right, laddie," Owen agreed, nodding. "You can't argue with that."

"Blast it! That's it!" roared an infuriated voice from the corridor. "I've had just about all *any mortal man can take!*"

Gwendolyn turned to see yet another white-haired man burst into the hall.

"MacDunn, thank God you're back. You've got to do something about the frightful mess they're making of the castle," he said, glaring at Owen and Lachlan. "You can't walk anywhere without stepping in slime, there's no light and even less air, and not even a man's private chamber is safe. The vapors in my room were so thick this morning, I thought I'd fallen asleep naked *in the bloody smokehouse!*"

"You're exaggerating, Reginald," scolded a smiling woman with an ample bosom and neatly arranged gray hair, who entered the hall behind him.

"No, by God, I'm not, Marjorie," Reginald returned.

"And it's a sad day in a man's life when his very own wife tries to smoke him to death while he sleeps!"

Apparently untroubled by his anger, Marjorie bustled past the group of them with an armful of dried grasses, which she promptly heaved into one of the fireplaces. Fresh smoke began to spew thickly into the room.

"There, now, do you see?" demanded Reginald. "Day and night they've been at this. Burning and draping, stewing and sliming, until this castle and everything in it stinks like rotten herring. I tell you, it's enough to drive a man stark, raving *mad!*"

Owen's and Lachlan's eyes grew wide.

"Your pardon, MacDunn," Reginald apologized hastily. "It was merely a figure of speech."

"I know," said Alex.

"Well, then, now that everything is ready, where is the witch?" asked Owen brightly, rubbing his gnarled hands together with anticipation. He looked around the room and frowned. "You did remember to bring her, didn't you laddie?"

"Yes," Alex assured him. "I did."

"Thank God," said Reginald. "I would hate to think I had endured all of this for nothing."

"Send the old hag in," ordered Lachlan, who was carefully trying to avoid having any of his frothing potion spill onto his hand. "This elixir works best while it's still fresh."

"*She is already here,*" proclaimed a thin, crackling voice.

A hush gripped the hall as a ghostly apparition began to emerge from the thick shroud of smoke still swirling at the opposite end. As the specter drew closer, Gwendolyn saw it was actually an ancient old woman with a silvery veil of hair that seemed to float around her as she moved. She wore a magnificent robe of scarlet silk trimmed with gold, and walked with the assistance of a dark, elegantly carved staff. Though her carriage was bent and her body frail, a remarkable energy emanated from her, which seemed to dissipate the smoke as she moved through it. Her skin was pale and webbed by time, yet it had a softness and luminosity that Gwendolyn could not recall in any other woman of such advanced years.

On reaching Gwendolyn she stopped, leaned against her staff, and studied her a long, silent moment. Gwendolyn returned her scrutiny with deliberate calm. The woman's eyes were of the deepest green, and they sparkled with an intriguing combination of wisdom, merriment, and something more, as if she had seen more of life than she might have wished, but had yet to be conquered by it.

"You did well, Alex," she finally stated. "She holds great power within her spirit. But you must treat her with care," she added, her gaze still locked on Gwendolyn. "She is strong, but she has been injured. Her wounds have yet to heal."

Gwendolyn controlled her urge to smile. How many years, she wondered, had this eccentric old woman fabricated fanciful stories and visions for the MacDunns? Of course it was to Gwendolyn's advantage that this seer had just proclaimed her a witch, for she sensed by the look on MacDunn's face that he respected the poor thing's opinion. However, Gwendolyn felt she needed to correct her on the matter of having been injured.

"I'm afraid I have no wounds," she told her.

The old woman regarded her calmly. "Some wounds cut deeper than those of the flesh, my dear."

Owen, Lachlan, and Reginald were now staring at Gwendolyn in slack-jawed astonishment.

"Good God, do you mean to say this comely lass is the witch?" sputtered Owen, appalled. "Why, she's barely more than a child!"

"I really think you're mistaken, Morag," decided Reginald. "And no wonder. With all the smoke fogging this hall, it's a wonder you can even see her!" he added irritably.

"Here, lassie," said Lachlan, smiling. "You must be parched after your long journey. Why don't you have a nice, long draft of this special drink I made just for you?" he invited, raising the effervescing concoction to her face.

Alex snatched the goblet from Lachlan and hurled its contents into the hearth. The fire exploded into a blinding ball of flames, forcing all of them to shield their eyes as they stepped back.

"Really, Lachlan, I wish you would leave the potions to me," Morag chided. "You don't know what you're doing."

Gwendolyn stared blankly at the thick timbers in the fireplace, which were rapidly dissolving beneath the smoldering sludge of Lachlan's elixir.

"If she's really a witch, the potion wouldn't have harmed her!" Lachlan protested.

"I don't know, Lachlan," Owen mused. "That brew seems awfully potent."

"I think the lass must have us under some kind of spell," said Reginald, "that makes us think she looks like that, when in fact she is really a hideous old bat. Which is not to say that all old women are hideous, Morag," he quickly qualified.

"Why are you saying that to me?" demanded Morag, clearly incensed. "I'm not old."

Alex glanced at Gwendolyn. She seemed to be holding up remarkably well, considering that after escaping being burned at the stake, his own clan now seemed determined to both suffocate and poison her. Her expression was composed as she watched the elders heatedly arguing about when, exactly, one could be considered old. For a moment he thought she might actually see the humor in this ludicrous reception.

Then he noticed that her hands were clutching her gown again, as if searching for something to hold on to.

He moved to stand beside her, so close her bare arm nearly grazed his. "This is Gwendolyn, formerly of the Clan MacSween," he announced. "She is the witch I went to find. When we reached the MacSween holding, we discovered she had been tried by her clan for witchcraft and was sentenced to be burned at the stake," he explained, purposely omitting that Gwendolyn had also been accused of murder. He saw no merit in alarming his people more than necessary. "When my offer to purchase her was rejected, I decided to save her, thereby raising the ire of the Clan MacSween. I am afraid we may experience trouble from them in the future."

"Are you saying we're at war with the MacSweens, laddie?" demanded Owen incredulously.

"Because of this comely witch?" added Lachlan, looking at Gwendolyn in outrage.

Alex nodded.

The little group absorbed this information in shocked silence. Only Morag seemed undisturbed.

"Well, I call that splendid!" Owen declared, suddenly beaming. "It's been years since we MacDunns were involved in a good clan war."

"I don't know what's splendid about it," Lachlan grumbled sourly. "We're all likely to be split open and disemboweled where we stand."

"I'll just fetch my sword and shield," said Reginald. "Those crafty MacSween devils could strike at any moment."

"I don't think we need to worry about an attack today," Alex said. "We encountered a few of them on the way home and they were quickly taken care of. It will be a while before a new force can make its way here—if Laird MacSween decides he wants to pursue the matter."

"Oh, he will have to pursue it, laddie," Owen assured him. "It's a matter of honor. After all, you've stolen his witch."

"Are you sure she is a witch, Morag?" asked Lachlan, studying Gwendolyn suspiciously. "She doesn't seem bothered by all this smoke."

"Cameron, Brodick, and Ned can all attest to her powers," Morag replied. "Can't you?"

"Aye," said Cameron, nodding. "One night during our journey here, she whipped the spirits into a fair frenzy, she did."

"I've never seen anything like it," added Brodick. "One minute there was a raging storm, and the next minute the night was as still as can be."

"Really?" Owen was clearly impressed. "Can you do that for us now, lassie?"

"I can't see how that will be of any use to us," remarked Lachlan, frowning. "Creating a storm in the middle of a perfectly adequate day."

"But it would be amusing," said a silky voice.

The woman who entered the hall was smiling, but as her eyes fell upon Gwendolyn her mouth tightened slightly, as if she had unexpectedly tasted something bitter. She quickly recovered, however, and proceeded to make her way across the room. She was exceptionally attractive, with thick honey-tinted hair that spilled down her lushly curved body. Her movements gave the impression of unhurried grace, but Gwendolyn sensed her pace had more to do with the fact that all eyes were upon her, and she was very much enjoying the attention.

"Welcome back, Alex," she murmured, stopping directly in front of him. "We have missed you." She frowned at the tattered bandage circling his otherwise naked chest. "Were you badly injured?"

"No, Robena," he assured her. " 'Tis barely a scratch."

Gwendolyn noticed the gown the woman wore was cut low and a shade too tight, so that the fabric strained over the pale swell of her breasts. But it was neither faded nor worn, suggesting that this clinging fit was intentional. For some reason this observation irritated her. She had an overwhelming desire to grab a swath of plaid and cover her.

"So this is the witch," observed Robena, turning toward Gwendolyn. She smiled, but her smile did not quite reach her eyes. She stared at Gwendolyn's naked arms, recognizing that the fabric of her torn gown matched MacDunn's bandage. Now that she was closer, Gwendolyn could see a fan of fine lines under her eyes, betraying her age to be closer to thirty than she had previously thought. "You poor thing," she cooed, taking in Gwendolyn's disheveled appearance. "You look half starved. Alex, did you not feed this child on your journey here?"

Her tone was playfully chastising, but Gwendolyn sensed there was something about her appearance that displeased Robena.

"She will eat well enough now that she is here," Alex replied. "How is my son?"

A pall fell over the room. The clan members eyed each

other uncertainly, not knowing how to answer. Only Morag's expression remained serene.

"His condition remains unchanged, Alex," Robena volunteered, her voice soft with regret. "I managed to get him to take a little food last night, but his body quickly rejected it. Elspeth said it was the poisons in his body that caused this, and so she bled him last night, and then again this morning. He is now resting quietly in his chamber."

Alex absorbed this information in silence. The report was no different than what he had expected. That was why he had brought the witch here. And the news could have been far worse. They could have said his son was dead.

"I will see him now," he announced, striding toward the staircase at the far end of the hall. "The rest of you, see if you can't do something about cleaning up this mess. I dislike having my hall smell like a putrid cavern."

Robena picked up her skirts and rushed to follow him. Suddenly Alex stopped and looked expectantly at Gwendolyn. "Are you coming?" he asked impatiently.

The trio made their way up the staircase and along a dim, torchlit corridor. The air grew heavier and staler as they continued, and by the time they stopped in front of a wooden door, Gwendolyn felt she could scarcely breathe. Even Robena had produced a dainty linen square from her sleeve and raised it to her nose, so she could better tolerate the stifling smoke. Alex hesitated a moment, his enormous hand gripping the iron latch, as if steeling himself for what lay on the other side of the door. Finally he lifted the latch, swung the heavy door open, and went inside.

The chamber was dark, hot, and airless, as the windows were shut tight and a fire roared in the hearth, even though the day outside was warm. The acrid haze produced by countless pots of smoldering herbs was so thick it made the great hall seem almost breezy in comparison. But there was another smell to the room, a close, sour odor of sickness. A few dripping candles cast a feeble glow into the gloom, allowing just enough light for Gwendolyn to make out a bed piled high with blankets and animal skins. A lean, spindly armed woman was bent over the pile, briskly arranging yet another covering. On seeing Alex, the woman straightened and gave him a respectful nod.

"Welcome back, MacDunn." She cast a confused glance at Gwendolyn. "Is this the witch?"

Alex nodded. The woman's expression hardened.

"Forgive me, m'lord," she began, her tone far more acquiescent than the rigid set of her pinched face, "but your son is quite weak just now and I really don't think—"

"She will see him now, Elspeth," Alex interrupted firmly.

Elspeth pressed her lips together, as if trying to contain whatever argument she wanted to give her laird. Realizing she had no choice, she moved away from the bed.

Alex stepped toward it as if he were approaching a coffin. Summoning all of his courage, he looked stonily at the thin, ashen face of his son. If not for Elspeth's certainty that the lad was resting, he would have thought he was dead. David's skin was white and bloodless, his cheeks gaunt, his eyelids as thin and fragile as paper. Alex swallowed hard, fighting the despair threatening to engulf him. First his beloved Flora, and now his only son. What had he done, he wondered desperately, to make God loathe him so? Overwhelmed by the sight of his child laid out like a corpse, he raised his eyes to Gwendolyn, silently imploring her to help.

Gwendolyn stared at MacDunn. It was as if she were looking upon him for the first time. Instead of the powerful mad laird, a man who feared nothing and found amusement by instilling fear in others, she suddenly saw a man in unbearable pain.

She looked down at the pallid, sweat-soaked head lying still on the damp pillow. She guessed his son's age to be about nine, certainly no more than ten, though his illness might have delayed his growth. He had a delicacy of structure that reminded Gwendolyn of an eggshell, fine and white and smooth, and she feared if she laid her hand against his feverish brow he might suddenly shatter. His breathing was so faint it was almost imperceptible—and no wonder, she thought angrily. The terrible heat and stench corrupted what little air remained in this dreadful chamber.

"He can barely breathe—could we not open a window?" she suggested, looking hopefully at MacDunn.

"No," interjected Robena. "The boy is weak and vulnerable to drafts."

"He must be kept warm," Elspeth added firmly. "A sudden chill could kill him."

Gwendolyn bit back her response that between the raging fire and the suffocating mound of blankets and furs, there was little chance of the lad catching cold. Instead she gently laid her hand against his hot cheek, then his brow, wondering how much of his unnatural heat was due to fever and how much was due to the ungodly warmth in this room. The lad's eyes slowly fluttered open. He stared at her a moment, puzzled, as if he thought he should know who she was but could not remember. And then his eyes grew wide and he began to tremble, not with cold, Gwendolyn realized, but with fear.

"Are you the witch?" he asked in a small, frightened voice.

"My name is Gwendolyn," she replied gently.

He interpreted this as an affirmation. "Elspeth says you're evil."

"Elspeth has never met me before," returned Gwendolyn, "so I don't see how she could know such a thing."

The lad appeared to consider her response a moment. And then he looked at Alex and whimpered, "I don't want a witch near me."

"You will tolerate her presence," Alex ordered.

The boy's eyes drifted shut, as if the effort of wakening for that brief moment had completely drained him.

Gwendolyn cast a disapproving look at MacDunn. The lad was obviously extremely ill and terribly frightened. She could well imagine what horrid tales this Elspeth woman and possibly others had told him about witches and what they did to helpless young children. MacDunn's unnecessary gruffness would only succeed in frightening the child even more. As she frowned at him, she suddenly noticed a striking similarity between the structure of MacDunn's face and that of his son's.

The boy's cheeks and jaw were softer, prettier almost, and his coloring was different, for his damp hair lay dark against the pillow, and his brows were red. But his nose was a virtual copy of MacDunn's, smaller, but perfectly straight and narrow, and his chin bore the same distinctive cleft.

"You will heal him," Alex commanded.

His voice was flat and emotionless, as if he were ordering her to do something simple and of little consequence. But Gwendolyn was not fooled by his dispassionate mien. The agony in his eyes a moment earlier had already revealed how deeply he cared for this child. This was why he had brought her here, she realized. Not because he wanted to use her supposed powers to bring him riches, or to render him invincible, or to destroy other clans, as she had believed. MacDunn had gone in search of her and brazenly stolen her from her executioners because he prayed she had the ability to perform a miracle and save his dying son.

And by playing along and pretending to be a witch, she had encouraged him to believe such an impossible feat was within her grasp.

She lowered her gaze.

"You *can* heal him," Alex persisted, troubled by her failure to respond. "Can't you?"

"She will destroy him," Elspeth warned, casting a hateful glance at Gwendolyn. "She is evil and can only work the devil's mischief. David's soul is young and pure, and she will steal it for her own foul purposes, just as she has no doubt stolen the souls of countless other innocents—"

"That is enough, Elspeth," commanded Alex.

Elspeth clamped her mouth into a tight line, then moved toward the fire and began to hurl more sticks of wood on it.

Streams of sweat were leaking down Gwendolyn's face, making her acutely aware of the unbearable heat in the room. Her head was starting to spin, and her breath had been reduced to shallow gasps as her body rejected the foul air she breathed. She could only imagine the effect these insufferable conditions were having on MacDunn's poor son.

"We will discuss this matter elsewhere," MacDunn stated

abruptly. He crossed the chamber, flung open the door, and left.

A gust of marginally cooler air entered the room.

"Mind the draft," ordered Robena, frowning at Gwendolyn.

Grateful to be leaving the stifling chamber, Gwendolyn hurried out, feeling strangely guilty that she was abandoning David to the ministrations of these two women.

"Can you cure him?"

His manner was calm as he posed the question. Had Gwendolyn not witnessed his pain as he looked upon the lad a few moments earlier, she would have thought him only vaguely interested in her response.

The chamber he had taken her to was at the top of one of the castle's towers, where she would be isolated from the rest of the clan. She did not know whether this was for their protection or her own. Like the rest of this bleak fortress, it was dark and airless, and choked with the smoke emanating from two vessels of burning herbs. Feeling dizzy and nauseated, Gwendolyn went to the shuttered windows and threw them open, then greedily inhaled several long, cleansing breaths of fresh air. Once she felt sufficiently recovered from the stench of smoke and sickness, she turned to face MacDunn.

"Is this to be my chamber?" she asked, ignoring his question.

He nodded.

On learning that, she marched over to the table, scooped up the two smoldering vessels, and hurled them out the window.

"It is clear your clan despises me," she began, turning to face him, "but if I am to earn their trust—"

"*Bleedin' ballocks!*" bellowed an enraged voice from below. "What in the name of Christ are you trying to do up there, *kill me*?"

Gwendolyn gasped and peered out the window. A short,

round little man was glaring up at her as he crossly rubbed his aching head.

"I'm so sorry," she apologized fervently. "I didn't realize you were there."

The man's scowl melted into an expression of sheer horror. "The witch! The witch!" he screamed, scrambling away. "She tried to kill me! She's put the mark of death upon me! Help! *Help!*"

Gwendolyn watched in frustration as the man ran off, shrieking at the top of his lungs.

"I think you should relinquish any hope of the clan coming to trust you," Alex suggested dryly. "They are quite a superstitious lot, and not likely to believe that a witch can be trusted. Besides, I don't give a damn whether you befriend the clan or not. I brought you here because of your powers. And now I want to know, can you cure my son?"

Gwendolyn regarded him in silence. It was clear the boy was deathly ill, and he had already been treated by healers who were far more experienced than she.

"How long has he been ill, MacDunn?"

Alex wearily shrugged his shoulders. "I don't really know. He has never been a well child, from the time he was born. He takes after his mother, both in appearance and in the delicacy of his constitution. His mother died from it," he finished gravely.

"But surely he has not always been like this," argued Gwendolyn.

"No," he admitted. "He began to take more ill than usual some four months ago. At first it seemed a simple stomach ailment. He could not seem to keep anything inside, and when he tried to eat, he suffered terrible pain. Gradually his appetite diminished completely. He lost weight, and then strength. Elspeth is a fine healer, but she did not seem to be able to help the lad, so I sent for two healers from Scone. They stayed nearly a month and tormented the poor lad with hideous potions and treatments—bleedings and purgings and blisterings. At times it seemed as if they were determined to break the illness by breaking his body, but my son was no better for all their torture. Finally I could bear his cries no longer and I sent them away. Elspeth assumed his care once more, assisted by Robena. I prayed that he would recover, but he did not. I had given up all hope. And then one day I heard there was a witch living amongst the MacSweens. It was said her powers were great, though often used for evil purposes. Morag told me to seek you out and bring you to my clan. And now I want to know—can you cure my son?"

Gwendolyn hesitated. She had no magic powers, and other than her clandestine study of her mother's notes, she had no practical experience as a healer. By all appearances it seemed the boy was certainly going to die, perhaps before this very night was out. But if she admitted this to MacDunn, he would realize he had risked the welfare of his clan for nothing and would have no reason to protect her.

"The lad's illness is severe," she began, "and he has been forced to endure treatments which may have weakened him rather than strengthened him. I cannot say for certain that I will be able to cure him," she admitted carefully, "but I will try, MacDunn."

She saw no trace of hope flicker across his face. Perhaps he had felt hope before and realized how painful it could be. Instead he merely nodded.

"Then I put my son in your care. While you are here, you may roam the castle as you wish, but you are not permitted to go outside without my consent and an escort. If the boy worsens or dies, or if you try to escape while I have entrusted his life to you, then you will suffer the consequences. Is that clear?"

"And if the lad recovers?"

"If my son is cured, your life will be spared."

"And I will be set free?"

"No. You will remain here, to heal others should they fall ill."

"That is hardly a satisfactory exchange, MacDunn," Gwendolyn protested. "If I save the life of your son, then I must be granted my freedom."

"I have already saved you from death three times," he

reminded her. "Twice from the MacSweens, and once from that wild boar. Your life belongs to me, and your only reward, should you earn it, will be the gift of your life."

"Then slay me and be done with it," she retorted angrily, turning away, "for I won't live my life as a prisoner."

Irritation swelled within him. Did she not understand that she had no choice in the matter? He grabbed her roughly by the arm and spun her around. She gasped with outrage and tried to wrench free, but he tightened his grip until he could almost feel her flesh bruising like ripe fruit beneath his fingers. He captured her chin with his other hand and forced her to look at him, making it clear he would not tolerate her insolence.

"You have no choice, Gwendolyn," he said harshly.

"It is you who have no choice, MacDunn," she countered, her gray eyes glinting with fire. "For unless you agree to free me, your son will die, and I will do nothing to stop it."

He knew his hold on her was painful, but her fury seemed to outweigh her discomfort. Suddenly he was aware of how small and fragile she felt within his grasp. The delicate structure of her jaw could almost shatter beneath the strength of his grip, and the crushed satin of her arm had heated the palm of his hand. Her breath was angry and shallow, her cheeks slightly flushed, whether from the warmth of his son's room or her own anger, he was not sure. The soft swell of her breasts brushed against his chest as she breathed, the coarse fabric of her gown the only barrier between her flesh and his.

Desire ripped through him, dark, powerful, and overwhelming.

Unable to control himself, he released her chin and sank his fingers deep into her hair while wrapping his other arm around her, pulling her against him as he ground his mouth to hers. She moaned in outrage and tried to shove him away, but the hunger surging through him was staggering, consuming every vestige of his reason. She was fighting him, yes, but he could not understand it, could not believe that the need now raging within him had not inflamed her as well. His tongue delved into the sweetness of her mouth, tasting her, possessing her, pleading with her to give in. She froze for an instant, as if shocked, or perhaps her body was remembering when he had kissed her so before, and how she had responded. He moaned and deepened his kiss, drawing her closer, until her slim, soft form was pressed tight against his own hard length. And then suddenly her hesitation vanished, and she was clinging to him and returning his kiss with a desperation that seemed to match his own.

It was wrong, it was unthinkable, he understood this well, and yet he continued to touch her and hold her and taste her, like a drowning man who at last has found something to grasp on to. In a moment his reason would return, he felt almost certain of it, but until then he released himself to this glorious madness, this stolen ecstasy, which he had never thought to know again. When Flora had been well she had stirred his blood, but never like this, never to the point where he could scarcely think, could scarcely breathe, or remember who and what he was.

He was Flora's husband.

Appalled by his brutish behavior, he abruptly released Gwendolyn and stepped away. He regarded her warily, wondering if she had cast some spell over him. The thought gave him some comfort, for it almost explained, if not pardoned, his staggering desire for her. But she had raised her fingertips to her lips and was staring at him in bewilderment, as if she, too, could not understand what was happening between them.

"Very well," he said, his voice strangely hollow. "Cure my son, and I will grant you your freedom."

She said nothing. He interpreted her silence as acquiescence.

"You will dine in the great hall tonight with the rest of the clan," he commanded, moving toward the door. The chamber had grown smaller, somehow, and he was overcome with a need to have distance from her. "I will instruct my people that they are not to try to poison you while you are here."

"I do not wish to dine with your clan," Gwendolyn informed him, shaken by what had just transpired between them. "As I am here as a prisoner, I will take my meal alone in my chamber."

"You will eat where and when I tell you to eat," Alex countered. "And I order you to join me in the great hall."

Gwendolyn shook her head. "I won't come down."

He jerked open the door. "Then I'll send someone to carry you down."

Sunlight was pouring through the open windows, wrapping her small form in a brilliant haze as she glared at him. It shimmered through the black silk of her hair and etched the slim outline of her body in gold, making him achingly aware of how fine and womanly she was, even in that tattered, smoke-stained gown. Desire pulsed through him once again, so intense it was almost painful.

"You will need another gown," he murmured thickly. "I will arrange for it."

He slammed the door as he left.

". . . The pot flew in a great loop, and then it stopped, just sat there in the air, as if it were being held by terrible, ungodly hands," said Munro, cupping his own plump hands to better illustrate his tale.

A murmur of awe rippled through the great hall.

"And what did you do?" prodded Reginald.

"Why, I just stood and stared at it, frozen, for my legs had been turned to stone, and when I opened my mouth to yell, no sound came out. That was when I knew the witch had cast one of her wicked spells upon me and there was nothing I could do but pray for mercy."

"Then what happened?" asked Lachlan.

"Well, the vessel hung there a moment, casting its great, black shadow over me," continued Munro, waving his arms for effect. "And all at once I felt chilled to the very bone. Just as I was certain I could bear no more, the pot suddenly began to fly toward me, like a falcon swooping down on a hare. I let out a long, terrified scream before it banged me most cruelly on the head, knocking me out cold." He tilted his head forward and pointed to the egg-sized lump swelling from his scalp.

The women of the clan gasped in horror.

"Do forgive, Munro, but how could you scream?" Owen wondered. "I thought you said you could make no sound."

"It was a silent scream," Munro clarified. His eyes narrowed and his voice grew ominously low as he finished, "The most terrifying scream of all."

"But why has the witch chosen to harm you?" asked Reginald. "You've done her no wrong."

"Don't think for a moment that Munro will be the only one to suffer from her spells," warned Elspeth grimly. "Witches need no reason to create mischief. They bring harm to others purely out of sport!"

"Dear me," said Owen, shaking his head. "She seemed like such a nice lass."

"I didn't think so," countered Lachlan petulantly. "A nice lass would have tried my elixir, just to be polite."

"Good God, Lachlan, that potion you made would have dissolved steel!" observed Reginald. "MacDunn would have been most annoyed if you'd poisoned his guest the moment she arrived."

"It may have been a trifle strong," Lachlan conceded. "But I have been working on another one, and this time I have the measurements just right." He patted the small ewer next to his goblet.

"If she truly is a witch, her powers must be great, for she seemed unaffected by the herbs and amulets in the hall," fretted Marjorie, laying a platter of roasted meat on the table. "I wish MacDunn had permitted us to leave them a while longer."

"I don't," said Reginald. "The place looked bloody awful, and smelled even worse."

"The witch was not unaffected," Elspeth assured Marjorie. "She merely used her powers to disguise her distress. But she did not fare so well in the lad's room. I could see the smoke was bothering her."

"What the devil does that prove?" Reginald demanded

impatiently. "That stinking haze you women have created in every room bothers me, and I'm certainly not a witch."

"It is not the same," Elspeth replied testily.

"What are we going to do?" lamented Robena. "Poor David is terrified of her, but MacDunn is determined that we submit the boy to her care."

"She will certainly kill him," Elspeth predicted. "If not with her spells, then with ignorance. Today she wanted to open a window in his chamber."

"Does the lass not realize how dangerous that could be?" sputtered Owen, clearly horrified.

"It would seem not." Elspeth's expression grew pensive. "And then again, perhaps she does."

"This is terrible," Marjorie fretted. "Someone has to talk to MacDunn."

"MacDunn won't listen to reason," said Lachlan. "Not when it comes to his son."

"Aye, that's true," Owen agreed. "The poor lad just hasn't been the same since dear Flora died."

"MacDunn is much better than he was," pointed out Robena. "If we can just get him to see that this witch will only use her evil ways to inflict misery and suffering—"

"Good evening, lassie," called Owen brightly, waving. "We were just talking about you."

Startled, everyone in the hall turned and looked fearfully at Gwendolyn, who was standing at the top of the stairs.

She shouldn't have come, she realized miserably. She had not wanted to. It was only the threat of MacDunn sending someone to carry her down that had finally wrested her from her chamber. That, and the spicy sweet aroma of roasted meat and freshly baked bread. The sudden, agonizing loss of her father had left her far too numb to care much about the needs of her body these past few days. But as she sat in her chamber gloomily watching the fading purple ribbons of summer light from her window, she suddenly grew aware of a great, almost painful emptiness. The tantalizing scents filtering up from the kitchen and the great hall only intensified this sensation, until finally hunger was clawing impatiently in her stomach. It was

at that moment that two men appeared at her door, carrying a
metal bathing tub. MacDunn thought she might be wanting a
bath, they explained, hurriedly setting it down in her chamber. A parade of men followed with sloshing buckets of water,
which they swiftly dumped into the tub before racing from the
room.

Just as Gwendolyn was about to climb into the bath, there
was another knock at her door. She opened it to find an extremely timid serving girl cradling a beautiful gown of crimson wool. A gift from MacDunn, she stammered, thrusting it
nervously into Gwendolyn's arms and scurrying away. At first
Gwendolyn was tempted to call the girl back and tell her she
wanted no such gift. But the woolen fabric poured like warm
wine over the bare skin of her arms, and she found herself
fascinated by its softness, which was so unlike the familiar
coarseness of her own gown. She draped the garment across
her body, marveling at the intricate gold embroidery decorat-
ing the low neckline and cuffs. She had always been responsible for making her own clothes, and without a mother or
woman friend to guide her, her handiwork had never been
accomplished. Suddenly her own gown seemed not only tattered, but ugly and crudely constructed. Perhaps there was no
harm in accepting this gift, she decided. After all, if she was to
dine in the great hall with the clan, she could not appear
dressed in what was little better than a rag.

But now as she stood at the top of the stairs, staring down
at the wary glances of the MacDunns, she wished she had not
come. She endured their silent, hostile scrutiny with an air of
cool detachment, a manner she had learned to call upon from
the time she was a child. Reminding herself that MacDunn
had ordered her to join the clan for the evening meal, she
slowly descended the staircase.

Uneasy murmurs rippled through the room. On reaching
the floor, Gwendolyn realized she had no idea where she was
supposed to sit. Owen, Lachlan, Reginald, and Morag were
seated at the laird's table, which was situated on a raised dais
in the center of the hall. Owen had cheerfully waved at her as
she entered, but stopped when Lachlan poked him disapprov-

ingly in the ribs. The rest of the clan members dining in the hall that night were crowded on benches arranged around long, cloth-draped tables. Seeing an empty place at one of them, Gwendolyn moved toward it. As soon as the MacDunns there realized her intent, they immediately shifted positions so that the opening previously there was now gone. Gwendolyn stopped, straightened her spine, and began to move purposefully toward another table. The people there quickly closed ranks, effectively preventing her from seating herself. She hesitated a moment and then approached a third table. The MacDunns glared frostily at her as she drew near, making it clear her company was not welcome.

Shaken and humiliated, her hunger all but forgotten, Gwendolyn moved quickly toward the archway leading to the corridor, only to plow straight into MacDunn as he rounded the corner with Brodick and Cameron.

"Where are you going?" he demanded.

"I—I am returning to my chamber," she stammered.

"Then your sense of direction is askew," observed Cameron, amused. "The stairs to your chamber are on the other side of the hall."

Alex studied her a moment. The gown he had sent to her poured over her slender form in a glorious wash of crimson and gold, its brilliant color accentuating the paleness of her skin and the inky cape of her hair. But the fabric draped too loosely across the narrow width of her waist and hips, reminding him of her fragility. He found himself wondering if she had always been this thin, or if the death of her father and the bleak days spent in a dank dungeon had melted her flesh away.

"Have you eaten anything?" he demanded.

"I am not hungry."

"Are you ill?" he persisted, troubled by her lack of appetite.

Her gaze lowered, Gwendolyn shook her head.

"Then you will stay and eat something," he commanded. "I will not have you starving yourself to death."

"Please, MacDunn," Gwendolyn implored softly, "I wish to return to my chamber."

Her voice was small and strained, as if on the verge of breaking. Alex frowned. Though he had vowed he would not touch her again, he found himself grasping her chin and gently raising her head. Her wide gray eyes were sparkling with pain, and her expression was pleading. Stunned to see her so obviously hurt, he raked his gaze questioningly over the rest of the clan. Their guilty expressions quickly told him that they had driven her to this state. Anger reared within him, anger and an oddly protective sensation, which made him want to wrap his arms around her and soothe her battered spirits with gentle words. Instead he gave her a small bow and offered her his arm.

"Do forgive me, m'lady, for arriving so late." His tone was purposely contrite, as if she had every reason to be angry with him. "But now that I am here, I hope you will reconsider and agree to join me at my table."

Gwendolyn regarded him in confusion. There was no hint of mockery in MacDunn's expression. Instead he seemed genuinely remorseful, as if her sudden flight from the hall were somehow due to his unforgivable neglect of her. He was trying to salvage her wounded pride, she realized, by apologizing before his clan and giving her the choice of either accepting or rejecting his gesture.

Moved by his sensitivity, she reached up and laid her hand on the firm muscle of his arm.

Alex escorted her across the silent hall to the laird's table, where he pulled out a chair and seated her. Then he took his place beside her and sternly addressed his clan.

"Gwendolyn MacSween is our guest. During her stay here, I have faith that you will treat her with the honor we normally extend to our guests, and give her any assistance she may require as she heals my son."

The clan remained silent. Satisfied that he had made his expectations clear, he turned and began to pile food on Gwendolyn's trencher.

Although   Gwendolyn   felt   somewhat   fortified   by

MacDunn's support, there was no mistaking the animosity swirling through the room. Out of the corner of her eye she saw Elspeth and Robena glaring at her, and they were not alone. The MacDunns feared and resented her presence. A command from their laird could not change their feelings toward her.

"Well, now, lassie," began Owen, breaking the awkward stillness, "I'm wondering if you know a witch named Fenella."

Gwendolyn shook her head.

"Come, now, surely you have at least heard of her?" he persisted. "She was an ugly old thing, with a singularly nasty disposition, which was unfortunate, because she was a sorceress of immense power." He began to chuckle. "When I was a lad, a friend of mine mocked her behind her back. He was just a silly boy and meant no harm, but Fenella punished him by making his ears and nose ridiculously large, so that he would learn what it was like to be the victim of taunts. You're sure you don't know her?"

"Why would she know her?" asked Lachlan impatiently. "Fenella was as ancient as a rock when we were lads. She died long before this lass was born."

"We don't know how old this witch is," pointed out Owen. "Perhaps she is using her powers to maintain a youthful appearance. Why, just look at Morag. She is nearing eighty and doesn't look a day over sixty-nine."

A splash of color appeared on Morag's cheeks. "Thank you, Owen. It isn't sorcery that maintains my youthful appearance, but a special cream I have developed."

Reginald eyed Gwendolyn curiously. "Are you using your powers to look as you do?"

Gwendolyn shook her head.

Owen looked disappointed. "Then I guess you're too young to know Fenella. Ah, well, no matter."

"Here, lassie," invited Lachlan, raising the ewer beside his cup, "I've a wonderful wine here you must try."

Alex raised a brow and regarded him sternly.

Lachlan huffed with frustration and set the ewer down.

"MacDunn mentioned that you were sentenced to be burned at the stake," began Reginald conversationally.

Gwendolyn nodded.

"A nasty piece of business, that," remarked Reginald. "As a warrior, I'd much rather die with a sword in my belly." He speared a chunk of meat with his dirk. "Clean and simple."

"I don't know what's so clean about having your bowels carved out of you," observed Lachlan, his thin mouth puckered with distaste. "It sounds perfectly ghastly to me."

"Do forgive, Lachlan, but I believe it's better than being trussed to a post and having someone set fire to you," Owen reflected, reaching for a serving of salmon. His elbow accidentally knocked Lachlan's ewer, sending it onto its side. A thick brown liquid oozed from it. Everyone at the table watched in fascination as the substance began to smolder, then rapidly burned an enormous hole in the cloth covering the table.

"Honestly, Lachlan, you don't know what you're doing when it comes to potions," Morag scolded. "You really must stop making them."

"I just need practice." He glanced sheepishly at Alex. "I was certain I had it right this time."

"I'm sure you did," agreed Alex, struggling for patience. "But I would prefer it, Lachlan, if you would refrain from concocting special drinks for Gwendolyn while she is here."

Lachlan lowered his eyes to his food. He looked so defeated, Gwendolyn found herself almost feeling sorry for him.

The meal continued in awkward silence. Gwendolyn managed to eat a little from the mountain of food MacDunn had piled in her trencher, but every bite seemed to lodge in her throat. Finally, unable to bear the strained atmosphere a moment longer, she rose from the table.

"I am tired," she murmured. "Please excuse me."

Without waiting for MacDunn's approval, she turned and walked slowly toward the stairs, affecting a cool confidence that completely belied the misery clutching her heart.

• • •

She had to escape before the boy died.

There was no question that he would die, she realized, staring out the window at the black sky. No one seemed to know what ailed him, and since Gwendolyn was neither a healer nor a witch, she did not see how she could possibly help him. If anything, her lack of experience in these matters might hasten his demise, a possibility that alarmed her. MacDunn had warned her she would be punished if the boy worsened or died. Although he had not specified what form that punishment would take, she had no desire to find out. Given the hostility that greeted her this evening in the great hall, the MacDunns might well decide to burn her.

She trembled, remembering her terror as flames lapped at her gown.

Tomorrow night while the clan slept she would slip out of the castle, steal a horse, and escape into the surrounding woods. Next she would make her way back to the MacSween lands and retrieve the stone. And then she would find Robert and kill him. The thought invigorated her weary spirit somewhat, so she lingered over it, imagining the different methods she could use. Poison was an option, but it would have to be a foul enough concoction that would cause him great pain, burning him from the inside out. Perhaps she should ask Lachlan about his recipes. Stabbing was another good possibility. She imagined Robert's stunned expression after she had buried a blade deep into his chest. It would be a sweet moment, watching his life drain out of him and knowing that he threatened her no more.

Once her father's death was avenged, she would leave the MacSween lands and find a place where she could live in peace. The thought of being by herself, with no one to fear her or taunt her, was immensely appealing. She would find a plot of land and hire someone to build her a small cottage, where she would keep a cow and a few chickens. Of course, these things would require some form of payment. At dinner she had noticed the goblets used at the laird's table were of silver, and some were even studded with jewels. She decided that she would take a few valuable objects from the castle before she left.

A vague sense of guilt wrapped around her as she recalled her pledge to MacDunn that she would try to heal his son. It seemed a shameless betrayal to break her word to the man who had thrice saved her life. But it would be worse to stay and pretend she could heal the boy, when in fact she might only be further jeopardizing his already precarious health. She did not wish to be the cause of the lad's death. Once she was gone, MacDunn would return the boy's care to the clan's healers, and they would do the best they could for him, she assured herself, blowing out the candles beside the bed.

But as she lay back against the cool sheets and closed her eyes, she found herself remembering David's pale, sweat-soaked form buried in a casket of blankets, struggling to breathe in the unbearable heat and stench of his room. And it was deep into the night before she finally escaped into the waters of sleep, still tormented by the thought of his suffering.

CHAPTER 5

A river of light stretched all the way to her bed and radiated through the rumpled blankets, warming her.

Gwendolyn sighed and closed her eyes, assuring herself it could not possibly be as late as the brilliance of the sun suggested. Burrowing deeper into the sheets, she tried to enter the hazy respite of sleep once more. Just a few minutes, and then she would rise and prepare her father's breakfast.

The scent of baking bread filtered into her chamber. Frowning, she opened her eyes.

Despondence surged over her in a cold, black wave, washing away the drowsy shreds of languor. Her father was dead. He lay deep within the ground, trapped forever in the darkness. She would never hear his rumbling voice, or kiss his bearded cheek, or find comfort in his gentle presence again. She was alone in the world, a prisoner and an outcast, feared and despised because she had been branded a murderess and a

witch. For a moment the pain was unbearable. She squeezed
her eyes shut and curled into a ball, feeling small and afraid,
like a helpless child. She wanted to fall asleep again and
awaken to find that the bitter realities of her life were nothing
but a hideous dream.

But her mind was sharp and her body restless, rendering
slumber impossible. The sounds of the MacDunns going
about their day slowly penetrated her despair. She had to remain strong, she reminded herself. She would never escape
this place and have vengeance on Robert if she allowed herself
to crumble. That realization enabled her to master her anguish
as she threw back her covers and padded across the cool stone
floor to the window. The sun was burning through the last
gauzy veils of mist shrouding the mountains, telling her that
the morning was advanced and the day was certain to be a fine
one.

She filled the stone basin hewn into the wall of the tower
with cold water from a jug that had been left in her chamber
and quickly washed her face and hands. Then she dressed in
her drab gray gown, deciding the crimson one was too fine a
garment to wear during the day. Until her escape tonight she
must act as if she were reconciled to her situation, and that
meant assuming her duties as healer to David. Although
sleeveless and singed, her gray gown was still serviceable and
seemed a more appropriate choice for the work of tending a
severely ill child. She searched through the chest at the foot of
the bed and found a comb, which she dragged impatiently
through the tangles in her hair. She had no ribbon or scrap of
cord to tie it back, so she left it to fall where it might, indiffer-
ent to the matter of her appearance.

She climbed down the narrow tower staircase and headed
straight for young David's chamber, praying her sickly charge
hadn't died during the night. The stench of burning herbs
filled her nostrils as she approached, and the air grew heavy
and warm. On reaching his door, she hesitated, preparing for
the confrontation she would surely face if Elspeth was with the
lad. Reminding herself that she was caring for the boy by
MacDunn's order, she rapped firmly on the door. No one

answered, but she heard a muffled cough. Encouraged by the fact that David might be alone, she lifted the latch and entered the dark room.

The fire was blazing away, and the containers of herbs were smoldering thicker than ever, rendering the hot, dank air almost noxious. Clearly someone had been there earlier that morning tending these things, but David was alone at the moment, lying forlornly beneath a crush of heavy blankets and animal skins. He was hacking and coughing against his pillow, sounding as if every hoarse breath might be his last. Anger streaked through Gwendolyn, obliterating her melancholy. She might not have much experience in healing, but she could certainly see when a child was suffering. Blinking against the stinging smoke, she managed a smile.

"Good morning, David," she called cheerfully, heading straight for the windows. "My goodness, one would almost think your room was on fire, the smoke is so thick. Let's see if we can't clear it."

She threw open the wooden shutters to all three windows, flooding the dingy room with light. Fresh air blew in with a soft gust, whirling the smoke around as it chased it out of the chamber.

David eyed her fearfully from the bed. "Elspeth and Robena won't like that."

"Probably not," Gwendolyn agreed. "But don't you hate lying in the dark breathing that horrible air all the time? I know I would."

He hesitated, as if uncertain how to answer. "Elspeth says it is good for me, and my father says I must heed Elspeth." He began to cough again.

"Well, that is about to change." She picked up an iron rod beside the fire and poked at the logs to separate them, reducing their hot blaze. "If Elspeth's methods are certain, then why are you so ill?"

"God gave me a weak constitution—like my mother."

He said it tonelessly, with neither anger nor self-pity. Gwendolyn suspected this explanation for his failing health had been drummed into him from the time he was very young.

"Is that all?" she scoffed. "For a moment I thought it was something serious. If weakness is what ails you, then we must work on making you strong. But I cannot see how you will get better lying in the dark, breathing foul air that would fell even the heartiest of warriors."

She proceeded to carry the smoldering jars of herbs out into the hallway. By the time the last container was removed, the warm breeze puffing through the windows had almost cleared the chamber, and David's coughing had subsided considerably.

"Elspeth will be angry that you did that," he warned.

"I'm sure she will be," agreed Gwendolyn, giving him a conspiratorial smile. "But your father has asked me to help you get better, and my methods are not the same as Elspeth's."

His face froze. "Are you going to cast an evil spell on me?"

"What a ridiculous idea," she scolded. If she was to care for this lad, even just for today, it was important that she gain his trust. "I'm not going to do anything of the sort, David. All I want is for you to get better."

He studied her as she approached him, as if wondering whether or not to believe her. The room had cooled considerably, but David's face was still beaded with sweat, and the linen of his pillow was damp. Gwendolyn lay her hand against his brow, then frowned at the mound of blankets and skins pinning him to the mattress.

"Would you like me to remove some of these blankets?"

He regarded her with surprise. "I'm very hot," he confessed, "but Robena says I'm not allowed to disturb my coverings."

"I will deal with Robena," Gwendolyn told him, peeling away the heavy layers of wool and fur.

She suspected they had not been aired for weeks, for the smell of smoke and sweat and sickness clung to them. Once she had stripped the bed down to a sheet, she selected two relatively fresh blankets, which she arranged neatly over him.

As she positioned his thin arms on the soft wool, she noticed one of them was bandaged with a strip of bloodstained cloth, while the other was heavily etched with small, ugly gashes at various stages of healing. These were the cuts Elspeth and the other healers had made when they bled him, she realized. She recalled Robena telling MacDunn that the boy had been bled both yesterday and the day before, to release the poisons from his body. She frowned at the marks, wondering if it was wise to bleed a child so frequently.

"There, now," she said, giving a final tuck to the corner of the blankets. "Are you warm enough?"

He nodded.

"Good. Have you eaten anything today?"

"I'm not hungry."

His face was gaunt and his body thin, suggesting that his illness had eroded his appetite for some time. Gwendolyn recalled MacDunn telling her that David's affliction had begun as a stomach ailment. MacDunn had also said that the boy had had trouble keeping food in him, until finally he could scarcely eat at all.

"You cannot get better if you don't eat," Gwendolyn remarked, pulling a chair over to the bed and seating herself. "Your body needs food to get strong."

The lad regarded her with weary indifference. No doubt he had been told this many times before. "I feel too sick to eat."

"Does your stomach hurt?"

"Sometimes."

"Does it hurt now?" she persisted, trying to better understand his symptoms.

"No."

"Do you have pain anywhere else?"

"Sometimes."

"Where?"

He shrugged his thin shoulders. "All over."

Gwendolyn thought about this a moment. "Piercing pain, like an arrow shooting through you, or an overall ache?"

"An overall ache."

"Do you ache now?"

He nodded.

"Do you ever feel any better after Elspeth has bled you?" she asked curiously.

His blue eyes widened. "I don't want to be bled today," he whimpered.

"I have no intention of bleeding you," Gwendolyn quickly promised him. "I was just wondering if it has ever made you feel better."

He shook his head. "It hurts when she cuts my arm, and I always feel sicker afterward. But Elspeth says you don't feel the good of a bleeding right away. And I would rather be bled than purged. Being purged is *awful*." He wrinkled his nose in revulsion.

Gwendolyn considered this a moment. In truth, she had no experience with bleedings and purgings, although she knew these practices were common among healers. But the hatch marks on David's arm indicated he had been bled often. If his condition hadn't improved in spite of this, and if it made the poor lad feel even sicker, then why continue to do it?

"I don't think you should be bled again for a while," she decided. "But your body cannot get well if you do not eat, so that is something you must try to do, whether you are hungry or not."

"Eating makes me feel worse," he protested.

"But eventually it will make you feel better," she countered. "So when you eat you must think of all the things you love to do when you are well, like riding and swimming, and spending the day hiking in the mountains."

"I'm not allowed to do those things."

"You're not?" she said, amazed. "Why not?"

"I'm not allowed to tire myself."

"Why not?"

"Because I have a weak constitution," he repeated. "Like my mother."

"I see," said Gwendolyn, although in fact she did not. From the time she was a little girl, she and her father would find happiness in the pine scent of the woods, or the bracing feel of a cold wind blasting against a mountain. Her father had loved the glorious beauty of nature and encouraged Gwendolyn to know it and embrace it as a friend. Perhaps he foresaw that as she got older, she would have no friends among her clan.

"Well, then, what things do you enjoy doing?"

David thought for a moment. "I like listening to stories."

"So do I," Gwendolyn admitted enthusiastically, pleased that they shared this in common. "My father was a wonderful storyteller. When I was a little girl we would sit together by the fire and he would tell me tales about terrible dragons and savage warriors. Does your father do that?"

"My father is laird."

Gwendolyn regarded him blankly.

"A laird has many duties to his clan," he elaborated. "He doesn't have time for telling stories."

She supposed that might be true. "Then who tells them to you?"

"My mother used to. Before she got sick and went to live in heaven. And Elspeth does, sometimes," he added. "But hers are not the same."

No, thought Gwendolyn acidly, *I'm sure they're not.*

"If you like, while I am here, I will tell you stories," she offered.

A spark of pleasure lit his eyes. "Really?"

"Most of the stories I know are scary, though," she qualified, sensing this would appeal to him.

"I like scary stories," he assured her eagerly.

Gwendolyn cast him a doubtful look. "Are you sure? I don't know. Maybe I should just tell you the one about the beautiful princess who lived in a magnificent pink flower, with petals as soft as feathers—"

"That's a story for girls," interrupted David, rolling his eyes in disgust.

"You can't be certain of that," Gwendolyn chided, feigning offense. "Maybe the princess gets swallowed up by a giant rat who chews her into little bloody pieces."

That idea seemed to please him. "Does she?"

"Of course not. Princesses are never killed. That's the rule."

"And that's why it's a story for girls," grumbled David. "Or babies."

"I can see you are not going to be easy to please," Gwendolyn observed, sighing. "What kind of story would you like?"

"Tell me a story with a monster in it," he suggested.

"Very well." She thought for a moment. "My father used to tell me a really terrifying one about a great, black monster who was bigger than this castle. His teeth were long and sharp, like a thousand jagged swords—"

"What are you trying to do," demanded an infuriated voice, *"kill the lad?"*

Startled, Gwendolyn looked up to see Elspeth standing in the doorway holding a tray, her face twisted in outrage.

"How dare you open these windows—don't you realize a draft could kill him? Close them at once!"

Gwendolyn remained seated, regarding Elspeth coolly. "Laird MacDunn has entrusted me with his son's care, Elspeth," she said, her voice quiet but firm. "Thank you for bringing up his tray. You may leave it on the table."

Elspeth stared at her a moment, speechless with disbelief. She recovered her tongue quickly enough, however. "I will not let you do this," she snapped, banging the tray down on the table and stalking over to the windows. "You have been told the boy must be kept warm—"

"Your methods have not cured him, Elspeth," Gwendolyn pointed out, rising to face her. Although she had no direct experience with healing, she had studied her mother's notes extensively. Her mother had been a skilled healer, and she never advocated entombing someone in a hot, foul-smelling room as a cure for illness. "From now on, David's room is to have light and fresh air," Gwendolyn instructed. "And there will be no more jars of burning herbs left in here."

If she had suggested David be dropped stark naked into an icy well, she did not think Elspeth could have looked more appalled.

"I will speak to MacDunn about this, witch," Elspeth vowed. "I will not stand by and let you kill the lad for your own evil purposes—"

"Go ahead and speak to MacDunn," Gwendolyn interrupted. "And he will tell you that I am in charge of David's care and that you must heed my instructions."

In truth she was not entirely certain about that. MacDunn might find her methods questionable and decide to side with Elspeth. But this was not a moment to show doubt or weakness.

Elspeth's small, dark eyes narrowed. "We shall see," she declared ominously, then hurried from the room.

Gwendolyn forced a smile to her lips and turned to David, who was staring at her in awe.

"I've never seen Elspeth so angry," he murmured.

"She won't stay angry for long," Gwendolyn replied dismissively, trying to alleviate his concern. She was accustomed to the contempt of others and did not let Elspeth's animosity trouble her.

"Now, let's see if we can't get some of this food into you while I finish my story," she said, picking up the tray.

David shook his head. "I'm not hungry." He closed his eyes.

Gwendolyn set the tray down and went over to him. The boy still looked pale and ill, but he seemed more comfortable now that he was no longer sweating beneath his coverings or choking on foul air. She reached out and gently brushed a damp lock of hair off his brow. He was warm, but he did not seem as feverish as he had been when she touched his face yesterday.

Encouraged by that, she sat in the chair and prepared to watch over him as he slept, feeling strangely protective of her helpless charge.

"She is going to kill him!"

"She is the devil's spawn!"

"You must stop her, MacDunn, before it is too late!"

Alex pressed his fingers hard against his pounding temple and sighed.

He had spent most of the day training his men and inspecting the defenses of the castle. The MacSweens could attack at any time, and it was his duty to ensure that his clan and holding were secure. The MacSweens were a formidable enemy, but like any attacking army, they were finite and tangible. Unlike sickness and disease, they could be anticipated and, with adequate preparation and training, ultimately vanquished. It had felt good to focus his attention on the complex logistics of battle and defense. The fortification of his home had demanded his full concentration, and therefore freed his mind, however fleetingly, from the anguish of contemplating his dying son.

After leading his men in a grueling session of training, Alex had ridden hard across his lands for several hours, trying to escape all thoughts of David, especially the unbearable helplessness he felt each time he laid eyes upon the suffering lad. He had ridden high into the heather-caped mountain that had been Flora's favorite. When he reached the crest, he flung himself down from his horse and fell onto his knees, his breathing ragged and his despair almost overwhelming. Once he had mastered his emotions, he stretched out on his back and stared at the sky, taking some comfort from the knowledge that Flora was watching him. He talked to her awhile, and although she did not answer him, he found her silent company soothing. When the blue sky above him turned smoky orange, he mounted his horse and thundered toward the black fortress of his home. He sensed his calm was brittle, and so he rode hard, trying to exhaust himself so that when he returned to the castle he could simply retire to his chamber and escape into a deep, dreamless sleep.

Instead he entered his home to find this wildly agitated gathering of clan members, eagerly waiting to tell him that Gwendolyn was in the process of murdering his son.

"She waved her arms and the windows flew open, filling the chamber with freezing air," continued Elspeth, flailing her fleshless arms around as she re-created the scene for her deliciously horrified audience. "Then she blew softly into the hearth, like so . . ." she puckered her thin lips into a tiny, dark hole, "and the enormous fire roaring in it was instantly extinguished, just like that." She snapped her fingers for effect, startling everyone.

"Dear God," murmured Robena, glancing anxiously at Alex.

"I fell on my knees and begged her to stop," Elspeth went on, her voice rising to a wail. She refrained from actually falling to her knees as she said this, but did clap her bony hands together to demonstrate how she had pleaded. "I told her the poor lad would surely die from the bitter cold, and asked how could she not take pity on such an innocent soul? And the witch just laughed a terrible, wicked laugh, and told me to get out or she would kill me, too!" She made a quick slicing motion across her throat.

Alex leaned back in his chair and continued to massage his temple, idly wondering how much worse his headache could become. Already it felt like someone was hacking at his skull with an ax.

"Don't forget about how she stripped poor David of all his blankets, leaving him to lie naked and shivering on the bed," prodded Robena.

"And how she cast a spell causing the containers of burning herbs to fly out the windows, so that nothing could keep her from doing the devil's work!" added Marjorie.

Alex raised a skeptical brow.

"After hearing about her devilish ways, I went upstairs to confront the witch myself," began Lachlan, assuming control of the narrative. "But as I stood outside the chamber door, I could hear a dreadful moaning sound, like a thousand tortured souls screaming in agony."

Owen frowned. "Do forgive, Lachlan, but you never mentioned that to me," he objected. "You just said you could hear something, but you weren't sure what it was."

"That's because I didn't want to frighten you," snapped Lachlan, irritated at having his account contested. "Had I told you everything, you would have run screaming from this castle, never to return."

"I most certainly would not!" huffed Owen, indignant. "It takes more than a few ghostly cries to frighten an old warrior like me! Why, I'd have fetched my sword and told the witch to cease her nonsense at once or I would be forced to slice her to pieces."

"You can't slice a witch to pieces," Reginald objected. "Their bodies are like iron."

"If you prick them with a needle, they don't bleed," supplied Marjorie. "And they don't feel any pain."

"That's only if you prick them where the devil has left his mark," qualified Garrick, who was one of Alex's younger warriors. "But sometimes that mark is invisible," he added, his voice dropping to a whisper, "so you have to prick them all over."

"The only way to destroy them is to burn them," said Ewan, another of Alex's men.

"It seems a shame to burn the lass," Owen reflected sadly. "She's very comely."

"Perhaps we should just send her back to the MacSweens and let them burn her," suggested Reginald.

"I haven't finished telling my story," complained Lachlan. Alex sighed.

"Let's see, now—there was the moaning of a thousand tortured souls . . ." Lachlan muttered, trying to remember where he was, "oh, yes, and then the witch began to chant, in a low, ghastly voice that sounded nothing like her own. And that's when I knew Satan himself possessed her and I had best get away before he decided to come after me as well!"

The clan members nodded sympathetically, clearly thinking Lachlan had done all he could.

"Is that everything?" inquired Alex blandly, wondering just how much of this nonsense he was expected to believe.

"Not quite," said Robena, anxiously twisting the linen square she held. "A short while ago Gwendolyn came down and ordered that a bathing tub be carried into David's room and filled with water. Garrick and Ewan were afraid to disobey her, so they saw to it."

Alex straightened, suddenly concerned. "Does she not understand how dangerous a bath could be for him?"

"I told her that plunging the lad into freezing water would kill him," said Elspeth. "But she just laughed and said you had given her the power to do as she wished with him."

Alex stormed across the hall, the pounding in his head all but forgotten as he went to see just what the hell this witch was doing to his son.

". . . Oh, great ruler of the darkness, I offer as a sacrifice this innocent soul, if you will in turn reward me with your unearthly powers—"

Alex roared with rage and charged into the chamber, flashing his sword menacingly before him.

Gwendolyn and David regarded him in startled bewilderment.

"Good evening, MacDunn," Gwendolyn managed, trying to steady the terrified pounding of her heart. "Is something wrong?"

Alex regarded her blankly.

She was kneeling on the floor beside a metal tub, her hands buried in a whipped froth of lather as she gently washed David's hair. His son's thin cheeks were rosy from the heat of the steaming water, and the lad's gaze was remarkably bright and alert. Warm summer air gusted through the open windows, but the tub had been carefully positioned before a crackling fire in the hearth, ensuring that David was in no danger of getting chilled. Silver puddles of water sparkled against the stone floor, and Gwendolyn's black hair and ragged gown were damp, suggesting that there had been some playful splashing before Alex entered. No hint of sickness or misery fouled the air, instead the room smelled wonderfully clean and fresh, like soap and flowers. Every surface had been scrubbed, and small vases bearing colorful blossoms had been arranged throughout the room. The bed had been moved from the far corner of the chamber over to the windows, where David could study the stars at night and feel sunlight graze his face in the morning.

"I—I came to see if all was well," Alex stammered, feeling like an idiot.

"Gwendolyn is telling me a story about an evil sorcerer who turns himself into a dragon and tries to burn up a kingdom," David reported, peering at his father over the rim of the tub.

"Really?" Alex sheathed his sword, then stole a sheepish glance at Gwendolyn. Her expression had cooled, telling him she had guessed why he had charged in here waving his weapon like a madman.

"Perhaps you would like to stay and listen to the end of the story," she invited politely.

Alex hesitated. A palpable change had fallen over the room. It was as if Gwendolyn and David had been safely ensconced in their own private little world and he had cracked it open and blasted them with freezing air. For a moment the need to stay and be a part of it was almost overwhelming. But he was acutely aware of the fact that he was an outsider. Alex had never been actively involved in his son's physical care. He had certainly never participated in something as intimate as his bathing. And storytelling was a recreation for women and children, he reminded himself impatiently, not for a laird who had the welfare of his entire clan weighing heavily on his shoulders.

"I have a number of urgent matters I must attend to," he assured them, although at that precise moment he could not think of one. "I merely wanted to see how my son was faring."

Gwendolyn nodded. She was certain the clan had been downstairs filling MacDunn's head with all kinds of dreadful tales about what she was doing to the lad. The surprise on MacDunn's face when he stood staring at them indicated he had expected to find the child half dead.

"Gwendolyn says I can watch the stars from my bed," David chirped, breaking the awkward silence. "She says the stars have special healing powers that will help me get better.

And she says my mother is up there, watching over me as I sleep."

Alex looked at Gwendolyn with uneasy surprise. Did she know he studied the sky each night, searching for Flora's star? That he desperately clung to the belief that his wife's spirit was all around him, watching over him? Had she guessed the root of his madness?

She returned his gaze steadily, her gray eyes veiled, betraying no hint of her thoughts.

"He must not stay in the bath too long," Alex said gruffly, feeling ill-at-ease. "He might get cold."

"Are you ready to come out, David?" Gwendolyn asked.

"I guess so."

"Lean into my arms, then," she instructed, easing him back, "so I can rinse your hair."

Alex watched as his son lay in the cradle of Gwendolyn's arms and allowed her to pour a jug of fresh water over his head. She handled the lad tenderly, taking care that no soap slipped into his eyes and making sure that the dark slick of his hair was well rinsed before she helped him out of the tub. David looked as thin and fragile as a twig when he stood on the floor and let Gwendolyn wrap a warm towel around him. He was too weak to stand without her support.

Alex's heart clenched.

"I wish to speak with you in my chamber," Alex informed her. "Once you have the lad dried and settled in his bed."

"Very well." Gwendolyn playfully draped a second towel over David's head so that he was completely cloaked in fabric. "Why—where did he go?" she sputtered, sounding completely bewildered. "That's very strange. I know he was here just an instant ago—do you see him, MacDunn?"

Alex frowned. He was totally unfamiliar with the games of children and had no idea how to respond.

"David, you're being very naughty," Gwendolyn scolded with mock severity. "Stop being invisible at once."

A muffled giggle emanated from the ghostly little figure standing before her.

The unexpected, sparkling sound filled Alex with such

emotion that he turned and fled the chamber—for it was a sound that he had long forgotten, and never imagined to hear again.

Gwendolyn knocked hesitantly on the scarred wood.

"Enter."

Inhaling deeply, she lifted the latch and stepped inside.

MacDunn's chamber was large, as befitted a laird, but it was dimly lit and sparsely furnished, suggesting its occupant either enjoyed austerity or took little notice of his physical surroundings. A massive bed of dark wood occupied one end, which had no doubt been specially constructed to accommodate MacDunn's unusual height. There was a small table beside the bed, bearing a candelabra, and a simply carved chest for MacDunn's belongings positioned at its foot. A more substantial table and a heavy chair occupied the center of the room, on which a few more candles wavered. MacDunn himself stood before an enormous hearth of roughly hewn stone, his hands clasped behind his back as he contemplated the low fire spilling golden light into the chamber. There were no tapestries gracing the walls to add color to the room or warm the stone, but there were several large windows framing the silver-flecked night. Perhaps, Gwendolyn reflected, the view of the mountains and the sky during the day was sufficient to mitigate the oppressively dreary environment.

"You wished to speak with me?"

"I want to discuss your assessment of my son's condition," Alex murmured, his gaze still locked on the fire. "As you may be aware, some members of the clan have . . ." he paused, searching for the appropriate word, "misgivings about your methods of treatment."

"And what about you, MacDunn?" Gwendolyn challenged sharply. "Do you believe I am intentionally causing your son harm by giving him fresh air and light?"

"Not intentionally, no," Alex replied. "Your freedom depends upon my son's recovery, therefore you have nothing to gain by his suffering. But David's health is extremely delicate.

The healers who have attended him in the past have been vigilant about protecting him from all sources of cold and draft, assuring me his lungs and chest could not endure the strain of a chill."

"And these healers have not cured David, have they?"

"No," he admitted. "But they have kept him alive through horrendous bouts of illness, when there was every indication that he would die."

"Perhaps," Gwendolyn allowed. "Or perhaps David survived in spite of their treatments."

Alex turned and regarded her curiously. "Is that what you believe?" The thought had occurred to him many times, but he had never voiced it.

"I don't know," Gwendolyn answered. "The air in David's chamber was hot and foul and thick with smoke. I cannot see how anyone could lie imprisoned in such a haze for weeks on end and not be sickened by it. I also fail to see how it can possibly be healthy for a child to be deprived of fresh air and sunlight for extended periods of time."

"His previous healers said he was too weak to endure the impurities that exist in outside air," Alex explained. "By keeping his room sealed and burning various herbs, the air was kept warm and purified, and the constant darkness enabled him to rest."

Gwendolyn snorted with contempt. "The air was stale and corrupt. Even I could barely tolerate it, and I am far stronger than David. Having spent time in a dungeon, I can attest to the fact that perpetual darkness rapidly weakens both the body and the spirit."

Alex studied her in silence. He could find no indication that the woman standing before him suffered from anything akin to a frail spirit. Her tattered gray gown clung loosely to her slender frame, its dampness accentuating both her feminine curves and the exquisite delicacy of her. Her hair was spilling in ebony ripples over her thin shoulders and down her pale arms. He found himself remembering how selflessly she tore off her sleeves to bind his chest, after stitching him closed with her own hair. He knew for a fact that her appetite was poor and her body excessively thin. He did not know whether she had always been like this or whether the trauma of her father's death and her subsequent arrest had reduced her to this state. Whatever the cause, she looked as if she would snap beneath the force of a stiff gust of wind. And yet, incredibly, a powerful strength emanated from her as she stood there facing him. It was a strength of conviction and courage, and he found himself both fascinated and aroused by it.

Desire pounded through him, clouding his mind and interrupting his thoughts. He wanted to reach out and touch her, to draw her into the fold of his arms and press himself against her, to hold her fragile form tight as he hungrily kissed the sweetness of her mouth, the silk of her cheek, the enticing hollow at the base of her throat. They were alone in his chamber. He could easily take her. She was his prisoner, alive only because he had torn her from the jaws of death. No one would question his right to bed her if he chose. And he knew he could make her want him, for he had felt the same hunger burning in her when he had kissed her before. He thought of her cradling his son, holding him with tender strength as she poured warm water over his hair, remembering how the soapy stream washed across her slick flesh. And suddenly Alex wanted to caress her there, on the velvet cream of her arms, to run his rough palms down the length of them and drag his tongue languidly over the soft, clean skin.

Gwendolyn regarded MacDunn uneasily, flustered by the intensity of his gaze. She had seen this look before, and the memory quickened her breathing and heated her blood. She was vaguely aware of the fact that she should speak, or move, or do something to shatter the charged stillness, but her throat was dry and her body leaden, rendering action impossible. MacDunn moved toward her with slow, sure purpose. Gwendolyn shivered, not because she was afraid, but because she remembered what it was like to be crushed against the muscular wall of his body. MacDunn reached out and laid his hands on the bare skin of her shoulders, his touch searing her cool flesh. Gwendolyn stared at him helplessly, mesmerized by the painful need burning in his gaze. He languidly drew his palms down the slender length of her arms, then wrapped his powerful fingers around the narrow bones of her wrist, chaining her to him. The amber pulse of the fire flickered around him, sculpting the hard lines of his face in shadows and light, and turning his hair to gold. He seemed achingly beautiful to Gwendolyn in that moment, like a magnificent pagan god who had somehow fallen to earth. His grip was just on the threshold of bruising, as if he feared she might suddenly try to flee, but she kept her arms still and regarded him steadily, betraying not the slightest hint of fear.

And so he bent his golden head over the softness of her inner arm, inhaled deeply, and tasted her with his tongue.

A low, feline sound curled up the back of her throat as MacDunn caressed her with his hot, wet touch. He dragged his tongue up the length of her arm, then lifted her hair so he could rain hungry kisses along the smooth curve of her neck and jaw. Now that her wrists were free, Gwendolyn wrapped her arms around his massive shoulders, clinging to him for support as he roughly captured her lips with his. He tasted her with urgent possessiveness, stealing her breath away as he plundered the deepest recesses of her mouth. His hands began to roam her back, her shoulders, her hips, touching her and tasting her and drawing her further into his embrace, until she was pressed intimately against the hard length of him, separated only by the thin barrier of their clothes.

Somewhere in a corner of her mind Gwendolyn was vaguely aware that this was wrong, that she was a prisoner and he a mad laird, but an incredible need had veiled her perception, so that nothing made sense except the wine-sweet taste of MacDunn's mouth, the rough feel of his jaw scraping her cheek, and the shifting ripple of his muscular back beneath her fingers. She was MacDunn's prisoner, yes, but in this moment no more so than he was hers, for she could feel the desperate yearning in his touch, and knew that somehow he did not want to want her. And that made their forbidden kiss hotter and darker, because the deeper he tasted her, the more she desired him, until finally her fingers were threaded in the thickness of his hair and she was pulling him down onto the softness of his bed. MacDunn growled with pleasure as she hungrily returned his kiss; then he wrenched his mouth away so he could nibble on her chin, her neck, the delicate bones at the base of her throat. He lowered his head to the lush swell at the neckline of her gown and caressed it with his tongue, sending a shiver of fire through her.

A sudden pounding at the door made her gasp.

"MacDunn, you must come quickly!" called Elspeth, her voice shrill.

Alex inhaled deeply, but remained stretched over Gwendolyn, fighting to regain his senses. "What is it, Elspeth?"

" 'Tis David, m'lord," she reported anxiously. "The lad has taken horribly ill. That witch has cast some evil spell on the wee thing, and I don't know how to save him!"

The smoky languor in Alex's blue eyes froze. Without a word, he rolled off Gwendolyn and raced to the door.

Gwendolyn hurried into David's chamber just behind MacDunn and Elspeth, and found the poor child retching violently into the chamber pot Marjorie was holding for him. He had vomited all over his fresh bedclothes, and his dinner tray had been knocked to the floor, suggesting this attack had come on without warning. Robena was busy closing the shutters, and the sour smell of sickness was rapidly permeating the air.

"You evil witch—see what you have done to him?" hissed Elspeth. "I told you your ways would make him ill!"

Gwendolyn stared at David in shaken bewilderment. When she had left him alone just moments ago, he had been weak and tired, but relatively well. Now he was hunched over the bed, whimpering pitifully as he struggled to catch his breath. What could have brought on such an attack? Was it possible that the cool air and warm bath had been a shock to his delicate constitution and had therefore induced this reaction? The thought filled her with guilt. If her inexpert ministrations had reduced David to this awful state, then she should confess to her ignorance now and relinquish all responsibility for his care. Not because she feared MacDunn would punish her if the boy died—which the laird surely would—but because she could not bear the thought of being responsible for David's suffering.

"God alone knows what foul brew she has tainted his body with," railed Elspeth as she reached under David's bed and withdrew a small wooden box. Its surface was battered and heavily scratched, suggesting long years of regular use. "The devil's work is as vile as it is powerful." She set the box upon the table by David's bed and opened it. "But I am not afraid to fight you," she assured Gwendolyn, withdrawing a small, black-stained blade. "I will not let you steal this lad's innocent soul."

Gwendolyn watched helplessly as Elspeth bent over David's arm and began to slice through the fresh bandage Gwendolyn had carefully wrapped around it after his bath. She did not want Elspeth to bleed the child, but she was unsure how she could stop her. It was clear everyone in the chamber believed Gwendolyn had deliberately caused David this torment. But the lad had been suffering these violent bouts of illness long before she came here, she reminded herself desperately. David's chronic inability to retain food was the reason he was wasting away. It was entirely possible this episode was directly related to his illness and had nothing whatsoever to do with her care. Whatever the cause of his sudden vomiting, it was certainly not due to her tainting his body with evil spells and potions, as Elspeth seemed to believe. Therefore Gwendolyn could not see how bleeding the already weak child could possibly help him. David had told her he hated being bled and that he always felt sicker afterward. Determined to protect him from unnecessary suffering, she took a step forward and declared in a low, firm voice, "You will not bleed him, Elspeth."

Elspeth hesitated over the half-peeled bandage and regarded her in astonishment. "How dare you try to give me an order! Do you think I will stand by and just watch him die?"

Gathering the frayed remnants of her confidence,

Gwendolyn went over to the tub, wrung out a cloth in the tepid water, then moved purposefully toward the bed. "Thank you for tending David in my absence, Marjorie," she said stiffly. "I will look after him now."

Marjorie gripped the pot she was holding for David and glanced uncertainly at Elspeth.

"You won't go near him again, witch!" screeched Elspeth. "You've done enough devil's work already!"

"Perhaps it would be best if you left, Gwendolyn," suggested Robena, eyeing her coldly from her position near the windows.

Refusing to be intimidated, Gwendolyn ignored Robena and met Elspeth's hostile gaze. "MacDunn," she said, her voice remarkably even, "did you not bring me here to see if I could heal your son?"

A taut silence fell over the chamber, punctuated only by the thin sound of David's whimpering.

"I did," Alex admitted.

"Then tell these women to stand aside, so I can continue with my work."

There was a long, frozen moment in which Elspeth, Robena, and Marjorie regarded him expectantly. It was clear from their expressions that they believed he would settle the matter by ordering Gwendolyn to leave. Which, Alex had to admit, was his initial inclination.

He had been horrified to come in here and find his son so hideously ill. In that first moment, the possibility that Gwendolyn was responsible for David's condition had filled him with blinding rage. But when Alex looked at her, he had seen that her gray eyes were wide with dismay as she watched David suffer. It was hardly the look he would have expected from a witch who was purposely trying to harm his son. If Gwendolyn had somehow instigated this attack, she had done so unwittingly, he realized. Further reflection reminded him that episodes like this one, as appalling as they were, had not been uncommon for the lad these past few months. The ugly, raw slash marks scarring his thin little arms were testament to that. Therefore it was possible Gwendolyn's unconventional methods of healing were not the cause of his son's current condition.

But what if they were?

"Laird MacDunn is not fooled by your lies, witch," Elspeth announced, interpreting Alex's silence as a victory for her. She removed a small, filthy basin from her box and positioned it beneath David's arm.

A faint mewl of protest came from his son, piercing Alex's indecision.

"Your concern for my son's welfare pleases me, Elspeth," he began. "I know you want nothing more than for David to be strong and well . . ."

Elspeth cast a triumphant look at Gwendolyn, her tarnished blade poised over David's arm.

". . . which is why I must ask you to stand aside."

Elspeth's expression dissolved into stunned disbelief.

"Really, Alex, you can't mean that," protested Robena. "Just look at the lad!"

David's retching had ceased for the moment, and he had collapsed weakly against his pillow. The warm blush Alex had witnessed earlier when Gwendolyn was bathing his son had vanished, leaving the lad's sunken cheeks even paler than the linen upon which his damp hair rested. His breath was coming in tiny, shallow puffs, as if it hurt to draw in more air than was absolutely necessary. At that moment, it was difficult to believe the boy could possibly survive the night.

If he dies, Alex thought, *so will I.*

Alex lifted his gaze to Gwendolyn. Her expression was contained, but he sensed that was because she chose to guard her emotions in front of the others in the chamber. A small crowd of clan members had gathered just outside the door. They were watching him in silent dismay, no doubt thinking his order was yet another indication that their laird was truly mad.

She is a condemned witch and a murderess, Alex reminded himself harshly. *My son's life means nothing to her. If she could somehow benefit from his death, she would not hesitate to kill him.*

But he found himself recalling the tenderness of Gwendolyn's touch as she held his son in her arms, the softness of her voice as she spoke lightly to him, the gentle concern that seemed to infiltrate her very being when she was with the lad. Alex stared at the dark blade poised over David's bloodless arm, and struggled with his decision. He was a warrior and a laird, not a healer. He could not pretend to know about the wisdom of cool air and baths, or foul potions and stinking hot air and endless bleedings.

All he knew for certain was that his son was dying and no one had been able to save him.

"You women stand aside," he commanded, praying to God he was not making the wrong choice, "and offer Gwendolyn whatever assistance she may require."

Everyone stared at him, dumbfounded. Even Gwendolyn appeared startled.

"I implore you, Laird MacDunn," pleaded Elspeth, "you must not let this devil's whore near him!"

"I have given you an order, Elspeth."

She clutched her small blade in her fist and regarded him helplessly.

"Really, Alex, you must listen to reason," protested Robena.

"I am not accustomed to having my orders challenged, Robena. If you do not wish to assist Gwendolyn, then you may leave." His voice was dangerously low.

Robena opened her mouth as if to argue further, then apparently thought better of it and clamped it shut.

"I will not stay and be part of this," Elspeth said, her voice shaking. She tossed her bloodstained knife and basin back into the box and hurried toward the door. "May God have mercy on the poor lad's soul."

"What about you, Robena?" demanded Alex. "Do you choose to stay and assist Gwendolyn, or leave?"

Robena did not hesitate. Humiliated by Alex's brusqueness in front of other members of the clan, she picked up her skirts and quit the chamber.

"You may also leave, Marjorie," Alex offered.

"If I may, MacDunn," Marjorie began, still holding David's chamber pot, "I would like to stay and help."

A gasp of surprise erupted from the clan members crowded in the corridor.

Alex nodded. "Gwendolyn, tell Marjorie what you require and she will see to it."

Gwendolyn thought quickly. "A fresh set of bedclothes and a nightshirt," she began, anxious to have David clean and comfortable once more. "That chamber pot should be emptied and rinsed out very well, and I would like a pitcher of clean drinking water and a cup. I will also need a new length of linen to bind his arm again."

Marjorie immediately left to see to these things.

Alex watched as Gwendolyn went to his son and gently began to wipe his face with her warm cloth. "There, now, David," she murmured, her voice soothing. "I need you to sit up a little so I can take off your nightshirt," she instructed as she peeled back the soiled bedding.

David moaned weakly. Gwendolyn eased him up into her arms, then held him steady as she gently began to remove the garment. Suddenly she hesitated. "I believe your son is entitled to some privacy, MacDunn," she said, glancing at the crowded doorway.

Her concern for the boy's modesty surprised him. None of David's previous healers had thought anything of exposing him naked before an audience, perhaps believing him too ill to either know or care. But David was ten, and although he might be too sick to protest, he was certainly old enough to feel embarrassed before a gaping crowd of onlookers.

"Return to your business," Alex ordered, moving toward the door. "You will be informed if there is any change in my son's condition."

With obvious reluctance, the clan dispersed. MacDunn cast a final glance as Gwendolyn pulled off David's shirt. The lad's shoulders and ribs were tautly covered with milky white skin. If this sickness didn't kill him soon, then his son would simply die of starvation. Unable to bear the thought, he retreated into the corridor and closed the door.

Marjorie returned a few minutes later to help Gwendolyn finish stripping the bed, then took away the soiled linens. Once David was lying comfortably beneath clean sheets, Gwendolyn gave him some water to rinse his mouth and bound his injured arm once more. She then added more wood to the fire and opened one of the shuttered windows, inviting sweeter air into the chamber.

"How do you feel, David?" she asked softly, moving toward the bed.

He did not answer. His wan face lay pressed against the pillow, and his breath was coming in deep, slow pulses, telling her he had fallen asleep. Whatever had caused his terrible bout of vomiting seemed to have passed, for the moment at least. Gwendolyn brushed a silky curl of red hair off his forehead. His brow was cool and dry. It was not fever, then, that had reduced him to this pitiful state. She thought she should try to get him to drink some water to replace the fluid his body had lost, but decided it could wait until he awakened. Given how unexpectedly this attack had come on, she did not want to leave his side, in case he suddenly became ill again. She also feared Elspeth might decide that she knew better than her laird when it came to healing, and return to secretly bleed David when he was unattended. Unwilling to permit such an assault, she dragged her chair closer to the bed, sat down, and lay her warm hand protectively over his slender fingers, preparing to watch over her charge through the night.

Darkness had thickened to a charcoal cape as Alex slowly made his way along the corridor to his son's room. There was only one surviving torch to illuminate the grim passage, and its oily flicker was leaking a shallow pool of red-orange light onto the stone floor. He was not surprised to find the corridor empty. He had given an order to his clan, and although they might question his grip on his senses, they still respected him enough to obey.

If David died, his senses would abandon him completely and he would no longer warrant that respect.

He paused before entering the chamber, trying to summon the courage he needed to face the sight of his dying son. It had been the same with Flora, he reflected painfully. Each time he had gone to visit her, he hesitated outside her door, begging God to have miraculously given her the strength to overcome her illness during his absence. He had not thought that his request was selfish. After all, Flora had been everything that was good, and pure, and fine. If for some reason a life had to be sacrificed from this castle, then it should have been his own. Alex's life had been far from virtuous, for he was a man and a warrior, and had given little thought to his soul's salvation when in the throes of passion and battle. Of course his clan needed him, but he had felt that if he died another would be found to act as laird while his precious wife raised his son to manhood. Flora had to live, because she was the only woman he had ever known who could love absolutely, without question or reservation, and he wanted his son to know that love. But God had ignored his pleas. Each time Alex had entered Flora's chamber, he found her a little weaker, a little farther beyond his hold, like a shadow slipping from the last filmy threads of daylight.

How ironic that he needed this moment to muster his strength, while his son so bravely endured the constant torment of illness. Sometimes he felt he should tell the boy how unbearably proud he was of him. But he knew if he spoke to the lad with such unguarded tenderness, his heart would break completely and he would be reduced to an unstoppable flood of tears.

Better to remain silent and at least give the appearance of being strong.

He lifted the latch and cautiously eased the door open. The stench of sickness was gone, replaced by the cool breath of rain-washed air floating through the open window. Only a single candle remained burning, and the fire had waned to a glowing pile of pink and gray embers, which emitted some heat but contributed little to the dusky veil of light. Alex moved reluctantly through the gloom, dreading the sight of his child. The lad's small form lay still beneath the neatly arranged blankets, pale and frozen, a tiny, perfect corpse laid out for burial. David did not moan or shiver, did not even cause the blankets to stir with the weak rhythm of his breathing.

He could not, because he was dead.

Grief spewed up from the pit of Alex's belly, the same raw anguish he had battled so hard the night Flora had died, when he had felt his mind snap like a dry piece of kindling. It was more than he could bear, he realized, dragging his leaden feet across the stone floor, to lose the only other person he really loved, this sickly child who was his last link to Flora. He knew his weakness was pathetic and unmanly. Life was a battlefield—there were scores of men who suffered losses far more hideous than his, yet somehow managed to get on with the grim business of their lives. But those men had not known what it was to share their life with a woman such as Flora, and therefore could have no comprehension of the gaping wound her death had left. And that wound was now torn wider, until there was nothing left that merited his struggle to hold his fractured mind together.

Gwendolyn had fallen asleep in a chair beside David, her slender hand holding his, unaware that her patient had escaped her earthly grasp. Alex stared blankly at her, feeling none of the rage or blame he had thought he would experience if his son died while under her care. She had done what she could. Perhaps, given more time, her unorthodox methods might have helped the lad. If anyone was to be blamed, Alex realized harshly, it was himself, for waiting so long before fetching the witch and bringing her here.

A faint sigh erupted from the chalky face resting on the pillow. Startled, Alex shifted his gaze. His son regarded him with dull, glazed eyes, still overwhelmed by illness, but unmistakably alive.

"David?" Alex whispered.

David stared at him in confusion, as if struggling to recall where he was, or perhaps trying to make some sense of why his father was at his bedside in the middle of the night. Ultimately exhaustion defeated his concern. His eyelids fluttered down and he turned his head, leaving his hand securely guarded in Gwendolyn's grasp.

Hope shot through Alex like an arrow, draining away the worst of his grief. His son was alive. He took a deep breath, cleansing himself of the fear that had nearly paralyzed him. As long as David lived, Alex could go on. He gazed restlessly about the room, feeling the need to help expedite his son's recovery, but uncertain what he should do. The fire was too low, he decided. He carefully arranged several logs on it, then prodded them until they were wrapped in brilliant flames. Satisfied that this would keep the room adequately warm for the rest of the night, he returned to steal a final glance at his sleeping child. But it was Gwendolyn who commanded his attention as he approached.

She had huddled into the chair, with one bare arm still extended so she could hold on to David, and the other crossed tightly over her chest, as if trying to find some heat. The inky silk of her hair flowed over her shoulders and rippled down her back, but it was an insufficient cloak against the damp night breeze flowing through the open window. She looked small and vulnerable as she sat curled there, her skin nearly as ashen as his son's, her pale brow etched into a deep line of worry. Even in sleep she found no respite, Alex realized, feeling an unbidden affinity toward her.

He removed the folded plaid at the foot of David's bed, opened it, and gently arranged it around her, enveloping her in its soft warmth. And as he bent close and inhaled the clean, summer-sweet fragrance of her, he found himself once again overwhelmed with desire. He longed to reach out and wrap his arms around her, to lay her down on the floor and ease himself beside her and draw her close, as he had that first night she lay shivering on the ground. His body hardened as he remembered the velvety crush of her slight form pressing against him, the sweet warmth of her mouth as he plundered it with his tongue, the glorious shivering sound she made as he pressed his lips to her breast.

Appalled that he could have such lascivious thoughts in the presence of his dying son, he turned abruptly and left the room, wondering if his grip on his mind was more tenuous than he realized.

CHAPTER 6

Someone was squeezing her hand.

Gwendolyn opened her eyes. David was sleeping peacefully, his breathing steady, his cheeks and brow pale but dry. She uttered a quick prayer of thanks, because she knew his recovery had little, if anything, to do with her care.

What troubled her was the possibility that she had somehow caused his seizure, as everyone in the clan seemed to believe.

She straightened her stiff back, then gently stroked the soft skin stretched across his knuckles. It was possible, she supposed, that bathing the lad had exhausted his already weak body, or perhaps been too great a shock for his weak system. But she had been careful to keep him from getting chilled, and he had seemed frail but steady when she tucked him into his bed and left him to speak with MacDunn. What had caused David's body to go into such a violent spasm? she wondered.

She recalled telling him that he must try to eat at least a little of his dinner as she left. Evidently his attack had begun while he was eating, for the tray had been knocked to the floor when she returned. Was there some mysterious growth or poison in his body that caused him to reject his food? If so, what could she possibly do to cure it?

The first smoky ripples of morning light were filtering through the window, and rain was beating heavily outside, washing the world clean and scenting the air with the fragrance of wet earth and grass. Concerned that the chamber might become overly damp, Gwendolyn rose, then stared in confusion at the warm plaid that slid down her body and puddled onto the floor. The plaid had come from David's bed, she realized, but she could not remember wrapping herself in it before she fell asleep. Deciding she must have been too tired to recall, she scooped it up and draped it over David, taking care not to wake him. Then she went to the fire and added more wood. Once it was burning brightly, she took another quick glance at her charge and, satisfied that he was sleeping comfortably, she stole quietly out of the room.

The castle was eerily still as she hurried along the corridor and up the steps leading to her tower chamber. She was glad she had awakened early, for she did not wish to encounter anyone until she had the opportunity to tidy herself and change her gown. The tangled black waves leaking over her shoulders suggested that her hair must look a sight, and her already soiled, tattered gray gown was now wrinkled and water-stained from the soapy splashing during David's bath. She only had the crimson gown to change into, which seemed inordinately fine for the task of tending to David, but since she had no other garment, it would have to do.

The acrid scent of smoke greeted her as she approached the door. Gwendolyn pushed the heavy door open to find the sealed chamber choked with a gray haze. Exasperated, she went to the windows and threw them wide, then quickly scanned the room for the culprit pots of burning herbs. But the billow of smoke was coursing from the hearth. Gwendolyn approached it in bewilderment, wondering who would be considerate enough to enter her chamber so early in the morning and lay a fire, albeit a suffocating one? As she drew closer she stared at the smoldering material lying in a forlorn heap upon the logs. The fabric was charred beyond recognition, except for a small swath that had somehow managed to elude the heat and flames—a fragment of crimson wool edged in gold.

Bitter fury whipped through her. How dare the MacDunns enter her chamber and destroy one of her few precious possessions, and worse, one that their own laird had given to her? The petty meanness of such an act was abominable. She whirled toward the door, determined to find MacDunn and inform him of his clan's contemptible behavior.

But she froze when she saw the note crudely speared to her pillow.

She moved toward it cautiously, her anger tempered by wariness. She withdrew the small wooden stake skewering a wrinkled sheaf of paper on which someone had written a message in a blunt, inelegant hand.

Make haste and leave, witch, before you suffer the unfortunate fate of your gown.

Gwendolyn fought to stifle the panic swelling in her chest. She knew this was no idle threat. She had been here long enough to realize that the MacDunns' loathing of witches was even greater than that of the MacSweens. With the welfare of both their current and future lairds at risk, these people would have no qualms about lashing her to a post and setting fire to her, just as the MacSweens had done to her mother, and had tried to do to her.

What was amazing was that they were giving her warning.

The note fell to the floor, followed by the carefully whittled stake, which now seemed grotesquely appropriate. She must escape now, this morning, before these awful people had a chance to harm her. MacDunn had promised to keep her safe, but not even he could control the misguided fears of his clan. She was not guarded in the castle. It would be all too easy for someone to enter her chamber unnoticed, or capture her as she moved along a dark hallway, or slip poison into her food as it was carried from the kitchen. The methods by which she might be killed were infinite. She would not stay and give the MacDunns the opportunity to succeed where her own clan had failed.

"Oh, are you casting a spell?" asked a shy voice.

Gwendolyn inhaled sharply, trying to steady the pounding of her heart. A young woman with hair the color of darkly polished wood stood in the doorway, balancing a tray precariously before the enormous expanse of her pregnant body. Despite the rather startling roundness of her shape, Gwendolyn could tell by the slim arms holding the tray the girl was normally quite tiny, leading her to believe that she was either carrying more than one child or the bairn was about to arrive momentarily.

"I thought you might be hungry," the girl explained.

"I'm not," Gwendolyn assured her tautly. Was this some ploy to poison her? Or did the MacDunns plan to drug her with some herb and then murder her as she slept?

"Well, I'll just leave it here, then," the girl said, waddling into the chamber and setting the tray down on a table. "It's early yet, but you might find your insides sorely empty later." She sighed and pressed her hand into the small of her back, massaging her aching muscles. "Why are you burning your lovely gown?" she asked, regarding the fireplace curiously. "Is it part of some ritual?"

"Don't pretend you don't know about this!"

The girl stared at her blankly. Then she spied the note lying on the stone floor. With considerable effort, she bent down and scooped it up. "Oh," she murmured, scanning the message.

"You MacDunns have made it clear that you don't want me here," Gwendolyn observed coolly. "It's obvious you'll do anything to be rid of me."

"That's true for most of the clan," the girl agreed, not looking overly troubled by the note. "The MacDunns are afraid you mean to harm wee David, and as you can see, they're not the kind of folk who will just stand by and watch you do it. But I don't believe you mean the lad any suffering."

"Oh, really?" said Gwendolyn, unconvinced.

"At first I did," the girl confessed. "But that was before I watched you tending him last night. I knew that a woman couldn't care for a child with such gentleness and mean him ill at the same time."

"Everyone in the clan believed his illness last night was my fault."

"Not everyone," corrected the girl, easing her bulky form into a chair. Her straining gown rose slightly as she did so, revealing ankles and feet that looked uncomfortably swollen. She laced her bloated fingers together over her stomach and regarded Gwendolyn calmly. "MacDunn obviously didn't, or he wouldn't have let you near his son. And I didn't. David takes ill like that all the time. He has for months now, since he first became really sick."

Gwendolyn hesitated. The girl seemed earnest, but Gwendolyn did not know if she should believe her. It was possible she had been sent by others in the clan to gain her trust and then use it against her.

"I've never seen anyone stand up to Elspeth the way you did," the girl remarked, her pretty mouth curving into a smile. "I know I've never had the courage to do it, though I've wanted to often enough."

"You have?" Despite her determination to remain wary, Gwendolyn was actually starting to like her visitor.

"Aye," the girl answered. "Elspeth loves nothing better than to be in command, especially when people are sick and helpless. She believes illness is either the devil's work or a punishment from God. Whatever the reason, she says 'tis only through suffering and atonement that one can be made better. That and lots of bleedings to leech out the evil and purify the body."

"Judging by the slashes on David's arms, I would think the lad should be absolutely immaculate by now."

"There's many a time that bleeding has worked," the girl

pointed out. "But other times, when the poisons and evil have spread too far, not even a good bleeding can save a lost soul."

She meditatively stroked her taut belly, as if soothing some ghostly pain. It was apparent to Gwendolyn that the girl spoke from experience. She found herself wondering what ailment had forced this young woman to endure Elspeth's harsh ministrations.

"My Cameron says you have the power to take away pain," continued the girl conversationally. "He says that on your journey here, you conjured up some spirits and asked them to soothe that scratch on his great thick head. Is that so?"

Gwendolyn stared at her in astonishment. "You're Cameron's wife?"

"Aye," returned the girl, amused by Gwendolyn's surprise. "I'm Clarinda. Most people think such a big brute of a man should be married to a giant." She chuckled, shaking her head. "I may be small, but I've both the temper and the will to match wits with any man, big or scrawny. Besides, my Cameron may be a great lion of a warrior, but when it comes to his wife, he's as gentle as a lamb."

Gwendolyn thought back to Cameron slashing his way through Robert's warriors as he fought to rescue her from the MacSweens. At the time she had likened him to a ferocious bear. But Clarinda was right—with that great mane of fiery hair, he was actually closer to a lion.

"So, is it true, then?" Clarinda persisted, clearly intrigued. "Can you take away pain?"

Gwendolyn hesitated. It occurred to her that Clarinda was probably worrying about the delivery of her child. Gwendolyn did not want to mislead her into thinking she could shield her from the suffering inherent to childbirth.

"Sometimes," she replied carefully. "It depends on how severe the pain is—and my spells don't work all the time."

Clarinda pondered this, absently stroking her enormous belly. "That's a wonderful power, the ability to ease suffering," she remarked. "Especially since some healers seem only capable of inflicting more. I suppose it's all in God's hands, really.

When He decides your time has come, He takes you, and that's that." Her voice was matter-of-fact, but Gwendolyn detected a thread of sadness.

"Often that's true," she agreed, sympathetic to the girl's fear. "But sometimes, if you fight really hard, He may change His mind and let you stay awhile longer."

Clarinda stared silently into space. And then she suddenly blinked and gave herself a small shake, banishing whatever thoughts had induced her melancholy. "Are you hungry yet?"

Gwendolyn glanced suspiciously at the tray. The sight of cold sliced meat, dark bread, cheese, and an artfully arranged flower of apple slices suddenly reminded her of the hollowness of her stomach.

"Lachlan had no chance to slip any of his potion into it," Clarinda assured her teasingly. "Here," she said, helping herself to a large chunk of cheese, "I'll take a bite myself."

"Wait!"

Clarinda regarded her with surprise.

"Someone may have tainted the food without your knowledge," Gwendolyn explained anxiously. "You mustn't eat it."

Clarinda smiled. "I don't believe a witch who meant the clan harm would mind having someone drop dead while tasting her food for her," she observed. "But I prepared this tray myself, Gwendolyn, and I know it's fine." With that she popped the chunk of cheese into her mouth.

Gwendolyn watched her worriedly a moment, wondering what she should do if Clarinda suddenly fell ill. But Clarinda just swallowed and helped herself to another piece of cheese and a thick slice of meat, suggesting that her pregnancy gave her a good appetite and the food was uncorrupted.

"I am rather hungry," Gwendolyn confessed. She perched herself on the edge of the bed and began to nibble on a slice of apple. "I'm sorry if I seemed rude when you came in. It's just that it was rather a shock to find my gown in the hearth. Do you have any idea who might have left that note for me?"

"It could have been any number of people," Clarinda replied, shrugging. "The MacDunns have a long tradition of fearing witches, fairies, kelpies, and other evil spirits. And, of course, since MacDunn's wife died, we have had to be particularly careful about keeping evil away."

The mention of MacDunn's wife gave Gwendolyn pause. Perhaps her delicate health could lend some clue as to what was wrong with David. "What did MacDunn's wife die from?"

"Some say she died because she had a weak constitution," replied Clarinda. "But she seemed fit enough when MacDunn first brought her here as his bride. 'Twas after David was born that Flora began to fare poorly. Twice more she grew round with child, and both times the poor bairns died, born far too soon to live even an instant." She laid her hands protectively over her swollen stomach. "After the second one, she complained of a terrible pain and was too sick to rise from her bed. MacDunn was overcome with worry, so he sent for the finest healers in the land, who came from as far away as Scone. Great, conceited brutes they were, assuring MacDunn that there was no illness they had not seen. They bled her and purged her and leeched her, and forced her to drink all kinds of stinking potions. But Flora just grew weaker and weaker."

Gwendolyn felt a surge of pity for the woman. She had no doubt Flora suffered miserably.

"Of course, Elspeth also tended her during her illness," Clarinda continued. "She firmly believed 'twas evil spirits robbing her of her health, and said we all had to help her drive them away. Poor Flora continued to ail for nearly a year. And then she finally died. Some say it was her own sadness that destroyed her, because of the two wee bairns she lost." She circled her palm over her belly. "I suppose that's possible," she conceded. "But Flora adored MacDunn and the son she already had. I can't see how any woman with a wee child would let herself die if she had any choice in the matter. And Flora also worried terribly about what would happen to MacDunn if she died."

"What do you mean?"

"There are some men who tolerate their wives well enough," Clarinda explained, "but they would not be overly tormented if they lost one and had to find another. Life for a woman can be short, especially since the duty of childbearing has been left to us. I think many men realize this and guard their feelings accordingly."

Gwendolyn considered this. There had been a number of MacSween women who had died either during or shortly following childbirth. It was not uncommon to find their grieving husbands married again a few months later—especially if the infant had survived. It was not love that inspired these swift unions, but the simple practicalities of life. The child needed a mother, the man needed a wife.

"MacDunn's feelings for Flora ran far deeper than that," Clarinda continued. "The longer her illness continued, the more absorbed he became with her, until he could barely attend to his responsibilities as laird. When Flora finally died, MacDunn was devastated. And that," she finished quietly, "is when the madness claimed him."

"What happened?" asked Gwendolyn.

"He raged a long while. Screamed at both God and the devil at the top of his lungs, calling them the most hideous names and uttering all kinds of terrible threats. He was taunting them, you see, because he wanted them to take him as well."

So this was the pain MacDunn carried deep within him. On several occasions Gwendolyn had glimpsed a raw anguish in his eyes, but she had not understood its source. And now his precious son, who was his only surviving bond to the memory of his wife, was dying as well. The cruelty of it was almost unfathomable.

No wonder he had risked himself, his closest warriors, and the security of his clan to steal Gwendolyn and bring her here.

"How long did his rage last?"

"It never went away," Clarinda replied. "He just learned to control it better, so that we couldn't see it so well. But then he began to act in a strange manner and we knew our laird was not the same."

Gwendolyn frowned. "What did he do?"

"For nearly a year he drank himself into a stupor every night. That in itself might not seem extraordinary, but none of us had ever seen MacDunn drunk before. He was a proud man, and intensely aware of his duties. A drunken man is not fit to be a warrior, or a father, or a laird, and MacDunn knew this. He would lock himself up in his chamber, or mount his horse and disappear for days at a time, drinking and completely neglecting his duties to his clan, to say nothing of his son. And then," she added quietly, "people heard him talking to Flora."

"His dead wife?"

She nodded. "He would have long conversations with her, at all hours of the day and night. We hoped it was just his grief trying to find a way out and that eventually it would pass. But it didn't. Every time someone went to his chamber to consult him on some matter, he would order them away, saying that he was not to be disturbed when he was talking to his wife." Her expression grew sober. "We knew then that madness was claiming him. And soon word of it reached other clans, and they began to call him Mad MacDunn."

"Does the clan still think he is mad?"

Clarinda hesitated. "About a year after Flora's death, something happened that caused MacDunn to stop drinking to excess. He continued to talk to Flora, but he was so much better in almost every other way, no one minded. After all, maybe she really is hovering over him, answering him back. For a time it seemed MacDunn was practically sound again, although of course he had changed. But then David fell ill. Once again MacDunn sent for the best healers he could find, and once again they were unable to cure the lad. Finally he sent them away. We all fear that if the lad dies, it will be more than MacDunn can bear."

"And now MacDunn has brought a witch here to heal his son," Gwendolyn supplied. "And that makes the clan question the stability of his mind even more."

"Because people fear that which they do not understand," pronounced an amused voice. "It is up to those who do understand to try to ease their anxiety. But that is a lesson you have not yet learned, have you, my dear?"

Gwendolyn turned to see Morag standing in the doorway. The ancient seer was dressed in a voluminous robe of sapphire velvet, over which her long hair poured in a silver river. One arm leaned against her elegantly carved staff, while the other was festooned with rumpled mounds of emerald, gold, and rich purple fabric.

"It seems you are in need of a gown," Morag observed, her sea-green eyes sparkling as she entered the chamber. "These were among my favorites when I was about your age. It would please me to see them being worn once again."

Gwendolyn arched her brows with suspicion. "How did you know I needed another gown?"

" 'Twas just a feeling," replied Morag airily, depositing her gifts on the bed. "Do you like them?"

Gwendolyn reached out and laid a tentative hand on the soft crush of fabric. "They are beautiful," she admitted, tracing the elaborate embroidery on one with her fingertip. If these gowns had indeed been Morag's when she was young, they must be over fifty years old. But the fabric and stitching were scarcely worn, and the colors were brilliant, suggesting they could not possibly date from that time.

"I have always taken good care of my clothes," Morag explained, as if reading her thoughts. "And as you will see, classic styling endures from one generation to the next."

"I've always said the same thing," remarked Clarinda, rising heavily from her chair to join Gwendolyn by the bed. "Which is a good notion when you come from a family of nine brothers and sisters," she added wryly.

"I cannot accept these," said Gwendolyn, running her hand reverently over the dry silk of the gold gown.

"Of course you can." Morag waved a blue-veined hand in the air. "My days of wearing such slim garments are long gone, I can assure you. These gowns have been waiting for you."

Gwendolyn paused, tempted. Then she shook her head. "It is too generous a gift. And I should hate for anything to happen to them," she added, glancing at the shriveled black fabric lying in the hearth.

"A shame about that," Morag remarked, not sparing a glance at the fireplace. "I thought you looked perfectly lovely in crimson. Perhaps I will find something similar for you in one of my chests. Until then, I think those will suit you very well."

Gwendolyn hesitated. It would be wrong for her to accept these gowns, she realized. She had not minded accepting MacDunn's gown, because he had kidnapped her and was partly responsible for the fact that her own gown was in such a miserable state. But Morag was offering this gift as a gesture of friendship. Gwendolyn was not accustomed to such generosity and had no wish to feel indebted to her.

"A true gift is one which is bestowed with no expectation for something in return," Morag pointed out.

Gwendolyn looked at her in surprise, disconcerted by the way Morag seemed to read her mind.

"You will wear the emerald dress today," Morag decided. "It is wool and will protect you well when you go outside."

"Gwendolyn can't go outside today, Morag," protested Clarinda. "It's pouring rain. It has been ever since last night."

Morag eyed Gwendolyn with amusement. "That's because the rain complements her mood. If a witch doesn't like the weather, then she should change it."

Gwendolyn stifled her urge to smile. Evidently Brodick's and Cameron's story about the storm she supposedly conjured up on their journey here had made the clan think the weather was subject to her powers.

"I like the rain," she declared, as if she were responsible for it.

"So do I," chirped Morag brightly. "Washes the world clean and lets you start again." She turned to make her way toward the door. "I think you'll find, however, that the rest of the MacDunns are not quite so enamored with it."

She laughed, a high, melodious sound that filled the chamber as she left.

. . .

"A terrible evil has invaded our clan."

The MacDunns nodded solemnly as Lachlan made this dire pronouncement.

"I warned MacDunn not to fetch her," said Reginald. "I told him a witch in our midst would only bring mischief."

"The mischief I could live with," Garrick assured them. "I don't mind the odd flying pot, if that's as far as it went."

"Easy enough for you to say," growled Munro. "Ye're not the one who was chased clear across the courtyard before the thing swooped down and banged you on the bloody head! I'm lucky to have lived to tell the tale!"

"Do forgive, Munro, but being crowned by a pot seems an odd way for a witch to try to kill a man," observed Owen. "Perhaps she was just making sport with you."

Munro's face reddened with outrage. "She turned my legs to stone so I couldn't run away!" he bellowed. "'Twas an attempt to murder me, make no mistake!"

"Why should she want to murder you?" asked Reginald.

"Because she knows I can see beneath her comely appearance," explained Munro.

Owen's eyes grew wide. "Are you saying the lass doesn't really look like that?"

"She's as old and ugly as a withered toe," he replied. "With horrible, knobby growths all over her face!"

"I knew it!" burst out Lachlan, gleefully rubbing his bony hands together. "Tonight I shall begin working on a new potion, which will reveal her true, wizened self!" He scrunched his white brows together in confusion. "Did you say she looks like an old toe?"

"If she really wanted to murder you, then why are you still alive?" persisted Reginald, unconvinced.

"It takes more than one scrawny witch to do away with this MacDunn," Munro boasted. "Besides, this head is as hard as rock." He cracked his beefy fist against his skull, then winced.

"I can't believe MacDunn risked war with the MacSweens

to bring her here," fretted Lachlan. "An army is probably on its way to butcher us as we sleep! How am I supposed to get my rest at night?"

"Those cowardly MacSweens are no match for us," Reginald scoffed. "Laird MacSween is a spineless fool. Let them come," he declared, reaching for his sword, "and this is what they'll meet!" He groped at his empty belt a moment, then frowned and lowered his gaze to search for his weapon, as if he thought it might be hiding somewhere in his plaid. "That's odd—I'm sure I had it with me."

"It's David we have to worry about at the moment," Elspeth interjected. "His illness last night leaves no doubt that the witch has come to destroy him."

"Strange weather we've been having since she arrived," noted Owen, staring in sudden fascination at the rain-slick windows. "Before she came here, the days were fine." He scratched his white head, trying to remember. "Or was that last summer?"

"There's many a peculiar thing happening since the witch arrived," added Letitia, a pretty girl with dark, curly hair. "Last night my wee Gareth cried all night, and normally he's as quiet as a mouse."

"For God's sake, Lettie, 'twas just last week he screamed every night until dawn," countered Ewan, her husband. "Nearly drove me daft."

"He was cutting a tooth," Lettie returned defensively. "But it's all through now. There was no cause for him to shriek so last night."

"Except to keep his neighbors awake," grumbled Quentin, who lived in the cottage next to them.

"I heard an eerie howling last night," said Garrick, changing the subject.

"That was Lettie's bairn," joked Quentin, causing the clan to laugh.

" 'Twas a screech not of this world," Garrick countered. "I was searching for my dog Laddie in the storm, but the screaming froze my blood, so I ran home, bolted the door, and prayed to God for mercy."

"And then what?" prodded Reginald, who had finally given up trying to find his sword.

Garrick shrugged. "I drank a pitcher of ale and fell asleep."

"Exactly how many pitchers had you drunk before you heard this screeching?" demanded Lachlan suspiciously.

"Two or three," he confessed.

"Did you ever find your dog?" Owen asked.

He shook his head. "Witch took him for one of her spells."

Everyone gasped in sympathy.

A long, loud belch resounded through the hall, followed by the bang of an empty cup against wood.

"The ale is off," Farquhar reported, wiping his dripping mouth on his sleeve. "I can barely drink it." He blearily grabbed a pitcher and filled his cup to overflowing again.

"I've noticed that," agreed Quentin. "Ever since the witch came. And the meat has been burned every night, as well."

"It most certainly has not!" huffed Alice, the cook.

"Now, I'm not saying it's your fault, Alice," Quentin swiftly assured her. "It's just that since the witch arrived, things have been a little charred—which is entirely her doing," he added meekly, "not yours."

"If it was so awful, then why were you cramming your mouth last night like it was an empty sack?" she demanded testily.

"I think we can agree that there have been many peculiar occurrences here since the witch arrived," interrupted Lachlan.

"Even MacDunn has been acting strangely," commented Robena.

"The witch has cast some spell over him," Elspeth concluded. "That's why he allowed her to stay with David last night, when he should have locked the evil shrew in a dungeon!"

"MacDunn always acts strangely," Reginald pointed out. "You can't put much weight in that."

"Aye, that's true," agreed Lachlan. "He's been a little odd since Flora died."

Owen sighed. "Broke his heart, it did. And cracked his mind in the process."

"He hasn't been talking to her again, has he?" asked Marjorie worriedly.

"No," drawled an ominously low voice. "I haven't."

Awkward silence gripped the clan as Alex entered the hall. Cameron, Brodick, and Ned followed him, their expressions hard with disapproval.

"If any of you have concerns about the welfare of the clan," Alex began, raking his gaze over the uneasy assemblage, "I would prefer that you discuss them with me openly."

"Quite so, lad, quite so," agreed Owen, bobbing his white head. "Absolutely correct. We were about to do just that."

"That's why we've gathered in the hall," added Lachlan, feigning innocence. "So we could talk to you."

"And now you're here," Reginald finished. "Bloody convenient, I call it."

Alex folded his arms across his chest. "Well?"

"Well, laddie," Owen began hesitantly, "we were just having a wee chat about that comely witch you brought here."

"Munro says she actually looks like a shriveled old toe," supplied Lachlan.

"For God's sake, Lachlan," grumbled Reginald, "MacDunn doesn't care about that!"

"Why not?" demanded Lachlan. "If I were him I'd want to know that, before her false comeliness had made a bloody fool of me!"

"If her appearance is that grotesque," Alex said, struggling for patience, "then I am grateful to her for shielding me from it. Is there anything else?"

"She is going to kill your son, MacDunn," Elspeth warned. "That is why she is here."

Alex shook his head. "You're wrong, Elspeth. Gwendolyn MacSween is here because after I saved her from being burned I asked her to come and she generously agreed."

That was stretching the truth considerably, but Alex didn't think the knowledge that Gwendolyn had been dragged here against her will would allay any of the clan's anxiety. "She is here to help David," he assured her, "not to harm him."

"You can't believe that, Alex," Robena objected. "A witch cannot be trusted. She was sentenced to burn by her very own clan. She must have done something horrible to have merited such a punishment—no doubt she has killed others!"

"She was tried for witchcraft, Robena," Alex returned, making it sound as if this had been her only crime, and not a terribly serious one. He disliked deceiving his people, and felt especially guilty at lying to Robena, whose friendship had been relentlessly steadfast. But his son was dying, and Gwendolyn's powers, whatever they were or wherever they came from, were his only hope. He had to get his clan to accept her presence until David was well again.

"I can't imagine that lovely lassie killing anyone," Owen remarked. "Not on purpose, anyway."

"That's because you can't see her as she really is," objected Lachlan. "One swallow of my potion and you won't be able to look at that warty old crone without hurling up your breakfast!"

Owen frowned in bewilderment. "Why would I want to drink a potion like that?"

"Not you!" sputtered Lachlan impatiently. "Her!"

"If she means David no harm, then why is she subjecting the lad to cold air and frigid baths?" Elspeth challenged. "Why has she stripped his chamber of healing herbs and forced him to lie shivering on his bed with scarcely a plaid to cover him? And why did she stop me from bleeding him last night, when his body was seething with poison that needed to be drained?"

"Because her ways of healing are different than those we are accustomed to," Alex replied. "I realize you are all afraid of her, and I cannot change that. But Gwendolyn MacSween is a skilled and caring healer who has used her powers to cure dozens of others who were thought to be nearly dead. And," he finished solemnly, "she has sworn upon her very soul that she *will* cure my son."

It was a complete lie, of course. He had no idea how many people Gwendolyn had actually cured, and as his prisoner she had reluctantly agreed to *try* to heal his son, nothing more. But the clan did not argue. Instead they regarded him in silence, suddenly intrigued. Seizing upon this unexpected shift in mood, Alex boldly continued, "It will not happen in one day, and it will not be the result of just one spell. But I ask that you be patient and assist her in any way you can. Gwendolyn MacSween may be a witch, but her unnatural powers also make her an exceptionally skilled healer. More than that," he finished, "she is my last hope of seeing my son strong and whole again."

"That is quite a burden, MacDunn," observed a quiet voice. "Being someone's last hope."

Alex turned to see Gwendolyn standing behind him. Her expression was contained, making it difficult to assess her mood. Her gray eyes were staring at him intently, however, suggesting that she had heard enough of his fabrications to know he was blatantly lying to his own people. In that moment he feared she would strip away his false assurances and expose him before his clan. She desperately wanted to leave, and his people wanted her gone. All she had to do was tell them she could not cure David and his clan would cheerfully send her on her way. They would question their laird's grip on his mind and relieve him of his duties, convinced that they were acting in the best interests of both his son and the clan. Gwendolyn would leave. David would die.

And Alex's mind would shatter completely.

He regarded her in stony silence, waiting for her to vilify him before his people. He had been a fool, he realized bleakly. Only a fool would keep hoping that God would be merciful and spare his son.

God loathed him and was determined to destroy the last fragment of his life.

"Your son fares better this morning, MacDunn,"

Gwendolyn reported. "He is sleeping right now, but when he wakens he may be ready to take a little broth. We shall have to wait and see."

Alex stared at her, uncertain he had understood her correctly. Was she saying she would stay?

Gwendolyn sensed MacDunn's confusion, but did not think it could begin to match her own. Other than her father, no one had ever risen to her defense before or even said anything remotely kind or generous about her. Certainly no one had believed her capable of doing something pure and good, like saving the life of a helpless child. From the time she was a little girl she had been blamed for every incident of evil and misery that befell her clan, until finally she wondered if perhaps there wasn't some truth to the ugly accusations. Other than loving and caring for her father, she had not had any opportunity to explore or demonstrate her capacity for compassion. In truth, the MacSweens had not elicited many tender feelings from her, and other than David, neither had any of the MacDunns.

Until this moment.

"That is . . . good news." Alex felt oddly vulnerable as he stared at her, as if he had exposed some intimate secret he had not meant for her to know. Disconcerted, he pulled away from her intense gaze and tried to focus on something else, like the smooth contour of her cheek, the inky fall of her hair, the slender cut of her emerald gown.

He frowned. "That's not the gown I gave you."

A nervous tremor rippled through the clan, silent, but perceptible to Gwendolyn nonetheless. She had come down here with every intention of telling MacDunn about the disgraceful behavior of his people. She would not tolerate harassment and sincerely hoped that MacDunn would discipline them. But as she stared at the gathering of anxious faces before her, she found herself suddenly reluctant to expose their cowardly action. MacDunn would be furious when he learned what they had done. He would no doubt want to punish the perpetrators, and if they did not come forward willingly, he might even decide to punish the entire clan.

"Gwendolyn," persisted Alex, growing suspicious, "what happened to your gown?"

A few members of the clan coughed. A number of others became inexplicably fascinated with their feet. Perceiving their discomfort, Alex swept his gaze questioningly over his people. "Well?"

"MacDunn," began Garrick uneasily, "I fear there is something we must confess to you—"

"I burned it," burst out Gwendolyn.

Alex regarded her in astonishment. "You what?"

"Accidentally, of course," she swiftly clarified. "I was standing too close to the hearth and didn't notice when a hot cinder flew out and set it afire. By the time I realized what had happened, the gown was completely ruined. Morag was kind enough to give me a few gowns that she no longer wears, and that's where I got this one." She ran her hands briskly over the fabric, brushing away some imaginary specks of lint. "Do you like it?"

Alex regarded her skeptically, then studied his clan. Their apprehensive expressions told him he was not hearing an accurate account of the fate of Gwendolyn's dress. "Would any of you like to tell me what really happened?"

"I burned it," Gwendolyn insisted, wishing he would let the matter drop. "There is nothing more to tell."

"I see," said Alex. "Let us hope that no more 'accidents' happen to either you or your gowns, or I shall be most displeased." He regarded his people sternly.

"You look lovely in that new frock," Owen commented, breaking the tension. "I've always been particularly fond of green."

"Or at least you *appear* to look lovely in it," qualified Lachlan. He narrowed his eyes, as if trying to see her better.

Gwendolyn didn't know what to make of that bizarre comment. "I was planning to go into the woods this morning and collect some herbs and roots to make medicine for David," she said, turning to Alex. "As you have asked me not to leave the castle unattended, I assume you will want someone to escort me."

Alex glanced uncertainly at his clan. Given their profound animosity toward Gwendolyn, he was not sure he wanted any of them going off alone with her.

"Cameron will accompany you," Clarinda announced. "Won't you, my sweet?"

"Aye," said Cameron, lumbering over to Gwendolyn.

Without a word, Ned flanked her other side.

"You can't be thinking of going out now, lassie," Owen protested.

"Why not?" wondered Gwendolyn.

"Why, it's pouring rain," Reginald told her. "Practically a flood."

"But of course, you know that," added Lachlan accusingly.

"The rain is about to stop," Gwendolyn said, gesturing to the windows. "Look—the sun is coming out."

The clan watched in astonishment as the rivulets coursing down the windows suddenly stopped, and a brilliant wash of sunlight appeared.

"Good God," murmured Owen, awestruck. "Did you see what the lassie did?"

"I call that splendid!" remarked Reginald enthusiastically. "Could you make the winter a little warmer this year? I find the cold makes my joints stiff."

"How do we know the weather has really changed?" Lachlan pointed out cryptically. "Maybe she has cast a spell on all of us, to make us *think* that it's no longer raining."

"That sun is warm, Lachlan," Owen said, turning his wrinkled cheek toward the light. "If I'm just imagining this, then it's a damn fine trick!"

"It is not a trick," Gwendolyn assured them, heading toward the corridor with Cameron and Ned.

Cameron pushed open the heavy front door and cautiously stepped outside, looking as if he did not quite trust the sudden fairness of the day. Gwendolyn blinked as she stepped into the golden glare of sunlight. She wondered why no one else had been able to see that the weather was about to change.

Obviously the MacDunns' attention had been focused elsewhere. She recalled the sudden storm that had erupted in the woods when she had pretended to conjure a spell, and nearly found herself smiling.

The weather was being remarkably cooperative.

CHAPTER 7

"... and with those brave words the mighty Torvald whacked his blade down on Mungo's neck, closing his eyes against the hot spray of blood as Mungo's head rolled forlornly away from his twitching body."

"And then what happened?" David asked, enthralled. "Did Mungo get up and continue to fight without his head?"

"He tried to," Gwendolyn responded. "But as he fumbled blindly for his fallen sword, the mighty Torvald drove his blade deep into his gut, then wrenched it up in one powerful motion, splitting him open like a rotten, stinking melon."

"Oh, my, Gwendolyn," said Clarinda, looking queasy, "that's a truly horrid tale!"

"That's nothing," scoffed David. "You should hear the one she tells about the monster who lives in the loch. He swallows people whole and has them live inside his black, slimy stomach as he slowly digests them. Sometimes they spend years in there, with their flesh rotting off—"

"I don't think Clarinda is up to hearing that one, David," interrupted Gwendolyn. "Perhaps another time."

"It's just a story," he assured Clarinda, deciding she was taking it a little too seriously.

"I'm afraid my tolerance for such grisly tales is not what it used to be." Clarinda sighed, returning her attention to the tiny gown she was stitching. "Perhaps once this bairn is out and I don't feel like *I* just swallowed something whole, you can try telling it to me again."

"Is that what it feels like?" asked David, suddenly fascinated. "Like you're the monster and the bairn is some helpless creature you ate?"

Clarinda laughed. "I suppose that's one way of describing it. But more often I feel like the bairn is eating me, and growing so large in the process. I don't know how I'll be able to accommodate it another minute!"

"How much longer do you think it will be, Clarinda?" asked Gwendolyn.

"I'm not sure." She gently stroked the rigid swell of her belly. "Another few weeks, I should think. But you never know—sometimes they are in a great hurry to arrive, and other times they like it so much where they are, you start to think they'll never come out."

"Does it hurt?" David asked. "Being all swollen like that?"

"No. It feels wonderful. Here." She rose from her chair and waddled over to him. "Lay your hand against it and you'll feel the bairn moving." She sat beside him, grasped his little hand, and laid it firmly against her abdomen.

David frowned. "I don't feel anything."

"You have to be patient. Wait."

"You're stomach is awfully hard." He gave her a tentative poke. "I thought it would be soft and squishy, like Alice's."

"Alice doesn't have a bairn inside her," Clarinda explained, smiling. "She just likes to eat."

David suddenly gasped in horror and snatched his hand away. "Something moved in there!"

"That's the bairn," Clarinda said, trying not to laugh. "It's all right. Here, maybe it will move again." She took his hand and pressed it against her a second time. "There, now— it's kicking me—can you feel that?"

David felt her pulsing belly in shock. "Doesn't that hurt?" he asked, alarmed.

"No, it just feels a little strange. Here, Gwendolyn, you come and feel it."

Gwendolyn looked at Clarinda in surprise. She had never felt a pregnant woman's belly. In fact, she could not recall ever actually touching another woman. She supposed she must have been hugged and held by her mother, but her mother had been burned at the stake when Gwendolyn was only four, and Gwendolyn could barely remember her. From that day forward her father had cared for her, and as she endured the escalating ostracism of the MacSweens, he grew to be her only friend. None of the MacSween children were permitted to play with her, and so there had never been another girl with whom she could laugh or share secrets. All her life she had told herself she didn't care. But sometimes, when she lay awake at night, she felt alone and despised, and she wondered why she was doomed to spend her whole life being shunned by others. Surely this was why Clarinda's invitation confounded her so. After a lifetime of being feared and rejected, it seemed unfathomable that a woman might invite her to lay her hand against her womb and feel the precious life stirring inside her.

Clarinda was laughing now. "Hurry, Gwendolyn. The bairn is kicking up quite a fuss."

Despite her reticence, Gwendolyn found herself moving over to the bed and seating herself beside Clarinda.

"Here," said Clarinda, taking Gwendolyn's hand and holding it against the bulge of her body.

David was right, Gwendolyn realized. Clarinda's belly was far harder than she had expected. It felt like a great, smooth dome, not muscular, but firm and taut, as if there was an enormous pressure pushing against it.

"Oh," she gasped, startled by the sudden thump against her palm. "What was that?"

"A foot, I think," said Clarinda, laughing again. "Or maybe a fist. 'Tis difficult to know."

"It's quite strong," marveled Gwendolyn, tentatively pressing her hand against Clarinda once more.

"Aye. This one is strong, like its father. I only hope I can do a fair job of bringing it into the world."

"I'm sure you'll do just fine, Clarinda," Gwendolyn said encouragingly.

"Aye, I'm sure I will."

"How does the bairn breathe in there?" David wondered, frowning. "Is there a hole to let air in?"

"Until it's born, it breathes like a fish in water—it doesn't need air," Clarinda explained.

David yawned. "Does it have gills?"

"I hope not," she exclaimed, "or Cameron might have a word or two to say about it!"

The three of them giggled.

"I think you should rest now, David." Gwendolyn adjusted his blankets over him. "And I am going to make you a special broth for dinner."

"I'm not tired," he protested, stifling another yawn.

"Very well." Gwendolyn moved back to her chair. "You lie there quietly and I will tell you another story."

"I'm leaving," announced Clarinda, waddling toward the door, "so make it as gruesome as you wish."

"Tell me the one about the great two-headed serpent," suggested David, wearily closing his eyes, "who swallows two maidens at the same time and gets them stuck in his throat."

"All right," said Gwendolyn, certain she would not be even half through the tale before David was asleep. "Once, in a land far away, there lived a giant serpent, who had not one, but two terrible heads. A great monstrous beast he was, covered in thick green scales as hard as armor, with four eyes as yellow as fire and two slimy forked tongues that could grab a man by his head and legs and tear him in two. . . ."

Her voice was hushed as she spun her macabre tale, lulling David to sleep with her tone, if not her words. Gwendolyn watched with amusement as the lad struggled to stay awake, occasionally lifting his heavy lids to look at her, as if to demonstrate that he was still listening. But just as the serpent was wrapping its slimy tongue around one of the screaming maidens, exhaustion conquered David. Gwendolyn continued to talk for another minute, until his steady breathing assured her that his sleep was deep. She gently swept a fiery lock of hair off his white cheek, then settled back in her chair to watch him awhile.

Well over a week had passed since the MacDunns had burned her gown. Since that day she had devoted herself entirely to caring for David. When she wasn't looking after him, she would venture into the woods with Cameron and Ned, scouring the ground for various herbs, roots, and bits of leaf and bark that her mother had described in her writings. Once she had accumulated a selection, she would return to her chamber and spend hours grinding, drying, steeping, and mixing—transforming them into powders and potions that she had memorized from her mother's notes.

She had administered several of these elixirs to David, but so far the results had been far from encouraging. Although he might fare better for a few hours, or perhaps even a day, inevitably he would grow ill once again, his thin body wracked with painful spasms and vomiting. Twice now he had also suffered a skin ailment of red, itchy bumps, which made him sorely uncomfortable. The first time Gwendolyn saw the welts appearing, she panicked, thinking she had accidentally caused them with her potions. But Marjorie and Clarinda assured Gwendolyn that David had suffered these puzzling skin conditions before, and that although they were unpleasant, they usually went away within a day or so. Gwendolyn had bathed David in cool water and applied a drying paste of finely crushed oatmeal to his skin, which eased his itching and seemed to heal the sores.

She believed he was faring a little better now that he was breathing fresh, clean air and wasn't being bled and purged night and day. But he was still frighteningly thin and weak, and every day his inability to retain food caused her increasing alarm. Her mother's notes had stressed that a body could not be strong unless it consumed sufficient quantities of healthy food, so Gwendolyn had tried to build David's strength by giving him things laden with the richness of milk, eggs, cheese, meat, and fish. Although the lad had no appetite, he bravely tried to please her by eating them. Sometimes the meal stayed down, but more often David became violently ill, leaving Gwendolyn to wonder if she was helping him or hurting him by making him eat.

If the clan still believed she was the cause of his suffering, no one openly accused her of it. In fact, most of the MacDunns simply avoided her. It was clear they still feared her, for they quickly left a room or scurried down the hall if they saw her approaching, especially if it was dark or stormy outside, which made them wonder at her mood. But for the most part the clan seemed to have accepted her presence as a necessary evil. Only Clarinda, Marjorie, and Morag did not seem concerned that she was about to cast some hideous spell over them. Of course Morag fancied herself as a seer and probably thought that since she had not foreseen Gwendolyn harming her, there was no danger in their relationship. Marjorie was devoted to David, and although she was uncertain of Gwendolyn, she had made it clear that she wanted to help tend the lad. Clarinda, however, was a mystery.

Clarinda was the only person who not only showed no fear of her, but actually seemed to enjoy her company. Every afternoon she waddled into David's chamber and sat with them, chatting away as she carefully stitched some tiny gown or miniature stocking. Although Gwendolyn enjoyed her company, she was not so foolish as to let herself think that Clarinda actually considered her a friend. People didn't make friends of witches, because witches were inherently wicked and could never be trusted. But Clarinda's gentle, warm presence was like a ray of light in the otherwise gloomy castle, and Gwendolyn found herself looking forward to sharing her days with both David and Clarinda.

MacDunn, however, was another matter.

She had scarcely seen MacDunn since the day she found him addressing his clan in the great hall. She was relieved that their paths rarely crossed. Her body still stirred from the memory of being held hard against him, his mouth plundering hers as she wrapped her arms around him. She could not account for her shockingly wanton behavior when she was alone with him, both in the forest and in his chamber. No man had ever dared touch her, no doubt fearing she might suddenly transform him into a toad or cause his manhood to shrivel up and fall off, as she had boldly threatened Brodick.

Her childhood isolation had effectively crushed any illusions that she might marry someday and have a family. No man would ever want her as a wife. And she could not bear the thought of sentencing an innocent child to an existence like hers, forever tormented as the progeny of evil. Men's lack of interest had suited her fine. It was better to live chaste and alone, where she had no one to worry about but herself. Once she had agonized over the fate of her father if something happened to her. Now there was no one who would mourn her passing, no one who would even shed a tear at her demise. It was a lonely realization, but it was also somewhat liberating.

She was responsible for no one.

By contrast, MacDunn's responsibilities to his clan were immense. He was always working with his people—settling disputes, inspecting the cattle and the crops, overseeing new fortifications to the castle, orchestrating the production of weaponry and the preservation of food for storage, and of course leading his men in training. His warriors staged regular mock attacks on the castle, analyzing every possible weakness of the forbidding fortress and developing a strategy to strengthen it. At first Gwendolyn had assumed these exercises were part of the clan's regular training. But one day she had overheard two men complaining about MacDunn's arduous new regimen and the fact that it was her presence that had instigated it.

It was a cold reminder that Robert would eventually come for her.

In the beginning she believed the overwhelming burden of seeing to the demands of his clan kept MacDunn from spending time with his son. He saw David but once a day, and the visit was brief and oddly formal. MacDunn would calmly ask Gwendolyn how his son was faring, and then he would study him a moment, as if he did not quite trust her report. Once he was satisfied that the lad was in no imminent danger, he would turn abruptly and leave, as if there were matters of greater importance that commanded his attention. Not once had Gwendolyn seen MacDunn share a gentle word with David, or tenderly lay his hand upon his cheek, or bend and kiss his smooth brow. MacDunn's brusque demeanor with the lad bewildered Gwendolyn. She remembered the intense pain that had shadowed his eyes when he first introduced his suffering child to her. At the time she had believed his devotion to David was overwhelming. But as the days progressed and MacDunn's visits grew increasingly curt and strained, it became apparent that he barely knew the lad at all. She began to wonder if MacDunn's determination to save his son was not motivated by love, but by the more pragmatic necessity of preserving the life of the next laird.

"Good day, Gwendolyn," said Robena, entering the chamber bearing a tray. "I came to see how David fares."

Like MacDunn, Robena had also made a habit of visiting David once a day. She seemed to be fond of the lad and was always concerned about his progress. Although she had initially made it clear she did not support Gwendolyn's methods, she appeared to have accepted MacDunn's decree that Gwendolyn was now in charge of David's care, and was invariably polite to her.

"He is sleeping," Gwendolyn murmured softly as Robena set her tray on the table.

"How is he?"

"He is well for the moment," Gwendolyn answered carefully. "I am going to let him rest awhile, and then I will try to get him to eat something."

Robena went over to the bed and studied him. "He looks terribly pale."

"He has been ill for many months, and he has not been outside since early spring," Gwendolyn pointed out. "It is not surprising that he has no color."

"Perhaps not," Robena allowed. She adjusted David's blankets, pulling them up to his nose, then moved over to the tray. "Clarinda mentioned to me that you had not had anything to eat since early this morning. I have brought you some bread and fruit."

Gwendolyn regarded her in surprise. Robena was not in the habit of worrying about her welfare.

"The bread was freshly baked this morning, so it is still soft," she continued, filling a goblet with wine.

"That was very thoughtful of you."

Robena smiled and offered her the goblet. "Here."

Before Gwendolyn could wrap her fingers around the cup, it slipped and fell into her lap, drenching her in wine.

"Oh!" exclaimed Robena. "I'm truly sorry, Gwendolyn."

Gwendolyn stood and stared ruefully at the huge crimson stain spreading across the gold fabric of her gown.

"If you take your gown off right away and rinse it in cool water, the wine may not set," Robena advised helpfully. "It would be a shame for the garment to be ruined, especially since Morag has kept it all these years. It must have been one of her favorites."

She was probably right, Gwendolyn realized guiltily. Morag had carefully preserved this gown since her youth, so it was obviously precious to her. Gwendolyn dreaded the thought of having to tell her that it had been ruined.

"Why don't you go up to your chamber and change, and I will watch David for you while you tend to your gown?"

Gwendolyn hesitated, uneasy at the thought of leaving David with Robena. "But if he wakens—"

"If he wakens and needs something, I will fetch you. In the meantime, you must change out of that wet gown and see if it can be saved."

"Very well," said Gwendolyn reluctantly. She moved to the bed and drew back the blankets Robena had swaddled over David's face, so he could breathe fresh air once again. Then she went to the door. "Thank you, Robena. I won't be long."

"Take as much time as you need," Robena said amiably, settling into her chair. "I'll be here when you return."

Gwendolyn hurried along the corridor and up the narrow staircase to her chamber, anxious to be out of her wine-soaked gown. As she pushed the heavy door open, she noticed a note lying on the floor. Remembering the ominous contents of the last missive left for her, she picked it up with a degree of trepidation.

> *Dear Gwendolyn,*
> *You must come to my chamber immediately. I have had a vision that I must warn you about.*
>
> Morag

Gwendolyn smiled. When she first met Morag she had thought the elderly woman was simply pretending to have these mystical visions. It seemed a harmless enough deception, and since Morag had conveniently assured the MacDunns that Gwendolyn was a witch with great powers, Gwendolyn saw no reason to challenge her feigned abilities. But it was becoming clear that Morag actually believed she could see things that others could not.

Gwendolyn laid the note on the table and quickly stripped out of her gown. She placed it in the stone sink and carefully poured water from a jug over the wine stain, watching as the clear water turned crimson and drained away. Once the worst of the blot was gone, she plugged the sink and drenched the skirt with fresh water. Robena was probably right, she decided, briskly rubbing the fabric between her fists. If the gown soaked awhile, the stain might not set. After she visited Morag, she would fetch some fresh water and wash it again, she decided, putting on her green gown.

The spicy sweet scent of roasting meat and simmering vegetables wafted through the air, reminding Gwendolyn of how hungry she was. Anxious to return to David and the tray of food Robena had thoughtfully brought to her, she moved swiftly along the dim corridors. The torch at the top of the stairs leading to the lowest level of the castle had died, leaving the narrow steps to disappear into a vast, black cavern. Gathering her skirts into her hands, she hurried down the steps, vaguely wondering what nonsense Morag was going to tell her.

Suddenly she was hurtling into the blackness, her startled cry silenced as her head slammed against the frigid stone floor.

There was darkness, and there was light.

Throbbing strands of wakefulness slowly roused her from a slumber that had been absolute, yet not restful. Pain began to seep across her, slowly at first, then faster, wrapping its tentacles around her head, her neck, her shoulders, moving down, until finally she was cocooned in it. She shifted onto her side. A fresh stab of pain streaked through her, clean and sharp. There was no question of sleep now. Using what seemed an extraordinary amount of effort, she opened her eyes, then blinked vacantly at the surrounding gloom.

MacDunn was sitting in a chair beside the bed, his long, muscular legs stretched out before him, sound asleep. The lines of his face were deeply etched in the soft candlelight, making him look far older than his years. His hair fell in tangled gold locks over his wrinkled shirt, which was smudged with scarlet. Gwendolyn stared at the stains in confusion, wondering if his wound had torn open and bled onto his shirt. Perhaps she should have stitched his injury again with proper thread once they reached the castle. Her gaze moved to the windows. How had night fallen so quickly? she wondered. David had no doubt wakened long ago and was wondering where she was.

She sat upright and then closed her eyes, disoriented by the extreme effort the action cost her. When she opened them again, MacDunn was staring at her, his harsh expression tempered only marginally with what might have been relief.

"David," she said, her voice a dry rasp. "Is he all right?"

"David is fine, Gwendolyn."

She stared at him dubiously, wondering if he was lying to her. The fierce set of his face did little to alleviate her concern.

"I must see him." She pushed away the covers. "Now." A

sickening dizziness hobbled her movements, forcing her to stop and raise her fingers to her temples.

MacDunn's strong hands fastened on her shoulders and gently eased her back. "He is sleeping. You may see him in the morning."

"I want to make him a special broth."

"You can make it later. When you are feeling better." He held a cup of cool water to her lips. When she had taken her fill, he reached into a basin of water, wrung out a cloth, and laid it over her forehead.

"I'm not ill," Gwendolyn told him, wondering why he was treating her with such uncharacteristic gentleness. "I never get ill."

"No, you're not ill," he agreed.

She nodded. A terrible splitting sensation streaked across her skull. She raised her hand to her head, trying to press the pain away. Her hair was matted and sticky, and a crust of blood had formed on her scalp.

"I found you lying at the bottom of the stairs in the lower level," Alex explained, seeing her confusion. "You had struck your head on the way down. Made quite a mess of the floor."

That explained the pain. She ran her fingers tentatively over her hair, feeling the extent of the stickiness. "Head wounds do tend to bleed," she murmured, remembering the night she had stitched Cameron's scalp.

"Aye. It makes it difficult to tell how serious the injury is. Especially when the victim refuses to wake up."

"You can hardly blame me for resting a bit, MacDunn," Gwendolyn grumbled defensively.

"Perhaps not," Alex acknowledged. "But when a person who has struck her head cannot be stirred, one does start to become somewhat . . ."

He paused, searching for the right word. Frantic? Distraught? Terrified? All these things he had been, and more, though he had tried his damnedest not to let his clan see—for they would only think it was the madness rising up to claim him once again. And yet he had refused to let anyone else sit with her, not even Brodick, or Cameron, or Ned, each of whom he trusted with his life. The witch held the secret to his son's recovery, he had told them. This was why he wanted to watch over her himself.

But even as he said it, he knew it was a lie.

"Concerned," he finished. It seemed an innocuous enough word.

When he first learned she was gone, he had been overwhelmed with fury. He believed she had escaped, and her betrayal had been unforgivable, not just because she had broken her pledge to him, but because she had callously abandoned his son. Alex had ordered the castle and grounds searched and participated in the hunt himself, determined to find her and drag her back.

When he had discovered her lying unconscious in that dark passage, her pale cheek resting in a pool of blood, he had been so frozen with fear he could barely force himself to touch her neck for a pulse.

"You have been in a deep sleep since late yesterday afternoon. It will soon be dawn," he told her, tilting his head toward the window.

A soft veil of amber light spilled across his gold-stubbled cheek. Gwendolyn gazed at him, perplexed. MacDunn was a busy laird, who barely made time to spend a moment with his own ill son. Why was he sitting here watching over her like some nursemaid?

"What were you doing down there, Gwendolyn?"

Her mind was cloudy with pain, making it difficult to concentrate. "I believe I was going to see Morag." She closed her eyes, struggling to remember. "She had left a note in my chamber saying she wanted to warn me of something."

Alex arched a brow.

"Perhaps she wanted to alert me about those stairs," Gwendolyn reflected dryly.

"Where did you put the note?"

She thought for a moment, then raised her shoulders in a weak shrug. "I suppose I left it on the table."

Alex rose to look for it. He inspected the table, the chest, and thoroughly searched the floor. "It isn't here."

"Maybe I took it with me and dropped it in the passage," Gwendolyn suggested, not terribly interested.

"Were you alone when you went downstairs?"

Gwendolyn closed her eyes. "I suppose I must have been. I remember it was very dark—I think the torch above the stairs had gone out." She yawned. "That must be why I tripped."

Alex considered this a moment in silence. "You will rest now," he said, rising from his chair.

"I have to see David," Gwendolyn protested, her voice thickened with sleep.

"You will see him later. When you have rested."

Too exhausted to argue, Gwendolyn sighed and pressed her face farther into the pillow. Alex watched as sleep quickly claimed her once again. She was tired and bloody and aching, but he assured himself he could wake her if he chose. He lifted a matted clump of black hair off her bruised cheek, then lightly traced his finger along the delicate contour of her jaw. He had seen more than his share of head wounds in battle and knew that hers was not serious. But the sight of her lying there, so small and weak and helpless, brought back memories of Flora. This was not illness, he reminded himself sharply.

This was an injury, and he meant to find out who or what was bloody well responsible for it.

The torch above the staircase leading to the bowels of the castle was lit, flickering oily patterns of light over the damp stone steps. Alex stood at the top of the stairs, trying to decide if the illumination was adequate. He was accustomed to the dark, having spent much of the past four years lying awake in the night, or sometimes wandering through the empty corridors, talking to Flora. Many of the steps had a dark scum growing on them, rendering them somewhat treacherous. If the torch had been out and someone who did not know the stairs well was hurrying down them, it was easy to understand how she might have slipped. If not for the fact that Gwendolyn was feared by the clan, coupled with her memory of a note from Morag, he might have simply ordered the stairs scrubbed and another torch bracketed to the opposite wall. Instead he slowly descended them, then ascended once more, carefully examining each step for something beyond the greenish black residue coating the surface.

On the fifth step from the top he found it.

A length of slender black twine lay hidden in slime. Alex fished it from the filthy muck and discovered it was attached to a small nail embedded in the mortar between the stones in the wall. The twine was made of perhaps a dozen or more threads braided together, rendering it fine but surprisingly strong. The length was not sufficient to span the width of the stairs, but the frayed ends suggested it had broken from a longer piece. He bent down and examined the opposite wall. There was the second nail, with its fragment of twine still dangling from it. The nails had been positioned at approximately ankle level, right at the edge of the step. The unsuspecting victim would not tread directly on the dark twine strung between the nails, but could not avoid catching her foot on it. Whoever had done this had not bothered to retrieve the nails after Gwendolyn was found. Either they were extremely careless or they wanted someone to find out that Gwendolyn's fall had not been an accident.

Alex angrily yanked the nails out of the wall and hurried down the steps, heedless of their slippery state. He strode swiftly along the passage leading to Morag's chamber and threw the door open.

"Good evening, Alex," said Morag cheerily, unperturbed by his unexpected entrance. "Or should I say, good morning?"

She was standing at a long, scarred table cluttered with cracked jugs and jars of every size imaginable, pouring a thick brown liquid through a piece of green cloth, which was stretched over a jug. Her silver brows were furrowed and her gaze intent as she watched the filtering potion change from a murky brown to a creamy shade. Alex waited.

"Yes," she finally said, her green eyes still fixed on her work, "I knew about the twine."

"Who did it?" he demanded.

Morag set down the flask of brown liquid and sighed. "That I don't know. The vision was unclear, as so many of them are now. I could not see who had placed it there."

"Is that why you left Gwendolyn a note in her chamber? To warn her of the danger?"

"You know I left no note, Alex. I do not know how to scribe."

He nodded. "I thought perhaps you had someone write it for you."

"No."

He raked his hand through his hair, agitated. "There is someone in the clan who wants her gone."

"There are many within the clan who want her gone," Morag corrected him. She picked up the jug, grasped her staff, and moved toward the fire. "Surely this cannot surprise you."

"I was hoping that even if they feared her, they would learn to tolerate her. For my son's sake."

"Only for David's sake?"

"I brought her here to heal my son. That is all."

Morag bent and began to pour the creamy liquid from the pitcher into a steaming cauldron. A thick, mossy foam rose from the pot, and the air grew spicy and sharp. She took a wooden spoon and slowly stirred the mixture. "Perhaps David is the reason you brought her here, Alex," she conceded, "but he is not the reason you want to keep her here."

"I have told her that once she cures my son she may go."

"Because you had no choice. But even as you said it, you were not sure you meant it."

"I want to know who is trying to drive Gwendolyn away, Morag," Alex growled.

"Then you must watch her carefully. The witch's powers are great. There are many who would destroy them, and then there are those who would have them for their own."

He needed no further warning. He strode purposefully toward the door, cursing himself for leaving Gwendolyn alone in her chamber. As he jerked the door open, he hesitated. "If her powers are so great, then why has she not healed David yet?"

Morag smiled. "Some things cannot be accomplished swiftly. Healing takes time."

"So does dying," replied Alex, not certain whether he was speaking of his son or himself.

He eased the door open quietly, as he used to when he would enter Flora's chamber, not wishing to disturb her if she slept.

She was gone.

Panic gripped him. He spun about and descended the tower steps two at a time, trying to think. She must have staggered away on her own, confused and disoriented, and fallen again. Either that or whoever wanted her gone had grown even bolder and decided to abduct her from her chamber. Alex cursed his carelessness in leaving her alone. He had vowed to keep her safe, yet it seemed he could not protect her even within the walls of his own castle.

"Cameron! Brodick! Ned!" he shouted, storming down the hallway.

Ned silently slipped from the shadows and appeared in a thin shaft of early morning light.

"Gwendolyn is missing again," Alex said, the ferocity of his tone masking his fear.

"She is with David. I followed her there."

Alex nodded brusquely, as if he might have expected that.

"There you are, Alex," Brodick called out, hurrying down the corridor with Cameron at his side. "We've been looking all over for you."

"What is it?"

"A missive from Laird MacSween," said Cameron, handing him a stiff scroll of paper. "A messenger arrived a few moments ago. He is awaiting your response."

Alex impatiently broke the crimson seal and unraveled the document.

MacDunn,

Your gift was most generous, but I cannot permit you to keep her. Her freedom was won at too great a cost, to say nothing of how you have dishonored my clan. I implore you: Send her back, or I shall be forced to declare war on you.

MacSween

The civilized plea made it clear that Laird MacSween had drafted this document himself. Had Robert composed it, the tone would have been far more menacing. Although Alex had hoped the chest of gold and the apologetic letter he had sent would soothe the MacSweens' ire, Laird MacSween was absolutely right to give him this ultimatum. Alex had stolen one of his clan members, obstructed MacSween justice, and killed a number of warriors, all while he was a guest of the clan. Laird MacSween might believe Alex was mad and therefore not entirely responsible for his actions, but that did not mean they could go unpunished.

"Is he thanking you for your gift?" Brodick asked dryly, sensing there was trouble ahead.

"He thought it was considerate of me to send it," Alex replied, "but he wants her back anyway."

Cameron's expression brightened. "So it's war, then, is it?"

"Not for as long as we can delay it," Alex mused. "The clan is unhappy enough about Gwendolyn's presence without thinking she is causing war. Her fall yesterday proves there are those here who would be only too happy to deliver her back to the MacSweens themselves."

Brodick eyed him in disbelief. "Surely you don't think someone in the clan would purposely harm her?"

"Someone gave her reason to be on those stairs and then made certain she fell."

"By God," growled Cameron, "when I catch the cowardly dog who did it, I'll tear him to pieces!"

"What do you want us to do?" Brodick demanded.

"She is never to be left alone," Alex instructed. "Ned, you

will take the first shift of watching her, then Cameron, then Brodick. Whoever is trying to harm her may attempt to do so again. I want to make damn sure they don't get the opportunity."

"She won't like that," Ned said. "Being watched all the time."

"She won't know," Alex countered. "You will be as discreet as possible. That way whoever wants to drive her away may reveal themselves to us unintentionally."

"What about the MacSweens?" asked Cameron. "Are you going to send a message back?"

"Not right away. Brodick, tell the courier I am indisposed and cannot respond at this time. Allude to the idea that I have gone temporarily mad and there is no telling when I will be lucid again. Invite him to wait and join you in a meal. Then get him drunk and put him in the stables to sleep it off. We will delay his departure for as long as possible, and then we will give him a message that will make MacSween think we want to avoid war at all costs and have every intention of sending Gwendolyn back."

"Are you worried we may not be able to best the MacSweens in battle?" Brodick asked.

"I have no doubt the clan will fight to protect our holding, but I'm not certain how much they will be willing to sacrifice for the sake of a witch. Best to avoid the attack for as long as possible."

"Then this messenger isn't going anywhere today," Brodick announced, smiling. "And not tomorrow or the next day, either."

"Good," said Alex. "Cameron, you will take stock of our weapons. Order a sufficient supply of new arrows made, have all the swords, dirks, and spears sharpened, and tell the men to assemble at once for early morning training. I will be with you shortly."

Brodick and Cameron set off to carry out his orders, while Ned slipped back into a dark niche in the corridor.

Alex inhaled deeply, once again preparing himself for

whatever his son's condition might be, then quietly opened the door to his room.

". . . so I bounced down the stairs like Mungo's head," Gwendolyn said as she gently bathed David's face with a wet cloth. "It must have been quite a thing to watch!"

"Was there blood?"

"Gallons of it. I thought for certain I was going to drown."

His blue eyes widened in pure horror.

"Actually, not that much at all," she quickly amended, realizing that David did not enjoy gore so much when it concerned real life. "I barely scratched my head."

David regarded her dubiously. "Then what's that awful stuff in your hair?"

Gwendolyn self-consciously raised her hand to her sticky hair. "Why—there was a puddle of slimy muck on the floor, and I'm afraid I rolled right into it. When your father found me, he didn't know whether to take me to my chamber or toss me in the well!"

"In retrospect, I think the well would have been a better choice."

Gwendolyn then hastily drew up the plaid that had fallen around her waist and draped it around her shoulders. She regarded Alex guiltily, like a child who had been caught disobeying an order.

"I was feeling much better," she told him defensively, "so I decided to visit David."

Her discomfiture added to Alex's pleasure as he stood there watching her. She was perched on David's bed, her bare feet peeking out from the bottom of her thin chemise, untidily wrapped in a red and black plaid that kept slipping off the silky skin of her shoulders. The purple stain on her cheek seemed worse in the morning light, but perhaps it was because her impossibly pale skin made the bruise darker by contrast. She set down the cloth she had been using to bathe David's face and gently brushed back a wayward lock of his hair, as if wanting to make him more presentable for his father. Alex found himself moved by the gesture, and by the fact that the moment she had the strength to rise from her bed, her first thought was to care for his son. It had been the same with Flora, he reflected, in the early days of her illness, before her ever-weakening body finally entombed her in her bed.

He shoved the painful memory into the dark recesses of his mind.

"You are going to get a chill running around dressed like that," he said brusquely. "You will return to your chamber and get back into bed at once."

"But I'm not ill," Gwendolyn protested, crossing the plaid modestly over her chest. "And I'm feeling much better."

"You have had a bad fall. You need to rest."

"Is that blood?" David asked, staring curiously at Alex's stained shirt.

"No—it's wine," Gwendolyn quickly assured him. "I rested all night," she told Alex, disliking the idea of being treated as if she were infirm. "I don't want to rest anymore. Besides, David needs me."

"You will be of little use to him if you become ill with fever or suddenly faint dead away. You will rest today, and if you seem well enough tomorrow, then you may return to tending David."

"Really, MacDunn, I am not nearly as fragile as you think. All I require is a hot bath," she said, rising from the bed, "and I shall feel perfectly—"

Pain shot through her skull. She stifled a moan and sat back on the bed, cradling her head in her hands.

Within two strides Alex was kneeling before her. "What is it?" He cupped her chin with his hand. "Are you all right?"

"I'm fine," Gwendolyn managed, although she was not entirely sure of that. "My head just hurts a little." She closed her eyes, struggling to conquer her pain.

"Ned!" Alex called sharply.

Within an instant Ned appeared in the doorway.

"You will help Gwendolyn to her chamber at once and see that she returns to her bed and stays there."

"I don't need any help," Gwendolyn said stubbornly.

"You can either permit Ned to assist you or I will pick you up and carry you myself. The choice is yours."

Gwendolyn shot him a disgruntled look. Realizing she had no choice, she turned to David and gave him a weak smile. "I will be back to see you this afternoon, David. Until then, I shall ask Clarinda to come and sit with you."

David regarded her fearfully. "Will you be all right?"

"Of course I shall be all right," Gwendolyn assured him, stroking his cheek. "I'm just a little tired."

"When you come back, I will tell you the story about the giant who mashed up the eyes of warriors to make a spread for his oatcakes," David offered. "That always makes me feel better."

"What kind of ghastly stories have you been telling the lad?" Alex asked.

Gwendolyn cautiously rose from the bed and accepted Ned's arm. "Just a few silly tales," she replied innocently. "As I'm sure you know, David likes his stories with a bit of blood and gore."

Alex frowned. He had no idea what kind of stories his son preferred.

"Maybe you could sit with him until Clarinda comes, and David could tell you one," she suggested.

"I will tell you one about the mighty Torvald," David offered eagerly. "He is a powerful warrior like you, who lived far away in a land called—"

"I don't have time for storytelling," Alex interrupted impatiently. "Already the morning is half wasted. I must lead my men in training."

"Of course," said Gwendolyn. "Perhaps another time. When you can spare a moment for less important matters." Her voice was cool with disapproval.

Satisfied that both Gwendolyn and his son were safe for the moment, Alex quit the room, turning his thoughts to the upcoming challenge of a MacSween attack.

But all that morning he was plagued by the strange feeling that he had disappointed her, although he could not imagine how, or why it should matter to him.

• • •

"Who would do such a foul thing?"

The small gathering assembled in Ewan and Lettie's cottage regarded each other uneasily, troubled by Owen's question.

" 'Tis one thing to burn a gown," Reginald observed, "for no one is actually hurt. But if someone purposely tries to harm the lass, that is another matter entirely."

"We don't know that it wasn't an accident," argued Lachlan. "The witch might have been entranced in some evil spell, and as she was concentrating all her unearthly powers on slaughtering us as we sleep, she tripped."

"Why would such a sweet lass want to kill us?" Owen asked.

"She isn't sweet," Lachlan countered. "And she isn't fair, and she isn't young. Munro has already told us that she looks like a shriveled old toe."

Owen scratched his white head, considering this. "How is it that Munro can see this but the rest of us cannot?"

"I have a gift," Munro boasted.

"More like a curse," observed Garrick, "if she looks that bloody awful!"

The clan members laughed.

"Maybe she fell because she was drunk," suggested Farquhar. He took a deep swig of ale, then wiped his mouth on his sleeve. "She drinks, you know."

"I've spent more time in her company than you, and I've never known her to take more than a cup of wine," Clarinda countered impatiently.

"Those lower stairs are very slippery," Robena pointed out. "It's easy to see how someone could have fallen down them—especially if the torch had gone out."

"It couldn't have just gone out," objected Quentin. "I checked the torches just yesterday and made sure they were all well oiled, with plenty of rag for burning. That torch had hours of light in it."

"Perhaps there was a sudden gust of wind," Robena suggested.

"From where?" asked Ewan. "There are no windows in that passage."

"The witch must have stirred the air into a wind as she walked," Lettie decided. "Haven't you noticed how strange the weather has become since she arrived?"

"It always rains when her mood is foul," Lachlan grumbled.

"How do you know what her mood is?" wondered Owen.

"A wee drop of rain may be one thing, but I've never seen her extinguish a torch just by walking by it," said Reginald.

"Did you see how upset MacDunn was when he found her?" asked Marjorie. "Sat with her like a man possessed, not letting anyone else near her."

"Perhaps he is possessed," said Lachlan. "No doubt that's part of her wicked plan!"

"It's the madness." Clarinda sighed, shaking her head. "Poor man. Her lying helpless and still like that must have reminded him of Flora."

"The witch looks nothing like Flora," contradicted Robena sharply.

"But does MacDunn know that?" wondered Garrick. "Or is his mind playing tricks on him once again?"

"MacDunn knows the difference between a witch and his dead wife," Marjorie argued. "He was only disturbed because the witch is his last hope to cure poor David."

"But if his mind were sound he would realize she is killing David," said Elspeth. "Plunging the poor lad into freezing baths, exposing him to drafts, and letting the poisons fill his body. Did you see the dreadful red bumps that rose on him the other day?"

"He has had those before, Elspeth," Marjorie reminded her. "When he was in your care."

"He should have been bled immediately for it," Elspeth snapped. "He hasn't had a good bleeding since she arrived—I hate to think how tainted his poor flesh must be."

"He actually seems a little stronger at times than he used

to," observed Clarinda. "I think Gwendolyn may be doing him some good."

"If she strengthens him, it is only so she can sacrifice him to the devil," Elspeth returned. "That is her plan."

"What about this chap who arrived today from the Mac-Sweens?" said Owen. "Does anybody know what message he brought?"

"Last I saw of him, he was sitting in the hall drinking with Brodick," Quentin reported. "Don't know what became of him after that."

"MacSween has no doubt sent him to declare war on us," fretted Lachlan. "And tomorrow morning we shall waken to find we have been slashed to pieces as we sleep!"

"Do forgive, Lachlan, but if we are slashed to pieces, how will we waken?" asked Owen.

"I shall find the scurvy knave and serve him his bowels for breakfast!" declared Reginald fiercely. "Let's see what the Mac-Sweens think of that!" He reached for his sword, frowned, then checked between his spindly calves to see if it had somehow slipped behind him. "That's odd, I was sure I had it with me."

"I doubt Brodick would share a jug with someone who was about to attack us," said Ewan reasonably. "MacSween likely sent the messenger to thank MacDunn for his gift. Why else would Brodick be treating him like a guest?"

"If he's a guest, then why hasn't he been introduced to the rest of us?" wondered Garrick.

"Perhaps MacDunn has forgotten about him," suggested Lettie. "He was very preoccupied today."

"He was absorbed with readying the clan for battle," said Lachlan, "because he knows we are about to be slain!"

"MacDunn always seems a little preoccupied," Clarinda pointed out. "It is because he is listening to Flora."

"If the MacSweens attack, then we shall have to fight them. It is as simple as that," declared Reginald.

"I say we just give them the witch and be done with it," said Lachlan. "No point in sacrificing our lives for a sorceress who is just going to kill us anyway."

"MacDunn would never permit us to do such a thing," protested Marjorie. "He still believes she can heal his son."

"And maybe she can," added Clarinda. "Sometimes David actually seems to be getting better."

"That's splendid!" declared Owen enthusiastically.

"And other times it is clear he is dying," said Elspeth. Owen's expression fell. "That's terrible."

"I believe we need to be patient," proposed Reginald. "If the lass somehow manages to cure David, then perhaps MacDunn will recover from the melancholy that has claimed him since the lad first fell ill."

"He has been melancholy for four years now," Clarinda argued. "Ever since his Flora died."

"There have been times when he has been happy," countered Robena.

"Happy?" repeated Owen. He frowned, considering. "He has pieced his mind back together relatively well, and he certainly has been a dedicated and hardworking laird. But I've known the lad all his life, and I would not say he was happy."

"His mind is cracked," added Reginald. "If David dies, it will be broken completely. We will lose him forever."

"Then we must let Gwendolyn do what she can to save David," said Clarinda firmly. "And let us make sure no more accidents happen, either to her or to her gowns."

"The lass is right," decided Owen. "We shall bide our time awhile longer, for the sake of MacDunn and the lad."

"And if David dies as a result of the witch's care?" demanded Elspeth.

"Then we must send her back to the MacSweens," said Lachlan firmly, "and tell them to burn her."

CHAPTER 8

"I hurt."

Gwendolyn paused in her story and regarded David with concern. "What do you mean?"

He sat up, then flopped restlessly back against his pillow. "I mean I hurt."

"Where?" she persisted, trying to understand him.

His small brow furrowed with irritation. "Everywhere," he replied shortly, as if he thought it was obvious. "My back, my legs, my arms—everything hurts."

Gwendolyn drew down the plaid and sheet covering him and gently lifted his arm. "Does this hurt?" she asked, slowly moving the twiglike limb from side to side.

"No."

She bent the arm at the elbow, then opened it again. "What about this?"

"No."

She eased him onto his stomach, placed her hands on his back, and began to lightly massage the bony surface. "Does it hurt when I rub your back?"

"No," he murmured, sighing into the pillow. "It feels better."

Gwendolyn pressed a little harder, making slow, firm swirls over the narrow swath of his back. Not an ounce of excess flesh padded the tight cage of his ribs, and each bone formed a hard ridge that resisted the soothing motion of her touch. Gradually she shifted her hands to his shoulders, his neck, his arms, and finally his legs, kneading his aching flesh with firm gentleness, bringing movement and blood back to the stiff muscles. David did not complain of pain as she touched him, but instead his body gradually relaxed, indicating he found relief in her ministrations.

It did not surprise her that his body was aching. After being a prisoner in this bed for so many months, it was inevitable that his muscles and limbs would start to weaken and pain him. Her mother's notes had strongly advocated that the body required fresh air, sunlight, and, if a patient was well enough, a reasonable amount of exertion. Too little activity, her mother had warned, was as debilitating as depriving the body of food.

"Other than your body hurting, how are you feeling today, David?" Gwendolyn asked, working her hands along the thin length of his calf.

He shrugged his shoulders.

"Is your stomach bothering you?"

"No."

"Does your chest ache?"

"No."

"Do you feel tired?"

"I'm tired of lying in bed," he complained. "I'm tired of doing nothing."

That seemed a good sign to Gwendolyn. She continued to massage him, considering. Finally she asked, "How would you like to go outside today?"

He turned onto his back and regarded her in confusion. "Outside of this chamber, or outside of the castle?"

"Why, outside of the castle, of course. It's a fine, bright day, and even I find myself growing weary of being inside since my fall. We'll bundle you up nice and warm, and I'll ask Cameron to carry you into the courtyard. I'll even bring a basket of food, and we can sit on the grass and have some lunch. A little fresh air and sunshine will do us both a world of good."

A glint of pleasure lit his eyes, but he still regarded her doubtfully. "My father won't like it," he warned.

"Your father has entrusted me with your care," Gwendolyn returned. "And I believe you will benefit from a small excursion from this chamber. If we see him, I shall make him understand."

She began to rifle through the neatly folded garments in the chest by his bed, searching for something to dress him in. She was not entirely certain MacDunn would support her decision to take David outside, but if the lad fared well enough, she did not think his father would deny him the pleasure of being outdoors.

Within a half hour David was dressed, wrapped in a heavy woolen plaid, and comfortably ensconced in Cameron's strong arms. Gwendolyn followed the burly warrior and her charge down the staircase, carrying a large basket in which she had packed fresh milk, several wedges of cheese, some cold meat and fish, and some boiled eggs. She was hoping the fresh air and modest exercise would help to stimulate David's weak appetite.

"Great God in heaven!" sputtered Owen, staring at the trio in astonishment. "Do forgive, my dear, but what in the world are you doing with that sickly lad?"

"We're going outside to get some fresh air, Owen," Gwendolyn replied. "Would you care to join us?"

"You can't!" protested Reginald, clearly horrified. "MacDunn would never permit such a thing."

"But he did." She was only stretching the truth a bit.

MacDunn had given her the authority to care for his son however she saw fit. Today she saw fit to take him outside.

"That's a heavy-looking basket," Lachlan observed, eyeing it mistrustfully. "What heinous things are you planning to do to the lad?"

"I was thinking of feeding him, Lachlan."

"I think you had best wait until MacDunn returns from inspecting the southern border," Owen fretted, rubbing his gnarled hands together. "Yes, I'm quite certain that's the best thing to do."

"But we don't know when he'll return and the sun is shining brightly now," Gwendolyn pointed out. She pushed open the heavy front door, letting a brilliant shaft of light into the dark foyer.

The three elders gasped in shock and raised their hands to their eyes.

"By God, she's blinded me!" Lachlan bellowed. "The witch has burned my eyes!"

"And mine as well!" shouted Reginald. "They're melting in their sockets!"

"It's only sunlight," Gwendolyn assured them, wondering when they had last ventured out of the gloom of the castle. "It cannot hurt you."

The three elders hesitated, then slowly lowered their hands and blinked.

"She's right," Reginald decided after a moment, immensely relieved. "I can see again!"

"But there are spots everywhere," said Owen, gazing about in fascination. "Like large colored balls." He swatted at the air, trying to capture one.

"The witch has cast a spell on us," Lachlan insisted, grinding his fists into his eyes. "I know it!"

"You will be fine, Lachlan," Gwendolyn promised. "The spots will disappear in a moment." She stepped outside, leaving Cameron and David to follow.

A veil of stinging smoke was spewing from the bake house. There was also a sour, earthy aroma fouling the yard, the source of which became clear as Gwendolyn watched young Eric emerge from the stables and heave a shovelful of fresh manure and urine-soaked straw onto the enormous brown mountain he was building. The hot smell of livestock and the garderobes that emptied along the walls of the castle added another element to this amalgamation of scents, creating a stench that was quite overpowering.

"This won't do," she informed Cameron. "Let's walk over to the crest of that hill, where we can sit down and enjoy our meal amongst the grass and flowers."

Cameron shook his head. "MacDunn won't like us taking the lad beyond the castle walls."

"I can't stay here," David protested, wrinkling his nose in disgust. "It smells like a dragon's rotting entrails."

"You're absolutely right," Gwendolyn agreed, marching toward the gate. "We shall have to remember this disgusting smell for one of our stories, David. Come on, Cameron. I promise we won't go far."

The MacDunns working in the courtyard stopped and stared at them in surprise as Cameron reluctantly followed Gwendolyn to the gate.

"Stop her! *Stop the witch!*"

Gwendolyn turned to see Elspeth racing toward them, her pinched face twisted with fury.

"Take the lad back to his chamber at once!" she commanded. "He is far too ill to be outside!"

"Cameron, would you be kind enough to carry David to the other side of the wall and wait for me there?" requested Gwendolyn.

Once she was certain David and Cameron were well away, she turned and confronted Elspeth with cool authority. "David is in my care now, Elspeth," she said firmly. "MacDunn has told you this."

"You will kill him," Elspeth hissed. "Is that what you want?"

"Of course not. Despite what you may believe, I am trying to heal him. A little air and sunlight will do him good."

"He will catch a chill and die, just like his mother."

"David is not his mother. Her illness began when she lost two bairns. Whatever killed her is not what is ailing David."

"It doesn't matter. He shares his mother's delicate constitution."

"How do you know?"

"One need only look at him. But of course, that is something you couldn't understand. He is the very image of her!"

"The fact that he resembles his mother does not mean he shares her physical frailties," Gwendolyn pointed out. "David is also of MacDunn's flesh and blood, and MacDunn is powerful and strong."

"You may have fooled MacDunn with your talk, witch, but you cannot fool me. Your evil clings to you like a terrible caul!"

Gwendolyn flinched inwardly. It was clear Elspeth hated her, and Gwendolyn knew she could do nothing to change that. Long years of being feared and loathed by the members of her own clan had taught her that such deeply rooted animosity could never be overcome.

"Believe what you will, Elspeth. It does not change the fact that I have come here to try to heal David, not to harm him."

With that she turned and walked through the gate, struggling not to let Elspeth's harsh words further erode her already vulnerable composure.

"... and that cloud over there is a stout little man with an enormous belly," Gwendolyn continued, shading her eyes against the sun as she studied the sky. "Actually, it looks somewhat like Munro. Do you see him, David?"

He did not answer. Gwendolyn glanced at him and saw he had fallen asleep.

"I see it," said Cameron. "But I'm thinking it looks more like my great round ball of a wife."

"That's a very gallant observation," Gwendolyn remarked wryly. "I shall be sure to tell Clarinda you said so."

"She won't mind," Cameron said, pillowing his head in

his enormous hands. "She's too happy to finally have a bairn inside her again to take any notice of her shape."

Gwendolyn regarded him in confusion. Clarinda had never mentioned having another child. "Again?"

He nodded. "We had a bairn over two years ago—a wee girl. She died as Clarinda labored to birth her—strangled on her own cord."

So this was why Clarinda often seemed troubled as she stroked her belly, Gwendolyn realized. *I only hope I can do a fair job of bringing it into the world,* she had said. Gwendolyn had assumed Clarinda was merely expressing her concern as a young woman about to bear her first child. But Clarinda had been heavy and round once before, had laid her hand against the firm swell of her stomach and laughed at the movements of the bairn inside her, and had waited excitedly for the day she would be able to hold her beloved babe in her arms.

Instead she had given birth to a baby without life.

"How horrible for her," Gwendolyn murmured.

"It was," Cameron agreed sadly. "She begged to see the child. Perhaps after all those months of feeling it grow and move inside her, she could not believe it was truly dead. But Elspeth told her it was sinful for a mother to want to gape at her dead bairn—a child that had died for its mother's earthly sins." His mouth tightened with contempt. "I was up at the keep with Alex and Brodick, waiting for news of the birth. Everyone advised me that this was best. 'Twas cowardly of me, I suppose, but I did not think I could bear to listen to my sweet Clarinda screaming in agony. Even Clarinda had asked me to stay well away until it was over. But the fact that I wasn't with her meant I couldn't tell Elspeth to shut her pious mouth and give the dead bairn to my wife to hold." He stared grimly at the sky a moment, then shook his head. "Perhaps it was for the best. The sight of the poor thing might only have made it worse for Clarinda."

Gwendolyn said nothing. Had she been Clarinda, she had no idea whether she would have had the courage to look upon her dead child or not.

"By the time I got there, they had taken the bairn away

and Clarinda was crazed with grief. 'Twas impossible to know what was best for her. But for months afterward she wept about the fact that she had not been permitted to see or hold her little girl. She even gave her a name—Cathaleen. She said she needed a pretty name when she met all the unbaptized bairns who were not allowed to enter heaven, and she hoped her daughter wouldn't feel unloved because her mother hadn't kissed her good-bye." He paused a moment to rub his eyes. " 'Twas a difficult time for us, to be sure. Sometimes she would lie in my arms and weep all night—until I thought my heart would break. And even though I knew it was God's will that our little lass should die, I couldn't help but feel as if I had failed Clarinda by not being there when it happened."

"It wasn't your fault, Cameron," Gwendolyn quietly assured him. "Clarinda knows that."

He studied the sky in silence. "This time it will be different," he vowed, his voice gruff. "They say that birthing is women's business and that men are best left out of it. That may be, but this time, by God, I'll not leave her side."

At that moment David suddenly opened his eyes.

"Gwendolyn," he began, his voice small and trembling, "I feel sick—"

That was all the warning he could manage before the vomiting began.

You will not die.

Over and over she had repeated this pledge as she tended to the weak, exhausted child lying before her. She had begun it as she held his head while he retched into the grass on the hill, and had continued as she anxiously followed Cameron back to the castle, with the heaving David cradled in his arms. Through the courtyard, past the condemning stares of the MacDunns, into the great hall, past the horrified council elders and the smugly satisfied Elspeth and Robena. Up the stairs, along the corridor, and into David's chamber, where Cameron had gently laid the gasping child on the bed, then regarded Gwendolyn helplessly, wondering what should be done next.

At that moment the poor child's bowels erupted.

Once David's insides were finally empty, Gwendolyn sponged him clean, taking particular care as she skimmed the cloth over his hot, red-pocked face. With Clarinda's help she changed him into a fresh gown for sleeping, then covered his shivering form with several thick plaids. She built up the fire, then managed to get David to drink a little water, so concerned was she by all the fluid that had drained from him. And all the while Elspeth had stood in the corridor and ranted about how the child needed to be bled before the evil festering within his corrupted flesh killed him.

For one desperate moment Gwendolyn was almost ready to let her do it, so frantic was she to alleviate his suffering.

"Will he die?"

The voice was low and strangely detached. Still clasping David's hand, Gwendolyn rose from her chair to face MacDunn.

"No, MacDunn. I will not let him."

He remained standing in the doorway, the handsome lines of his face frozen into harsh valleys. Finally he approached the bed, slowly, his great fists clenched at his sides, like a man forcing himself to look upon something he does not think he can endure. His stricken gaze swept over his son, taking in his chalky color, the ugly red marks blotting his face, the dark bruises around his eyes, the sunken hollows of his cheeks. David's breathing was faint and shallow, as if it pained him to draw in more air than absolutely necessary.

Alex studied his son a long, agonizing moment, somehow managing not to throw himself over the lad and weep. If he permitted despondency to overwhelm him, his mind would begin to splinter, and this time he would not be able to piece the fragments together again. He inhaled deeply, fighting to control his emotions, to focus on something other than the sickening fear clawing at his heart. And there, burning within his anguish, he found a core of rage. It was dark and bitter, but it gave him something to grasp, and he clung to it like a drowning man. His previous descent into the vortex of despair had taught him there was little solace to be found in directing rage at the intangible. But this was different. David had nearly died today because he was recklessly removed from the safety and warmth of his chamber and exposed to the harsh elements of the outdoors.

For that terrible crime, Gwendolyn would be punished.

"You will accompany me to my chamber," he commanded harshly. "Now."

"I—I cannot leave David," Gwendolyn stammered, unnerved by the abrupt change in his manner.

"I believe you have done enough for my son today," Alex observed, his tone coldly mocking. "As of this moment, you are relieved of your duties."

Elspeth entered the chamber. A stained rag was draped carelessly over her arm, and her blackened dirk and basin flashed in her hands.

"No," protested Gwendolyn, still holding fast to David's thin hand. "You must not bleed him, Elspeth. He has already lost every drop of fluid from his stomach and bowels. You will only further weaken him by draining his blood."

"His body is struggling to purge itself of the evil poisons flowing through him," Elspeth said. "I must cleanse him or he will die." She marched purposefully toward the bed.

"No!" Gwendolyn looked desperately at MacDunn. "Please, MacDunn—I know you are angry, and I know you are afraid for your son. It was reckless of me to take him outside, and for that I am profoundly sorry. Punish me however you see fit, but I beg you, do not let Elspeth bleed him! It will only harm him!"

"She lies!" Elspeth snarled. "She says this so David will continue to suffer!"

"You cannot believe that, MacDunn," Gwendolyn pleaded, her voice trembling with emotion. "Whatever you and your clan may think of me, you cannot believe that I would purposely hurt this beautiful child."

Alex hesitated. Once again he was in the hideous position of deciding what was best for his son's rapidly deteriorating health. He had been forced to make the same impossible decisions when Flora lay dying. And ultimately he had lost her. Would it have been different, he wondered, if he had insisted upon a different course of healing? If he had stopped those who knew more than him from constantly slashing open her veins, and forcing her to drink the most fetid potions imaginable, that only succeeded in making her curl into a tight spasm of nausea and pain, or sent her into a delirium where she no longer recognized her own child, or the man who loved her beyond reason?

He swallowed, suppressing the sob threatening to erupt from his throat.

Both Gwendolyn and Elspeth were staring at him, anxiously awaiting his decision. He closed his eyes, desperately wishing he could escape this moment, this chamber, this life, and this awesome, unbearable responsibility.

I don't know what to do. What would you do, Flora?

For a moment he felt as if he might stagger beneath the weight of his decision. But when he finally opened his eyes, the answer seemed remarkably clear.

"Elspeth," he began slowly, "I am entrusting you to care for my son . . ."

Gwendolyn gave a small cry of alarm and moved closer to David. Elspeth shot her a triumphant smile.

". . . but you will not bleed him until I have considered the matter further."

Elspeth's expression melted into disbelief. "There is evil within him—"

"You will not bleed him," Alex repeated, his voice firm. "That is my command." He held out his hand.

Elspeth hesitated.

"Give it to me, Elspeth."

Reluctantly, she stepped forward and laid her dirk in his palm. The metal felt cool against his skin. He wrapped his fingers around the heavily stained blade, trying not to think of the many times it had been used on both his wife and his son.

"Accompany me to my chamber," he commanded

Gwendolyn, moving toward the door. Without looking to see if she followed, he disappeared into the hall.

"Don't think you have won, witch," Elspeth sneered, her face taut with loathing. "MacDunn has seen through your deception, and he has returned his son to my care. Now you will be punished for the evil you have wrought. Then MacDunn will send whatever is left of you back to your clan, where you will finally be committed to the fires of hell. And I will purge your evil from this lad's tiny soul," she swore, "so he can enter heaven with a pure spirit."

Cameron, Brodick, and Ned stood waiting in the corridor as she fled the chamber, their expressions grim. They were no doubt present to assist in punishing her, Gwendolyn realized. Although she understood that their loyalty to MacDunn demanded they obey his commands, their presence nevertheless wounded her. She held her head high as she followed MacDunn, unwilling to let them see her desolation.

"A word, Alex," Cameron said, stepping forward. "I should like to explain—"

"Later," Alex snapped. "After I have dealt with Gwendolyn."

Cameron blocked his passage. "But I am responsible for taking David from the castle. I carried the lad myself. It is I who must be punished."

"Without Cameron's assistance, Gwendolyn could never have removed him," added Brodick, moving to Cameron's side. "She cannot be held responsible for what happened."

Ned joined Brodick. "You must punish Cameron instead."

Alex stared at his three warriors in shock. Were they actually trying to defend her?

"If you are so anxious to be punished, Cameron, I am sure I can accommodate you," he said dryly. "But your actions do not absolve Gwendolyn of the risk she took with my son today. Now stand aside."

All three cast an anxious look at Gwendolyn, then reluctantly moved out of their laird's way. Despite her agitation, she was moved by their unexpected support.

"I will be all right," she whispered, trying to reassure them. "You needn't worry."

Their somber expressions did little to ease her fear.

Alex heaved the door to his chamber open and hurled the stained dirk across the room. It struck the wall with such force it chipped a block of stone before clattering loudly onto the floor.

"Close the door," he ordered tautly as Gwendolyn entered behind him.

He went to the table and poured himself a goblet of wine. He drank all of it, filled the cup once more, then quickly drained it again. Marginally in control of his reeling emotions, he filled the vessel a final time, then gripped the goblet tightly between his fingers and studied Gwendolyn.

"Why in the name of God did you take my dying son beyond the castle walls?" His voice lashed at her like a whip.

"I—I thought it would be good for him," Gwendolyn stammered. "He looked quite well this morning. I thought a little fresh air and exertion might make him stronger."

"You are well aware of how extraordinarily frail the lad is—how he may appear almost stable one minute and is vomiting and gasping for air the next. How could you possibly risk his life by exposing him to the outside?"

"He complained that he was weary of lying in his chamber all the time," Gwendolyn explained, the words tumbling out in a desperate rush. "Having been forced to stay within these dark walls myself these past few days, I know how awful it feels to be deprived of the touch of sunlight against your cheek and the scent of earth and grass and flowers. You have these things every day, so you do not know what it is like to be denied them. And David truly did seem to be faring well—he only got sick after we ate."

The realization made her pause. Had David's illness been instigated by consuming tainted food? She frowned, trying to recall what she had packed in her basket. As she went through the items, she realized that she and Cameron had eaten everything David had, and neither of them had become ill. Even so, the possibility of a connection between what David ate and the severe reaction he'd had was a troubling one.

"However innocent your intentions may have been, I cannot ignore the fact that my son came perilously close to dying today," stated Alex bitterly. "My son, should he survive, is the next laird of this clan. I cannot permit you to endanger him again. You are hereby relieved of your duties as his healer." He tilted his head back and drained his goblet.

He was sending her back, Gwendolyn realized helplessly. She had failed in her attempt to heal David, so MacDunn was returning her to the MacSweens. That she would be burned the moment she arrived did not trouble her nearly as much as the fact that she was abandoning David to Elspeth's care. *I will purge your evil from this lad's tiny soul, so he can enter heaven with a pure spirit.* With Gwendolyn gone, Elspeth would be free to leech David's life away in her misguided attempt to cleanse the child of evil. David would be entombed in a dark, stifling chamber once again, where he would be constantly purged, and bled, and suffocated with foul air and unbearable heat.

And he would die.

"You cannot do this," she said desperately. "You must not turn David over to the care of that horrible woman."

Alex narrowed his gaze. "Do you dare tell me what I can do with my own son?" His tone was dangerously low.

"Elspeth is so determined to purify his soul, she doesn't care if she kills him in the process!" Gwendolyn retorted. "I will not permit you to subject him to such cruelty. I don't care what you do to me, MacDunn. Punish me for what happened today however you see fit. But if you try to return me to my clan, I will escape and come back here. David needs me."

Alex regarded her in bemused silence. He had no intention of sending her back to her clan. He was stripping her of the responsibility of healing his son, but that was all. He had not actually considered the matter much past that, but it had certainly not occurred to him that she should leave. The moment she stepped beyond his lands, she would be captured by Robert and his warriors, returned to her clan, and burned.

Alex was devastated that she had not been able to cure David, but he was not about to sentence her to death.

A remarkable strength emanated from her as she stood before him, her face pale but determined, her small hands fisted tightly on her hips. It was a strength that completely bewildered him. Gwendolyn was far slighter and more delicate than Flora had ever been, at least before that ghastly illness. The pallor of Gwendolyn's skin clearly indicated a thinness of blood and a weak constitution. And yet this tiny witch had endured being arrested, imprisoned, and nearly burned. She had ridden long and hard for three days to reach his castle without once complaining or asking for rest. She had even cracked her head open and bled all over his stairs, and then been up a short while later, cheerfully relaying the episode to his son.

How could this impossibly frail slip of a girl have such incredible resilience?

She was staring at him with grim defiance, awaiting his response. Her ebony hair had all but slipped free of its ribbon and was falling in loose waves across her shoulders. The sleeves of her emerald gown had been carelessly shoved up to her elbows, and the garment itself was stained and wrinkled. Strangely, Alex found her disheveled appearance immensely pleasing. It was clear Gwendolyn gave no thought whatsoever to herself as she cared for his son—unlike Robena, who always emerged from David's chamber looking as immaculately arranged as when she first entered. The light woolen fabric of Gwendolyn's gown was cascading over her in liquid ripples, creating an enticing swell at the small curve of her breasts. Alex found himself remembering their exquisite softness when he cupped them with his palm, and the salty-sweet tang of her skin as he dragged his tongue languidly across her.

Desire shot through him.

Appalled, he struggled to suppress it. He would not be controlled by base physical hunger. He had brought the witch here to punish her, he reminded himself harshly. But instead of crying and begging for forgiveness as he might have expected, Gwendolyn had confounded him by coolly declaring that she had no intention of obeying him, and inviting him to do what he would with her. Her apparent lack of fear was incomprehensible. Women had always been intimidated by his very presence. Aside from his formidable physical bearing, Alex was laird of the powerful MacDunn clan and was therefore accustomed to a degree of deference from both men and women alike. Any reasonable woman would be quivering right now in the face of his anger. Yet this witch seemed completely unconcerned as she gazed up at him, boldly refusing to obey his commands. Had his descent into madness so destroyed his bearing that even diminutive girls no longer feared him? The thought infuriated him.

In that moment he was overwhelmed by a need to make her fear him—just a little.

Gwendolyn managed to hold her ground as MacDunn stalked toward her, his blue eyes smoldering with an emotion she did not recognize. Part of her longed to flee, but her determination to stay with David would not allow her to be so cowardly. She had been threatened and intimidated her entire life, she reminded herself firmly. She had been called every vulgar name imaginable and accused of the ghastliest of sins. She had been taunted, leered at, and jostled, had rocks thrown her way so often she had learned how to sense them slicing through the air long before they could strike her. Ultimately her father had been murdered and she had been thrown into the foulest of prisons, beaten by a mob, lashed to a stake, and almost burned to death. There was nothing MacDunn could do to her that could be any worse than what she had already endured, she decided as he grabbed her shoulders with bruising force. Nothing. She regarded him with masterful calm, determined to show him that she did not fear him in the least.

Alex stared at her a long, frozen moment, his hands clenched so hard on her thin shoulders he thought the bones might shatter beneath the force of his grip. He wanted to shake her, to alarm her so that when he looked down into those clear gray eyes he would see dread instead of that icy, mocking calm. The fury pounding through him was alarming, because rage always eroded his tenuous grasp on his mind.

But Flora was dead, and his son was dying, and this witch, who had been his last hope, had failed him. His child was going to die, taking the last shred of Flora with him. It was more than he could bear, this sickening, soul-destroying grief. It stripped him of his ability to think, reducing him to a vortex of agony. He wanted to lash out at the world, to destroy everything within his reach, and he also wanted to lie down and close his eyes and weep forever. He did neither. He just stood there clutching Gwendolyn, feeling lost and angry and helpless, feeling as if he couldn't bear his life another moment.

Suddenly he lowered his head and crushed his mouth savagely against hers.

Gwendolyn gasped and tried to pull away, but MacDunn wrapped his arms tightly around her, imprisoning her. She beat her fists against his chest, only to find his body was shielded by a heavy armor of muscle and the assault seemed to cost her more than it did him. Infuriated, she drew back her foot and kicked his shin as hard as she could. MacDunn grimaced and relaxed his hold—only slightly, but enough to enable her to wedge her hands between them and give him a good shove. It was like trying to push a mountain. Abandoning that tactic, she prepared to attack his other shin.

The next thing she knew, her feet were sailing in the air as MacDunn scooped her up into his arms as easily as he might lift a child.

Gwendolyn struggled and tried to protest, but the sound was stifled by the unrelenting seal of his lips. MacDunn held her hard against him as he carried her across the room, all the while plundering her mouth with his tongue. She wanted him to stop, she was certain of it, but as she sank into the soft depths of the mattress and felt MacDunn stretch over her, bracing his weight on his thickly muscled arms as he held her captive beneath him, a hazy resignation seeped over her. It was as if some part of her had always known this moment between them would come, and she could no longer fight it. MacDunn wrenched his mouth from hers to kiss her cheek, the contour of her jaw, the silky column of her neck, his lips grazing hungrily over her. His tongue tasted her in hot, languid swirls, growing more ravenous as his head lowered and his hands began to roam the crumpled fabric of her gown. She was aware of cool air drifting across her skin, and then MacDunn was closing his mouth hungrily over the peak of her breast.

Pleasure washed through her, stirring her blood and sapping her limbs of strength. She threaded her hands into the pale gold of his hair and held him to her, watching with dark, forbidden excitement as he caressed the rosy bud with his lips, feeling herself tighten against the hot slickness of his tongue. He brushed his rough cheek over the mound of her breast, into the small valley between, and then he was devouring her other breast, kissing and tasting and suckling until it was taut with desire. An unfamiliar ache bloomed deep inside her, strange and hollow and urgent, and she was aware of a honey-eyed heat between her legs. MacDunn's hand trailed up her calf, raising her gown and chemise, and then he was caressing the velvety skin of her inner thigh. Before she could protest, his finger slipped inside her hot, sweet wetness. A throaty moan escaped her lips, and then his mouth was covering hers again, tasting her deeply as his finger flicked lightly across the satiny slick folds.

Gwendolyn wrapped her arms around his shoulders and kissed him fiercely, wanting him to touch her more, kiss her more, wanting to feel the powerful wall of his muscular chest and arms and legs pressing against her as his fingers circled in and out, slowly, then faster, lightly, then harder, binding her to him with every aching caress, until finally she was lost in a mindless swirl of ecstasy. She began to pulse against him, rising and falling to the exquisite rhythm of his hand, kissing him urgently as she opened herself wider to him. Her pleasure began to swell, deeper and faster and harder, until there was nothing except MacDunn and his caresses and kisses, and the granite heat of his body against her as she clung desperately to him. Suddenly she froze, every limb and muscle and tendon straining for more of this incredible, glorious torture. Higher, faster, deeper, more, until she couldn't move, couldn't breathe, couldn't do anything except ravage MacDunn's mouth as her fingers dug deep into the chiseled mass of his shoulders. And then she began to shatter, like a summer star exploding against the velvet curtain of night, and she cried out in wonder and joy, and felt him tighten his hold on her, keeping her safe.

Alex kissed Gwendolyn deeply as he pressed against her exquisite wetness, fighting for control. Her clan had accused her of being a whore, but they had lied. Despite his staggering desire to swiftly bury himself inside her, he knew he must be gentle. And so he entered her slowly, giving her time to adjust to him. Her lids flickered open and she regarded him intently, her gray eyes liquid and smoky with desire. He searched her dark gaze for some trace of reluctance, vowing to stop if he saw any. He withdrew slowly and then entered her again, a little more this time, then summoned the vestiges of his crumbling control and retreated once more, feeling as if he might die from the magnificent, unbearable agony of it.

And then Gwendolyn wrapped her arms around him and pulled him down into her, sheathing him tightly in her silky wet heat.

Alex groaned. He had wanted to go slowly, to make this sublime moment last forever. But it had been years since he had lain with a woman, and he could not control the fire raging through him. And so he surrendered to his passion and began to flex within Gwendolyn, filling her, stretching her, melding their flesh as he kissed the dark recesses of her mouth, the softness of her cheek, the silky black river of her hair. Over and over he drove himself into her, lost to her heat and beauty, the impossibly slender delicacy of her, and the staggering passion she laid bare as she eagerly rose to meet his every thrust. Her nails bit into his back as she tasted him, deeply, fervently, the caress of her tongue broken by the rapid little pants escaping in tiny puffs from her throat. Harder and faster he penetrated her, holding her tight to him, aware of her every breath and touch, wanting her to the point of madness, until finally he thought his mind would splinter beneath the awesome force of his desire. It had never been like this, not even with Flora, and the realization both shocked and terrified him. He shoved himself into her as far as he could, feeling lost and afraid. And then he was hurtling over the precipice of ecstasy, and he cried out and buried his face against her throat. Her arms wrapped protectively around him as she clasped him tightly inside her.

In that instant he wanted to stay like that forever, joined to Gwendolyn, inhaling her fragrance of sunshine and meadows, instead of sickness and death.

Gwendolyn lay very still, feeling the steady pounding of MacDunn's heart as it beat against her chest. Nothing had prepared her for this. She had thought he intended to punish her and send her back to her clan. Instead he had roused a tempest within her that she had not known existed. She bit down hard on her lower lip, willing herself not to cry. It was as if MacDunn had trapped her, binding her to him with bonds far stronger than chains. She could not come to care for him, she told herself desperately. She could not care for anyone here, not even David, although she knew it was too late for that. She was going to leave this place, retrieve her mother's stone, and make Robert pay for killing her father. Nothing could alter that plan. The hardness of MacDunn inside her became intolerable, his heavy weight crushing. Overwhelmed, she shoved him away and rose from the bed, frantically adjusting her bedraggled gown.

Ice-cold reason flooded back to Alex as he studied Gwendolyn's tormented expression. What had he done? He had vowed never to touch a woman again after Flora died. Not only had he broken his vow, he had just raped a mere slip of a girl he had sworn to protect. His behavior was as cowardly as it was unfathomable. Had his grip on his mind become so feeble that he could no longer control the base hunger of his body?

He covered himself with his plaid as he rose from the bed. He wanted to say something, to try to explain, but he did not understand it himself. And so he became preoccupied with clumsily adjusting the folds of his plaid, waiting for Gwendolyn to speak. She didn't. Finally, his plaid restored to some semblance of order, he raised his eyes to look at her.

She was staring at him, her gray eyes sparkling with tears,

her fingers raised to her swollen lips, trying to keep them from trembling. She seemed barely more than a child to him in that moment. His guilt intensified a thousandfold.

"I didn't mean for that to happen, Gwendolyn," he told her bleakly. "I never should have touched you."

A shudder coursed through her body. She lowered her hands to her sides and clutched her gown, as if searching for something to cling to. Alex watched miserably as her knuckles grew taut and white.

He wanted to take her into his arms and hold her, to cradle her against him as he buried his face in the black silk of her hair and whispered gentle words of reassurance. But his body was already hardening with desire, and he feared if he touched her, he would strip her gown from her and take her once again.

As for words of reassurance—he had none to give.

"You will resume your duties as my son's healer," he said, his voice incongruously formal given the previous moment's passion.

Gwendolyn stared at him in bewilderment.

"That is all." He turned away, dismissing her.

"I—I want nothing other than for David to be well," she said, her voice small and ragged.

He did not respond, but remained with his back to her, staring out his window into the darkness.

Finally, not knowing what else to say, Gwendolyn lifted the latch and let herself out of his chamber.

When he was finally certain she was gone, Alex fell to his knees and stared imploringly at Flora's glittering star, silently begging his wife for forgiveness.

CHAPTER 9

Someone was banging his skull with a mallet.

Alex groaned and shifted onto his side. The pounding in his brain continued, hard and infuriatingly relentless. He cursed and buried his head under his pillow, struggling to lose himself in sleep once more.

"*MacDunn!*" shrieked a woman's voice. "*MacDunn!*"

The screeching pierced the thick haze of his weariness. Exasperated, he flung his pillow onto the floor and cracked open an eye. The chamber was shrouded in charcoal light, telling him it was not yet dawn. He sat up slowly, his hand pressed hard against his aching forehead.

"*MacDunn!*" screamed Elspeth from the corridor. "*Wake up!*" The banging against the door grew louder, until Alex felt certain his skull was about to explode.

"For God's sake, *cease that racket!*" he roared. He tossed down the covers and stalked angrily across the chamber, only to have his foot collide with an empty wine ewer. Swearing, he gave the object a churlish kick before heaving his chamber door open. "What the hell is it?"

His expression must have been formidable, for neither Elspeth nor Alice seemed able to speak. Their eyes were as wide as cups, and the iron ladle Alice had been using to whack against the door was frozen in midair.

"Speak!"

"Th-the lad," stammered Elspeth, finally finding her tongue.

"What about him?"

"The witch is . . . starving him," Alice managed.

"How the hell could she be starving him?" snapped Alex. "For God's sake, it's still the middle of the night!"

"What's amiss, lad?" Owen asked, sleepily shuffling out from his chamber. He studied Alex a moment, rubbed his eyes with his fists, then looked at him again. "Haven't been the same since the witch melted them," he muttered.

"By God, *I'm ready!*" Reginald's door flew open and he emerged, dragging his sword behind him. On seeing Alex, he stopped and stared, aghast. "Good Lord, lad, you can't go into battle like that!"

"I wasn't thinking of going anywhere except back to bed."

"But we're under attack!" Reginald raised his sword, then gazed around in confusion at the small party gathered in the corridor. "Aren't we?"

"I told you it was nothing," chided Marjorie, stepping from their chamber with a plaid draped around her. "Now come back to bed, before you catch your death of—" She stopped suddenly, staring at Alex.

"What is all this blasted noise about?" demanded Lachlan crossly. "A man requires a minimal amount of sleep, and I don't see how I'm supposed to get it with all of you out here carrying on as if it were a bloody— I say, MacDunn, aren't you cold, running around naked like that?"

"He isn't naked," Owen assured Lachlan. "It's just your eyes."

Alex looked down, swore silently, then retreated into his room.

"Tell me what happened," he ordered, wrapping his plaid around his waist.

"The witch came down to the kitchen and told Alice that David is to have nothing but bread and water," Elspeth explained. "Nothing."

"Not so much as an egg, or a bit of meat, or a crumb of cheese," elaborated Alice. "Or even a wee drop of milk, or a cup of ale, or a piece of fresh fish, or a few sweet berries—"

"I understand," Alex interrupted her. "Did she say why?"

"Because she is trying to starve him to death!" Elspeth exclaimed. "And it won't be a difficult task, with the lad so sick and so pitifully thin. He'll be dead within a day—two at the very most!"

"I begged her to reconsider and to let me take him some of the fine rabbit stew I made yesterday," said Alice. "And she told me I was to take him nothing at all, unless I was willing to face your wrath!"

"My wrath?"

"She said you had entrusted David's care to her once again and that you had sworn if anyone disobeyed her orders, you would see to it that they were severely punished."

Alex vainly tried to recall making such a pledge. Gwendolyn flooded his mind, her slender fingers laced into his hair as she held him to the paleness of her breast, her body pulsing frantically as a breathless cry tore from the back of her throat—

". . . Alex?" said Owen, a little louder this time.

Alex inhaled sharply, trying to extinguish the desire raging through his body. "Yes?"

"Did you say that?"

Everyone was staring at him, their expressions grim. The throbbing in his head intensified. Had he told Gwendolyn that? He couldn't remember. All he knew was he had brought her to his chamber and forced himself on her like an animal. And afterward he had fetched several jugs of wine and proceeded to get thoroughly drunk—which accounted for this godawful pounding in his head. He rubbed his temple, trying to think.

If you try to return me to my clan, I will escape and come back here. David needs me.

She had stood before him as she told him this, her determination almost eclipsing her fear. At that moment, she had wanted to stay—for no reason other than to care for his son. After what Alex had done to her last night, he could not blame her if she decided to flee. Instead she was downstairs before first light, embarking on some new, bizarre course of healing. He could not imagine what she hoped to achieve by feeding his son only bread and water. Perhaps it was some sort of cleansing rite in preparation for a spell. All he knew was that she had told him the truth.

No matter what he did to her, she would not abandon his son.

"You will respect Gwendolyn's instructions," he ordered, praying he was not making the wrong decision. "If she says the lad is to eat nothing but bread and water, so be it. No one is to interfere, or secretly feed my son when she isn't there. Is that understood?"

"He will starve to death!" protested Elspeth, horrified.

"Or he may get better," countered Alex, although in truth he failed to see how. "We shall have to wait and see."

"... and then the terrible giant chewed the warriors until their flesh and bones were nothing but runny, blood-soaked pulp."

David stared critically at the platter of misshapen bread figures. "These are too fat to be warriors."

"They grew a bit stout as they baked," Gwendolyn admitted. "But the giant preferred nice, plump warriors to little scrawny ones." She handed him one.

"Why are they naked?" he asked, tearing a leg off and popping it into his mouth.

"I tried dressing the first batch in plaids, but when they

came out of the oven their plaids had risen so much they looked just like turtles."

"Can I see them?"

"They were also a little burned," she confessed, "so I threw them out. But look, I have a nice plate of fish for you."

His blue eyes widened with anticipation. "Real fish?"

"No. Bread fish."

He scrunched up his nose. "I'm tired of bread," he complained, ripping the head off a warrior and squishing it flat with his thumb.

"Maybe if you are still feeling better tomorrow, we will try a little broth."

David rolled his eyes. "Broth isn't food," he informed her. "I want something I can chew."

"Very well," relented Gwendolyn, encouraged by the fact that he was actually developing an appetite. "I will put something in the broth that you can chew. Now finish eating."

She watched him as he savagely mutilated the remaining warriors before slowly eating them. She could not blame him for feeling frustrated. For five days now she had fed him nothing but bread and water. On the first day he was too ill to care much, but by the second day he was beginning to feel a little better and quickly began to complain. Unwilling to abandon her experiment too soon, Gwendolyn tried to make his diet more interesting for him by baking the bread into interesting shapes. Early each morning Alice provided her with dough, which Gwendolyn labored to mold into figures that might amuse David. Unfortunately, these forms baked with widely varying degrees of success.

On the first day the fine herd of horses she had created puffed up far more than she expected, until their bellies were bloated and their legs resembled little stumps. She told David they were wild boars, but he pointed out that their tails were too long. The next day she attempted an intricate castle and shaped a laird and an assortment of little clan members to dwell within it. The finely detailed castle emerged from the oven as a giant blob, its inhabitants a scorched collection of smaller blobs. Deciding she needed to simplify her efforts, she went on to shape stars, moons, and a few flowers. But it was difficult to weave an enticingly gory story with such innocuous figures. That was when David suggested she try her hand at monsters. These turned out as bulbous lumps with long necks, and the sharp fangs and talons she had painstakingly fashioned for them spread and baked together, turning into webbed feet and ridiculously misshapen heads. When Gwendolyn told David what they were supposed to be, he burst into laughter and then, sensing her distress, politely assured her they really did look like terrifying monsters.

While her attempts at baking were an unequivocal failure, thus far David's frugal diet was showing promising results. The red spots on his face and neck had disappeared, and he had not suffered from any fits of nausea, vomiting, or diarrhea. Of course Elspeth told her this was because he had nothing inside him, and that he would surely be dead within a day if she didn't give him some decent food. But Gwendolyn made certain David consumed a sufficient quantity of bread and water that his body could reject it if it chose. Miraculously, it did not. Although he remained pale and weak, David had passed five days without sickness. While this did not prove that his illness was caused by the food he ingested, it was possible that whatever was wrong with him made certain foods intolerable to his body. Therefore, Gwendolyn reasoned, if she carefully controlled what he ate, his body might have a chance to rest and grow strong again. If he still fared well tomorrow, she planned to let him have one new food—perhaps an egg or a chunk of cheese—and see how he responded to it.

"When can I go outside again?" he asked, nibbling half-heartedly on a warrior's bloated arm.

"Not for a while," replied Gwendolyn. "We must wait until you are feeling better."

"I'm feeling better now. And I'm tired of staying in bed all the time."

"I know you are. But your father has said you are not to leave the castle without his permission. If you want to go outside, you must ask him if he will allow it."

"He hasn't visited me for days," complained David. "Has he gone away?"

"No."

He frowned. "Then why doesn't he come to see me?"

"I imagine he is very busy. Perhaps he will visit you today and you can ask him about going outside."

"If he doesn't, will you find him and ask him for me?"

"No."

"Why not?"

Because I cannot bear to face him, she thought helplessly.

She had not seen MacDunn since the night she had followed him to his chamber. He had wanted to punish her, and he had, although not in a way that she ever could have imagined. Instead of striking her, he had cast a spell of dark desire over her that made her long for him. With every gentle caress of her skin, with each aching suckle upon her breast, and with the warm, powerful feel of him as he stretched over her, holding her safe within his hard embrace, he had bound her to him more strongly than if he had used chains. A brilliant fire had raged inside her that night, and every time she thought of MacDunn the heat of it blazed through her once again. He had tried to take her by force, but ultimately no force was necessary. She had lain with him and offered herself, had grown hot and slick and ravenous for him, and when it was over and she was curled alone on her own bed, shame had consumed her like a burning fever.

Her clan was right, she realized miserably. She was a whore.

While she had purposely avoided MacDunn, she had felt certain that the moment he heard of the unusual course she was taking with his son, he would confront her about it—especially since everyone in the clan believed she was starving David to death. But MacDunn had not sought her out. It was clear he had told the others not to interfere, for no one had challenged her right to care for David since that first morning when Elspeth and Alice vowed they would have MacDunn stop her. Although he had no desire to see either her or his son, he was willing to grant her one more opportunity to heal David.

"If I can't go outside, can I at least sit by the window and see what's happening in the courtyard?" asked David, pulling her from her thoughts. "They're making a lot of noise out there."

Gwendolyn rose from her chair and went to the window. A crowd of MacDunns were watching in astonishment as Garrick and Quentin rode through the gates, leading a young woman on a magnificent white horse. The woman's brown hair fell over her shoulders in thick, matted clumps, and her elegant scarlet riding cloak was torn and splattered with mud. Despite her unkempt appearance, the woman's bearing was frostily regal as she glared at the MacDunns gathering around her.

"Good Lord," Gwendolyn exclaimed, "it's Isabella!"

David instantly tossed down his covers and padded over to the window. "Is she a friend of yours?" he asked, peering down into the courtyard.

"She is Laird MacSween's daughter." What on earth was Isabella doing here?

"Does she always look so mean?"

"I'm afraid she does."

"Look, Lachlan is bringing her something to drink," said David, pointing. "That should make her feel welcome."

Gwendolyn gasped and raced out of the chamber.

🖾 "Take your hands off me, you filthy, hairy brute!" commanded Isabella, swatting at Garrick's hand.

"I was only trying to assist you off your mount," he grumbled.

" 'Tis another witch," Munro said, eyeing her fearfully. "Come to spread more evil among us!"

"I am most certainly not a witch!" declared Isabella, indignant. "I am the daughter of Laird MacSween."

"Now, that's a foolish tale, lass," said Ewan, shaking his

head. "No laird would permit his daughter to go riding about the countryside by herself."

"Where is your fine escort?" Lettie asked.

"And why are you so dirty?" Farquhar added.

"Here, now, lassie," said Lachlan, emerging through the crowd carrying a goblet. "You must be sorely parched. Have a wee drink, and you'll feel much better."

"Finally, someone who knows how to properly greet an honored guest," sniffed Isabella. She haughtily reached for the cup.

"Isabella—*no!*"

Everyone looked at Gwendolyn in surprise.

"Gwendolyn!" gasped Isabella. "You're alive!" Her eyes were round with shock, making it impossible to tell whether this revelation pleased or disturbed her.

"Lachlan," began Gwendolyn, her tone disapproving, "you should not be offering our guest such strong drink."

" 'Tis only wine," he replied innocently, squinting at her through the bright sunlight.

Gwendolyn regarded him sternly.

"It won't hurt her," he assured her. "After all, she is a witch."

"No, she isn't. She is the daughter of Laird MacSween."

Lachlan stared at Isabella in disbelief.

In truth, Gwendolyn could not blame the MacDunns for their incredulity. Isabella's hair lay in stringy clumps over her heavily stained cloak, and her cheeks and forehead were streaked with dirt. The sun had burned her nose a bright red, which contrasted sharply against the dark purple shadows ringing her eyes. She maintained an admirable air of practiced disdain, but Gwendolyn detected a hint of desperation in her gaze.

"Are you sure she's not a witch?" demanded Lachlan.

"Quite sure."

He sighed and lowered the goblet, disappointed.

"Gwendolyn, you must take me to see Mad MacDunn immediately," commanded Isabella.

Gwendolyn fought to control her anxiety. Why had Isabella come here?

"MacDunn isn't here," said Ned, moving beside Gwendolyn. "He has gone hunting with some of the men."

"When will they return?" asked Gwendolyn.

Ned shrugged. "Probably late tonight."

"Unless, of course, it's earlier," Garrick said.

"It might even be tomorrow," pointed out Lachlan. "You never quite know with MacDunn."

"Why don't you come inside and rest awhile, Isabella?" Gwendolyn suggested. "You must be exhausted after such a long journey."

"I shall require a hot bath immediately," Isabella informed Lachlan, dismounting from her horse. "With precisely four spoonfuls of your finest rose oil mixed into the water—no more—and two extra kettles of heated water to keep the bath warm. I shall also need a new gown—preferably red—with pleasing stitching at the neck, cuffs, and hem. Make certain the fabric is soft," she warned firmly, "or I won't wear it."

Lachlan stared at her, dumbfounded. "Are you suggesting I fetch these things for you?"

"Of course not. I can see you are far too decrepit to manage a heavy tub on your own. Have these two young brutes help you." She gestured at Garrick and Quentin. "Gwendolyn will tell you which chamber I am to have. I will also have a tray of roasted chicken, fresh, lightly warmed bread, a peeled, sliced apple, and a dish of ripe berries in cream. And I want ale to drink." She cast a critical eye at the liquid frothing in the goblet Lachlan was holding. "That wine is far too young to be served."

She adjusted her mud-streaked cape around her shoulders and swept regally through the crowd of MacDunns, leaving Lachlan to stare in bewilderment after her.

"You ran away?" said Gwendolyn, stunned. "But why?"

"Because my life is over!" Isabella wept dramatically as

she lay sprawled on Gwendolyn's bed. "I can never return to my clan!"

"What happened?"

"Some time after MacDunn so cruelly abandoned me in the woods, Robert finally found me."

"MacDunn wasn't abandoning you, Isabella," Gwendolyn pointed out. "He was setting you free, as he had promised your father he would. And he knew Robert had come to fetch you and would find you shortly."

"That madman deserted me!" Isabella railed. "Leaving me alone to fend for myself in the woods! I might have starved to death or frozen in the night!"

Gwendolyn refrained from mentioning that MacDunn had left her ample food, water, and a well-fed fire.

"Robert was in the foulest of tempers because MacDunn had slain all of his men," Isabella went on. "He had no interest in hearing about what I had been through! All during the journey back he kept telling me it was all my fault that you had escaped—as if I had any choice about that scoundrel Brodick holding a dirk to my throat! He didn't seem to be the least bit concerned that I might have been killed—or worse!" She sniffed into a scrap of linen.

No, thought Gwendolyn, Robert would not have been sympathetic to the travails of his niece. He was too concerned with finding Gwendolyn and stealing the stone.

"When we arrived home," Isabella continued, "my father was relieved that I had been returned safely and was prepared to leave well enough alone. But Robert told him that I was ruined because I had been abducted and forced to spend the night with Mad MacDunn and his men. I assured them that I hadn't been ravished, but Robert said I was lying. He convinced my father that no man would ever want me for a wife, and that I would have to be sent away immediately, in case I harbored MacDunn's seed within me. That way, once the child was born it could be secretly killed. My father refused to send me anywhere, saying that he would offer a fortune in gold to the man who would marry me and restore my honor.

And so Robert got his foulest, most brutal warrior, Derek, to offer for me, so that Robert could share his reward!"

"Surely your father rejected him?"

Isabella burst into tears. "I begged him to. I told him I would rather die than marry Derek. My father said it pained him greatly to see me so distraught, but that when I was older I would see this was the only way to salvage my life. And Robert vowed that as soon as Derek and I were married, he would lead an army here to destroy the MacDunns and avenge my honor."

So that was it, Gwendolyn mused. Robert was using Isabella's supposed defilement as an excuse to attack the MacDunns and capture Gwendolyn once again.

And when he had Gwendolyn as his prisoner, he would use any means necessary to force her to give him the stone.

"Since I would rather die than marry Derek, I decided to run away," finished Isabella miserably.

"But why did you come here? Surely you must hate MacDunn and his warriors after they dishonored you and your clan."

"I would like to see them all carved into tiny pieces with their bloody, steaming entrails rotting in the sun!" Isabella raged. She delicately dabbed her nose with her crumpled piece of linen and sighed. "But they are the only ones who know that my honor remains intact. And besides, where else could I go?"

"But how did you know the way here?"

"I remembered the direction we took when MacDunn abducted me. After I got past the woods, I just kept riding in the same direction. Of course I was absolutely terrified of being eaten by wolves, but I kept reminding myself of how I would rather die than be forced to marry Derek. Finally this morning these two horrid brutes found me. I told them I was looking for Mad MacDunn, and they said they were from his clan and agreed to bring me here."

"And after you have rested, those same horrid brutes will escort you home," drawled a harsh voice.

Gwendolyn's breath caught in her chest as MacDunn entered the chamber with Cameron and Brodick.

"Bella," said Brodick, concern in his voice, "you look absolutely frightful. What has happened to you?"

"Don't you come near me, you horrible beast! I hate you!" She flung herself against Gwendolyn's pillow and burst into a fresh torrent of tears.

"Looks like the lass didn't get over it, Brodick," Cameron commented wryly.

"What the hell is she doing here?" Alex asked, his gaze fixed hard on Gwendolyn.

"Isabella has run away from home," she explained. "And she now seeks sanctuary with you."

Alex looked incredulous. "Has she lost her mind?"

"Don't cry, sweet Bella," crooned Brodick, seating himself on the bed beside Isabella. "Whatever is wrong, we shall fix it."

"It cannot be fixed," wailed Isabella pitifully. "My life has been destroyed because of you, you cowardly defiler of beautiful, innocent women!" She sat up and whacked him with the pillow, then fell back and dissolved into tears once more.

"I think she still likes you, Brodick," observed Ned.

"Would someone kindly explain to me what is going on?" Alex asked, wincing at the racket Isabella was making.

"It seems Robert has convinced Laird MacSween that his daughter has been ruined by all of you," Gwendolyn explained.

"That's ridiculous!" scoffed Cameron. "No one ever laid a hand on the lass."

"And in a bid to salvage her sullied reputation, Robert has gallantly persuaded one of his most brutal warriors to take Isabella as his bride in return for a fortune in gold," she finished.

Alex regarded Gwendolyn in disbelief. "Surely MacSween turned this warrior down—"

"No," said Gwendolyn. "MacSween agreed to the match. And so Isabella ran away."

Isabella's wailing grew louder.

"Hush, now, sweet Bella," crooned Brodick, stroking her back. "Everything is going to be fine. You're safe now."

"She cannot stay here," Alex said. "Robert has been lusting for war since we took Gwendolyn, but MacSween has been holding off. We have just sent his messenger home with another apologetic letter and a bag of gold, but if we keep his daughter here against his wishes, MacSween will have no choice but to send an army for her. We must take her back."

"No!" cried Isabella.

"Really, Alex, you can't mean that," protested Brodick.

"I have no choice, Brodick. I cannot risk the safety of the clan because Isabella doesn't like her father's choice of a husband."

"But you are responsible for her situation," Gwendolyn pointed out.

"It is hardly my fault that she has a milksop for a father and a bastard for an uncle," countered Alex.

"Isabella did not ask to be abducted by you, MacDunn," Gwendolyn argued, rising to face him. "You used her as a hostage so that you and your men could escape with me. Whether you like it or not, by taking her you destroyed her honor, and now she is suffering because of it. She has come here asking for your protection, and it is your duty to take responsibility for what you have done and help her however you can."

"The lass is right, Alex," agreed Cameron. "We've done wrong by this girl."

"We're talking about war, for God's sake!" Alex thundered.

"That was a risk we were willing to take when we decided to steal Gwendolyn," observed Brodick. "What does it matter if we fight a war over one woman or two?"

"Taking Gwendolyn was different," Alex said.

"How?" asked Ned.

Because I needed a witch to heal my son, and for that I would have risked anything, Alex reflected grimly. But suddenly he realized how terribly selfish that was. He had not chanced war because it was his duty as laird to save the next

MacDunn. He had done it because he could not bear to watch his son suffer and die.

And because the moment he saw Gwendolyn he knew he could not stand by and watch her be engulfed by flames.

Everyone was staring at him in disapproving silence.

"Fine," he muttered. "She can stay here."

Isabella blinked, as if she hadn't understood.

And then she erupted into ear-splitting, hysterical sobbing.

"I'm glad to see my decision makes you happy," commented Alex dryly.

"She's a loud one, isn't she?" remarked Cameron, wincing.

"I feel a sudden need to make an inspection of the outer wall," announced Alex. "Coming, Cameron? Ned?"

"Aye," said Cameron, eager to escape the racket Isabella was making.

"I'll come as well," offered Brodick.

"No need," Alex said. "I can see Isabella enjoys your company, Brodick. I insist that you stay with her."

"I don't think that's necessary—" protested Brodick.

" 'Tis clear she finds your presence comforting," teased Cameron, following Alex out the door.

A slicing pain carved through Alex's head as Isabella's wailing reached new heights. When Robert came with Isabella's betrothed, Alex would tie him up and force him to listen to her screeching.

A few hours of that and the poor bastard would be well cured of any desire to marry her.

"Aim for his throat! That's it—now thrust your sword into his gut, where he has left himself open!"

Cameron obligingly shoved his sword forward.

"Brodick, *watch out!*" shrieked Isabella.

His attention diverted, Brodick leaped back a second too late and ended up sprawled on the ground.

"You're a trifle slow today, my friend," teased Cameron,

the tip of his sword pressing into Brodick's stomach. "Is something distracting you?"

"Your lovely wife," said Brodick. "There's something wonderful about a beautiful woman carrying life within her."

Grinning proudly, Cameron turned to look. Brodick instantly raised his sword in a wide arc, sending Cameron's weapon flying into the air.

"Cameron!" barked Alex. "Stay focused on your opponent!"

"I thought the fight was over," muttered Cameron, casting Brodick an irritated glance.

"Have some pity, Alex," Brodick said, rising. "The poor fellow is hopelessly in love with his wife."

"He won't be much good to her if he gets his belly carved open."

"No one will get close enough to me to carve anything open," Cameron scoffed, winking at Clarinda. "They'll be dead long before they can so much as scratch me."

Gwendolyn watched as Clarinda gave Cameron an exasperated smile, then lowered her head once again to the arrow she was fitting with a feather. The moment between husband and wife was fleeting, but Gwendolyn was moved by its tender intimacy.

"If you're quite finished swaggering before your wife, Cameron, perhaps we could continue training," suggested Alex.

"Certainly," said Cameron, still smiling.

"Fine. Brodick, take a group of about seventy-five men over to the west wall and have them practice fighting with just their spears. Cameron, you continue to lead this group in swordplay. Ned, you will take another one hundred to the targets outside the wall and sharpen their archery skills. I am going to have the remainder work on fighting without weapons."

Isabella added the poorly fletched arrow she had been working on to her meager pile and sighed. "My hands are cramped from all this work," she complained. "I think I will stop for a while and take a stroll."

"You should stay here and watch my father show the men how to fight without weapons," David said. "My father is wonderful at that."

"I'm sure he is," Isabella agreed politely. "But I find wielding a spear so much more fascinating." With that she quickly began to follow Brodick and his men to the west wall.

"She seems quite taken with our Brodick, poor thing," observed Clarinda, shaking her head. "No doubt he charmed her from the moment they met."

"Actually, he held a dirk to her throat and threatened to kill her," said Gwendolyn, removing the mangled feather from one of Isabella's arrows and replacing it.

"He did?" gasped David, clearly intrigued. He watched as Isabella daintily made her way through the churning maze of grunting warriors to be closer to Brodick. "How can Isabella like him if he did that to her?"

" 'Tis a strange thing, losing your heart to a man," mused Clarinda, smiling. "Sometimes it happens when you're most certain you cannot abide him."

"Isabella, for God's sake be careful!" Brodick dashed into the fray to grab her. "You shouldn't be so close to the men when they are training."

"After ruining my life, I can't see why you should care whether I get savagely mutilated by one of these spears," sniffed Isabella. "I should think you would be pleased if I were sliced wide open and lay here bleeding to death on the ground as these great brutes crushed my bones into mush."

"Bella, how can you say such terrible things?" asked Brodick, taking her arm and leading her out of the training area. "You know I would do anything for you. . . ."

Gwendolyn shook her head, unable to comprehend why Brodick remained so gallant toward Isabella. "Are you cold, David?" she asked, adjusting the plaids she had arranged over him. "The wind is getting stronger."

"I'm fine."

"We shouldn't stay out here much longer. Your father gave you permission to watch him train the men, but only for a short while."

"But look," David cried, pointing, "the men are starting to charge. Can't we stay and watch?"

His blue eyes were bright and pleading, his thin cheeks faintly flushed by the cool wind blowing against his pale skin. It had been six long days since that terrible afternoon when Gwendolyn had last taken him outside. Since then she had kept the lad in his chamber, watching over him as he slowly recovered from his violent bout of illness. But with Isabella's arrival yesterday, the castle had been swept into a whirlwind of activity as the clan prepared for the imminent arrival of the MacSweens, and David seemed to have been energized by it. No longer willing to remain in his bed, he had pleaded with his father for permission to watch the men as they practiced their fighting skills in the courtyard. MacDunn told the boy he could view the activity from his chamber window, but David had remained surprisingly steadfast in his request. He had assured his father the small excursion would do him good, and promised to tell Gwendolyn the moment he felt the least bit ill or tired.

Finally, MacDunn had relented.

"Well, I'm cold." Gwendolyn rubbed her arms. "If we are to stay out here awhile longer, I must fetch a wrap. Clarinda, will you watch David for me while I run up to my chamber?"

"Of course. Look, David, see how well your father fights with just his hands!"

"He is just like the mighty Torvald," said David proudly, "in the story Gwendolyn tells about the time he must battle a ferocious sea monster. . . ."

The great hall was empty as Gwendolyn hurried through it and mounted the stairs leading to the tower. The looming arrival of Robert and his army had forced the MacDunns to set to work preparing for the attack. Alex had assigned tasks to all in the clan according to their abilities. While the fittest men trained to fight, the older men worked on fortifying the castle and preparing weapons. Youths who were too young to participate in the battle had been enlisted to gather heavy stones from the surrounding area and haul them up to the parapet, from where they would be dropped onto the MacSweens as they tried to climb the wall. The MacDunn women were busy making great stores of food in the event of a lengthy siege and were also helping to produce thousands of arrows. Even the young girls were hard at work filling the enormous cauldrons positioned over the gate with endless buckets of water, which would be kept boiling until the moment they were dumped on the MacSweens as they attempted to breach the gate. When Robert came, he would find the MacDunns prepared to meet his attack.

How much they would be willing to sacrifice for an unwelcome witch and a runaway laird's daughter was another matter.

Gwendolyn frowned and blinked against the gloom as she pushed the door to her chamber open. Someone had closed the shutters of her windows, blocking the afternoon light. At first she suspected this was to conserve the essence of some smoldering herb meant to ward off her evil, but the air was relatively clear. Unable to fathom why someone would want to deprive her room of light, she went to the window and attempted to open the shutters. They wouldn't give. She went to the next window, only to find its shutters also locked tight. She bent down and studied the latch, trying to discern what was keeping the shutters closed. Suddenly aware of a whisper of sound, she started to turn.

Pain exploded in her head, brilliant and paralyzing.

And then there was nothing.

"Did Brodick really hold a dirk to your throat?" David asked.

"The beast most certainly did," Isabella replied, still annoyed at having been ordered to return to her seat on the opposite side of the courtyard. "And he said if I so much as breathed he would carve my head off and trample it beneath the dung-filled hooves of his horse."

David considered this a moment. "It would be a lot of

work to cut off someone's head with a dirk. In Gwendolyn's stories the warrior uses either a sword or an ax."

"I suppose he might have resorted to his sword once I had collapsed onto the ground," Isabella speculated. "But not until after I had suffered the most terrible pain, my last vision being of him seated on his mount high above me, his mouth twisted in an evil smile as he watched my blood flow like a river of scarlet around me!"

"That's good!" exclaimed David. "Do you tell stories?"

"Certainly not," she replied, insulted.

"But you would be wonderful at it! Just like Gwendolyn."

Isabella regarded him uncertainly a moment, then realized he was actually complimenting her. "Do you really think so?"

"You certainly have a colorful way with words," Clarinda observed, adding another neatly fletched arrow to the enormous stack beside her chair.

Isabella looked pleased. "Why, thank you, Clarinda. You're very kind."

"Maybe you could come to my chamber tonight and tell me a story," David suggested. "I'm sure Gwendolyn won't mind, since you are a friend from her clan."

"Did Gwendolyn tell you that?" asked Isabella, surprised.

"Of course," said David, although in fact he could not recall her exact words. "We watched you arriving from my chamber window, and she told me who you were. I was not allowed to come outside to greet you, of course, because I'm sick."

"You seem quite well today," Isabella noted.

"I have been feeling better since Gwendolyn stopped feeding me."

"She stopped feeding you?"

"It's part of a spell," he explained. "To help me heal."

"She does feed him," interjected Clarinda, "but only certain foods in limited amounts."

"Don't you get hungry?" Isabella asked.

"Sometimes," he admitted. "But today she let me have a

little bowl of porridge with my bread, and if I am still feeling well tomorrow, I may have one slice of apple."

"That spell would never work for me, I'm afraid," said Clarinda, giggling. "With this bairn growing so large, I now eat more than Cameron!"

"I'm a little hungry myself." Isabella sniffed the air, frowning. "MacDunn should really speak to the men in the bake house. They are burning the bread to cinders."

"*Fire!*" shouted Cameron, pointing suddenly with his sword. "In the west tower!"

Alex stared in horror at the black cloud spewing from the shuttered windows of Gwendolyn's chamber. He lowered his gaze to where she had been sitting with David, expecting to find her there.

And then he began to run.

Smoke was pouring from the bottom of the door. Alex's heart clenched as he jerked up the latch. The heavy door didn't budge. He slammed his shoulder against it, grunting with effort. As the door gave, a searing cloud blasted from the chamber, choking him. Coughing violently, he stumbled inside. The room was dark except for the brilliant flames dancing on the bed, feasting ravenously upon an unmoving mound. Paralyzing fear overwhelmed him. His voice raw with despair, he called her name. He clenched his fists as he stared helplessly at the blazing pyre, blinking against the acrid sting of the smoke. He had failed her. He had saved her from fire once before, but it didn't matter. Ultimately the flames had found her. He sank to his knees and moaned, fighting to grasp the taut threads of his sanity, which were threatening to snap as he watched the flames consume her.

Suddenly there was a muffled cough.

Startled, Alex rose to his feet. "Gwendolyn!" he shouted, searching the foggy darkness.

There was another cough, a tiny, birdlike sound, which was enough to guide him to her.

His eyes streaming from the terrible smoke, he staggered

past the burning bed and found her in a crumpled heap upon the floor. He pulled her into his arms and cradled her tightly against his chest, then ran with her from the blazing tomb.

"Jesus, Alex!" said Brodick. He raced forward to take Gwendolyn from him as a dozen men carrying buckets of water surged into the chamber to battle the flames.

"I will carry her," Alex rasped, gripping her even tighter.

"Clear the staircase!" commanded Cameron, waving the men who were crowding it back down. "Make way!"

Alex hurried down the staircase with his precious burden, acutely aware of how small and fragile she was as he held her within his arms. *She will not die,* he told himself fiercely, racing along the corridor. *She cannot.*

"Dear God, Alex, is she dead?" cried Robena, appearing suddenly in the hallway. Her face was pale with shock.

"No," he replied harshly. "She is alive."

Robena regarded him in silent sympathy, as if she thought his madness made him unable to accept the truth.

And then Gwendolyn coughed again.

"Take her into my chamber," Robena offered, swiftly regaining her composure. "I will tend to her."

Alex did not stop, but continued along the corridor toward his chamber.

"Alex, you cannot take her into your chamber," Robena protested. "It isn't seemly!"

He kicked open his chamber door. "I don't give a goddamn whether it is seemly or not," he growled. "She is mine, and I will bloody well look after her!"

He went inside and laid Gwendolyn gently on the bed. She was making horrible choking sounds, fighting to rid her lungs of smoke.

"Easy, now," Alex soothed, helping her as she struggled to sit up. "Breathe slowly, Gwendolyn. Easy."

Gwendolyn couldn't respond, for her chest and throat were drawn tight, making it difficult to inhale even the tiniest breath. She hacked and gagged, certain she was going to drown any moment in the vile, burning phlegm that was rising in her throat.

Suddenly she threw herself over the side of the bed and vomited.

"Elspeth must bleed her," said Robena as Elspeth marched through the doorway.

"Her body must be purged," agreed Elspeth.

"You won't touch her, Elspeth!" said Clarinda fiercely, waddling in behind them. "You only mean to harm her!"

"How dare you!" Elspeth's eyes seethed with outrage. "That you could say such a thing, after the care I gave you when you brought that dead child into the world!"

"Oh, aye," Clarinda responded caustically, "and all the while I screamed in torment as I labored to birth her, you told me 'twas God punishing me and I should bear it quietly, and when my poor bairn was strangled, you told me that I had angered God with my sins and my lust, and so he took my babe as punishment! 'Twas fine care, indeed!"

"Clarinda and I will tend to her," announced Marjorie, who had also entered the room. "We don't need your help, Elspeth."

"MacDunn," Elspeth said firmly, "you cannot allow—"

"Get out!" shouted Alex. "All of you!"

The women stared at him, startled.

"*Out!*" he roared, moving menacingly toward them.

They turned and scurried from the room.

Alex slammed the chamber door, blocking out the curious clan members who had gathered in the corridor. They were shocked by his behavior. No doubt they would spend the rest of the day debating whether or not he was going mad again.

Perhaps he was.

Gwendolyn had stopped retching and was lying limp on the bed, coughing. Alex wet a cloth, seated himself beside her, and began to gently wash her face.

"Take a deep breath, Gwendolyn," he ordered quietly, sponging her smudged cheeks and lips with the cool water. "That's it . . . slowly . . . now let it out. Very good. Now breathe in again."

He continued to murmur soothing words to her as her

breathing gradually steadied. When her chest was rising and falling with relative ease, he fetched her a cup of water.

"Rinse your mouth and spit into this basin." He pulled her up once again and held her hair back, making sure none of the black silk fell near the bowl. Gwendolyn leaned weakly against his arm, took the cup from him, and obediently rinsed her mouth.

"Now take a few small sips of water. It will help ease the burning in your throat. Very good," Alex soothed. "Your gown is blackened by the smoke. Let me help you take it off."

Far too miserable to be concerned with modesty, Gwendolyn raised her arms and permitted Alex to unlace the back of her gown and pull it up over her head, leaving her clad only in her chemise. He tossed her gown onto the floor, quickly removed her shoes and stockings, then drew back the coverings on his bed and laid her against the clean sheets.

"Feel better?" he asked, carefully laying a plaid over her.

She nodded, then winced with pain.

Alex gingerly ran his fingers over her head. Gwendolyn flinched as he grazed an enormous swelling on the crown. His expression contained, he studied the blood staining his fingers. If Gwendolyn had fainted as a result of the smoke, she would not have fallen on the crown of her head.

Someone had struck her and left her to die in that fire, he realized harshly.

He bent down and began to clean up the vomit on the floor, trying to gain control of his rage. Mopping up sickness was a task he had grown well accustomed to in the long months he cared for Flora. In the beginning he had every healer he could find at her bed, but toward the end, when it was obvious she was going to die, he refused to let any of them near her, preferring to care for her himself. Scrubbing the worn stones helped him to clarify his thoughts. God had denied both Flora and his son the blessing of adequate health, and for all Alex's rage and determination, ultimately there was little he could do to protect them. But it wasn't God who had trapped Gwendolyn in her chamber and set the bed afire.

It was one of his clan.

"Can you tell me what happened, Gwendolyn?" he asked, setting the cloth and basin aside.

"I—I'm not sure," she rasped.

He moved a chair closer to the bed and seated himself. "Was your chamber on fire when you went in?"

"No. I remember it was very dark, because the shutters were closed. But that was strange, because I never close them."

Which meant whoever started the fire had closed them first, Alex realized. Either they had wanted to contain the smoke to make it more deadly, or they were trying to ensure that no one noticed the haze escaping from the tower until it was too late. The rage within him intensified. "What happened then?"

"I went over to the window and tried to open the shutters. But it was difficult. I moved to another one and couldn't get it to open, either. And then—" She stopped suddenly, remembering.

"And then what?"

Gwendolyn hesitated. She knew the MacDunns feared and despised her. They had never made a secret of it. But although she was not welcomed by them, this past week she had allowed herself to believe that they had at least accepted her presence. She had been wrong, she realized, swallowing thickly. The MacDunns wanted to destroy her, just as her own clan had.

"Who struck you, Gwendolyn?"

She looked at him in surprise.

"You have a bleeding lump on the top of your head," he explained, "which you couldn't have received by falling to the floor. And when you previously fell down the staircase," he added reluctantly, "you were assisted by a strategically placed length of twine."

Shock stripped the last trace of color from her face.

"Morag never sent you that note," he continued grimly. "She does not know how to scribe."

She considered all this a moment before quietly asking, "Why didn't you tell me?"

"I was afraid that you might leave," he explained, apologetic. "And I needed you to stay—for David's sake. So I ordered Cameron, Ned, and Brodick to guard you."

So that was why one of them was always near. Gwendolyn had thought the warriors were watching her to make certain that she didn't run away. Instead they were trying to protect her.

"Unfortunately, this afternoon you slipped out of the courtyard while all three were engaged in training," Alex reflected in frustration. "We didn't realize you were gone until we saw the smoke."

"You should have told me, MacDunn."

She was right, he realized. Perhaps if she had known, she would have taken greater care. "Did you see who struck you, Gwendolyn?"

She shook her head. "It was dark and whoever did it was behind me. When I woke up, the chamber was on fire and you were carrying me."

She closed her eyes, fighting the misery surging through her. Whether by fire at the stake or in her chamber, or breaking her neck falling down some stairs, there would always be those who wanted to kill her. It was inevitable as long as people believed she was a witch. And she would never be able to convince the MacDunns that she wasn't. Ironically, she had accepted the role to save her life. She clutched the blanket, feeling lost and afraid.

Alex watched her knuckles whiten against the dark green of his plaid. "I will find the person who did this, Gwendolyn. And when I do, I will kill him."

"And what will you do if you discover it is your whole clan who wants me dead, MacDunn?" she asked in a quiet voice. "Will you kill all of them?"

"It isn't the whole clan."

"You don't know that for certain. Every time David gets ill, your people believe I am killing him. They seem to forget that he was gravely sick long before I arrived."

"They are afraid of you and your methods. But that does not mean they are conspiring to kill you. If that were true, you would have been dead long ago."

"I might have been, had I drunk one of Lachlan's potions."

"True. But haven't you noticed he has stopped offering them to you?"

"That is because he is afraid of your anger."

"Perhaps. Or maybe it is because he is starting to like you."

Gwendolyn eyed him doubtfully. "Lachlan doesn't like anyone."

"Of course he does." Alex rose from his chair. "He just isn't very good at showing it." He tucked the blanket more securely around her. "Rest awhile, Gwendolyn," he murmured, brushing an inky strand of hair from her cheek. "I will stay and watch over you, so you know you are safe. Try to put this from your mind and just sleep."

She was not safe, Gwendolyn reflected miserably, and she never would be as long as she remained here. But Alex's gentle words poured over her like warm water, reminding her of the low timbre of her father's voice when he used to put her to bed when she was little. Gwendolyn surrendered to her exhaustion and closed her eyes. She heard Alex settle back into his chair, preparing to watch over her.

And just as she began to drift into the shadowy haze of sleep, he laid his strong hand protectively over hers, and for one fleeting instant, she felt safe.

CHAPTER 10

Rain lashed against the enormous black fortress, making it glisten like a dark jewel against the leaden sky.

It was a bleak, forbidding structure, intended to intimidate rather than to entice. No effort had been wasted to grace the castle with a hint of warmth or whimsy. Instead it was a bastion of defense, with soaring sixty-foot walls crowned with heavy battlements, and four massive rounded towers slashed at regular intervals with deadly archer slits. Cleverly constructed wooden platforms had been built out from the wall head, from which warriors would be better situated to drop heavy boulders and boiling water onto the attackers scrambling to reach the wall below. The base of the wall had also been extended some twenty feet, making it foolhardy to attempt to mine underneath it. Robert sat upon his mount and studied the stronghold, heedless of the icy rain whipping against him.

MacDunn's castle was not going to be easy to penetrate. But even the most formidable of fortresses had a weakness.

He smiled.

How fortuitous that his niece had elected to seek sanctuary with the very man who had abducted her. When Isabella first returned from her abduction, his blithering fool of a brother had refused to permit Robert to lead an army to MacDunn's holding. Isabella was home safe as MacDunn had promised, and MacDunn had sent a lavish payment along with a bizarre note of apology, stating that he needed the witch to communicate with his pet birds, whose company he found far more stimulating than that of people. For Cedric, this only confirmed the fact that the laird was completely mad and could therefore not be held accountable for his strange actions. As far as Cedric was concerned, the matter was finished. He blamed Robert for the slaying of his warriors— MacDunn would not have been forced to kill them had Robert obeyed his command and not gone after him. As for the witch, Cedric felt her capture was of little consequence, since the MacSweens had been planning to burn her anyway.

Robert went into a rage and tried to make his insipid sibling see that it was his duty as laird to exact vengeance from the MacDunns. It was only when Robert finally convinced Cedric that his precious daughter had been cruelly ravished and was undoubtedly pregnant with Mad MacDunn's bastard that his brother began to listen. Horrified by the prospect of a bastard grandchild, Cedric proposed an immense dowry in gold for any man who would marry his ruined daughter immediately. Robert quickly arranged for one of his warriors to offer for Isabella, with the agreement that all of the dowry would secretly go to Robert. He easily convinced Derek that marrying his niece would be reward enough. The girl was hopelessly stupid and spoiled, but she was comely, and her willfulness could be beaten out of her—a task the brawny warrior was certain to relish. Isabella was little more than a child who had spent her entire life being coddled and such a tender morsel would be easy to crush. One night of being forced to endure Derek's unnaturally rough bed play, and she would be weeping and begging for mercy.

Unfortunately, while Cedric accepted Derek's offer of marriage, he still refused to order an attack. What could be accomplished, his brother wondered, by sending so many men to battle a laird with a broken mind? Was the loss of one condemned witch worth the price of war? Try as he might, Robert failed to convince him otherwise.

And then Isabella ran away.

While Cedric couldn't fathom why his daughter would return to the very man who had violated her, there was no question that she must be brought home. And so Robert finally got his army, with orders to fetch his niece. Of course, Cedric was hoping that force would not be necessary. But now that he had his warriors, Robert was finally in control. In truth, he didn't give a damn whether Isabella returned with him or not.

All he wanted was Gwendolyn and the stone.

When MacDunn had first come seeking her, Robert had feared that he had somehow heard about the stone and wanted it for himself. MacDunn's daring rescue of Gwendolyn as she was about to be burned had only fortified his suspicions. But when Robert faced him late that night in the woods, he was not convinced that MacDunn had any knowledge of the powerful talisman left to Gwendolyn by her mother, despite MacDunn's insinuations. Gwendolyn and her father had vigilantly guarded their secret for many years, as well they should have.

For the past year Robert had been watching Gwendolyn, aware that the silent, strange child whom everyone believed was a witch had suddenly slipped into womanhood. At first he had eyed her from a distance, unable to comprehend what it was that drew him to her. All his life he had preferred fairhaired, amply fleshed lasses with rounded bosoms and pink, laughing mouths. There was something incredibly pleasurable about watching alarm cloud their doelike eyes and seeing the sweet blush of innocence drain away to pure terror as he held them down with bruising force and took them. No girl was ever the same after he was through with her.

With that ebony cape of hair falling against her bloodless skin, and a body so thin it looked as if it might snap if squeezed too hard, Gwendolyn was hardly the kind of girl he typically found appealing. And yet he had not been able to stop thinking about her. Night after night he imagined her trapped beneath him as he drove himself into her, his hands crushing those tiny white breasts, his legs pinning down her slender, thrashing legs. The image haunted him, until finally his taste for other women waned. There was no way to avoid it, he finally decided. He would have Gwendolyn, if only to slake this urge and prove that she was not nearly as enticing as he imagined.

He began to visit her cottage, feigning friendship with her father so that he might have better access to her. Gwendolyn's father had lived an isolated existence among the MacSweens because of his daughter and was more than eager to share the honored company of the laird's brother. But Gwendolyn was always cold, retreating to her room or leaving the cottage altogether when he visited. Strangely, the fact that she was neither attracted to him nor afraid of him stirred his lust even more. Robert brought generous gifts of wine and ale to her father, hoping he would eventually fall into a deep slumber, leaving Robert alone with his quarry. One night, after a half dozen jugs of a particularly strong ale, John MacSween drunkenly buried his head into his arms and began to weep. He lamented the cruel loss of his wife, and the burden of raising a motherless child who was destined to inherit great powers. Thinking he was referring to the rumors of witchcraft, Robert drained his cup and scoffed that his daughter was no more a witch than he.

And Gwendolyn's father wept even harder and told him of the enchanted stone Gwendolyn was to inherit.

He had claimed it was a gem of rare clarity and beauty that had once belonged to Kenneth MacAlpin, king of the Picts some three and a half centuries earlier. It was said that Kenneth had stolen the stone from a sorcerer and used its great powers to win a vital battle. The next time Kenneth called upon the stone to vanquish his enemy it failed him, however, for it only had the power to grant but one wish every hundred years. Somehow the stone fell into the possession of Gwendolyn's mother's family and was passed down over the centuries from mother to daughter, each possessor charged with keeping it safe until it was time to call upon its powers once more. And that, her father claimed, was Gwendolyn's legacy, for the stone was once again ripe with power.

His curiosity aroused, Robert demanded to see this stone, but Gwendolyn's father refused, saying it was too dangerous. Robert grew angry and commanded that he turn the stone over to him, saying what belonged to a clansman was by right the property of his laird, and he would present it to his brother. John accused him of wanting it for himself. Infuriated by his belligerence, Robert began to tear the cottage apart, searching for the gem. Gwendolyn's father tried to stop him, but the aged, drunken fool was no match for him. In the struggle that followed, Robert wrapped his arms around the old man's neck and jerked up, snapping it. He had not meant to kill him, but ale had clouded his judgment and he had not been aware of the force of his embrace. John MacSween fell back dead, just as Gwendolyn walked in.

Robert had no choice but to accuse her of the murder.

"Seems quiet over there today," observed a dark-haired warrior with an ugly gash below his eye. Derek halted his horse beside him. "Evidently they don't like getting wet," he snorted contemptuously.

"They may not be training, but MacDunn has warriors posted every ten feet along the parapet," replied Robert. "They are difficult to see because of the rain. And I'd warrant every slit in those towers has an archer standing ready."

"If he knows we are coming, why don't we just attack now?" asked Hamish, scowling at the rain. "We've already been camped here three days. The men are growing restless."

"Do you really think we would stand a chance attacking in the thick of this storm, while the MacDunns are warm and dry inside those walls?" demanded Robert. "Only a fool would send drenched men into battle, half blinded by darkness and rain."

"We should have attacked yesterday, when the tower was afire," Giles mused, shifting uncomfortably on his horse. "It would have been easy to overwhelm them while their castle was burning."

"And every able-bodied man was fully armed and primed for battle," drawled Robert sardonically. "I would prefer not to march in while MacDunn's warriors are gathered outside training. Besides, we had no way of knowing how serious the blaze was. Given how quickly it was subdued, it seemed little more than a blocked chimney."

"So when are we going to attack?" Derek asked impatiently.

"When I give the order," snapped Robert. "Now return to your positions."

The three warriors eyed each other sullenly, then turned their horses back toward the camp. Derek was anxious to claim his betrothed, while the others hated MacDunn for stealing their witch and killing their clansmen. Vengeance and the brutal restoration of MacSween honor were uppermost in their minds. Robert had made it clear that they could do whatever they wished with the MacSween women, but the witch was not to be touched. Instead, she and Isabella were to be brought to him, so he could take them back to their holding. The moment he had the stone, he would make himself ruler of all Scotland.

As for Gwendolyn, he would relish breaking her before her death.

🙐 "This is a sad chamber," said Gwendolyn, vainly trying to warm her hands by the fire.

"Do you think so?" Morag leaned back in her chair and gazed around. "I have always thought it is a very pretty chamber, myself—much nicer than that tower room. On a fine day those arched windows let in a wonderful amount of light. Of course you'd never know it, with this terrible storm still raging outside." She slanted a meaningful glance at Gwendolyn.

"I didn't start this storm, Morag."

"Never said you did, did I?"

"I am not entirely in control of the weather, you know."

"Of course you aren't."

Gwendolyn sighed. A violent storm had been raging for two days now, and the MacDunns were convinced that she was the cause of it. She didn't like the cold, gloomy weather any more than they, although it was certainly reflective of her mood. Until she was trapped in that fire, she had not understood the extent of the MacDunns' hatred of her. She had known they feared her, but it had never occurred to her that they might actually try to murder her. The intensity of their loathing cut her deeply, since she had foolishly allowed herself to think that the MacDunns had been gradually starting to accept her. She had been wrong. The MacDunns were no more accepting of her than her own clan had been.

Now that she understood how much they wanted to be rid of her, she had to leave. But who would look after David after she was gone? she wondered desperately. What if he suddenly fell gravely ill again? Elspeth would clamp on to him like a giant leech, tormenting him with her foul methods, blissfully trying to purge Gwendolyn's evil from his tiny body. Poor David would be helpless to do anything except lie there. He would feel abandoned by Gwendolyn. And if he died, what would happen to MacDunn? She knew Alex well enough to understand that for all his strength, the death of his son would devastate him. He might descend into the refuge of madness, never to emerge again. How could she leave them knowing this? She pulled the plaid draped over her shoulders tighter, feeling alone and confused.

"Perhaps the sadness you feel comes from within," suggested Morag quietly.

Gwendolyn considered this a moment, then shook her head. "I have felt sadness in this chamber from the moment I stepped into it. The space is heavy with unhappiness—it is in the walls, the ceiling, the floor—in the very air. And the room never feels warm, even when the fire is blazing." She rubbed her chilled hands together. "To whom does this chamber belong?"

"No one. It once was occupied by MacDunn's wife, Flora. She died in here."

So that was the misery Gwendolyn sensed. MacDunn's wife had lain here in hideous pain, knowing she was going to die and leave her husband and child alone. No wonder her anguish had seeped into these heavy stone walls.

"Did Flora not share MacDunn's chamber?" she asked.

"She did until her illness confined her to bed. After that the healers said her chamber must be sealed from the ill effects of too much light and outside air, and filled with healing smoke. Flora did not want Alex to endure the constant heat and haze, so she asked to be moved into a separate room next to his. But Alex stayed in here with her every night despite her protests. He told her he could not sleep without her, making it seem like she was helping him by permitting it. I believe it made him feel better, to hold her safe in his arms at night, trying to protect her," she reflected quietly. "It certainly comforted Flora. Toward the end, when it was obvious that nothing more could be done for her, Alex cared for her during the day as well. He knew Flora might leave him at any moment, and he wanted to be with her when the time came."

Gwendolyn considered this in silence. Because Alex never spent any time caring for David, Gwendolyn had always assumed that he had no practical experience dealing with the misery of illness, other than as a helpless, tormented witness. But after the fire, when he had tended her and cleaned up after her with calm, gentle skill, she had realized she was wrong. MacDunn was all too familiar with the duties of ministering to the sick.

And he had learned them in this very chamber.

"Is that the bed Flora died in?" she asked, studying the elegantly carved piece in the center of the room.

"No," replied Morag. "Flora's bed was draped with a splendid yellow canopy that MacDunn had specially made for her. The underside was embroidered with mountains, and wildflowers, and a little waterfall that seemed to splash right down the end of it. He wanted her to have something pleasing to look at as she lay there. But the healers kept her room so smoky and dark, 'twas difficult for her to see it. Flora never let MacDunn know this, however." She smiled sadly. "She told him she had memorized every flower and blade of grass, so she could see them even when her eyes were closed. She was a sweet girl, Flora was. The clan adored her." Her expression grew distant.

And she was obviously very much loved by MacDunn as well, mused Gwendolyn. "Why doesn't MacDunn keep the bed in here, Morag?"

"After she died, MacDunn ordered it burned."

Gwendolyn regarded her in surprise. "Why? Did he fear it might harbor her illness?"

"No. He said he couldn't bear to look upon it. It made him think of Flora's suffering."

Gwendolyn reflected on this a long moment before quietly stating, "He loved her very much, didn't he?"

"Aye. He did. And Flora loved him. That's why it's been so difficult for them to say good-bye."

"Do you mean because MacDunn still talks to her?"

Morag hesitated. "Aye," she murmured, turning to gaze at the fire. "That's what I mean."

" 'Tis good to see you're up, Gwendolyn," said Clarinda, waddling in with an enormous tray. "Look, I've brought you a wee bite."

"Really, Clarinda, you shouldn't be carrying such heavy things," scolded Gwendolyn. She rose to take the tray from her, then regarded the food piled high upon it in astonishment. "Are there others coming to dine with me?"

Clarinda seated herself. "Only me. And Morag may also wish to have something."

"I'm afraid not," said Morag, reaching for her staff. "I'm busy working on a new cream to smooth out wrinkles, and it's time to add more fish oil. If it works, I will give you both some. It is never too soon to begin caring for your skin," she advised, disappearing out the door.

"There is enough food here to feed a small army!" Gwendolyn exclaimed.

"Or one extremely pregnant woman." Clarinda laughed, reaching for a fat, roasted chicken leg. "I don't know why, but I find myself absolutely ravenous these days. Cameron says if I continue to eat this much, there won't be any room left inside me for the bairn!"

"You're looking very well. Your time must be near."

Clarinda daintily licked her fingers. "I believe so. Which is why I'm so glad to see you're feeling better today. I was hoping you would help me when this bairn finally decides 'tis time to come out and see the world."

"I—I cannot, Clarinda," she stammered. Gwendolyn had no knowledge of how to birth a bairn and could not pretend that she did. Also, she had resolved to leave the MacDunns as quickly as possible—perhaps tomorrow. "Elspeth wouldn't permit me to attend. I'm sure she believes having a witch present at a birth will only bring evil."

"It doesn't matter what Elspeth believes. She won't be there."

"But Elspeth is the clan healer. She delivers almost all the MacDunn bairns, does she not?"

"She does. But not this one. You are going to do it."

Gwendolyn stared at her, speechless. The magnitude of what Clarinda wanted her to do was overwhelming. Caring for a dying child whom no one else had been able to help was one thing, but birthing a tiny babe was another matter entirely. She could not feign knowledge or experience in such a serious matter—not when Clarinda's very life, or her child's, might depend on it.

"I cannot do it, Clarinda," she said, her voice apologetic. "I have never birthed a bairn before."

"That's all right," said Clarinda, helping herself to an enormous chunk of bread. "I intend to do the actual birthing. I just need you to help me through it. Perhaps you can cast a spell to ease the pain, or make the birth go a little faster."

Gwendolyn shook her head. "There must be someone else within the clan who can help you."

"I don't want anyone else. I want you."

"But I can't—"

"I cannot do this alone, Gwendolyn. And no one else would dare accept, for fear of angering Elspeth, and then she might refuse to care for them or their families when they needed her. If I am left without someone to help me, Elspeth will step in when I am overwhelmed with pain and unable to send her away. Do you understand?" She laid her hands protectively over the enormous swell of her stomach. "I could not bear to have her near, telling me how God is punishing me for my sins by giving me pain. And if anything were to happen to the bairn and she wouldn't let me see it—" She broke off suddenly.

Gwendolyn lowered her gaze. She could not bear to see Clarinda upset.

"I'm asking you to help me, Gwendolyn," Clarinda said, brushing away the tears welling in her eyes. "I need you to be with me when I am powerless to help myself. If you are truly my friend, you cannot refuse me. I would not refuse you if you needed me."

If you are truly my friend.

The words seemed strange to Gwendolyn, for she had never had a friend. No one in her clan had ever been willing to associate with her. After all those years of rejection and isolation, she had accepted the fact that there would never be anyone in her life except her father who would care for her. Yet here was Clarinda, who had never shown her anything but kindness and concern, asking for her help. Warmth suddenly flooded through Gwendolyn, dispelling the chill that had seized her these past two days. Seeing that Clarinda had started to tremble, Gwendolyn silently rose from her chair and draped her shawl over her friend.

"We will bring this bairn into the world together, Clarinda," she told her, kneeling so she could wrap her arms around her. "I swear to you I will not leave your side."

Clarinda regarded her uncertainly. "You're sure?"

Gwendolyn pressed her cheek against the soft auburn fall

of Clarinda's hair, like a mother comforting a child. "I'm sure," she whispered softly.

"The storm has finally broken," Owen announced with relief. "The witch must be feeling better."

"A foul tempest, that was," said Lachlan, carefully measuring a draft of his latest potion into a cup. "By all the saints, she must have been furious." He cautiously sniffed his drink, then wrinkled his nose in disgust.

"I believe I would have been furious as well," said Marjorie, "had someone tried to burn me to death in my own chamber!"

"It was a black day for our clan," fretted Reginald, polishing his sword with an enormous rag. "Nothing honorable about sealing a woman in a burning room. A right nasty way to kill someone—even if she is a witch."

"And I suppose it would be more honorable to tie her to a stake and set her afire?" challenged Clarinda. "With everyone there to watch?"

"Dear me, no," Owen assured her, looking horrified. "Witch or not, I could never sanction anyone doing such a terrible thing."

"Nor could MacDunn," added Morag. "That is why he saved her from the MacSweens."

"The question is, who banged her on the head and set her chamber afire?" wondered Munro.

"Why don't you tell us, Munro?" Robena suggested, her voice sharp with accusation. "You've hated her from the day she dropped that pot on your head."

"I would never do such a thing!" Munro's eyes bulged out of his round face. "I have no reason to want her dead."

"You said she looks like an old toe to you," pointed out Lachlan. "Any man might tire of looking at something like that."

"She isn't nearly as hideous as I once thought," Munro quickly assured them. "Actually, there are moments when she is almost comely."

"I've thought that as well," agreed Owen brightly. "Of course, she's not nearly as comely as you are, Morag," he quickly amended. "No one is."

"Really, Owen," said Morag, flustered. "What a ridiculous thing to say."

"MacDunn was in a rage when it happened," said Farquhar. "He has vowed to find the culprit who did it." He took a deep swig of ale before finishing, "I'd not want to be anywhere near when he does."

"He has also said that we are all to keep a careful watch over her and ensure that no more accidents happen," added Ewan.

"What an excellent idea!" said Owen, rubbing his hands together. "I would be happy to look after the lass. I shall begin straightaway." He took a few steps, then stopped and turned. "Where, exactly, is she?"

"She has gone outside with David," said Lettie, adjusting her baby onto her shoulder.

"Outside?" said Owen. "Dear me. I don't believe I want to go outside. All that bright sunshine—"

"Outside?" thundered Reginald, sounding appalled. "By God, the MacSweens could come at any moment!" He threw down his rag and hurried toward the door, dragging his sword with him.

"Are you all right, David?"

"I'm fine, Gwendolyn," he assured her. "Please take me around once more."

His cheeks were rosy and his blue eyes clear as he leaned forward and patted the neck of his horse. At first Gwendolyn was worried that the exertion would prove too much for him, but the fresh air and excitement of sitting astride a horse for the first time had infused him with a boyish energy she had not seen in him before.

"Very well," she relented. "But this is the last time. After this we are going to sit on the grass with Ned and have our lunch." She began to slowly lead the small horse in a circle at the very back of the courtyard, out of sight from where MacDunn was training with the men. "I can scarcely believe you have never been on a horse before, David. You are a natural rider."

"Do you really think so?" His face was beaming with pride.

"Absolutely. Don't you agree, Ned?"

"He looks fine up there," replied Ned, whittling a long stick.

"We shall have to ask your father to give you riding lessons," said Gwendolyn. "Perhaps, if you are still feeling well enough, you could start tomorrow."

David's face fell. "My father won't allow it."

"Why not?"

"My father doesn't want me to ride."

"That is because you have been very ill. As long as you are feeling better, I'm certain he will be pleased to help you learn. Every father wants his children to learn to ride."

David shook his head. "My father has never allowed me to ride a horse, even before I got sick. He said I might fall and hurt myself."

"Well, of course you would fall. Falling is part of learning how to ride. You get all of your falling done in the beginning, when you are just learning, and then you don't fall anymore."

"But my father doesn't want me to fall. He says I have a weak constitution and I might break my brittle bones."

"I don't believe you have anything wrong with your bones," said Gwendolyn, slightly exasperated with MacDunn for leading the boy to think there was. "And as for your constitution—"

"Hold there, lass!" shouted Reginald, suddenly appearing around the side of the castle. "I'm coming!" He shielded his eyes with his arm and trekked purposefully toward her, followed by an agitated group of MacDunns.

"What is it, Reginald?" she asked tautly. "Is something wrong?"

"Aye, there's something wrong, all right," Reginald told her, his white-browed eyes puckered into slits. "That sun is so bright I can barely see you! How am I supposed to protect you with my eyes burning out of my head?"

"Now, lass, 'tis good to see that you are feeling better," added Owen, squinting at her through his steepled hands, "but could you not fade the light just a wee bit? It's harsh for an old man who doesn't go out much."

"I don't know what you're talking about," said Lachlan, joining them. "You never go outside at all." He suddenly noticed David and the horse. "Good Lord, get that lad off that colossal beast! He will fall and smash his brains in!"

"David is fine, Lachlan," Gwendolyn assured him. "He is not about to fall, and even if he did, this horse is so small, he would only bruise himself a little."

"Bruise himself a little?" sputtered Reginald, incredulous. "The lad is so weak, his neck will snap like a dry twig!"

"The very height of that creature is enough to make him faint!" added Owen.

"Actually, David feels quite well today," Gwendolyn informed them. "And he enjoys being on the horse—don't you, David?"

"Aye," said David, nodding. "I feel just fine." He smiled at the anxious group assembled before him. "Would you like to see me ride around the courtyard?"

"No!" everyone burst out.

David's smile instantly melted.

Gwendolyn sighed. "Very well, then." She moved to help David dismount.

"Of course we want to see you ride, David," said Clarinda suddenly. "Show us what you have learned today."

David regarded Gwendolyn uncertainly. She nodded.

Turning his attention back to the group, David straightened his back. "You must sit tall when you are on a horse," he informed them, his blue gaze serious. "And you must hold on with your legs and pay attention to the rhythm of the horse, so that you learn to move with her. And you must pat her and praise her often, so that she knows you are her friend. You are not forcing her to go where you want," he told them earnestly, "you are both riding there *together*."

The cluster of MacDunns stared at him, speechless.

"Very good, David," praised Gwendolyn. "Now let's show them how well you ride." She began to lead his horse across the grass.

"Good Lord, have you ever heard the lad say so much?" asked Owen, astonished.

"Never," remarked Lachlan, equally bemused. "I always thought he was too timid to utter more than a word or two."

"So how is it that he is suddenly chattering away like an old woman?" said Reginald, leaning on his sword.

"And why is he out here riding, when just a few days ago he was nearly dead?" wondered Ewan.

"I thought he was supposed to be starving to death," added Munro, scratching his head. "He doesn't look starved to me."

"It is witchcraft," said Robena angrily. "She has cast a spell on him to make him seem well, when in fact he is dying."

"I don't believe that, Robena," interjected Marjorie. "If Gwendolyn could make him appear well through witchcraft, then why didn't she do so the day she arrived and be done with it?"

"Marjorie has a point," Reginald allowed.

"Then how do you explain the fact that she has been starving David for days, yet he has the strength to go riding?" Robena challenged.

"She hasn't starved him," Marjorie countered. "She has limited what he can eat."

"And she has spent many long hours talking with him and telling him marvelous stories," added Clarinda, watching as Gwendolyn and David made a slow, steady circle on the grass. "That's why David has become better at expressing himself."

The little group watched in silence as David happily followed Gwendolyn on his horse.

"Well, I call that splendid!" declared Owen suddenly. "Absolutely splendid! Lass!" he shouted, shuffling toward her. "Do you think you could cure my hands?"

Gwendolyn stopped and regarded the elder in confusion. "Pardon?"

"My hands," Owen repeated loudly, holding the gnarled appendages up to her. "They ache something fierce these days—particularly when the weather is foul. Not that I blame you for that," he quickly assured her. "You had every right to be upset. Horrid thing, to be nearly burned. Simply ghastly. Glad to see you're feeling better, even if this sun is blinding. Can you cure them?" He turned his hands over to display his pasty, wrinkled palms.

"I—I don't know." Was Owen actually asking her for help?

"It's just that you've done such a grand job with the lad, I thought a pair of old hands might be easy to fix." He stared at them a moment, then sighed. "No matter, my dear. I've almost grown accustomed to the pain. Just a part of being old and useless, I suppose. Do forgive." He began to turn away.

"Owen."

He turned and regarded her hopefully.

"I will make a warm liniment for them," she offered. "It must be massaged into the joints three times a day." She glanced at his stiff, blue-veined fingers. "If you like," she added hesitantly, "I can rub it in for you, so you don't make them ache even more from the effort."

"A liniment, you say?" He sounded disappointed. "Don't you want to purge my bowels? Or cast a spell?"

"I will cast a spell, if you like," Gwendolyn said, sensing that he wanted something more dramatic than a simple liniment. "But you must use the liniment as well or the spell won't work."

"What about my bowels?"

"Let's wait and see how we do with the liniment," Gwendolyn suggested.

"And the spell," Owen reminded her.

"And the spell."

"Excellent!" He turned to the others and shouted excitedly, "The witch is going to cast a spell on me to cure my hands!"

The group gasped with awe.

And then they hustled forward, surrounding her.

"My belly twists into a bluster after I eat," Reginald complained. "Can you make a spell that will cure that?"

Gwendolyn regarded him blankly. The MacDunns had never concealed the fact that they feared her and wanted to be rid of her. Why were these council members suddenly trusting her to cast spells on them?

"If you can cast a spell on Owen, I don't see why you can't cast one on me," added Reginald, feeling slightly injured by her hesitation.

"I can try," said Gwendolyn. She suddenly recalled a special drink her mother's notes had recommended for simple stomach distress. "But there is a potion I will make that you must drink with it."

"As long as it isn't like the foul concoctions Lachlan makes," Reginald replied. "I'd hate to burn a hole in my gut."

"There's nothing wrong with my potions," barked Lachlan, offended.

"Nothing wrong with them if you're already dead," muttered Reginald.

A terrible coughing cut short their banter. "This bloody cough has been plaguing me for weeks," Ewan reported, thumping himself on the chest. "Do you have a spell for that?"

"I may," allowed Gwendolyn, thinking of her mother's honey drink for coughs. "And there is a hot brew that works with it."

"By the end of the day I'm so groggy, I barely make it to my cottage," complained Farquhar. He paused to take a hefty draft of ale, then wiped his mouth on his sleeve. "Can you cast a spell for that?"

"Now, let's not keep the lass standing here holding this horse," said Owen. "Why don't we sit down over there on the grass?"

"What's in the basket?" asked Munro. "I'm hungry."

"I'm afraid it's nothing much," Gwendolyn replied. "David is eating only the simplest of foods. Today we are having bread with honey and apples."

"That sounds wonderful!" said Clarinda. "I'm starving." She began to waddle toward the basket, with the rest of the group following.

"Aim higher!" shouted Alex. "Release together—now!"

A flurry of padded arrows sailed high into the air, making a slow, graceful arc before pummeling the warriors below.

"Bloody hell!" said Cameron, lowering his sword to rub his head. "Those things smart!"

"That is one of the hazards of having a big head, my friend," teased Brodick. "Perhaps we should find a bucket for you to wear."

"You'll be needing a helmet more than me," scoffed Cameron. "I'd hate to see that pretty face of yours marred."

"I think Brodick might welcome a scratch or two on his cheek," joked Garrick. "Maybe if he weren't so comely, Isabella might leave him alone for more than a minute."

"More like she would be weeping all over him," snorted Quentin. "The lass does enjoy a good cry."

"I say she'd fly into one of her rages and swear to disembowel the poor chap who dared touch Brodick," predicted Cameron. "She has a colorful way with words, that one does."

"Really?" said Brodick, his brows raised in surprise. "I hadn't noticed."

The warriors laughed.

"I'm delighted you find preparing for battle so amusing," snapped Alex. "Do you think you could spare me your attention a little longer, or shall we just sit and entertain each other while the MacSweens attack?"

His men regarded him in astonishment.

"Your pardon, MacDunn," said Brodick stiffly. "We will not speak again."

His friend's uncharacteristic formality told Alex that his attitude was unreasonable. He instantly regretted his mocking words, but could not possibly take them back. To do so would suggest weakness, and he could not afford to be weak. An army of MacSweens was about to attack, to try to take

Gwendolyn and Isabella away. Despite his clan's loyalty to their laird, he had no idea how hard they would fight to protect these two unwelcome guests. Given how they longed to be rid of Gwendolyn, he could not believe they would put up much resistance. He had vowed to keep her safe, but Alex could not defend her against an entire army by himself.

The thought unnerved him.

Pushing the thought aside, he ordered, "We will resume the attack on the south wall. Assuming Robert comes with a minimum of two hundred men, we will need archers stationed on the battlements at approximately every eight feet. They will be able to hold off the MacSweens for a few minutes, but once the attackers have positioned their ladders—"

A shout of laughter exploded into the air.

"I require your complete attention!" he snapped.

"It isn't the men," Cameron said. "The laughter is coming from the bailey."

Alex listened. The laughter had now become animated shouting. How the hell was he supposed to train with all this noise?

"Practice your swordplay," he ordered, striding angrily toward the gate.

He entered the courtyard and was surprised to find it completely empty. Following the noise around to the side of the castle, he discovered an enormous crowd of MacDunns sitting on the grass at the back corner of the courtyard, eagerly listening to Gwendolyn tell them a story.

"'Surrender your weapon,' commanded the mighty Torvald, his own sword flashing like a streak of silver before him, 'or you will die.' 'I will never surrender to you,' hissed the terrible MacRory, 'for it is you who is about to die. Even now, you can barely stand for all the blood that flows from you.' 'I may die,' Torvald agreed, 'but you will die first.' And the terrible MacRory lowered his sword and laughed. 'Ha! I shall slice you into pieces and feed you to the wolves,' he promised, 'and then I will brutally murder your wife and children.' 'Never!' roared Torvald. And with that he rushed toward MacRory, blood gushing like a river from his neck, his left arm severed but for the slenderest thread of flesh. 'Die, foul knave!' he cried. Summoning the last of his strength, the mighty Torvald drove his sword deep into MacRory's stomach, skewering him like a rabbit for the spit of a fire."

The MacDunns stared at her, spellbound.

"What happened then?" asked Lachlan, breaking the silence. "Did the mighty Torvald live?"

"Of course he lived," interjected Reginald. "What kind of a bloody story would it be if he died?"

"I can't see how he would survive all those terrible wounds," mused Owen. "Surely he must have bled to death."

"He didn't bleed to death," Marjorie countered. "After that he probably crawled down the mountain and came to an old woman's cottage, and she took him in and healed him."

"How could he crawl with his throat slit and one arm about to fall off?" demanded Ewan.

"Maybe the old woman was out walking on the mountain and she found him and took him to her cottage," suggested Lettie.

"He would have been dead long before he could get there," scoffed Lachlan.

"No, he wouldn't," argued Munro. "After all, he is the mighty Torvald. He is strong enough to endure anything."

"He can't survive having his neck slashed and his arm sliced off," objected Farquhar.

"He could if he got help quickly," countered Clarinda.

"No old woman in a cottage could save a man with those kinds of injuries!" said Lachlan, almost shouting now.

"She could if she were a witch," Ned suggested quietly.

The group instantly fell silent, considering this.

"Aye," said Owen finally, pleased that Ned had solved the problem. "She could if she were a witch."

Alex stared at his clan incredulously. But for a few, his people openly despised Gwendolyn. The incident on the stairs and in the tower made it eminently clear that they wanted nothing more than to be rid of her. So why the hell were they clustered around her like enraptured children, listening to her tell these ridiculous tales?

"Father!" David called, suddenly noticing him, "Gwendolyn let me ride a horse!"

Alex blinked. "She what?"

"I rode a horse," David repeated, his little voice bright with pride. "All by myself."

"And a fine job he did of it, too," Owen said. "Reminded me of you as a lad, Alex." He frowned. "At least I think it was you."

"The lad looked right splendid up there, MacDunn," added Reginald. "Straight as an arrow."

"You put him on a horse?" Alex demanded. The look he gave Gwendolyn could have frozen fire.

"David was feeling quite well," she said, "so I thought it would be good for him to—"

"To what?" interrupted Alex, his voice harsh. "Fall and break his neck?"

"He wasn't going to fall, MacDunn." Gwendolyn rose to face him. "I had the horse on a lead, and David was only—"

"He is too weak to be on a horse!" Alex thundered furiously. "He could have collapsed suddenly and broken his skull, or been trampled beneath the animal's hooves! Or the exertion could have reduced him to another hideous bout of sickness, as it did the day you so carelessly took him beyond the walls! For God's sake, *are you trying to kill my son?*"

Gwendolyn regarded him woodenly, determined not to let him see how his condemnation of her in front of the clan wounded her. For a brief, impossible moment, as the MacDunns sat crowded around her on the sun-warmed grass listening to her tales, it had almost seemed as if they were coming to accept her. It had been strange to have so many people eager to share her company—strange and new and utterly wonderful. And in less than an instant MacDunn had shattered all that. The MacDunns would never accept her now, she realized dully. Their laird had just made it painfully clear that he did not really trust her himself.

"Come, David," she said quietly, extending her hand to him. "Your father would prefer that you rest now."

David slipped his hand into hers and squeezed it hard. It

was a small, silent gesture, but Gwendolyn took some comfort from it. Avoiding the gazes of the MacDunns, she turned and quickly led David back to the castle.

The great hall was unusually quiet that evening.

Alex focused his gaze on the battle plans laid before him, trying to ignore the silent, furtive glances his clan kept shooting his way. He knew they were thinking he had acted unreasonably this afternoon. He also knew they feared this meant his madness was raising its talons once more. No doubt they were wondering how deeply the monster would take him this time, and for how long.

He wished to God he knew himself.

He had felt it clawing at him from the moment he pulled Gwendolyn from the fire. Not that his madness had ever really left him—he was honest enough with himself to admit that. But for some time now he had been able to keep it more or less at bay, like a snarling wolf that has been forced into a corner. Since the fire he had felt that wolf inching forward. The pain in his head had become more and more frequent, his fleeting bouts of sleep more shallow and disturbed.

Worst of all, he could no longer speak to Flora.

His conversations with his wife had grown increasingly intermittent since he had brought Gwendolyn here. He had assured himself that was because he was so weary at night, but it was a lie, for sleep was elusive. And after he had forced himself upon Gwendolyn, savagely taking her in the same bed where he had spent so many tender nights with his beloved wife, he had been filled with a shame so overwhelming he could no longer bring himself to speak with Flora at all. What could he say to her? he wondered bitterly. What feeble apology could he possibly offer? He had betrayed his wife, whom he had sworn to honor forever.

"I hear David was up on a horse today," Morag remarked, breaking the heavy silence that entombed the room. "How did he fare?"

No one answered.

"He fared extremely well," Owen said after a moment. "Sat up there like a brave young warrior."

Morag smiled. "Evidently he takes after his father. Did he fall?"

"The horse wasn't moving fast enough for him to fall," snorted Reginald, glancing pointedly at Alex. "Gwendolyn had wisely put him on old Duff. That beast hasn't trotted since before David was born. But just to be safe, Gwendolyn led the horse by a rope."

"He still could have fallen off," objected Robena. "He might have been killed."

"Even if he had fallen, he wouldn't have hurt himself," scoffed Lachlan. "He would have just been a little bruised."

"Falling is part of learning to ride," added Ned, repeating Gwendolyn's words. "Everyone knows that."

"It was a dangerous thing to do," said Robena. "The witch has no right to take such risks with David."

"She is trying to kill him," added Elspeth. "I've told you that."

"Putting a lad on a horse seems a strange way to try to kill him," observed Owen.

"That means every one of us here was nearly murdered by our parents," joked Cameron.

Alex kept his gaze lowered to his papers and said nothing. What the hell was the matter with his clan tonight? he wondered. His son was too weak to ride, and that was the end of it. He refused to be part of this discussion.

The hall fell silent once again.

"It's awfully quiet in here," chirped Isabella, apparently oblivious to the tension stifling the vast room. She turned to Brodick, who was seated next to her. "Why doesn't your clan have musicians play during dinner?"

"MacDunn doesn't like it," he replied shortly.

"We used to have music," reflected Owen. "A few years ago, there was music and dancing almost every night in this very hall." He smiled, remembering. "In those days, I was something of a dancer."

"You were dreadful," interjected Lachlan. "You looked like a badger hopping on hot coals."

"That was the dance," replied Owen, insulted. "It required one to move one's feet up and down rather quickly. Of course, not being a dancer yourself, Lachlan, you wouldn't know that."

"I'd love to see it," said Isabella.

"No, you wouldn't," Lachlan assured her.

"If there were music, I'd be happy to show you, lass," said Owen, ignoring him.

"Thank God there isn't any," muttered Lachlan.

"In my clan, we always had musicians playing when we dined," Isabella reflected. "It made the evening more pleasant. Don't you think some music might make this evening more pleasant, Brodick?"

"It couldn't make it worse," he grumbled.

"Exactly," agreed Isabella, failing to recognize his sarcasm. She stood and tapped her goblet to gain the clan's attention. "Does anyone here have an instrument they could play?"

"Alas, my pipes have been stowed away for over nine years." Ewan sighed. "I doubt I could get anything but screeching from them now."

"And how would that be different from what you used to play on them?" teased Lettie.

"Anyone else?" Isabella asked.

No one answered.

"Well, then, I guess I shall have to sing," she decided. "It won't be quite the same without accompaniment, but I shall do my best." She thought for a moment. "This song is about a warrior who is tormented by the loss of his one great love—"

"That sounds a wee bit grim," interrupted Reginald. "Do you know anything livelier?"

"Do forgive, lass, but I can't dance to a song about some forlorn warrior," Owen said. "I need something I can stomp my feet to."

"Very well," said Isabella, trying to think. "I have it!" she declared suddenly. "This one is about a maiden who kills herself when she learns her lover has betrayed her."

"Are you sure it's lively?" asked Owen, looking doubtful.

"It's slow at the beginning," Isabella admitted, "but it picks up a fair bit toward the end when they're burying her."

"All right, then, lass," said Reginald. "Sing away."

Isabella inhaled deeply, then proceeded to fill the hall with her dreadful voice. Alex winced, clenched his jaw, and finally gathered his plans and rose from his chair, unable to endure the dreadful shrieking any longer.

At that moment Gwendolyn appeared at the base of the stairs, her head held high as she studied the room, his son standing nervously beside her.

She was draped in a gown of deepest black, which was intricately embroidered with luminous silver thread. The dark fabric scooped low over the creamy swell of her breasts, making her skin appear even paler than usual, and the long sleeves clung tightly to her slender arms, emphasizing her fine structure. The ebony fall of her hair poured across the white satin of her shoulders like a silken cape, shimmering in the torchlight. She seemed almost ethereal as she stood there, a mysterious, fragile specter from another world, and as Alex drank in her beauty he was almost afraid she might suddenly vanish. He watched as Gwendolyn gave David a reassuring smile and took his hand, offering his son strength and comfort as they faced the enormous gathering.

It was a small, silent gesture, almost unnoticeable were Alex not watching them so carefully, and yet he found himself profoundly moved by it. Flora had loved to hold David's hands when he was a babe, marveling at each little finger with its wee, wrinkled knuckles, laughing over the impossibly tiny pink shells of her nails. And then she would ask Alex to hold out his hand, and she would press his son's diminutive palm against his enormous one. It had felt like a velvety soft blossom floating upon his callused palm, and Alex would stare at it in fascination, wondering how anything so tiny and fine and perfect could possibly grow to resemble the hard, rough-skinned hand that held it.

He had not held his son's hand for years.

Isabella's wailing finally ended as Gwendolyn and David

approached the laird's table. Gwendolyn was aware that every clan member was staring at her, wondering how she dared show her face after MacDunn's enraged outburst in the courtyard. She endured their scrutiny with practiced indifference. Not one of them had risen to her defense when MacDunn had raged at her earlier that day. The MacDunns had pretended to trust her by asking her for help, but when their laird unjustly accused her, they had remained silent. She should have expected nothing less, she realized bitterly. To them she was a witch, and a witch was not worthy of defense. She had learned that lesson well when her own clan had sentenced her to burn for murdering her own father.

If not for David, she would leave this place tonight.

The lad had not wanted to dine with his father in the great hall, for MacDunn had intimidated his son sufficiently this afternoon to make him tremble at the mere suggestion of it. But Gwendolyn had been gently persistent, and David finally relented. It was time MacDunn realized that the boy he had sired was not made of glass.

Or stone.

MacDunn's expression was hard as they approached, and for a moment Gwendolyn feared he might order them from the hall forthwith. She laid her hands upon David's small shoulders, holding him steady as they faced his father.

"Good evening, MacDunn," she said, her voice cool. "David is feeling well tonight, and I thought you might enjoy the pleasure of his company. With your permission, I have told him he may stay as long as he doesn't tire himself and he limits his supper to what I have told him he may eat."

Alex stared in amazement at his son. The lad was freshly bathed, and his flame-colored hair was still damp and curling about his neck and forehead, as Flora's hair once had. David's cheeks and nose were kissed by sunlight, and a handful of freckles that Alex had never seen before were scattered across his customarily chalky skin. Gwendolyn had dressed the lad in a handsome saffron shirt and a green and yellow plaid that was a miniature version of his own, and had even supplied him with a little dirk to strap to his waist. His son bore little resemblance to the sickly child he had watched deteriorate these past few months.

A fragile spark of joy ignited within him.

"Join me," Alex commanded gruffly. When he saw David hesitate, he realized his error. He drew out the empty chair beside him and patted it. "Here."

David looked inquiringly up at Gwendolyn. She nodded. Releasing her hands from his shoulders, she watched as the boy hesitantly mounted the scarlet-draped dais and seated himself beside his father.

"Well, that's what I call splendid!" Owen burst out. "So nice to see the lad seated beside his father—don't you agree, Lachlan?"

"Aye," said Lachlan with uncharacteristic agreement. "Very nice."

"The lad looks to be half starved," remarked Reginald. "Your pardon, Gwendolyn," he quickly added. "Didn't mean to suggest you've been starving the lad. No, indeed. 'Tis clear to everyone in this hall that you've done wonders for the boy. Simply wonders. A bit more meat on his bones, and he'll be ready to train with the warriors. You'd like that, laddie, wouldn't you?"

"Yes, sir," said David, his blue eyes flickering with pleasure.

"Well, then, eat." Reginald shoved a platter of greasy roasted meat toward him.

"No, David," said Gwendolyn. "You don't want to be sick tonight, do you?"

David shook his head.

"Then we will stay with our meal of apples, bread, and a little broth. Tomorrow we will try something new."

Alex waited for his son to protest.

Instead the lad obediently reached for a chunk of bread.

Gwendolyn nearly smiled. Although she had known the sight and aroma of so many different platters of food would be tempting, David was far more excited by the fact that he was dining in the great hall with his father.

"I shall leave you, then, David," Gwendolyn said. "I will return later to fetch you for bed."

"Where are you going?" demanded Alex.

"To my chamber."

"Have you dined this evening?"

"I am not hungry."

"You will eat something," he ordered, disliking the fact that she was leaving. "You will become ill if you do not."

"I am not hungry, MacDunn," she repeated firmly.

"Nevertheless, you will eat."

"No, MacDunn," she returned, her voice taut. "I am not your prisoner, nor am I one of your clan. You cannot order me to eat, nor can you order me to stay in this hall against my wishes. Do you understand? You may direct me when it comes to the care of your son, but only I decide how I care for myself. And if I become ill, that is entirely my affair, not yours." She turned and began to walk away.

"Gwendolyn."

There was a faint pleading in his tone that made her pause. She turned and regarded him questioningly. "Yes, MacDunn?"

Alex hesitated. He knew she was angry with him. Until this afternoon, he had always defended her, at least in front of his people. But today he had forsaken her. He had accused her of being reckless with his son, when all she had ever tried to do was help the lad. He wanted to apologize, but he couldn't possibly do it in front of his entire clan. That would only reinforce their belief that his outburst had been unwarranted and that he was not in control of his emotions.

Which he wasn't.

"Do stay, lass, and at least have a cup of wine," Owen suggested. "I was just about to do a wee bit of dancing."

"Yes, stay, Gwendolyn," said Isabella. "You can sing with me."

"I don't sing," murmured Gwendolyn, her eyes never leaving Alex's.

Alex regarded her intently. *Forgive me.*

She stood there a moment, her gaze locked with his, oblivious to the others in the hall.

And then she climbed the dais and seated herself in the chair he offered.

🔺 Alex stood in the shadows, listening.

A strange emptiness had overwhelmed him as he watched Gwendolyn and David leave the great hall, their hands clasped tightly together. Duty demanded that he remain and discuss the pending MacSween attack with his clan, and he had felt oddly resentful that he could not follow them. The moment it was possible for him to leave, he had made his way to the corridor outside David's chamber. There he had found Ned standing by the doorway, sharpening a stick as he listened through the heavy wood to Gwendolyn spinning yet another gruesome tale for David. Alex had offered to relieve Ned and watch over Gwendolyn himself for a while. Ned assured him it wasn't necessary. Alex had to practically order his warrior to leave.

Finally Ned had relented, but only after making Alex promise to listen well so he could tell him how the story ended.

". . . and then the mighty Torvald raised his sword into the glare of the sun, cleverly blinding the giant snake as he hurled his dirk at him with his other hand. The dirk flew deep into the monster's hideous yellow eye, and the creature screeched in agony as boiling hot blood gushed from the wound, scorching the very grass upon which he writhed. . . ."

Gwendolyn certainly had a remarkable ability to tell stories, Alex reflected. He wondered what kind of tales Flora had told the lad before she became ill. Somehow he couldn't imagine his gentle wife spinning the ghastly narratives Gwendolyn fabricated. Of course David had been much younger then and would probably not have enjoyed such chilling tales. When had he developed this fascination with blood and gore? he wondered. After Flora's death and his own descent into madness, Alex had not had time to pay attention to the lad's changing fancies.

". . . and with those words the mighty Torvald cast the beast's dark, shriveled heart into the sea, where it fell to the bottom like a stone and lay forever in the slimiest of muck, too hard and bitter for even the hungriest of fish to nibble upon."

There were a few hushed words that Alex couldn't make out, and then a small giggle. He pressed his ear against the door, straining to hear. He wanted to go inside, but he could not bring himself to do so, knowing that whatever warm moment the two were sharing would be shattered the instant he appeared. An easy familiarity reigned between Gwendolyn and his son, which was something Alex had never enjoyed with the lad.

The memory of David's tiny palm pressed against his returned, achingly sweet and sad. How had that helpless bairn suddenly become the handsome, confident lad who sat so proudly beside him tonight in the hall?

The door opened and Gwendolyn appeared, carrying a candle.

"Oh," she said, looking startled, "did you come to say good night to David?"

Her pale skin was warmed by the glow of the flame she carried, making her look unusually radiant.

"Is my son asleep?" Alex managed to ask.

"Almost." She opened the door a little wider so he could see.

A trio of candles was flickering beside the bed, veiling the chamber in hazy gold. No hint of sickness fouled the air, but instead the fragrance of heather and pine was drifting through the windows and mingling with the faint tangy scent of soap. David lay curled upon the bed, breathing deeply, his red hair flickering against the white of his pillow. Alex took a tentative step closer, not wanting to waken the lad. The boy sleepily rubbed his eye, then left his hand loosely fisted beside his face. It bore scant resemblance to the tiny palm Flora had once pressed into his, but it remained the diminutive, soft hand of a child. If Alex reached out and held it, he would still wonder how it could ever grow to be as large and rough as his own.

Somehow he found comfort in that.

He turned and indicated to Gwendolyn that he was ready to leave.

"Where is Ned?" she asked, searching for him in the corridor.

"I dismissed him for the evening."

She looked at him curiously.

"He was tired."

She made no comment. Together they proceeded in silence down the hallway.

When he stood before the corridor to her chamber, Alex hesitated. He had not entered this room since the night Flora died. Behind this door were a thousand agonizing memories from which he longed to escape. His heart began to pound and tighten in his chest, making it difficult to breathe. *Open it,* he commanded silently. *Now.*

His arms stayed leaden at his sides.

He was a coward, he realized bleakly. Only a coward could be so terrified of an empty chamber. Scores of other men had lost their wives, or even several wives, and they didn't end up babbling endlessly to themselves or becoming afraid to enter a chamber in their own bloody castle. He wanted to leave, to retreat to a dark corner and drown himself in drink until his mind was cloudy and his fear trifling. Then, perhaps, he might try to breech this portal again. But he could not permit Gwendolyn to enter the room alone, lest some menace awaited her inside.

He contemplated telling her to wait while he fetched someone else to escort her across the threshold.

Open it, goddammit. It is just a chamber.

Summoning his nerve, he roughly jerked up the latch and entered the oppressive blackness. He inhaled a cautious breath, searching the air for some trace of the misery he knew lingered here. The sun-washed scent of heather and grass filled his nostrils, the same as they had in David's chamber. But he was not fooled by the superficial fragrance. Flora's misery had seeped into these walls, and the chamber would reek of suffering and death until the very stones of the castle disintegrated.

He would be dead long before that hour came.

Gwendolyn entered and began to light the candles in the chamber. Little by little the darkness faded, until finally the chamber was suffused with honeyed light. The furniture was different, Alex realized numbly. Of course it would be. He had ordered everything removed after Flora's death, and stored deep within the bowels of the castle. Except for her bed. That cursed prison he had ordered burned, in a feeble attempt to exorcise the memory of her lying trapped within it.

Unfortunately, the memory remained.

He turned his gaze to the simple construction of polished oak that now graced the center of the room. A neatly arranged plaid of red and blue was spread over it, and something pale lay upon the pillow. Curious, he moved closer. A heavy, smooth bone, more than two hand spans in length, lay nestled upon the soft wool.

"What is this?" he asked, picking it up. "A charm for one of your spells?"

Gwendolyn approached him slowly, staring at the bone. She reached out and took it from him, then ran her fingers lightly over the dry surface. "It is a bone from the leg of a horse," she said quietly. "It is used as a talisman against evil."

Alex frowned. "Are you using this to cure my son?"

She shook her head. "Someone has left it here hoping it will drive me away." She turned the bone over, studying it. "It is said that horses are related to the Celtic goddess Epona, and therefore have special powers—"

"How can you be so placid about this?" he demanded, his voice rigid with fury. "Someone came into your chamber and left this here to frighten you!"

"What would you have me do, MacDunn?" Gwendolyn challenged, her feigned composure cracking. "All my life people have been leaving objects like this for me. From the time I was a little girl, my own clan would place them on the doorstep of my father's cottage, or toss them through a window, or tie them to a stick and hurl them at me as I walked. Once when I was eleven a boy threw a rough piece of iron at me, which struck me in the head." She lifted back the thick curtain of her hair, showing him the jagged white scar that marred the edge of her hairline.

"I ran home screaming to my father," Gwendolyn continued, "with blood pouring down my face and into my gown. I told him I hated everyone in the world except for him, and wished they all would die. And do you know what he did?"

Alex shook his head. He sure as hell knew what he would have done. He would have found the little bastard who struck her and thrashed him until he couldn't sit for a month.

"My father bathed and bandaged my wound, and then he sat and put his arms around me. And as I wept and raged, he told me it was far better to love my enemies than to hate them, and that eventually they would grow ashamed of their cruelties and stop."

"But they never did," Alex surmised quietly.

A bitter laugh escaped her throat. "One might think eventually they would at least realize their talismans had no power over me, because I never left. But that didn't stop them from constantly trying to expel me, with their holy relics and their pious prayers and their bags of stinking herbs, rowan branches, bones, scraps of iron, and red wool." She turned abruptly and hurled the bone with all her might into the hearth. It clattered loudly against the grate before sinking into the cold ashes. Fighting the tears welling in her eyes, Gwendolyn laid her hands against the cool stone of the mantel and bit down hard against her trembling lip.

"I hate this, MacDunn," she confessed brokenly. "I hate all of it, and I hate being alone to face it. But I have grown so accustomed to the fear and ostracism of others, I don't know what it is to be without it." Her voice disintegrated into a ragged whisper as she finished, "I never will."

Her despondency surged over him. Overwhelmed by a need to comfort her, he laid his hands on her small shoulders and turned her around to face him. She did not push him away, but instead stared up at him with wide, pain-filled eyes, like a wounded deer who cannot understand why it has been made to suffer. He wanted to ease her torment, to banish all trace of the loneliness and cruelties she had been forced to endure, and make her see that there was at least one person on this earth who neither feared nor despised her. She was a witch, yes, but he had only seen her use her magic to try to help his son. How could that make her evil? The MacSweens had convicted her of murdering her father, but Alex had long ago known that was a lie. Gwendolyn had loved her father, and his death had left her completely abandoned in a world that was determined to destroy her. If Alex hadn't stolen her for the sake of his dying son, the MacSweens would have succeeded.

And David would be dead tonight instead of sleeping peacefully with his little hand curled beside his freckled cheek.

"Gwendolyn," he whispered, raising his hand to trace the contour of her jaw, "you are not alone."

She shook her head. "I am, MacDunn. I always will be."

"No," he murmured, lowering his lips until they hovered barely a breath from hers. "Not as long as I live."

With that solemn pledge he crushed his lips to hers, wrapping his arms around her and hauling her hard against him. He kissed her deeply, ravenously, wanting to lose himself to the pleasure of holding her and kissing her and touching her. Gwendolyn's mouth was soft and dark and wine-sweet, like ripe, sun-warmed fruit, and she smelled of summer meadows and sunlight, a scent that had driven him mad since that first time he had held her. She did not fight him as she had before, not even a little, but instead she whimpered and wrapped her arms around him, seeking the comfort of his hard body against hers. Alex complied by pressing himself against her, feeling her soft form set fire to every inch of his flesh, until his loins were throbbing and his knees were weak. He took her hand and guided it beneath his plaid, then pressed it firmly against the hardness of his thigh. She froze for a moment, her soft palm fixed against him, uncertain. And then she tentatively began to explore him, her fingers drifting up and down, flitting with agonizing curiosity across his burning skin. Up, then down, then up a little more, until finally he thought he would go mad from the need to have her take hold of him. He plunged his tongue deep into her mouth and sank his hand into the depths of her black gown, capturing the forbidden lushness of her breast. Releasing his mouth from hers, he pulled down the silver-embroidered fabric covering her shoulder with his teeth, causing her bodice to crumple to her waist. Then he lowered his head and closed his lips around the sweet peak of her breast, suckling the dark berry of her nipple until it was taut against his teasing tongue.

Gwendolyn moaned with pleasure and threw her head back, offering more of herself to Alex as she explored the smooth curve of his buttocks, the chiseled form of his thighs, the iron ridges of muscle layered across his stomach. He felt as if he had been sculpted from granite, except that he was warm and powerful as he groaned and flexed beneath the gentleness of her touch. His hand was swiftly trailing up her gown, but she was scarcely aware of it until his finger slipped inside her hot wetness just as he suckled hard upon her breast. Hot pleasure tore through her, causing her to cry out. Abandoning her shyness, she closed her hand firmly around the velvety hard length of his manhood. Alex groaned and buried his face into the soft hollow between her breasts, pulsing against her caress as he stroked her with his finger. She opened her thighs wider, offering more of herself to him, and he eagerly complied, pressing his fingers deeper into her with each languid thrust against her hand.

Alex's fingers were bathed in Gwendolyn's sweet wetness and the intricate petals of her flesh were slick and swollen, telling him how much she longed for release. Unable to bear her stroking a moment longer, he sank to his knees and lifted her gown, then pressed his face between the creamy silk of her thighs and began to lap at the rosy hot folds of her. She cried out and gripped his shoulders, struggling to remain upright, and then she sighed and opened herself even further, inviting him to seek out the hottest, deepest recesses of her body. He held her gown to her waist with one hand and cupped her buttocks with the other, pulling her closer to him as he licked and probed every delectable inch of her, inhaling the womanly fragrance of her as he took her closer to the crest of ecstasy.

Gwendolyn stood frozen, clinging helplessly to Alex's massive shoulders as his tongue flitted in and out of her. Her breath was coming in tiny gasps as her heart pounded hard against her chest, until she could almost feel the surge of her blood as it raced through her straining flesh. And still she opened herself wider, pressing herself shamelessly against Alex's mouth as he worshiped her with his tongue, wanting him to taste her faster, deeper, more, wanting it never to end, and yet knowing she could not possibly bear it another moment. She laid her hands against the roughness of his jaw and threaded her fingers into the golden thickness of his hair, holding him to her, experiencing a dark, forbidden thrill at the sight of him passionately lapping at her most intimate place. And then her pleasure began to soar. She gasped and held him even tighter. Alex responded by thrusting his finger deep inside her, filling the hollow ache that had bloomed within. In and out with his finger, up and down with his tongue, stroking and thrusting and kissing until she could no longer breathe, could no longer think, could no longer do anything except stand there clinging to him mindlessly. And still the sensations within her continued to surge and swell, higher, more, and Alex tasted her harder and faster, until suddenly sweet, pure ecstasy exploded through her, and she cried out, her entire being flushed with hot joy as she crumpled limply against him.

Alex held Gwendolyn tightly, stroking her silky hair as her breath feathered through the wrinkled fabric of his shirt and warmed his chest. His own body was hard and aching for release, but the feel of Gwendolyn resting sated in his arms was far too glorious and fragile a moment to relinquish. And so he remained as he was, kneeling upon the cool stone floor with his arms wrapped around her, resting his chin on the top of her head as he listened to her breathing gradually steady. What spell had this tiny witch cast over him, he wondered, that made him so ravenous for her? How was it that she could arouse such staggering passion in him, when no woman had been able to ignite even the flimsiest spark of desire after Flora had died? He wanted her with an intensity that was awesome, and it scarcely seemed to matter when or where. The fact that he had taken her here, in this room where Flora had suffered so hideously for so long, was ample testament to the depravity of his longing.

He closed his eyes, fighting the surge of guilt threatening to engulf him.

A sudden pounding jerked him from his thoughts.

"Alex!" called Brodick. "For God's sake, open the door! We're under attack!"

Alex released his hold on Gwendolyn and sprang to his feet. "Cover yourself," he said harshly, barely giving her time to adjust her fallen bodice as he flung open the door.

"What's happening?" he demanded.

Brodick and Cameron stared at him in confusion, their fists still pounding against his own chamber door a few feet down the corridor. Their eyes quickly took in his rumpled hair and disheveled attire.

"It's the MacSweens," explained Cameron, regaining his composure first. "Robert has arrived with an army. They are surrounding the castle wall."

"How many?" Alex hastily adjusted his plaid.

"It looks like about two hundred," Brodick replied, "but there could be more waiting in the woods."

"Anyone left in the cottages?"

"No," Cameron assured him. "Garrick was out looking for his dog and spotted some of Robert's men as they assembled on the east hill. He alerted everyone as he ran up to the castle, and they quietly made their way through the gate."

"Cameron, tell Robena and Marjorie to take all the women and children into the storerooms on the lower level," Alex ordered. "Have five warriors stand guard over them. Bordick, make certain the towers are adequately manned, and place three lines of thirty warriors each in the courtyard to wait for Robert should he breach the gate. Then both of you join me on the wall head. We will fight this battle from the higher level, and end it long before Robert and his men have a prayer of entering the castle itself. Move!"

The two warriors instantly went to carry out his orders. Alex returned to find Gwendolyn standing before the hearth, contemplating the bone half buried in the ashes.

"So," she murmured, "he has finally come for me."

"Fetch David and take him to the storeroom with the other women and children. You will be safe there."

"Safe?" she repeated, her voice mocking. She turned to face him. "Your people despise me, MacDunn. They want me either gone or dead, and Robert has just arrived to fulfill both those desires. Do you honestly believe your clan will fight to keep me here?"

"They will do as I say," Alex assured her. "I am laird."

"They think you are mad. They thought you were mad for bringing me here and entrusting your son to me, and they will certainly think you mad for risking their lives to protect me. They can see that David is faring better and does not need me anymore. Why should they sacrifice themselves to protect a witch?"

"I have no time for this," Alex growled, exasperated. "Get my son and take him below!"

Gwendolyn shook her head. "I will not hide, nor will I ask your people to protect me against their will. They did nothing to provoke this attack. This is my battle, MacDunn, not theirs." She began to move toward the door.

Alex grabbed her shoulders with brusing strength, holding her fast. "Listen well, Gwendolyn. You will take my son below and you will stay there, do you understand?"

"Can you not see this is a battle that cannot be won? Robert will not rest until he has made me prisoner once more. Why force your people to suffer and die because of me?"

"Because I protect what is mine!"

"But I am not yours, MacDunn." Gwendolyn's gray eyes snapped fire. "I belong to no one!"

She was trembling beneath his grasp, whether from fury or fear he could not be certain. She seemed achingly beautiful to him in that moment, with her ebony veil of hair spilling wildly over the pale silk of her shoulders, and the faint flush of pleasure still coloring her exquisitely sculpted cheeks.

"You're wrong, Gwendolyn." He released his grip on her shoulder to gently trace his fingers along the graceful curve of her chin. He crushed his mouth against hers, stifling any further protest. Then he pulled away and regarded her sternly. "Swear to me that you will take my son to the lower level with the other women and children."

"Your people do not want to fight this war, and Robert will grant them no mercy." She lowered her gaze, unable to face him as she finished in a tear-choked whisper, "They will be slaughtered."

Alex cupped her chin in his hand and tilted her head up to face him. "Have faith, Gwendolyn. My people *will* be able to stand against Robert." He released her and strode toward the door. "I trained them myself, you know."

He studied her a final moment, then disappeared into the corridor.

Gwendolyn stood alone, listening to the first cries of battle tear through the night.

And then she raced from the chamber to fetch David.

CHAPTER 11

"Alex!" called Robena anxiously, "what are you going to do?"

"I'm going to fight him, Robena," Alex replied, striding toward the stairs that led to the battlements. "He leaves me no choice."

"This is madness! You cannot let your people die for the sake of that whore!"

Alex stopped. "What did you say?" His voice was ominously soft.

Realizing she had gone too far, Robena made a cautious retreat. "I mean only that she is a witch, Alex." She began to wring the fine linen square she held in her hand as she continued meekly, "You brought her here to help your son, but he seems better now. We don't need her anymore. It would be best for everyone if you simply gave her back to the Mac-Sweens."

"So they can kill her?"

"Whatever they decide to do with her is their affair, not ours. She is one of them, and they have the right to punish her for her evil crimes. It is not your responsibility to protect her."

"You're wrong, Robena. From the moment I rescued Gwendolyn from that stake, she became my responsibility. And I will defend her the same as I would any member of my clan."

"But she doesn't belong here, Alex," she persisted. "Surely you can see that?"

"Whether she belongs here or not, she will be protected."

Rowena's gaze narrowed. "Elspeth said the witch would bring misery and death to the clan, and so she has. And she has bewitched you with her sluttish charms until you are too blind to see the truth!"

Alex stared at her, shocked by the sudden change in her demeanor. The linen square she held was crushed into a limp ball, and the feminine fear sparkling in her eyes a moment earlier had been obliterated by utter loathing.

"You disappoint me, Robena," he said tautly. "I would have thought that you, of all people, would have more faith in me than that."

"But Alex—" she began, laying a pleading hand upon his shoulder.

"Get yourself below. I have a battle to fight."

He shrugged off her touch and mounted the stairs, deeply troubled by the realization that Robena was likely not alone in her convictions.

"Get off my wall, ye louse-ridden heap o' fur!" shouted Munro, awkwardly shoving a heavy stone off the parapet.

Farquhar leaned over and blearily watched as the boulder plopped to the ground, missing a cluster of MacSween warriors by a good six feet. "You missed," he reported. He took a deep swallow of ale and belched loudly.

"Christ, those buggers are fast," complained Munro, mopping the sweat off his face with his sleeve.

"They're coming up the ladder now," observed Farquhar, not sounding overly concerned. "Why don't you try again?"

"How many are there?" asked Munro, critically scanning the enormous pile of boulders at his disposal.

"Three—no—four—no—one's been shot—but here's another—and that one there makes five—or more like four and a half—the last chap is rather scrawny. . . ." He paused to take another draft of ale.

"For God's sake, Farquhar, *how many?*" bellowed Munro.

He belched. "Definitely five."

"This one looks like a fiver," decided Munro, selecting an enormous boulder from the pile. He hauled the heavy stone up, grunted loudly, and heaved it over.

"A clean strike!" praised Farquhar, watching as the five MacSween warriors were knocked from the ladder.

"Let that be a lesson to ye, ye stinkin' clods of dung!" shouted Munro triumphantly. "Oh-ho," he said, spotting another group advancing with a ladder. "You're wantin' some of the same, are ye? Well, I'll not be disappointing ye!"

"Stand back so I can shoot them," said Ned, slipping between them with his bow and arrow.

"Now, Neddie, Farquhar and I have this little area well in hand," protested Munro. "Why don't ye move along and find your own space?"

"It's too crowded," grumbled Ned.

Munro sighed. "Very well. Come over here. But try to hit the MacSweens who are farther out, and leave the ones scrambling up the wall to us."

Ned obligingly took aim at a warrior who was pointing at them with a burning arrow.

"Now, that's a daft thing," commented Cameron, coming up behind them. "Does he not realize the flame from that arrow makes him a pretty target?"

Ned released the string of his bow, sending his arrow flying. The MacSween warrior let out a bellow of pain as the sharp missile pierced his chest. "I'd warrant he does now," Ned reflected.

"Spread yourselves out!" commanded Alex, driving his

sword into the belly of a MacSween who had nearly climbed to the top of his ladder. "They're coming up the east side!"

The MacDunns instantly thinned ranks, covering the exposed areas.

"We're here, laddie!" trumpeted Owen, emerging on the wall head. He squinted into the darkness, then awkwardly began to grope his way along the parapet. Suddenly he stumbled and grabbed Cameron's plaid, jerking it down to the enormous warrior's ankles. "Do forgive, lad," he apologized hastily. "Not much light out here, is there?"

"Not unless you count the moonlight bouncing off Cameron's backside!" joked Brodick, who had just finished knocking a MacSween off the parapet.

"Stand over here, Cameron. Ye can help me to better see these stones!" roared Munro, nearly doubled over with amusement.

"By God, those MacSweens have had it now!" shouted Reginald, appearing with his sword wobbling before him. "I'll slice them open and feed their rancid, stinking bowels to the frogs!"

"Disgusting," sniffed Lachlan, who was following him, carefully balancing a frothing pitcher in his hands. "You have been spending far too much time with that Isabella."

"That's not from Isabella," protested Reginald, his aged arms trembling as he struggled to wield his weapon. "That's what the mighty Torvald says when he goes to fight the Gunns."

"Do forgive, Reginald," interjected Owen, "but I believe that's *dogs,* not frogs."

Reginald dropped his sword and scratched his white head. "Are you sure?" he asked, bewildered.

"For heaven's sake, how long do you suppose it would take to feed just one man to a bunch of frogs?" demanded Lachlan impatiently. "Years!"

"That's what makes the threat so dreadful," explained Reginald. "All those green, slimy creatures hopping in and out—"

"*Get down!*" roared Alex, racing toward the elderly trio. "*Now!*"

Ned, Cameron, and Brodick instantly threw themselves at the council members, knocking them down and shielding them with their bodies. A flurry of burning arrows sailed up to the battlements and landed around them.

"Now, that was bloody close!" swore Cameron, angrily kicking one of the flaming arrows aside.

"Release the first cauldron!" commanded Alex, watching as a group of MacSweens reached the gate carrying an enormous timber.

"Wait!" cried Lachlan, still cradling his frothing pitcher in his hands. He scrambled to his feet, shuffled over, and dumped the mixture into the cauldron of boiling water. "Not yet," he ordered, waving away Garrick, Ewan, and Quentin. "It has to ripen."

"For God's sake, Lachlan, get the hell out of the way!" shouted Alex.

"Very well. I suppose it will have to do," Lachlan relented. "But don't blame me if it doesn't work."

The MacDunns heaved the giant pot on its side. The startled MacSweens instantly abandoned their log as the boiling water poured down. There were a few shouts of pain and much colorful language, but nothing that suggested too serious an injury. Gazing warily up at the wall head, the cluster of MacSweens moved back to pick up their timber.

"Watch this," said Lachlan, cautiously peering over the parapet.

When they were just a few yards away from the abandoned log, the MacSweens began to gag.

"Christ almighty," complained one, "what the hell is that stench?"

"You'll find out soon enough!" shouted Lachlan merrily, waving at them. "Just keep on coming!"

"Ram the gate, you fools!" bellowed Robert impatiently from somewhere in the darkness. "Now!"

Hacking and choking, the MacSweens manfully continued toward their objective.

"Prepare to release the next cauldron!" commanded Alex.

"No, no," said Lachlan. "Let's wait and see if my potion worked."

"Lachlan," Alex began, struggling for patience, "this isn't the time—"

"It will only take a moment," Lachlan assured him. "Just watch."

"Fine," Alex muttered, thoroughly exasperated.

Pinching their noses with their fingers, the MacSweens reached the log. The instant they released their nostrils to pick up the heavy timber, half of them bent over and began to retch.

"Poison!" screeched one, falling to his knees. "By God, they've poisoned us!"

"The log is dripping with filth!" observed another, staring in horror at his slime-coated hands. "My God, the stink!"

"It's on your clothes!" shouted another. "Bloody hell, we're covered in it!"

"It worked!" burst out Lachlan, dancing with elation. He leaned boldly over the parapet. "Ruined your pretty log, didn't I?" he cackled. "Now you'd best find a stream to scrub yourselves in, before that slime turns to fire and burns your flesh off your miserable bones!"

The MacSween warriors stopped gagging and looked up at him in horror.

And then they turned and ran, knocking each other over in their haste to find a stream.

"My God, Lachlan, will that muck really turn to fire?" demanded Alex, incredulous.

"No," he admitted slyly. "But it won't hurt them to think so, now, will it?"

"Well, that's a damn nuisance," complained Reginald, leaning against his sword. "If you do that to all of them, who will be left for me to feed to the frogs?"

"He means dogs," Owen assured Alex.

"*MacDunn!*" roared a low, furious voice.

Alex watched as Robert rode forth from his vantage point with a group of mounted, torch-bearing warriors flanking him on either side. He lifted his sword, signaling for the remaining MacSween warriors to abandon their attack and form a protective line in front of him. They moved forward with the deliberate, elegant precision of a highly trained army, their shields and swords flashing in the amber waver of torchlight. The moment Robert caught a whiff of Lachlan's foul brew he halted, some thirty yards from the castle wall. The torch-bearing warriors swiftly reassembled, safely enclosing him in a ring of horse and fire.

"Good evening, Robert," called Alex pleasantly. "How splendid that you have decided to join us. I was actually starting to miss your cheerful presence."

"Give her to me, MacDunn," demanded Robert coldly. "You have no right to her."

"You're quite right," Alex agreed. "I don't." He sighed. "The problem is, Robert, she doesn't want to go with you."

"I don't give a damn what she wants," Robert snarled. "She must be returned to me so she can be burned."

"Good Lord," said Alex, sounding startled, "that's a bit harsh, don't you think?"

"That is her punishment."

"Well, I can't say I approve of that," mused Alex, clicking his tongue. "I mean, if we all went around burning every young girl who rejected her suitor—"

"I'm not talking about Isabella!" snapped Robert.

Alex regarded him in bewilderment. "You're not?"

"Give the witch to me, MacDunn, or I shall not rest until every man, woman, and child in your clan is reduced to a hot stew of flesh and blood."

Alex frowned. "Does this mean you don't want Isabella?"

"Forget Isabella!" he thundered.

"Well, that is a feat easier said than done, I'm afraid," Alex told him. "Perhaps you haven't noticed, but the lass loves to be the center of attention—which I suspect she gets from you—"

"Hear me, MacDunns!" shouted Robert, deciding to appeal directly to the clan. "Your mad laird has placed you in

terrible danger by bringing an evil witch and murderer into
your midst . . ."

"Nonsense!" shouted Owen, wagging a gnarled finger in
the air. "The lass would never harm a soul!"

". . . who viciously murdered her own father," continued Robert, "by casting a hideous spell over him that sucked
out his spirit and delivered it straight to the devil."

"Did she, now?" snorted Reginald. "Then maybe we
should ask her to do the same to you!"

Robert stared up at the jeering elder in confusion. Why
the hell weren't these ignorant louts afraid of Gwendolyn, as
her own clan had been?

"The witch has cast a horrible pestilence on my people
and lands," he told them dramatically, "to punish us for trying to put an end to her wickedness. From the day your feeble-
minded laird stole her, scores of MacSweens have died in the
most horrendous agony, their flesh consumed by fetid black
sores. Our crops have rotted in violent storms, in which unearthly winds have uprooted house, tree, and animal alike,
smashing them against the ground as she tries to destroy
us—"

"*Liar!*" shouted an enraged woman's voice. "How can you
stand there and tell such vile falsehoods?"

Surprised, both the MacDunns and the MacSweens
turned to gaze at Isabella, who was leaning out of one of the
castle windows.

"Isabella!" yelled Brodick, "get back inside at once!"

"No," returned Isabella defiantly. "Not when my uncle
sits down there telling such ridiculous fabrications!" She
leaned out even farther to ensure that everyone could see her.
"Shall I tell them the truth, dear uncle?"

"Go and haul her back inside, Brodick," Alex ordered
between clenched teeth, "before she falls and breaks her
bloody neck."

"When I get her, I may break it for her," muttered
Brodick, moving swiftly away.

"Isabella, my child," said Robert smoothly, "I am deeply
relieved to see that you are well. Your dear father has been

overcome with worry. Come to me, my sweet, and I shall take you home."

"You would take me to a place where the starving Mac-Sweens are dying from some ghastly scourge, and unearthly winds are destroying forests and homes?" Isabella asked sarcastically. "Your concern for my welfare is truly touching."

"That does seem a wee bit odd," observed Owen, knitting his white brows together.

"There was no pestilence after Gwendolyn left," Isabella shouted, "nor were there storms, or winds, or uncommon occurrences of any kind! He only says this to make you think she is evil, when in fact the only evil one here is the man you see befo—"

Her tirade ended abruptly as Brodick grabbed her by the waist and yanked her back through the window.

"What are you doing?" Isabella shrieked, struggling to escape his grasp. "I'm not finished!"

"Yes, you are," Brodick assured her. "And if I ever find you doing such a dangerously foolish thing again, Isabella, I swear to you I will make certain you cannot sit for a month!"

"How dare you!" she raged, trying to break free. "I'm trying to help Gwendolyn! Robert is filling their heads with lies!"

"You have already helped her. You have exposed Robert's charges against her for the falsehoods they are. You needn't put yourself in any further danger by falling out the window or getting shot by one of Robert's men."

"No!" she cried, struggling violently against him. "I must help her more!"

"Isabella, stop!" He gave her a hard shake. "*Enough!*"

Startled by the anger in his voice, she suddenly stopped and gazed up at him, her eyes sparkling with tears.

"Forgive me, Bella," he apologized, instantly easing his grip on her. "I didn't mean to hurt you."

Isabella swallowed thickly and shook her head. "You didn't," she said, her voice small and forlorn. "It's not that."

"Then what is it?"

She hesitated a moment, then inhaled a ragged breath and whispered brokenly, "I didn't know."

"Didn't know what?" asked Brodick, gently capturing the silver drop trickling down her cheek. "Tell me."

"They were so cruel to her," she said, the words choked with misery. "Everyone was, because they—we—thought she was evil. 'Twas common knowledge, so none of us ever thought to question it. And whenever anyone grew sick, or died, or a crop failed, or milk soured, or bread wouldn't rise, we blamed Gwendolyn."

Brodick regarded her grimly and said nothing.

"But when they said that she had killed her father . . . I knew that couldn't be right." She bit her trembling lip. "I'd seen them, you see, walking together on the hill. I used to go sometimes and hide in the deep grasses when I wanted to be alone. And they would be walking—just the two of them, because no one else would go near her—and they'd be holding hands, and he'd be telling her the most marvelous stories about a great warrior called the mighty Torvald. Then they would sit on the ground, and he would tell her things that he thought she should know, about birds and clouds, or the world that lives under a rock when you turn it over. . . ." Her voice began to break. "And Gwendolyn would look at him with such *love*. . . ." The words disintegrated into tears.

"Shhh, Bella," soothed Brodick, wrapping her in his arms. "It's all right."

"No, it isn't. Because I knew there was something wrong when Robert said she had murdered her father—but I didn't do anything. I just let them find her guilty. But how could Gwendolyn have killed the only person in the world she really loved?"

"She couldn't have," Brodick agreed quietly.

"I believed she was a witch, and told myself it didn't matter," she confessed, her voice sodden with contempt. "I thought that even if she didn't kill him, she was responsible for all kinds of other terrible things, so she deserved to die. And then I just put it from my mind. I chose a pretty gown to wear, and I laughed and flirted with you while they tied her to that awful stake—and set her afire—" She began to sob.

"Hush, Bella," crooned Brodick, tenderly stroking her hair. "You couldn't have saved her. Your people had feared her for years and were determined to burn her. There was nothing you could have done to change that."

"But I should have tried. I should have said something in her defense. But instead I remained silent." She buried her face in the warm mantle of his plaid and wept uncontrollably.

"And yet tonight you leaned out of a tower in the midst of a battle and challenged Robert's false allegations against Gwendolyn." Brodick grasped her chin and tipped her head up so he could look into her eyes. "Do you realize Robert could have had you shot just to silence you?"

"I don't care," she told him fiercely. "At least the MacDunns would know the truth about Gwendolyn."

Brodick stared at her a moment, overwhelmed by her unexpected courage.

And then he bent his head and crushed his lips against hers.

". . . and therefore I shall be forced to destroy this holding and everyone in it," finished Robert menacingly.

A long silence followed.

"Do you hear me, MacDunn?" he thundered.

Alex peered over the parapet, politely stifling a yawn. "Forgive me, Robert," he apologized, stretching, "but you were talking for so long I found my mind wandering a bit. What were you saying?"

Robert's face contorted with fury. "Shoot them!"

A volley of burning arrows vaulted into the air, making a graceful arc of flame against the velvet sky before they dipped and rained upon the battlements.

"Sweet Jesus!" shouted Munro, grabbing his blazing shoulder. "I'm hit!"

Cameron quickly whipped off his plaid and threw it over Munro's shoulder, extinguishing the flames.

"By God, Cameron," Munro said between clenched teeth, " 'tis noble of you to bare that ivory backside of yours again just for me."

"Be grateful it's a warm night," joked Cameron, "or I might have thought twice about it. Steady, now," he commanded, gently easing Munro against the stone floor. "Breathe deep. If it's not in too far we can take the arrow out straight-away."

"Are you going to give her to me, MacDunn?" demanded Robert.

Alex gripped the hilt of his sword, focusing on the cold steel pressing against his heated palm. "Never," he swore. *Instead I'm going to kill you, you bastard.*

"Then prepare to die!" Robert raised his sword to signal the next volley of arrows.

"*Stop!*" cried a high, desperate voice.

Alex irritably shifted his gaze from Robert, wondering why Brodick still hadn't brought Isabella under control.

His heart froze.

It was Gwendolyn, struggling to balance herself on one of the tower merlons as a group of MacDunns rushed anxiously toward her.

"Stay back!" she warned. "Come one step closer and I'll jump."

"No one move!" commanded Alex, terrified that she might slip and fall if they startled her. "Gwendolyn," he began, affecting a nonchalance that completely belied his anxiety, "just what, exactly, do you think you are doing?"

"I cannot bear this," she replied, her voice trembling. "I cannot bear the thought that some of your clan may die because of me."

"We're happy to do it, lass!" said Owen grandly. "These MacSween scoundrels need to be taught a lesson, just as the mighty Torvald would do to them!"

"I'm going to whip up another batch of that potion," Lachlan added, "only this time I'll make it so strong they'll be spewing their bowels out their eye sockets!"

"And then we're going to feed them to the frogs!" finished Reginald enthusiastically.

"Come down, Gwendolyn," interjected Alex. "We can discuss this better if you are over here."

"You don't understand," she whispered, shaking her head. "He will never give up."

"Perhaps not." Alex slowly moved along the parapet toward the tower. "But I don't intend to let him have you."

"And how much blood will be shed because of me?" She gazed at him sadly, her eyes two silver pools against the paleness of her face. "How much death will I have brought to your people?"

"I knew the risks when I took you, Gwendolyn."

"No, MacDunn," she said, her voice laced with pain. "You didn't."

She turned away from him suddenly, and his heart constricted with terror.

"Shoot me, Robert!" she commanded, opening her arms wide in invitation. "Let us bring this to an end!"

"Hold!" roared Robert as his warriors instantly took aim at her. "The first man to release an arrow is dead!"

Their arrows taut against the strings of their bows, his warriors regarded him in amazement.

"What in bloody hell is the matter with you?" demanded Derek. "Are we here to kill the witch or not?"

"Shut your mouth," snapped Robert.

"Why don't you let them kill me, Robert?" Gwendolyn taunted. "That is what you came here for, is it not? To finally put an end to my evil powers? Now is your chance to save the MacSweens from all the devastation I have wrought on them, and punish me for murdering my father at the same time. Why do you hesitate?"

"You must be burned, witch," Robert told her, grappling for some reasonable explanation for his reticence. "Your cursed form must be consumed by fire."

"Then have one of your brave warriors shoot a burning arrow through me. That will suffice, I think. Once I fall, you can heap dry twigs and peat around me, to be certain I burn to nothing." She raised her arms slightly higher, wobbling on her tiny perch.

Alex stood paralyzed, afraid if he moved she would plunge to her death. A cool wind had begun to gust, blowing the silky black of her hair and gown out behind her like great, dark wings. She looked utterly glorious as she stood precariously on that merlon, her small, slender form a wisp of shadow against the brilliant wash of moonlight glowing behind her. His people were willing to protect her, yet she had chosen to face Robert's army alone, bravely offering her life in exchange for the safety of a clan that had been hostile toward her from the day she arrived. She was completely magnificent to him, as courageous and honorable as the finest warrior he had ever known. He swallowed thickly, humbled by her.

"You have erred, Gwendolyn," said Robert, the corners of his mouth curling in a predaceous smile. "You have just revealed your weakness."

"I have nothing to lose, Robert," countered Gwendolyn. "You have stolen everything from me."

"Is that so?" he drawled. "Then you won't mind what I am about to do." He raised his sword and gestured at the neat little cottages scattered upon the hill. "Burn them," he commanded harshly. "Destroy the fields and gardens. And slay anything that breathes, be it human or animal."

The torch-bearing warriors circling him immediately disbanded.

"My God," murmured Cameron, watching in horror. "He's going to destroy our homes and kill our livestock."

"Cowards!" shouted Owen, shaking his gnarled fist in the air. "Come back and fight like warriors, not demons!"

"My grandfather built my cottage," reflected Ewan, his voice filled with despair. "I was born in it, as was my son."

"It will be all right," said Quentin, resting his hand on his friend's shoulder. "We will build again."

Sick horror welled in Gwendolyn's throat as she watched Robert's men touch their torches to the roofs of the MacDunns' cottages. The flames leaped eagerly onto the thick nests of thatch, consuming the sweet, dry straw with voracious hunger. In little more than a breath a half dozen homes were blazing, their orange and gold flicker strangely beautiful against the charcoal cape of night. She closed her eyes, unable to bear the hideous sight. Somewhere in the darkness a dog was frantically barking.

"That's my Laddie," said Garrick. "He must think I'm trapped in my house."

"Kill that goddamn dog!" Robert commanded, wheeling his mount about.

"Run, Laddie!" Garrick shouted, leaning over the parapet. "Run!"

The barking stopped.

And then it started again, only now it was coming closer.

"No, Laddie!" said Garrick, his voice rough with emotion. "Go away! Run, damn you! Run!"

"I see it!" snarled Robert. "It's coming up the hill. Shoot the damn thing!"

Gwendolyn did not bother to open her eyes. Instead she raised her arms high, reaching into the clear black of the sky. A deafening roar filled her ears, blocking out the sound of the dog barking, the cottages burning, the MacDunns' despair as they watched their beloved homes being destroyed.

You cannot do this, Robert. I won't let you.

A brilliant ribbon of light suddenly tore across the cloudless sky, cracking it open for the torrent of rain that burst forth. It poured down in hard, icy needles, drowning the flaming cottages and extinguishing the MacSweens' torches and flaming arrows. The sharp water lashed against the attacking warriors with such force they could scarcely open their eyes. Another streak of lightning ripped through the night, and another, the searing flashes of light as blinding as the rain. Earsplitting waves of thunder crashed over the mountains, causing the MacSweens' horses to whinny and rear up in fear as their masters shouted at them to be still. The rain fell in heavy sheets and began to pool on the ground, swiftly turning the grass and earth to a slippery, muddy slop.

"Damn you, MacDunn!" bellowed Robert, as if he felt that Alex were somehow responsible for the sudden squall. "*It will be mine!*" He stared up at him a long moment, his face twisted with fury, heedless of the water whipping against him.

And then he jerked his mount's head to one side and galloped into the thundering darkness.

The MacSween warriors turned and scrambled after their retreating commander, their heads held low as they vainly tried to shield themselves against the lash of the rain.

The MacDunns raised their weapons into the air and cheered.

"That was simply splendid!" exclaimed Owen, dabbing at his dripping face with his sopping-wet mantle. "In all my years, I've never seen such a beastie of a storm."

"The lass has a fine way with the weather," yelled Reginald, trying to be heard above the crashing thunder. "Brought it on just in a whisker of time."

"A bit excessive, if you ask me," shouted Lachlan, irritably squinting into the gale. "A tempest of half this potency would have sufficed."

Alex was barely aware of their comments as he cautiously moved toward Gwendolyn. She rose from the parapet like a magnificent stone sculpture teetering over the precipice of death, her eyes closed and her arms outstretched, apparently oblivious to the fact that the MacSweens had retreated. The pelting rain had reduced her gown to a liquid black sheath that poured over the curves of her breasts and hips, turning her into a rippling shadow against the jagged strips of light flashing around her. Alex locked his gaze on her as he closed the distance between them, willing her not to fall.

"Gwendolyn." He reached out to her. "Take my hand."

Her lids fluttered open. Even through the heavy veil of rain he could see that her gray eyes were distant and blurred, like someone who has just been roused from a long and restless sleep. She regarded him in confusion, as if wondering who he was and how he had come to be there.

And then she sighed and fell into the blackness.

Alex roared as he threw himself forward, his arms outstretched. For an endless shred of time he felt nothing but rain and darkness and death, and his mind began to shatter, as surely as it had the night Flora had forever escaped his grasp. *No, by God, no.* He extended his body farther, reaching through the night until every bone and tendon and muscle was strained to the very limits of his skin.

And then he had her, her slender form whole and firm as she dangled helplessly in the crush of his aching hands.

With a savage groan he heaved her up, too overcome to be gentle as he hauled her over the parapet. Holding her tight against him, he sank to his knees, fighting the splintering pain tangling like a web through his skull.

She is all right, he told himself fiercely. *She is not going to die.* The stinging rain thrashed against them as he cradled her in his arms, soaking their hair and skin and clothes, and he leaned over her, vainly trying to protect her from the rain, the cold, the night, from every dark force that might seek to harm her or steal her from him.

He did not know how long he remained huddled over her. When Brodick's voice finally penetrated the aching fog in his brain, the wall head was all but deserted.

"Let's take her inside, Alex," Cameron was saying, resting his hand upon Alex's shoulder. "Come."

"The battle," Alex murmured stupidly.

"The battle is over," Brodick said. "Everyone is safe and accounted for, including Garrick's dog. I have posted men to watch from the towers for any further disturbances, although there is little Robert can do as long as this storm rages. Just to be certain, the entire clan will be spending the night within the confines of the castle. There is nothing more to be done tonight, Alex. Come."

Dizzy and disoriented, Alex rose to his feet, still holding his precious burden tightly against him. Gwendolyn's eyes were closed and her body was limp. "She is not dead," he said dully, staring down at her.

"I believe she has fainted," Brodick told him. "You've been holding her out here a long while."

"He has," Gwendolyn agreed, the chalky line of her lips barely moving. "But I'm awfully cold, MacDunn." Her gray eyes opened and she regarded him with a steady clarity that had been completely absent when she regarded him just before she fell. "Could we go inside now?"

He drew her closer to his chest as he carried her along the battlements, down the stairs, into the corridor. Neither Cameron nor Brodick spoke as they made their way along the torchlit hallway, the only sound being the spatter of their sodden garments as they dripped streams of water onto the stone floor. Alex did not pause at Flora's old sickroom, but continued to his own chamber. He carried Gwendolyn inside and closed the door on Cameron's and Brodick's confused expressions. He didn't give a damn what they thought of his taking Gwendolyn to his chamber. He didn't give a damn what anyone thought.

She was his, and she belonged here, with him.

He placed her in a chair before the hearth, then quickly heaped a mound of twigs and dry logs in the fireplace. He lit it with one of the candles flickering in the room, watching impatiently as the amber flames began to billow and snap. When the fire was blazing, he added several more lengths of wood to the pyre, ensuring its heat would last for several hours. Then he turned to her.

"We must remove that wet gown before you catch your death from a chill."

Gwendolyn obediently stood and began to remove her gown. Alex went to his bed and stripped off the plaid covering, then quickly wrapped her in it as her black gown and chemise dropped to her bare feet.

"There, now." He rubbed her through the softness of the plaid, trying to restore blood and heat to her chilled flesh. "Feel better?"

She stared up at him in numb silence. The lines of his handsome face were deeply etched in the flickering firelight, making him look far older than his years. His pale blond hair spilled like shimmering wet satin over his shoulders, and he seemed heedless of the fact that his shirt and plaid were lying cold and wet against his own skin. His touch was achingly gentle as he warmed her with his hands, the steady, sure stroke of a man who was well accustomed to tending someone weak.

The thought of Flora filled her mind—Flora lying trapped in a dark, stifling room, but in a bed that had been carefully embroidered with flowers and sunshine and waterfalls. A bed that Alex had insisted on sharing with her as she lay dying, so she would not be alone. A bed that he had ordered burned after she died, so he would never have to endure the agony of looking upon it and remembering her in it.

Pity lanced Gwendolyn's heart. MacDunn had risked everything for her this evening, she realized, bewildered by the incredible selflessness of his actions. He had been willing to sacrifice his people, his castle, even himself, all for the sake of her safety. And she had been equally ready to die, so that he and his clan might be spared Robert's brutality. In that moment on the battlements, as she stood trembling over the dark embrace of death, she had suddenly understood the depth of her feelings for this mad, tormented laird.

And she had been terrified.

With a little cry she wrapped her arms around him, clinging to him desperately as she pressed her trembling lips to his. She wanted to be enveloped by him, to lose herself to his extraordinary strength and courage, to banish all thought of David and Clarinda, Cameron and Brodick and Ned, and even silly, spoiled Isabella, who had so courageously leaned out of a window and shouted at the top of her lungs that Gwendolyn was not evil. She wanted to wash all of them from her mind, and the cruel, irrefutable fact that by staying here, she endangered each and every one of them. And so she pressed herself against Alex's hard, rain-soaked length, kissing him deeply as the plaid he had wrapped around her slipped to the floor in a rumpled pool of wool.

Alex groaned and drove his tongue deep into the sweetness of Gwendolyn's mouth as he swept her up into his arms. He had not planned this, he assured himself as he crossed the chamber and lowered her onto the bed, but he could no more douse the passion blazing within him than he could have stopped the storm still raging outside. He wanted her with a voracity that was staggering. For weeks now he had feared her, not because of her unearthly powers, which he could not begin to comprehend, but because of her physical fragility, which made her seem like a tender blossom that would wither in the sun, or be swept away by the faintest gust of wind. The agony of Flora's suffering was still raw in his mind, and he had been wary of Gwendolyn from the moment he saw her lashed to the stake, thinking such a feeble wisp of a girl could never endure even the simplest hardships of life. But he had been wrong. She had withstood the rancor of his own people with a stubborn resolution that would have tested his most seasoned warrior. She had endured fire and loathing, injury and humiliation, and the bitter knowledge that everyone she encountered either despised or feared her. Yet she had remained, tending to his son with tenderness and compassion, ignoring everything else in her bid to make a dying lad well. And then, when her mission was nearly completed, she had climbed upon the parapet and offered herself in exchange for the lives of those who had conspired to be rid of her.

The nobility beating within her tiny breast was staggering.

He shed his wet garments and stretched himself over her, covering her with his warmth and strength. He wanted to possess her, to hold her tight against him and lose himself inside her, to chain her to him with his body and mind and soul, so that she would never leave him, never know the touch of another man, and most of all so that she would never barter with her precious life as she had tonight. She was his, and she had to understand that, not with words, but with the heavy press of his thighs against hers, with the rough stroke of his tongue upon her taut nipple, the sun-bronzed splay of his hand grasping her creamy hip, and the harsh moan that escaped his throat as he buried himself deep within her velvet wet heat. A startled gasp escaped her lips, and he felt the bite of her nails as she clutched the muscles in his back, pulling him even closer against her small, silky body. He ravaged her mouth as he drove himself into her, tasting her deeply, thoroughly, feeling her cries of pleasure vibrate against his lips and teeth. Again and again he plunged into her as he drank in her beauty and strength and courage, feeling more a part of her with each aching penetration, stretching and filling her with his desperate need, until finally he did not know where he ended and she began. His mind began to spin as he lost himself to her, touching and kissing and gripping and thrusting, acutely aware of her slippery hot tightness as she held him safe inside her, the rapid flutter of her heart as it beat against his chest, the tangle of her slender legs as she twined them around his thighs, and the painful ache as he moved in and out of her, desperately trying to bind her to him, and feeling instead like he was being chained forever to her. He could not breathe, could not think, could not stop, could not do anything except lunge into her again and again, faster, harder, his body straining for release from this sublime torture. And suddenly he was soaring through the night, and he cried out her name in despair. He never wanted it to end, but his body could bear no more and so he rammed himself as far into her as he could, filling her with every fragment of his flesh and his soul before collapsing helplessly against her.

Gwendolyn lay utterly still, feeling the pounding of MacDunn's heart against her breast and the warm caress of his breath upon her neck. She wrapped her arms around his shoulders and held him, feeling briefly, impossibly safe, as if the muscular shield of his beautiful body and the inexorable power of his will could protect her from anything. Outside, the storm was still howling with awesome fury, making another attack on the castle impossible tonight. This was a fragile, stolen moment, she realized, tightening her hold on MacDunn, that would never come again.

It will be mine, Robert had vowed. Robert would not rest until he had forced Gwendolyn to give the stone to him. Which she would never do. It mattered little that he would certainly kill her once he held that powerful talisman in the crush of his palm. What was of consequence was the fact that he would use the stone to obtain the power he so lusted for, enabling him to vanquish all those who would rise against him. As long as she remained in this castle, Alex and his people were in grave danger. Robert had made it clear he thought nothing of destroying their homes and brutally slaying them. Although the MacDunns had demonstrated enormous courage in their stand against the MacSweens, she had felt their anguish as they watched their beloved homes being torched as surely as if it had been her own. She did not doubt Alex would fight to the absolute limits of his ability to protect her. In his desperate bid to save the life of his son, Alex had unwittingly brought death and suffering to his people.

And she was the cause of it.

She swallowed the despair welling in her throat, and vainly tried to summon the cold detachment that had always served her so well in the past. But somehow in this shadowed moment it eluded her, and she was left feeling deeply shaken and afraid.

There was no question that she must leave immediately. The moment this violent storm stopped, Robert would bring his savage forces back. Until then, the MacDunns were prisoners in their own castle. Only by luring Robert away could she restore the peace the MacDunns had known before she came here, and thereby protect the people who had come to mean so much to her. Once Robert discovered she was gone, he would waste no time dallying here. His desire for the stone would force him to set out after her immediately.

And when he found her, she would kill him.

She blinked back the tears blurring her eyes, vaguely wondering why the thought didn't bring her the dark comfort it once had. But all she could think of was young David staring at her in wonder as he listened to her tell one of her stories, and Clarinda smiling sweetly as she pressed Gwendolyn's hand against her swollen, pulsing belly, and dour old Lachlan vehemently promising her that he would make a potion that would have the MacSweens spewing their bowels out their eye sockets. All this she must leave behind. Hardest of all, she must leave MacDunn, who had awakened emotions within her that she had never imagined existed. He was lying heavily against her, his body still joined to hers, the roughness of his cheek grazing the soft curve of her neck. She inhaled a shallow, ragged breath, unable to suppress the anguish tearing through her heart.

Alex raised himself up on his elbows and frowned.

Gwendolyn turned her face away from him, trying to avoid his gaze. He laid his fingers against the elegantly sculpted line of her jaw and tilted her head back, forcing her to look at him. Her gray eyes were filled with a terrible hopelessness, and a tear trickled across the paleness of her cheek and dropped into the wet black river of her hair. He considered himself a hardened warrior, who had seen far more than his share of despondency during his life, both in Flora's eyes, and in his own. Nevertheless, the sight of Gwendolyn's torment slashed deep into him, carving fresh wounds over those that would never heal.

"Do not be afraid, Gwendolyn," he murmured, caressing her shimmering cheek with the back of his fingers. "I will keep you safe."

She swallowed miserably and shook her head. "No," she whispered, her voice a thread of sound against the wind and the rain, "you cannot."

"I can," he insisted harshly, "and I will. You are *mine*." He captured her lips with bruising force, silencing any further argument.

She felt him harden inside her as he ravaged the deepest recesses of her mouth. He began to thrust in and out of her, filling her and emptying her, his powerful form flexing with slow deliberation as he tried to make her his. Gwendolyn wrapped her arms and legs around him and desperately kissed him back, nearly choking on the hot tears that were now streaming down her face. *I love you,* she said silently, her heart breaking from the agonizing confession. *I love you I love you I love you.*

She moaned as she moved with him, knowing that she would never hold him deep within the blazing heat of her body again. *I love you,* she wept, threading her hands into the golden length of his hair. He pushed himself into her with gentle roughness, kissing her tenderly now, trying to possess her body and spirit, his hands roaming across her in a constant, sweeping caress. And then his fingers were stroking the slick soft heat of her as he thrust in and out, and she felt herself begin to tighten and stretch and reach, and her tears stopped as she became aware of nothing but the sheer wonder of him touching her and filling her and kissing her. *I love you,* she told him silently, not daring to speak the words aloud for fear he would reject them. A low growl curled up from deep within his chest, the masculine sound answering her own soft gasps. *I love you more than life itself.*

She cried out suddenly, feeling herself shatter into a thousand silvery fragments, and Alex buried himself deeply inside her and let out a harsh groan. Ripples of ecstasy cascaded over her as his muscled weight pressed her deeper into the softness of the mattress, and she knew an instant of pure, glorious joy.

As swiftly as it came it was gone, replaced with a trembling sense of loss. Alex rolled off her and gathered her in his arms, holding her against him as he gently swept back a damp lock of her hair.

"You will stay with me," he commanded, his voice low. "And I will keep you safe, Gwendolyn." He trailed his fingers along the slender length of her arm, then grasped her hand and laid it firmly over his heart. "I swear it."

Gwendolyn stared a long, solemn moment into the piercing blue of his gaze. And then she laid her cheek against the warm marble of his chest and closed her eyes, fighting the tears that were threatening to spill from her again as she felt the steady rhythm of his heartbeat against her palm. She said nothing. There was nothing she could say.

She loved him.

And tomorrow she would leave him forever.

CHAPTER 12

Gwendolyn opened her eyes to find David staring at her, his little freckled face puckered with bemusement.

"Aren't you cold?" he asked curiously.

She looked down and saw that she was just barely covered by the soft plaid draped over her. She gasped and hastily yanked the blanket up to her neck, then glanced over to see if MacDunn was still lying beside her. Mercifully, he wasn't. Summoning every shred of her tattered dignity, she regarded David as if there was nothing unusual about her being found stark naked in his father's bed. "Is everything all right?"

"The whole clan is talking about you," he reported.

Gwendolyn's eyes widened in horror. Obviously everyone knew she had spent the night with MacDunn. Mortified to the core, she lowered her lids and meekly asked, "Are you terribly upset?"

He shook his head.

"You're not?" she asked, confused.

"Your standing up to Robert is the bravest thing I've ever heard of—like something the mighty Torvald would do!"

His words penetrated her embarrassment. "Is *that* what the clan is talking about?"

"What else would they be talking about?"

"Nothing," she hastily responded. She sat up a little, still clutching the blanket. "What, exactly, is the clan saying?"

He seated himself beside her, forcing her to move over a bit. "Owen says that of all the witches he has ever known, you are by far the most magnificent," he said excitedly. "Then Lachlan demanded to know exactly how many witches he had known, and Owen could only think of you and one other, and Lachlan said that hardly accounted for much of a comparison. Then Reginald said he's only sorry that he didn't have the chance to hack off Robert's monstrous head and present it to you, all bloody and leaking his brains on a pike, so that you might keep it as a memento of your bravery. And Lachlan snorted and said that was a disgusting notion, and that instead he would spend all day creating a special wine to be drunk tonight in your honor!"

Gwendolyn stared at him in bewilderment.

"Did you really climb onto the parapet and tell Robert to shoot you with a burning arrow?" David asked eagerly.

She nodded.

"Cameron said you looked like a black angel standing on the merlon, and that when Robert set the cottages afire, you raised your arms and conjured up a storm to put out the flames!"

Of course they would think that, Gwendolyn reflected. After all, the MacDunns were convinced that she controlled the weather.

"Ned says as long as the storm continues like this, the MacSweens won't be able to attack again. But you won't let it rain like this forever, will you? I'm feeling quite well today, and thought that maybe I could try riding again soon."

"It won't rain forever," Gwendolyn assured him, although

the storm did not seem to have eased since last night. "Have you had anything to eat?"

"I got hungry while I was waiting for you to come with my breakfast, so I went down to the kitchen and asked Marjorie to give me some bread and oatmeal. I didn't have any milk, eggs, or cheese, or even any of the smoked herring that she was serving to the others."

"How do you feel?"

He shrugged his shoulders. "Fine."

He certainly looked fine, Gwendolyn reflected. His blue eyes were clear and sparkling, and although his skin was still pale from a lack of sunlight, his lightly freckled cheeks held a hint of color. His face was freshly scrubbed, and he had taken the time to comb his bright red hair, so that it spilled in a relatively tidy mass of curls over his saffron shirt. Gwendolyn remembered the first time she had seen him, lying in that foul chamber with his chalky skin stretched across his sunken face like the thinnest of fabric, and his limp hair saturated with sweat and filth. She had felt certain he was on the edge of death and that there was nothing she could possibly do to save him. There was no trace of that dying child in the glowing young lad who sat beside her now, restlessly banging his feet against the frame of the bed. He was dressed in the plaid he had worn to the great hall last night, which he had arranged to the best of his unskilled ability, so that it hung like a shapeless rag over his narrow hips, with the excess fabric falling in a long swath down his back. MacDunn would have to give him a lesson in putting on his plaid, she decided, taking pleasure in seeing David look so well.

God had tested her in many ways, but He had given her one incredible gift. He had enabled her to help David live. For that she would be eternally grateful.

"My father said that conjuring up that storm made you tired," David said sympathetically. "Is that why you're still in bed?"

She nodded. "Where is your father?"

"He has gone outside with some of the men, to survey the damage to the outer wall and return the rocks that were dropped off the battlements. He has ordered all the tables and benches in the great hall to be moved to the sides so the men can train in there while it rains."

Which means he knew Robert would return soon, reflected Gwendolyn. *I will keep you safe.* She did not doubt that MacDunn actually believed he was capable of such a feat. But he did not understand the depth of Robert's ruthless determination to get her back. Robert would stop at nothing to force her to give him the stone. And by standing before him last night and offering him her life, Gwendolyn had made a grave, irreversible blunder. She had armed Robert with the knowledge that she was ready to die for the sake of the MacDunns. All he needed to do was attack the vulnerable cottages on the hill or take just one MacDunn hostage, be it Cameron, or Ned, or even grumpy old Lachlan, and Gwendolyn would have no choice but to surrender to him. And then Robert would slaughter the MacDunns anyway, before using the power of the stone for his own vile purposes.

She must lure him away from here and kill him first.

"David, please find Clarinda and tell her I must speak with her at once."

"Are you going to tell us the story about what happened last night?" asked David, his eyes bright with anticipation. "I'm sure you would tell it better than Owen or Cameron."

"Not today. Now hurry."

David obediently rushed out the door, awkwardly hiking up his sagging plaid as he went.

A lump of emotion rose to her throat as she watched him go. Until she met David, her experience with children had been limited exclusively to the young MacSweens who used to taunt her and throw things at her, or run away whenever she appeared. She had thought children were either stupid or cruel, and most often both. But David had changed that perception. During their time together she had discovered that children were quick to abandon the fear and intolerance they learned from adults, and to judge people for themselves, as David had with her. MacDunn's son was a sweet and gentle lad, and caring for him had made her understand what it is to love a child more than oneself.

She would not permit any harm to come to him.

She had promised Clarinda that she would stay and help her deliver her child, but that was impossible now. She must leave today, so she could spare the clan any further attacks. Although the knowledge that she was breaking her pledge to her dearest friend weighed heavily upon her, she felt certain Clarinda would understand. Marjorie would be able to help her with the birth, and perhaps Letitia would stay with her as well. Both these women were far more experienced in matters of childbearing than Gwendolyn was, since they had actually given birth.

"And must one have been cut open by a sword in order to know how to deal with the wound?" demanded Morag cryptically from the doorway. "I've brought you some fresh garments to wear," she continued, not waiting for a reply as she moved gracefully past the sodden pile of black and cream fabric lying on the floor. "It would hardly do to have you traipsing about the corridor wearing nothing but that plaid, although you do look quite fetching in it." She laid upon the disheveled bed a clean chemise and the amethyst-colored gown she had given to Gwendolyn.

"Thank you," said Gwendolyn, trying to conceal her mortification at being found naked in the laird's chamber.

"Not at all." Morag smiled as she eased herself into the chair by the hearth. "I may be old, but I still remember what it is to be young and filled with longing."

"I am not filled with longing," Gwendolyn told her, pulling the chemise over her head.

"Of course you are, my dear. You have so much longing in you, you cannot trust yourself to give in to it, for fear that if you open that door you will drown in the flood of need that spills forth. You perceive need as weakness, and that frightens you, because you have always had to be strong and reserved— never giving in to your emotions, be they anger, or love, or even the simple desire for friendship. And sadly, you were correct. Had you listened to your heart and acted without restraint, the MacSweens would have found a reason to tie you to that stake long ago."

Gwendolyn continued to dress herself, saying nothing.

"Alex, on the other hand, was once so full of fun and fire, we used to wonder how the rascal would ever learn to behave himself when he was laird," she said, her mouth curving in a soft smile. "Whether with women or hunting or battle, he followed his own pleasures, giving no thought to the consequences. The clan was relieved when Flora finally captured his heart. She brought out the more responsible side of Alex, while still fanning the flames of his passion." She sighed. "Unfortunately, when she died, Flora took part of Alex with her. He fell into a madness from which we feared he would never emerge—and he never really did. When he finally was lucid again, the passionate young man we had known was gone, replaced by someone who seemed incapable of any emotion but anger."

Gwendolyn closed her eyes, her heart aching as she recalled the magnificent passion that had raged between them last night.

"You don't want to leave," Morag observed.

Gwendolyn opened her eyes and regarded her steadily. Although she didn't believe Morag could see the future, it was clear the woman was uniquely perceptive. "I must."

Morag considered this a moment. "At least you feel you must, and that, I suppose, is all that matters."

"Robert will not rest until he has me," Gwendolyn explained. "And when he returns, he will be far more brutal. If I stay, I will fulfill Elspeth's prophecy of bringing death and destruction to the MacDunns."

"Nonsense!" Morag waved her hand dismissively. "You have listened to the foul accusations of others for so long, you are starting to give them power over you." Her expression grew contemplative. "You must look at yourself, Gwendolyn, but do not use your eyes. Only then will you be able to see clearly."

"I cannot stay, Morag," Gwendolyn said, her voice laden with regret.

Morag regarded her a long moment. And then she nodded. "Very well. But there is one matter you must attend to before you go. A promise to a friend in need cannot be broken."

"If you mean my promise to help Clarinda birth her child, I cannot possibly keep it," Gwendolyn told her apologetically. "I must leave before the storm breaks, so that Robert cannot—"

"Gwendolyn, come quickly!" pleaded Isabella, bursting into the room. "Clarinda's birthing pains have started, and that horrible Elspeth is at her bedside insisting that she will deliver the child!"

Gwendolyn grabbed her skirts and raced out the door.

"Go away!" screamed Clarinda as she writhed in pain. *"I don't want you near me!"*

"If I leave, your child will die," Elspeth said coldly, knotting a length of rope to one of the posts at the foot of the bed. "Is that what you want, foolish girl?"

"Cameron," whimpered Clarinda, her voice barely more than a sob, "please make her go away. Please!"

"Cameron is in a far better state to be sensible than you are," said Elspeth, casting him a warning look through the hot, dark room. "He knows I have birthed more bairns in this clan than anyone else, and that he should not interfere in a female matter he cannot possibly understand. Not if he wants his child to live."

Cameron raked his hand through his hair, torn by his beloved wife's suffering and the undeniable weight of Elspeth's experience.

"Don't touch me!" screamed Clarinda, flailing wildly as Elspeth tried to grab her ankle. *"Don't you dare touch me!"*

"For the love of God, Elspeth, must you tie her down?" asked Cameron.

"All this thrashing about is doing grave injury to the bairn," Elspeth informed him curtly. "We'll be lucky if it isn't dead already. I can't imagine a mother being so sinfully selfish.

Now hold her while I secure her to the bed." She grabbed Clarinda's ankle and began to twist the rope tightly around it.

"Take your hands off her, Elspeth," commanded Gwendolyn, barely able to contain her rage. *"Now."*

"You have no business here, witch," declared Elspeth, moving to secure Clarinda's other leg. "This unborn child will not belong to you or the devil you serve. Begone!"

"Gwendolyn," mewled Clarinda pitifully, "don't leave me."

"I'm not going anywhere, Clarinda," Gwendolyn assured her, hurrying over to the bed. "We have a bairn to birth— remember?" She took hold of Clarinda's sweating hand and gave it a reassuring squeeze.

"You cannot stay," snapped Elspeth. "I won't allow it."

"You're mistaken, Elspeth," Gwendolyn responded, her voice as hard as steel. "It is you who isn't staying."

Elspeth continued to lash Clarinda's other swollen ankle to the bed. "If I leave, this child will die, for God will not absolve the sins of the mother—"

"Get out!" Gwendolyn cried, still holding Clarinda's hand. "Take your ropes and your vile threats and leave this chamber at once or I will cast a spell that will turn your evil tongue into a slithering snake!"

Elspeth raised her hand to her mouth and stared at her in shock, suddenly unsure. "I will speak to MacDunn of this," she warned, speaking through her fingers.

"Do so," Gwendolyn said. "And I will tell him how you take pleasure in terrorizing helpless women as they suffer during birth!"

Elspeth cast her a long look of undiluted loathing.

And then, her hand still shielding her mouth, she turned and fled the room.

"That was wonderful!" exclaimed Isabella, who had entered the chamber with Gwendolyn. "Although I must confess, I would have enjoyed seeing her tongue change into a snake. Do you suppose it might have slithered out and bitten her on the nose?"

"Isabella, would you kindly fetch Marjorie and Lettie?"

asked Gwendolyn, her voice deliberately bright as she gently untied the cords binding Clarinda's ankles. "Tell them we are going to need their assistance, as they have some experience in this business of childbearing—and ask them to bring whatever they feel we will need."

"Why don't you just use your powers to take the bairn out?" Isabella asked.

"I think it is better to let this wee life appear naturally," Gwendolyn explained. "But I have never assisted at a birth before, and I would like Marjorie and Lettie to help."

"I will help as well," Isabella volunteered as she headed toward the door. "I won't be long."

Clarinda regarded her friend with tear-filled eyes. "Thank you, Gwendolyn. For a moment I was so afraid—"

"Hush, now, Clarinda." Gwendolyn brushed a silky lock of hair off Clarinda's forehead. "Everything is going to be just fine. My word, it's hot in here—Cameron, would you kindly open the windows?"

"It's still storming outside," Cameron pointed out, "and Elspeth said the room must be kept very warm—"

"I hardly think it can be good for either Clarinda or your bairn to inhale this awful smoke," Gwendolyn said. "Does it bother you, Clarinda?"

Clarinda nodded. "It's making me feel sick."

"There, you see? Come, now, Cameron, a little fresh, rain-washed air will do us all a world of good. And see if you can't take that fire down a bit," she added, glancing at the blazing hearth. "One would think we were preparing to roast a stag in here!"

Cameron obediently opened the windows, releasing a sweet gust of moist, grass-scented air into the chamber. The wind had eased slightly, so that no rain came into the chamber, but instead thrummed soothingly against the stone exterior of the castle.

"That's much better," Gwendolyn declared. "Now, then, Clarinda, how do you feel?"

"I feel better. I would like to get up."

Gwendolyn frowned in confusion. Just a moment earlier

Clarinda had been thrashing about in complete agony. "Really?"

"The pain is gone, and it won't be back for a little while," Clarinda told her with relative certainty. "I would like to walk a little before the next pain comes." She began to sit up.

"No, Clarinda," Cameron objected. "Elspeth said you mustn't move. You must lie still and wait for the bairn to come."

"I don't want to lie still. I want to get up. I think I will feel better if I walk a bit." She eased her legs over the side of the bed.

"Gwendolyn, tell her to get back into bed," said Cameron, searching for an ally.

Gwendolyn considered a moment. "You're not planning to run up and down the corridor or go leaping about, are you, Clarinda?"

"Of course not. I just want to walk."

"Well, there, you see, Cameron? I can hardly see how a gentle stroll could do either Clarinda or the bairn any harm."

"She needs to rest," Cameron told her firmly.

"I'm not tired," Clarinda protested impatiently.

"But you will be," Cameron assured her. "You must rest now for the long and painful suffering ahead—"

"Thank you, Cameron, for sharing your opinion with us," Gwendolyn interrupted. "But since it is Clarinda who is going to birth this bairn, I think that if she feels better sitting up, or walking, or standing on her head, then that is what she should do." She helped Clarinda to her feet, then wrapped her arm around her friend's back and began to walk across the chamber with her.

"You shouldn't be doing this, Clarinda," Cameron said sternly.

"And when you're the one giving birth, I'll be certain to tell you all about how you should do it," Clarinda retorted. "Now, why don't you go and train with the other men in the great hall while Gwendolyn and I take care of things here?"

Cameron's red brows rose in disbelief. "You want me to leave?"

"Gwendolyn will call you when we need your assistance. Won't you, Gwendolyn?"

"Aye," promised Gwendolyn, having no idea what, exactly, Cameron would be needed to do. "I will."

Cameron looked unconvinced. "You're certain?"

"I'm certain," Clarinda assured him. "Now that Gwendolyn is here, everything is going to be fine."

"Very well." He stood in front of his wife and tipped her chin up. "But you are to have Gwendolyn call me the moment you need me—is that understood?" Without waiting for an answer, he bent low and gave her a long, gentle kiss.

"Everything is going to be fine this time, my love," whispered Clarinda softly. "I can feel it."

"Aye," said Cameron, his voice gruff. He laid his hand against the hard swell of his wife's abdomen. "I can feel it as well." He kissed the top of her head.

"Oh, look, she's up—did the bairn come already?" asked Isabella, entering with Marjorie and Lettie.

"Judging by her size, I'd say the wee thing's still tucked safely inside her," said Lettie, setting down a basin and a stack of neatly folded linens. "Either that or she's been eating far too many bannocks!"

"Was it a false pain, Clarinda?" asked Marjorie, while placing a small dirk, needle, and thread, and a soft little plaid on the table. "That happens sometimes, you know. With my third one, I felt sure it was coming, and then had to wait nearly a week before he finally appeared."

"I don't believe there was anything false about it," Clarinda replied. "This bairn is coming today. It's just taking a little rest at the moment."

"Then why are you out of bed?" Marjorie asked.

"Because she feels like it," Cameron said flatly. "And since Clarinda's the one birthing the bairn, she can do as she pleases." He hesitated at the door. "But if, by chance, she decides to stand on her head, be sure to fetch me. That's a sight I'd not want to miss!" He easily ducked the pillow Clarinda tossed his way, then closed the door.

"Isabella tells us you sent Elspeth away," Lettie said, regarding Gwendolyn in amazement.

"I most certainly did." Once again she began to escort Clarinda slowly around the chamber. "Clarinda did not want her near, and that was fine by me. Can you believe she was actually tying Clarinda to the bed when I came in?"

Lettie nodded and seated herself in the chair by the hearth. "Elspeth tied me down when I birthed my wee Gareth. She ties all birthing mothers down. She believes the mother should lie still and suffer the pain in silence, since 'tis God who is sending her the pain, as punishment for her womanly sins."

"Didn't you mind being bound?" Gwendolyn asked.

"I hated it," Lettie admitted. "It made me feel helpless— like a prisoner. And I couldn't move my arms or legs to a more comfortable position when I wanted to. I was struggling as much against the bonds as I was against the pain. My wrists were so raw and sore afterward, I could scarcely hold my bairn."

"I think it's a horrible thing to do to a woman," Gwendolyn said. "I may not know much about birthing, but it seems to me one should do everything possible to make the mother more comfortable, instead of lashing her to the bed and ordering her to keep still."

"I certainly wouldn't have wanted to be tied down when I had my bairns," agreed Marjorie, sitting on the bed. "That was long before Elspeth became the clan's healer. In my day, the women who attended you just made you lie in bed until the bairn came. Which is strange," she mused, frowning, "since my mother said she always worked right up until a few minutes before the bairn pushed its way out. She claimed that when I was born, she wrapped me up, put me in the cradle, and then carried on making supper. Said my father hated it if anything interfered with his supper being ready!"

The women laughed.

"Oh my!" Clarinda gasped. She grabbed Gwendolyn for support as her knees buckled beneath her. "Oh—my." Her eyes squeezed shut, she crumpled to the floor, unable to say anything else.

"What's happening to her?" Isabella asked anxiously. "Is the bairn coming?"

"Clarinda, are you all right?" Gwendolyn knelt beside her. "Do you want us to help you to the bed?"

Clarinda held her breath, her lips locked tight as she struggled against the pain.

"Breathe deeply, Clarinda," instructed Marjorie, hurrying over to them. "Come, now, lass, a nice, deep breath. That's it. Now let it out. It won't last long—you're almost through it—and everything is just fine—you're a good lass. Just a wee bit longer, and then you'll feel much better."

"Shouldn't we do something?" demanded Gwendolyn, distressed at seeing her friend in such agony.

"There's nothing much we can do," said Lettie, who had also moved closer. "You have to suffer until you think you cannot bear it a moment longer, and then you suffer even more. And finally the bairn comes out, and you forget about everything except the wee person you hold in your arms."

"Oh!" gasped Clarinda weakly, relinquishing her crushing grip on Gwendolyn's hand. She exhaled a long, steadying breath. "That was a fierce one."

"Where is the bairn?" asked Isabella, who hadn't moved from the opposite side of the chamber. "Do you have it?"

"Not yet, Isabella," said Marjorie, smiling. "We have to wait awhile longer."

"That was very good, Clarinda," praised Gwendolyn. "You were absolutely splendid—like the mighty Torvald when he was almost torn in half by the terrible two-headed monster!"

"Perhaps that's how I should think of it," Clarinda suggested weakly. "I am a great warrior who refuses to be conquered by this pain."

"And in the end, you are rewarded by a marvelous treasure," suggested Lettie.

"You mustn't think you need to be brave," Gwendolyn

countered. "Or at least, you needn't be quiet. Make all the noise you want, do you hear?"

Clarinda smiled. "I will, Gwendolyn. Thank you."

"Would you like to walk some more?"

"Actually, I believe I will lie down for a moment. That left me feeling rather wilted."

Gwendolyn and Marjorie obligingly helped her over to the bed.

"There, now," said Gwendolyn, adjusting the pillow behind Clarinda's head. "Are you warm enough?"

"I'm fine."

"We must wait awhile now," said Marjorie, sitting on the opposite side of the bed. "It can be a slow business, waiting for a bairn."

"Why don't you tell us a story, Gwendolyn?" prompted Isabella. "That will make the time go faster."

Clarinda's expression brightened. "Tell the one about when the mighty Torvald went to slay the kelpie who had stolen the poor man's daughter—"

"—only he found she was living as a princess in a magic kingdom deep at the bottom of the loch," finished Isabella excitedly.

Gwendolyn looked at Isabella in surprise. "How do you know that story, Isabella? I have only told it to David and Clarinda."

"I—I must have heard it somewhere else," she stammered.

Gwendolyn reflected on this in confusion. The mighty Torvald was a character her father had created exclusively for her, and that particular tale was one they had made up together during one of their many walks in the mountains. She could not imagine how Isabella could possibly have heard it.

"Do tell it, Gwendolyn," prodded Lettie, pulling her chair closer to the bed. "It sounds like a wonderful tale."

"Very well." She settled herself beside Clarinda. "Long ago, in a land far beyond the edge of the ocean, there lived a magnificent warrior of extraordinary strength and courage, who was known by all as the mighty Torvald. . . ."

Afternoon slowly melted into evening, but the circle of women scarcely noticed. Gwendolyn spun the fiercest, most glorious tales she could think of, trying her best to distract Clarinda from her advancing pain. When the contractions grew stronger, she held Clarinda's hand and spoke encouragingly to her, telling her to hold fast just a little longer, and promising her that it was nearly over. And when Clarinda would collapse against the mattress and whimper that she could not bear any more, Gwendolyn would gently massage the hard, aching swell of her belly, while Isabella sponged Clarinda's face with cool water and Marjorie and Lettie spoke about what a wonderful experience it was to finally hold your very own child in your arms. More candles were lit, keeping the chamber bright, and outside the rain continued to pour, so that the air was fragrant with the sweet tang of wet heather and pine.

". . . that's it, Clarinda, you're doing just splendidly," said Gwendolyn, supporting her friend's shoulders as Clarinda heaved and strained to free her child from her body.

"I can see more of the head!" announced Marjorie excitedly. "Oh, my," she said, laughing, "what a lot of hair!"

"Let me see," said Isabella, who had thus far avoided looking anywhere near where the child was to emerge. She cautiously moved to the end of the bed, then stared at the dark, wet crown of the baby's head in shock.

And fainted dead away.

"Let's hope she manages to stay awake for her own child," quipped Gwendolyn.

"Come, now, Clarinda, you're almost there," said Lettie. "Another few pushes, and it will slip right out."

"I can't," sobbed Clarinda, sagging back into Gwendolyn's arms. "I just can't." She closed her eyes and began to weep, overcome with pain and exhaustion.

Marjorie regarded Gwendolyn with alarm. "She mustn't stop now—"

"Look at me, Clarinda," Gwendolyn commanded. "Open your eyes and look at me."

Clarinda regarded her dully. "Forgive me, Gwendolyn."

"You have nothing to apologize for," Gwendolyn told her sternly. "You are doing a wonderful job, and you are not about to give up now, do you hear? Now look at me—summon every shred of strength you have left and push, do you hear? Push!"

Clarinda closed her eyes. "I can't."

"You can, and you will," Gwendolyn informed her, using the same implacable tone she had heard Alex use when training his warriors. "We've come this far, and in another minute you'll see your bairn, but you have to work a little longer. Now take a deep breath—that's good—you're strong, Clarinda, stronger than the mighty Torvald, do you hear? Now push, and scream as loud as you can!"

Clarinda obediently pushed. And screamed. And screamed some more.

"That's it!" shouted Marjorie, elated. "Here it comes! Oh, my, Clarinda, it's a girl! Oh, she's just beautiful!"

A tiny, mewling cry filled the air as the door crashed open and Cameron burst into the chamber, his expression wild with terror.

"It's a girl, Cameron," Gwendolyn told him triumphantly, still cradling Clarinda in her arms. "A tiny, perfect lass."

Cameron stared in awe at the gray, slime-coated creature that Marjorie was holding up for him to see. His gaze moved to Clarinda, who managed a trembling smile, and then to the bloody, unfamiliar fluids soaking the linens between Clarinda's legs.

And then the fearless warrior's eyes rolled up into his head and he joined Isabella on the floor.

Gwendolyn leaned back in her chair and watched the soft play of candlelight flickering over David's cheeks. Her back and shoulders ached, and her hands were stained with purple bruises, the result of Clarinda's agonized clutch. Weary beyond measure, she closed her eyes.

Thank you, God, for keeping Clarinda and her new daughter safe.

After little Eveline's arrival, Gwendolyn and the other women had made Clarinda clean and comfortable while they all marveled over the sheer perfection of her child. They had repeatedly counted the bairn's tiny fingers and toes, and touched the soft thatch of red hair fringing her forehead, and unanimously declared that she was by far the comeliest child any of them had ever seen. Clarinda had shone with pleasure and quietly thanked them all, saying she could never have managed without them, and that although she had decided she would not be having any more children, she would happily recommend their services to the other women in the clan. And Marjorie had laughed and said she used to feel the same way after each of her bairns was born, yet somehow she managed to produce six of them. Finally Isabella awakened, so of course they had to unwrap Eveline and marvel at her fingers and toes and arms and legs once more, and Clarinda assured Isabella that she felt quite well, despite how she may have appeared earlier. The chamber had been aglow with feminine laughter and warmth, and Gwendolyn had felt strangely content, bonded to these women by the wonderful journey they had taken together that day.

Finally Cameron groaned and rose from the floor, rubbing his head. He sheepishly apologized to the women for fainting, and attributed it to the fact that he had not eaten that day, assuring them that it took much more than a little blood to bring him to the floor. Marjorie had tried to soothe his pride by telling him that childbirth was a woman's business and that men were best left to their battles. Then the women had discreetly excused themselves, leaving the new father and mother to stare in tender wonder at the child they had created.

The hour was late and most of the castle was now asleep, save for the warriors standing guard in the towers. Fortunately, the rain was still pouring down with great force, and there was little concern that Robert would attack tonight. David's brow was cool and dry, his breathing steady and deep, so there was no reason for Gwendolyn to linger in his chamber. Yet she remained, watching over him as he slumbered, vainly trying to steel her heart to the unbearable knowledge that tomorrow she would leave him.

When MacDunn first brought her here, he had ordered her to heal his son. Gwendolyn had reluctantly agreed, coolly bartering David's life in exchange for her own freedom once he was healed, a feat which she did not believe could be realized. At the time she had wanted nothing more than to escape the MacDunns and seek her vengeance on Robert. And now David was well and her time to leave had finally come.

She thought her heart would break from the pain of it.

When had she begun to care so deeply for this sweet child? she wondered bleakly. At what moment had his life become so much more important than her own? She gazed down at him with a love that was absolute—a powerful, motherly devotion she had never anticipated. Gwendolyn had not experienced the joy of bringing a new life into the world. But she had taken this dying child and labored long and hard to make him well, to heal his starving flesh and nourish his soul. And in those hours and days and weeks he had quietly captured her heart, binding her to him as surely as if he were part of her. He was not of her flesh, but her love for David was as powerful as the love of any caring mother for her child. All her life she had been accused of being a witch, and she had wondered why God would allow people to torment her so. But now she understood that God had had a reason to label her. Had she not been believed to be a witch, MacDunn would never have brought her here to save his dying son. David would have died, and she would never have known what it is to love a man and a lad to the very depths of her being. She inhaled a ragged breath as she skimmed her fingers across the softness of David's freckled cheek, down to the sweet little dent in his chin that was a gift from his father.

And then she picked up a candle and left the room, fearing if she stayed a moment longer, she would begin to weep and never stop.

"I thought I would find you here," said MacDunn,

emerging from the dark shadows of the corridor. He frowned. "Are you ill?"

"I am tired." Gwendolyn bowed her head as she quickly brushed away her tears. "That is all."

He studied her a moment. "Between standing on the parapet in the freezing rain and then spending all day and night helping Clarinda to give birth, it will be a miracle if you don't develop a burning fever and take to your bed for a month."

"I never get sick, MacDunn," Gwendolyn replied wearily. "I've told you that often enough."

"Even so, you need to sleep. I am escorting you to your chamber, and you are to rest tomorrow morning—is that clear?"

Far too exhausted to argue, Gwendolyn nodded. MacDunn offered her his arm, and she laid her hand lightly against it as she walked with him along the torchlit hallway.

"I have heard that you were invaluable in helping Clarinda to birth her daughter," he said.

"Clarinda did the hardest work."

"That is usually the case when it comes to childbirth," Alex acknowledged, trying not to smile. "But according to Marjorie, you kept Clarinda's spirits high and managed to keep her strong when she felt she could bear no more."

"Most of us can bear more than we think we can. Especially when we have no choice."

"That is true. But it is an uncommon ability, to make others believe that. It is what enables a good leader to keep his men fighting, when all they want is to lay down their swords and die."

"Had Clarinda been lashed to the bed as Elspeth had planned, she and her bairn might well have died," declared Gwendolyn, feeling fresh anger overwhelm her. "Did Elspeth tell you I ordered her to leave the chamber?"

He nodded. "She also said you threatened to transform her tongue into a snake," he added, giving her a mildly disapproving look. "It is not like you, Gwendolyn, to threaten others with your powers."

"I believe her having a snake for a tongue would be an improvement. It would make her open her mouth less."

"Regardless, I would prefer you not inflame Elspeth's distrust of you by making such threats. Most of the clan has gradually come to accept you, and if you are patient, eventually Elspeth will accept you as well."

Gwendolyn shook her head. She had no time to be patient, and she feared that when she was gone, other women would be at the mercy of Elspeth's vile methods. Before she left, she had to make sure that MacDunn would put an end to Elspeth's cruelty.

"Did you know that Elspeth binds laboring mothers to the bed as they writhe in agony, so that they cannot adjust their bodies to better birth their children?" she demanded. "You are a man and might think that is necessary, but Marjorie has birthed six children, and she assures me it is not. Lettie told me she hated being bound when she bore little Gareth, that it made her feel like a prisoner. And then Elspeth tells laboring women their pain is God's punishment for their sins, and that they mustn't scream, but they must endure it in silence, making them feel like they have sinned if they utter a sound. And if something is wrong with their child, or it is born dead, she blames the poor mother, as if the agonized woman could have somehow prevented it!"

For a moment Alex was too appalled to speak. He knew little about the business of childbirth, but what Gwendolyn had just described was utterly obscene. Elspeth had tended Flora during all her births, and two of those children had been born dead. Not once had Flora made any suggestion to him that she had been mistreated by Elspeth during her ordeal. Perhaps his gentle wife had been too naive to understand the atrocity of her treatment. Or perhaps the painful shock of the bairns' deaths had obliterated all memory of being trussed like an animal and told that she was responsible for her child's death. A terrible guilt enveloped him, coupled with a sudden, searing pain that seemed to cleave right through his skull.

"I—I did not know this," he stammered, wondering how

such a thing could have been kept from him. "No one told me."

"Most women are far too embarrassed to ever discuss such a delicate matter with their laird, or even their husbands," Gwendolyn explained. "And then of course many must believe Elspeth is right and that they must simply endure her horrid methods. But whatever the reason for their silence, you must speak with Elspeth. You are laird of all those women who have suffered, and those who will continue to suffer in Elspeth's care. It is your responsibility to protect them from such barbarous treatment."

Her gray eyes were wide and earnest, and her lower lip trembled slightly, making it clear how vital this issue was to her. Alex found himself deeply moved by her desire to protect the MacDunn women.

"I will speak with Elspeth tomorrow," he promised, stopping before Gwendolyn's door. "And I will make certain she abandons these practices immediately."

"Thank you."

Her black hair was spilling wildly over her badly wrinkled gown, giving her a sweetly disheveled look that only endeared her more to him. The memory of lying naked with her last night flooded his senses, stirring his body and heating his blood. He wanted to lift her into his arms and take her to his bed, to hold her and kiss her and pleasure her until neither of them could bear any more. But dark crescents bruised the delicate skin beneath her eyes, and if it was possible, her face seemed even paler than usual. He sensed a deep melancholy to her as well, which he attributed to her severe fatigue. Last night he had kept her awake deep into the hours of early morning, and then she had endured a day that had been both physically and emotionally exhausting. The sight of her looking so frail troubled him.

"You will stay in bed until these marks under your eyes have faded," he ordered, tracing them with the tip of his finger. "If I see you appear before then, I will carry you back to bed myself. Is that understood?"

Gwendolyn nodded as she stared up at him. She would

never see him again after this moment, for she would be gone long before the castle began to stir. There was suddenly much she wanted to tell him, and yet she found she could not speak, for fear her tears would betray her and make him suspicious. And so she regarded him in silent anguish, memorizing the burnished gold of his hair and brows, the brilliant blue of his eyes, the elegantly chiseled line of his jaw, and that distinctive cleft in his chin that he had passed on to his son. *I will keep you safe,* he had vowed, and she knew he believed such a feat was possible, even if it meant he had to die to achieve it. But he had a son who needed him, and a clan who depended upon him. She could not let any of them suffer for something as insignificant as the preservation of her life.

"Good night, Gwendolyn." Alex bent and pressed a kiss to her forehead. He did not trust himself to kiss her mouth, knowing desire would overwhelm him. "Sleep well."

She tentatively raised her hand to his jaw, then slowly traced her fingers along the same path she had taken with his son; down the sandy plane of his sun-bronzed cheek, finally stopping at the depression in his chin. *I love you,* she told him silently, wondering if he could feel it in her touch. *I always will.*

"What is it?" Alex demanded, sensing her distress.

She abruptly took her hand away. "Nothing," she whispered, turning from him. "Sleep well, MacDunn." She slipped into her chamber and closed the door, then listened. She heard him hesitate a moment, perhaps waiting to see if she might emerge again.

Finally he left, his gait slow but sure as he made his way to his own chamber.

Gwendolyn approached the bed with leaden legs, using her candle to guide her through the shadows. There was something lying upon her pillow. Anticipating yet another talisman of iron or horse bone, or perhaps even a bloodstone, which was thought to have the power to break spells, she approached it with weary indifference. But as she drew closer she saw the shimmering handle of a dirk. She stopped and glanced nervously around the chamber, thinking that whoever had left this for her might still be lurking in the shadows. Then she reached out and pulled the dirk from the pillow, freeing the scrap of paper that had been skewered on its wickedly sharp point.

> Gwendolyn,
>
> Whatever the price, it will be mine. You will bring the stone to me at the south end of the woods before first light, or I swear I shall not rest until every MacDunn man, woman, and child lies butchered on the ground, and that mad fool's head has been hacked from his body and placed in the hands of his precious son.
>
> Their fate lies within your power.
>
> Robert

Sick, dark fear spiraled up from the pit of her stomach. MacDunn. She must show this to MacDunn. She raced toward the door, clutching the note in her hand. And then she stopped. What could MacDunn possibly do? she wondered helplessly. He could not prevent Robert from burning the cottages and laying siege to the castle. Nor could he keep his people trapped within these walls forever. Eventually the MacDunns would have to go out, whether to find food or to face Robert's army. The instant they did, Robert would cut them to pieces. There would be unimaginable suffering and death, because MacDunn had sworn to keep her safe, and he would fight to the hideous, blood-drenched end trying to keep his word.

She could not let him do that.

She inhaled a steadying breath, fighting to master her panic. She had planned to leave tonight, hoping to lure Robert away by leaving a note for him with the MacDunns, saying that she was returning to the MacSween lands to retrieve the stone, and Robert and his army should follow her there. That was impossible now. Robert was giving her an ultimatum, and he would tolerate nothing less than his terms. She had no choice but to go to him. Once he learned that the stone was hidden on MacSween land, he would not waste any more time here. He would depart before light, aroused by the promise of finally having that powerful charm within his evil grasp. No doubt he believed that once he had used it to give him unbridled power, he would massacre MacDunn and his people anyway.

But the moment she held the stone in her hands, she would use its power to destroy Robert instead.

CHAPTER 13

"What do you mean, she's gone?"

Ned grimly handed him a damp, rumpled square of paper. Filled with dread, Alex forced himself to take it.

> MacDunn,
>   I shall always be grateful to you for pulling me from the fire and bringing me to your home.
>   For one brief moment, I almost belonged somewhere.
>
> > Gwendolyn

Fear clenched his chest, making it difficult to breathe. He turned from his training warriors and raced into the castle, taking the stairs three at a time in his haste to reach Gwendolyn's chamber. The door flew open with a thundering crash as he entered, absolutely determined that he would find her obediently resting in her bed.

The chamber was empty, the bed untouched, except for a few feathers that were clinging to the plaid. Frowning, Alex went over and studied the pillow. More feathers were protruding from a small slash in the center of the cushion.

"Where did you find this note?" he demanded as Ned, Cameron, and Brodick entered the room.

"She must have given it to me," replied Ned. "Last night."

"What do you mean, 'must have'?" asked Cameron, quickly scanning the note with Brodick. "Can you not remember?"

Ned shook his head in frustration. "Late last night I saw her emerge from this chamber dressed in a dark cloak. She told me that she needed a special herb she had seen in the courtyard, to use in an elixir she was making to ease Clarinda's pain. I asked her if it couldn't wait until morning, and she said this particular herb must be gathered at night, or else it lost its healing powers. And so I agreed to go with her. She searched the grounds in vain, then told me there was a place where the herb grew in abundance just beyond the castle walls. I told her it wasn't safe to leave the courtyard, but she pleaded with me, saying Clarinda had suffered greatly while birthing her bairn and that if I were Cameron I'd not be so heartless as to deny her request. And then she added that with the storm raging so hard, Robert and his warriors were likely halfway back to MacSween lands. Finally I relented, and ordered Garrick to let us pass through the gate." Remorse shadowed his face. "I know it was wrong, Alex."

"Go on," Alex said tersely, uninterested in the issue of blame.

"Once we were beyond the walls, Gwendolyn withdrew a skin of wine from her cloak and asked me if I would like a drop, to keep me warm. I swear I took no more than a swallow or two, but it must have been drugged, for soon I could barely keep my eyes open. She suggested I sit beneath a tree and rest while she collected the herb." He gave a helpless shrug. "The next thing I knew, I woke up with the sun shining in my face, and Gwendolyn was nowhere to be found. She must have placed the note in my shirt when I was asleep."

Pain webbed through Alex's head, making him feel dizzy and unfocused. Gone. She was gone. But where? And why? He rubbed his temple as he scanned the letter again, searching for some clue, some explanation as to why she would suddenly leave in the middle of a storm.

For one brief moment, I almost belonged somewhere.

Is that what she thought? he wondered helplessly. His son adored her, Clarinda would have no other by her as she birthed her child, and although his clan had often tried to drive her away, ultimately they had been prepared to fight to the death for her against Robert. How could there be any question as to whether she belonged here?

"Clarinda will be devastated when she learns Gwendolyn is gone," reflected Cameron. "She has come to feel like a sister to her."

And David would be heartbroken, Alex realized dully. Which of course Gwendolyn must have known. He thought of her emerging from David's chamber the previous night, her gray eyes shimmering with despondence. At the time he had attributed her melancholy to weariness, coupled with the rawness of emotion a woman might experience after helping to bring a new life into the world. He was a fool, he realized. The despair in Gwendolyn's expression was one he should have recognized instantly, for he had seen it often enough as Flora lay dying. It was the tormented look of a woman who must leave those she loved behind. That was why she was so adamant that he promise to speak to Elspeth about her methods with birthing mothers. Gwendolyn had known she would not be here to help them herself. He closed his eyes, damning himself for his blindness as he recalled her exquisite touch skimming along the contour of his jaw.

She had been saying good-bye to him, and he had been too consumed with lust to recognize it.

" 'Tis strange that she would choose to leave in the middle of a storm," Brodick said, frowning. "I mean, why couldn't she have waited a day or two, until it was over?"

"Gwendolyn conjured up that storm to keep Robert from burning the cottages," Ned pointed out. "I don't suppose it bothered her much, since it was her spell that made it."

"Odd, though, that Robert hasn't paid us a visit now that the storm is over," Brodick reflected. "Do you suppose he really has gone home?"

A sickening realization began to swirl through Alex.

"By what I've seen of him, I'd not think Robert is the type to give up so easily," Cameron observed. "Surely the lass must have realized he and his men might well be camped somewhere in the woods. Was she not afraid of getting caught?"

"She wanted to be caught," Alex said, his voice hollow. "That's why she left."

"That makes no sense, Alex," protested Brodick. "She knows Robert will burn her, and she knew she was safe here. Why on earth would she want to be caught?"

Alex stared vacantly at the note. *I almost belonged somewhere.* Moments before Robert arrived, she had told him of what her life had been, living completely ostracized by everyone. Yet when Robert attacked, the MacDunns had not turned her over as she had feared they might, but instead had fought to defend her. It seemed Gwendolyn could not accept the MacDunns risking their lives for her. That was why she had climbed onto the parapet and challenged Robert to shoot her, hoping to bring an end to the battle. And that was why she was offering him her life now.

She was trying to protect Alex's people.

"Look at this," said Brodick, fishing a scrap of paper from the hearth.

The note was badly burned, but the dampness of the ashes had extinguished the flames before the paper was completely consumed by them. Holding it gingerly between his fingers, Alex read:

*mad fool's head has
been hacked from his body and placed in the hands of
his precious son.*

Their fate lies within your power.

Robert

"Christ," he swore, his fear suddenly shadowed by the
magnitude of his rage. "Robert threatened her with killing me,
to force her to go to him." He crushed the paper within his
shaking fist and hurled it into the hearth. "Divide the men
into two forces. Half will remain here to defend the castle. The
others will ride with me."

Cameron stroked his beard as he stared at the scorched
ball lying in the ashes. "How do you suppose he got a note
into her chamber?"

"That's a good question," snapped Alex, striding out of
the room, "and I damn well intend to find out."

"Gone?" repeated Owen blankly. "Gone where?"

"She can't be gone," Lachlan said, looking genuinely
crestfallen. "I've made a special wine for her."

Alex shoved his dirk into his belt. "You will have to save
it, Lachlan, for when I bring her home."

"But why would the lass want to leave us?" Owen asked.
"I thought we were all getting along splendidly."

"I found a note from Robert in her chamber saying if she
didn't surrender to him, Robert would kill me," Alex explained.

Reginald grabbed for his sword and roared, "By all the
saints, I'll mince the swine so fine, the frogs will have to lick
him off the ground!"

"You mean my uncle was in this castle?" asked Isabella,
her face paling.

There was a moment of stunned silence.

Farquhar belched and gazed blearily about the great hall.
"I don't recall seeing Robert skulking about." He sighed and
buried his face back into his cup.

"If one of those bloody MacSweens got in here, it wasn't through the gate," Garrick assured Alex. "Me and Quentin kept a careful watch, and the only people who went through last night were Ned and Gwendolyn."

"What about during the day?" Brodick asked. "We had the gate open while we inspected the outer wall."

"Well, now, that's true enough," agreed Garrick. "But you can't expect me to recall everyone who passed through during the day—especially since many of you had your heads covered to protect you from the rain."

"I don't, Garrick," Alex assured him. "What I want to know is, did any of you notice someone entering or leaving Gwendolyn's chamber yesterday?" He scrutinized the faces assembled before him, searching for a flicker of reaction. His gaze fell hard upon Elspeth, knowing she had every reason to want Gwendolyn gone. But her expression remained utterly flat, betraying no hint of either guilt or intrigue. "Alice?" he prompted, suddenly detecting a shadow of uncertainty cross the cook's face.

Alice regarded him nervously.

"Did you see someone in Gwendolyn's chamber?"

"I was taking her a tray," Alice said, wringing her apron with her hands. "I knew the lass had been helping Clarinda birth her bairn for most of the day. I thought she might need a wee bite to eat."

"That was very thoughtful of you," commented Alex. "And so you went into her chamber?"

She shook her head.

"You left the tray outside the door?"

She shook her head again.

"Then what did you do with the tray?" demanded Alex, struggling for patience.

"I gave it to Robena," Alice blurted out. "She was just coming out of Gwendolyn's chamber. She said she would take the tray inside for me. She was most adamant about it."

There was a hushed gasp as all eyes in the hall fastened on Robena, who was standing near Alex.

"Surely you cannot believe that I had anything to do with

Gwendolyn's leaving, Alex," she scoffed lightly. "I simply took the tray into her chamber and left. I've no idea how that note came to be on her pillow."

For a moment Alex was too stunned to speak. Robena and he had been friends since they were children, and he did not want to believe that she could possibly have anything to do with Gwendolyn's disappearance. But cold, simple logic forced him to finally ask, "How do you know it was left on her pillow, Robena?"

"I—you said it was," Robena stammered. "I'm sure you did."

"No, Robena," he replied, fighting to control his dismay, "I did not."

She stared at him a long moment, her blue eyes suddenly wide and frozen, like a trapped animal. He wanted to be furious with her, but instead he felt hopelessly sick and hollow. When Flora had fallen ill, Robena had been a steadfast source of strength and encouragement, and during the nightmare of madness that followed, she never once wavered in either her devotion to him or the conviction that he would eventually be well again. As she stood there staring at him, her lips trembling and her eyes shimmering with desperation, he suddenly understood why she had been so relentlessly faithful to him for all those years.

She loved him.

"Was the note really from Robert?" Alex asked quietly. "Or did you script it yourself?"

She shook her head. "I don't know anything about the—"

"Robena," Alex interrupted, "I would have the truth from you."

Her gaze dropped to the ground. "It was from Robert." Her voice was small and quivering. "I knew he was going to burn our homes to the ground and starve us to death. And so I slipped beyond the gate while you were inspecting the wall, and sought him out in the woods. I asked him what it would cost for him to leave us in peace. And he told me if he had the witch, he would leave. So I agreed to deliver the note for him." She regarded Alex with large, pleading eyes. "She would have killed you, Alex, and I could not bear that," she said vehemently. "That witch had cast a spell over you, making you unable to see the terrible destruction she was bringing to the clan. And every day the spell grew stronger, and more of the clan fell under it. I had to make her leave, before she destroyed all of us."

Alex considered this, wanting to believe her. Finally he shook his head. "You have been trying to get rid of her from the moment she arrived, Robena," he said, somehow unable to summon any rage. "You threaded a string across the stairs knowing she would trip and injure herself. When that didn't work, you trapped her in her room and set fire to it, hoping to either kill her or at least scare her away. Was this also an attempt to protect the clan?"

"She was a witch," Robena insisted desperately. "She came here to practice her evil ways. She wanted to enslave us to the devil!"

"No, Robena. She came here because I forced her to. And she stayed because she wanted to heal my son. That is all."

Tears sparkled in her eyes. "She cast a spell over you, Alex," she said, her voice breaking as he slowly approached her. "She changed you. You are still under that spell, so you cannot see it. But one day you will be better, and then you will know I did the right thing. Now that she is gone, it will be as it was before."

Alex reached out and laid his hand against her cheek. "I'm sorry, Robena," he murmured, his voice gentle, "but we were not meant to be together."

Robena shook her head. "You don't know that. You are angry with me, and you cannot see it. But with time—"

"No, Robena. Not now. Not ever. Do you understand me? It will not happen."

Robena stared at him as if he had slapped her.

And then she turned and fled the hall, filling the uneasy silence with the sound of her weeping.

"Dear me," said Owen, scratching his white head. "Do forgive, MacDunn, but I believe that lass is rather taken with you."

Alex closed his eyes and rubbed his temples. The pain in his head had worsened. "Cameron and Brodick, take the men outside and divide them into two forces," he ordered tautly. "One will remain here to defend the castle and the other will ride with me. We leave in ten minutes."

"Excellent," said Lachlan, rubbing his hands together. "That gives me just enough time to whip up another batch of my potion."

"I'm ready to leave anytime," declared Reginald, cheerfully patting his sword. "I'll just fetch some of that elixir Gwendolyn made to settle my belly. Marvelous stuff, really. You might want to try some of it for that pain in your head, MacDunn."

"I cannot see how a belly potion could possibly cure the lad's head," scoffed Owen. "He should use the liniment she made for my hands," he decided, holding his palms up and proudly flexing his fingers to demonstrate their newfound dexterity. "I'll bring some along for you, Alex, so you can try rubbing it into your scalp."

"That's a fool notion if ever I heard one," snorted Lachlan. "How is he supposed to face Robert with that stinking liniment dripping from his head? When you first put the ghastly stuff on, I can barely tolerate being in the same room with you."

Owen's white brows snapped together. "Do forgive, Lachlan, but I hardly think you're in any position to comment on the issue of aroma."

"He's right, you know," added Reginald. "Have you any inkling how much you reek after making that revolting potion of yours?"

Lachlan gasped with outrage. "That potion is a deadly military weapon. . . ."

Alex regarded the three bickering elders in complete bewilderment. Owen, Lachlan, and Reginald rarely ventured outside, and he certainly could not remember the last time they went beyond the safety of the castle walls. "Do you think you're coming with me?" he asked, confused.

The three elders ceased their arguing and looked at him.

"Of course we're coming, lad," Owen assured him. "We have to help you save our witch."

"Those MacSweens really have no right to her, you know," added Reginald. "We have to make them see that."

"The lass belongs with us," finished Lachlan. "I've said so from the beginning."

Alex blinked, unable to believe what he was hearing. How had Gwendolyn managed to bewitch these three old men to the point that they were willing to abandon the safety of their castle and fight to bring her back?

The same way she had bewitched him, he reflected soberly. By being strong, and honest, and caring. By bringing the healing power of her presence to those whom she sensed needed it. She had taken a dying lad and brought him back to life, not with bleedings and purgings and other foul tortures, but with gentleness and patience, and perhaps even a little magic. Gwendolyn had thrown open the shutters and flooded their world with light, banishing the darkness and misery that had clung to the castle like a dark shroud since Flora's death. And by doing so, she had inadvertently won a battle of her own, he realized. She had finally overcome the fear and suspicion of others, and made them see her for what she really was.

A woman of immense courage and compassion, who would risk anything for those she cared for.

He had told her she belonged to him, but he had been wrong, he realized humbly. Gwendolyn was far too fine and rare to ever belong to anyone. She belonged *with* him, and with these people who were ready to die for her. Once he saved her from Robert, he would do everything within his power to make her understand that.

However, he had no intention of setting out to rescue her with these three squabbling old men in tow.

"Your desire to make such a long and arduous journey to bring Gwendolyn home pleases me," he said. "Even the youngest and fittest of my warriors will scarcely be able to endure the grueling hours astride a horse, the scant moments of rest upon the damp, hard ground, and the savagery of the battle that is to follow . . ."

The council members blinked.

". . . and so I look forward to having you on this punishing mission, even though I had hoped one of you might remain here to help protect the clan from further attack—"

"I'm happy to stay and look after things here," Owen offered. "Only because you insist," he added.

"I'll stay as well," decided Reginald. "Not that your younger chaps aren't fine soldiers, but you need a warrior here who knows what he's about in battle."

"Perhaps I'll just give you some of my potion to take with you," suggested Lachlan. "You don't really need me there to show you how to use it. Just hurl it at them and run."

Alex regarded them in feigned surprise. "Are you sure?"

"Quite sure, lad," said Owen. "Just make certain you tell Gwendolyn we would have been there if we weren't needed so desperately here."

"Aye," said Reginald. "I'd hate for her to think we'd abandoned her to that scoundrel."

"I'll be sure to tell her," Alex said, heading toward the door.

"And tell that Robert chap that Gwendolyn is most certainly not an object, and should not be referred to as such," added Lachlan crossly. " 'It will be mine,' indeed. What is the matter with young warriors today? Have they no manners whatsoever?"

The comment barely registered with Alex until he reached the door. And then he frowned. "What did you say, Lachlan?"

"I said, tell that ill-mannered brute that he is not to—"

"After that," interrupted Alex. "How did Robert refer to Gwendolyn?"

"As an it," Lachlan replied. "I heard him very clearly, just before he and his men retreated into the storm. *It will be mine!* he shouted, as if she were a plate or a stool. I never heard anything so shamelessly rude in my life."

And then Alex remembered Robert's final words.

Damn you, MacDunn. It will be mine.

At the time Alex had been far too overwhelmed with fear for Gwendolyn to heed Robert's choice of words. But suddenly it disturbed him. Gwendolyn had made herself a perfect target when she stood upon the parapet and invited the MacSweens to shoot her with a burning arrow. Yet Robert had ordered his men to hold. If his sole aspiration was to see the witch burned, why would he scorn such an opportunity? *It will be mine.* Just what the hell did Robert mean by that?

Determined to find out, he went to seek out the one person who might know.

~~~ "I've been expecting you." Morag did not look up as she carefully poured a dark red liquid into a simmering pot. A gasp of steam rose into the air, making the sickly sweet odor choking the room even more cloying.

"Gwendolyn has surrendered herself to Robert," Alex informed her grimly.

Morag nodded as she stirred the pot with a heavy iron ladle. "It was time."

"The hell it was," he roared, infuriated by her calm demeanor. "She belongs here."

Morag looked up from her stirring and regarded him curiously. "How do you know?"

Alex shook his pounding head in frustration. "I have no time for games, Morag. I need to know why Robert is so determined to have her. It is clear from his actions the other night that he wants her alive, not dead. The bastard wants to force her to use her powers for his benefit, doesn't he?"

"And how does that make him any different from you?" she asked quietly.

"I did not ask her to bring me wealth or power. All I asked was that she save my son."

"You did not ask her. You gave her no choice. You told her that if she saved David, her life would be spared, but she would remain your prisoner. Remember?"

He looked away, suddenly ashamed. He did remember telling Gwendolyn that.

And she had told him to simply kill her and be done with it, for she would not live her life as a prisoner.

"That was before," he said, desperately wishing he had never issued such a foul ultimatum. "My son was dying and I—I was not myself. It is not the same now. You must realize that."

Morag thoughtfully tapped her ladle against the pot and set it down by the hearth. "You are right, Alex. You are not the same. And neither is Gwendolyn. That is why she could not stay and ask you to defend her."

"She thinks that by sacrificing herself to Robert, she is saving my life. But she is wrong." He cleared his throat, embarrassed by the tremor in his voice. "She is wrong, Morag."

"I know," said Morag softly. Leaning on her staff, she slowly made her way across the chamber, then seated herself in a chair. "It is not easy, having powers that are not readily explained," she reflected, her green eyes meditative. "Once people know what you are, they either want to use you or destroy you. Or, as in Robert's case with Gwendolyn, both."

Alex fought to control his panic. "That doesn't make any sense. How can he use her for her powers if he kills her?"

"He cannot. Unfortunately, Robert does not understand the nature of Gwendolyn's powers—any more than she does. That is what puts her in grave danger."

"Morag, please," said Alex, struggling to understand what she was telling him, "just tell me what Robert wants of her. I have to know. What did he mean when he said, 'It will be mine'?"

For a long moment she studied him. "Can it be true, Alex?" she finally asked, her voice threaded with wonder. "Have you really lost your heart to one other than Flora?"

Alex said nothing. He didn't have to.

Morag closed her eyes. "There is a stone," she finally began, "a brilliant red jewel of magnificent size and clarity that fills nearly all who look upon it with the overwhelming desire to possess it. This has been passed down from mother to daughter in Gwendolyn's family for over three hundred years."

"And that's all that Robert wants? This red stone?"

"It is not merely a pretty bauble. The women of

Gwendolyn's lineage are occasionally gifted with special powers. Gwendolyn has been so gifted, but her mother was not, nor was her grandmother before that. The stone's purpose is to protect these special girls when they are children, before their powers are fully mature."

Alex frowned. "What possible good is that to Robert?"

"It is not of any use to him. Unfortunately, a legend has arisen over the centuries, saying that once every hundred years, the stone has the power to grant its bearer a single wish. It is this power that Robert seeks. In his hunger to have it, he murdered Gwendolyn's father and accused her of the crime. But Gwendolyn had hidden the stone well, and Robert was unable to find it. Now only she knows where it lies, and only she can give it to him."

"And once he has it, he will kill her," finished Alex harshly.

Morag nodded. "Gwendolyn has long haunted Robert, as much because of her unusual beauty and strength as because of the stone. Robert is not a man who can tolerate weakness, and that is how he interprets his desire for her. Once he has secured the stone, he will seek to purge himself of his lust for her—by destroying her."

Alex turned and strode swiftly toward the door.

"There is something more you must know, Alex," Morag called out.

He stopped.

"Gwendolyn's mother was burned when Gwendolyn was a tender age, robbing her of the knowledge of her heritage. She does not understand her powers, nor does she comprehend the true purpose of the stone. She may think she can use the stone to destroy Robert. If she tries, she will fail, and Robert's rage will be horrendous."

Alex jerked the door open and raced down the corridor, desperate to get to Gwendolyn before she retrieved this useless stone.

CHAPTER 14

Brilliant strips of silver cracked the velvety darkness, briefly illuminating the mysterious assembly of carefully arranged rocks standing tall before them. The enormous stones had an austere, almost menacing quality; they stretched across the charcoal ground like a powerful army lying in wait, guarding their ancient secrets in hallowed silence.

It was, thought Gwendolyn, a fitting place for Robert to die.

"Is this it?" he demanded, his impatience eclipsing the bone-numbing weariness from which Gwendolyn and his men had suffered for several days.

She nodded.

"Get it, then. Now."

"You're an even bigger fool than I realized," she observed, casting him a scornful look. "No man is able to look upon the jewel's extraordinary beauty without wanting it. I shall barely be able to pass it to you before your own men fall prey to its allure. You will be dead long before you have the chance to curl your greedy fingers around it."

The corners of his mouth twitched. "Your concern for my welfare is moving, Gwendolyn." He reached out and grabbed her by her hair, nearly wrenching her off her horse as he forced her to look at him. "You think that if we are alone you will have a chance to kill me, don't you?"

"I don't need to kill you," Gwendolyn retorted in a cold, hard voice. "I have seen your death, Robert, and it is far more painful and hideous than anything I could manage on my own."

He slapped her hard across the face, holding her head steady so she could not evade the full impact of his hand. "You cannot see the future, Gwendolyn," he scoffed, but there was a flicker of uncertainty in his gaze. "If you could, you would have been able to save your father."

Gwendolyn regarded him steadily, refusing to betray any emotion other than hatred.

And then, sensing it would unnerve him, she smiled.

Robert abruptly released her. "Derek, come here."

An oily ripple of light from the black-haired warrior's torch pulsed across his face as he rode forward, illuminating the ugly, jagged scar beneath his left eye.

"A parting gift from you on the day you escaped, witch," Derek said as she stared at it. "Rest assured, I intend to repay you in full."

"Give me your torch," ordered Robert, "and take the men just beyond the crest of that hill. I will signal when I am ready for you to return."

The warrior scowled. "I thought we were going to take her back to the castle to burn her."

"I have some unfinished business I wish to settle with her first," Robert replied.

"If you're going to rape her, you should at least let us watch," grumbled Hamish. "After all, we never got to pillage MacDunn's castle and use his women."

"He's right, Robert," Derek decided. "And since it seems

I'm not getting Isabella, I deserve to have this one when you're finished with her." His mouth split into a rotting smile.

"Silence!" roared Robert, withdrawing his sword. "Move to the crest of the hill now, before I hack your insolent tongues out!"

Derek reluctantly tossed his torch to Robert. He cast one last dark look at Gwendolyn, then angrily wheeled his horse about and rode toward the lightning streaking over the hill. The other warriors quickly followed him.

"And so we are alone," observed Robert, sheathing his sword. "Satisfied?"

Gwendolyn slid off her horse and adjusted her cloak as she moved toward the forbidding spires of rock, ignoring him. She slowly approached a tall, craggy slab in the center of the stone army and laid her hand against it, drawing strength from its rough coolness. This one had been her father's favorite, she reflected, skimming her fingers tenderly across its pocked surface. The edges of its irregular shape had been smoothed by time and wind and rain, and silvery green lichen was creeping across its hard skin. Her father had told her that this rock had been placed here by the mighty Torvald after he successfully battled the evil MacRory. Each time she and her father came here, they would sit before a different boulder and he would tell her the glorious tale that resulted in the stone being added to the mighty Torvald's secret garden.

"What are you doing?" demanded Robert. "Is the jewel here or isn't it?"

"I'm not certain which of these standing rocks I buried it under," she lied. "I believe it is this one."

He swung off his horse and moved toward her, carrying the torch. "Then dig it up."

She obediently sank to her knees and began to scratch at the ground with her fingers.

"Use that," he ordered, tossing his dirk onto the ground. "But try to cut anything beyond the earth, Gwendolyn, and I'll splay you with my sword like a fish for the fire."

She stabbed the blade into the ground and began to crudely dig up the packed earth at the base of the standing rock. For an instant she imagined that she was the mighty Torvald and that she had the strength to turn and bury the dirk deep within Robert's chest. But she would not need the strength of the mighty Torvald to kill Robert, she reminded herself coldly. Once she held the stone in her hand, she would simply use its power to slay him. His death would not be quick, she vowed, for Robert did not deserve the dignity of a swift demise. No, she would wish for something hideously slow and painful. Perhaps she would have him consumed by fire, in retaliation for the death he tried to give her. She lingered over the image of his flesh blackening on his bones as he screamed in agony. Robert's warriors would thunder down from that hill and slay her when they discovered their master was dead, but it did not matter. MacDunn and David and the rest of their clan would be safe. As for the stone, the instant she made her wish she would return it to its shallow grave, so it could sleep safely beneath these forbidding rock sentries for another hundred years.

"Have you found it yet?" Robert asked, growing increasingly agitated. He lowered his torch, trying to ascertain her progress. "Is it there?"

"I'm not certain." Gwendolyn chopped at the ground with her blade. How deeply had she buried it? "This may not be the right place."

"Give me the dirk," he snapped, snatching the weapon from her hand as he roughly pushed her out of his way. "I will find the bloody thing myself."

"No!" protested Gwendolyn. If Robert touched the stone before she did, he would make his wish and all would be lost. "I'm certain I can find it faster than you."

"And no doubt you plan to use it against me once you have found it," he surmised astutely. "No, Gwendolyn, I have not come this far to have you cheat me at the last moment. Hold this," he ordered, shoving the torch at her. "And keep the flame low so I can see."

He hacked at the ground like a man possessed, cutting a huge trough beneath the dark rock watching over him. Another moment and he would reach the stone, Gwendolyn realized helplessly. Robert would make himself the cruelest, most vicious tyrant Scotland had ever known, and MacDunn and his clan would be ruthlessly crushed.

And then the mighty Torvald brought his sword crashing down, her father's voice rumbled from some distant memory, *smashing it against his enemy's back. . . .*

Summoning every shred of her strength, she smashed the torch against Robert's shoulders. A shower of fiery sparks exploded into the air as Robert fell face first into the shallow pit he had dug.

"By God, *I'll kill you!*" he roared, spitting dirt from his mouth. He scrambled to his feet and stalked toward her. Gwendolyn cautiously retreated, holding the flaming club in front of her.

"Goddamn bitch," he swore, his earth-crusted mouth twisted with rage. "I'm going to make you feel pain unlike anything you've ever imagined, and I'm going to enjoy every min—"

His tirade was cut short by another shocked bellow. Gwendolyn raced around him as he wildly beat himself about the head, trying to smother the flames now dancing up his hair. She dropped the torch and fell to her knees before the standing rock, clawing desperately at the ground.

Please God, let it be here.

Nothing but earth churned beneath her fingers. She let out a desperate sob. *Where are you?* Suddenly her nail caught on a damp fold of fabric. Tearing it up with her hands, she unraveled the grubby, limp cloth and grabbed the dark jewel lying within, closing her fingers around it as its chain spilled from her fist.

"Stay back!" she hissed, brandishing the stone like a holy relic. "One more step and I'll kill you!"

Robert hesitated.

And then a hard smile oozed across his dirt-streaked face. "Do it, then," he invited, slowly moving toward her. "Let us finally see if that precious pebble actually works."

"I will use it, Robert," Gwendolyn warned him. "Stay where you are!"

"We have come too far, you and I," he mused, still advancing, "not to see this thing to the end."

"Don't make me do it." She was almost pleading as she began to back away. "Don't."

"Do you know why I first went to visit your cottage?" he asked, his voice dropping to a gentle croon. "Why I risked my reputation to visit your father, when everyone in the clan believed the devil himself dwelled within those walls? It was because of you, Gwendolyn. Despite the vile things everyone said of you, I wanted to know you."

"You knew they were lies," Gwendolyn retorted. "You were the only one in the clan who knew I wasn't a witch. That is why you weren't afraid of me."

"I could not believe you could be evil," he said wistfully. "You were far too beautiful, and far too sad, to be capable of inflicting suffering on others."

"Don't pretend you cared about my unhappiness," she hissed, clutching the stone tighter. "You murdered my father!"

"That was an accident." His voice was filled with regret. "I never meant to harm him. He had been drinking too much that night and he fell."

"Liar!" she spat, still backing away. "You wanted him to give you the stone, and when he refused, you fought with him and killed him. And then you blamed the murder on me, knowing full well that no one in the clan would rise to my defense."

"No, Gwendolyn, you're wrong. I tried to tell the clan it had been an accident, but they wouldn't listen—I even argued with my brother over it. But everyone in the clan wanted you dead, and there was nothing I could do to stop them."

She shook her head. "You told me when I was imprisoned that you could make the clan spare my life if I would only tell you where this stone was hidden. When I refused, you left me to die!"

"I had fallen victim to the stone's legendary power," he explained, apologetic. "That is what made me act in such an unfathomable way. But I never wanted to see you come to harm, Gwendolyn," he insisted, still easing toward her. "You must believe me."

"Stay away from me, Robert, or I'll tell the stone to burn you to death!"

"Could you really do such a hideous thing, Gwendolyn?" he asked quietly. "Could you really stand there and watch me burn?"

"It is no more than you deserve!" she said, feeling her resolve eroding. "You were going to slaughter MacDunn's entire clan, and cut off his head and give it to his son!"

"How can you believe I am capable of such a heinous act?" he asked, sounding wounded. "I said that because I wanted you to come to me. It was an idle threat, Gwendolyn, nothing more. Look at me." Once again he was closing the distance between them. "Can you honestly believe I am this terrible monster you have painted?"

Tears blurred her eyes, softening his appearance. He looked utterly defeated, with his burned hair curling in ragged wisps around his dirt-smudged face, and a solemn expression that was filled with remorse. She almost believed he was telling the truth, or at least some portion of what he believed the truth to be. If she didn't kill him he would kill her, she reminded herself desperately, taking another step backward. She had to do it. And yet she hesitated, profoundly torn by the thought of bringing this man's life to an end when he was pleading with her for compassion. She stepped back again, colliding abruptly with a standing stone.

Robert instantly leaped forward and wrenched the jewel from her.

"At last," he breathed, staring lasciviously at the glittering gem, "you are finally mine."

"No!" Gwendolyn gasped, trying to grab it from him.

Robert struck her hard against the face with the back of his hand. She cried out as she went flying to the ground.

Swirls of pain clouded her head, and a warm, metallic taste seeped onto her tongue. Gwendolyn touched the corner of her mouth, then stared numbly at the blood wetting her fingers. Slowly she raised her eyes to him. Gone was the soulful remorse that she had imagined seeing in him but a moment earlier. The man who glared down at her now was the Robert she knew: cruel, avaricious, and utterly ruthless.

"Surprised?" he drawled. "Poor Gwendolyn. Did you actually think I could be the simpering idiot I was pretending to be?"

"I thought even you might have some fragment of morality buried deep within your blackened soul," she replied, shaken. "I was wrong."

"So you were," he agreed, amused. "But do not despair. In another moment I shall be king of Scotland, and then I will put you out of your misery." He braced his legs apart and lifted the stone reverently toward the roiling sky. "I, Robert of Clan MacSween, command you to make me the most powerful king and mightiest ruler of Scotland, invincible to all!"

A blinding sheet of lightning painted the sky white, followed by a deafening explosion of thunder.

Gwendolyn slowly rose and stared at Robert. He stood with his arms outstretched and his eyes closed, the jewel gripped tightly in one hand as he waited for his transformation to finish. It was over, she realized, overwhelmed by the magnitude of her failure. Not only was Robert king, but he had wished for invincibility as well. No one could stop him now. A sob rose from the back of her throat.

"Good Lord, such a blast!" sang out a cheerful voice through the darkness. "That was truly marvelous, I tell you. I expect my ears will be ringing for days."

No, thought Gwendolyn as horror surged through her. *Please God, don't let him be here.*

A lone rider was casually weaving his way through the standing stones, moving at such a leisurely pace one might think he was out for a pleasure ride. His ghostly silhouette was tall and broad, and the powerful horse he rode moved with a deliberately controlled stride, as if the beast were in no greater hurry than his master. A bright shaft of moonlight pierced the darkness as the warrior drew forward, turning his hair to gold and lighting every magnificent detail of him, from the insouciant expression on his handsome face to the relaxed stature of his enormous body. MacDunn had come here alone, Gwendolyn realized, no doubt believing he would fight Robert on fair and equal terms. It was of no consequence whether madness or foolish naïveté had caused him to behave in such a reckless manner. The conclusion was inevitable.

MacDunn was about to die.

"Good evening, m'lady," Alex said, offering her a courtly bow from his mount. "It is an absolutely splendid night, is it not? I must say, ever since that last storm of yours, I have grown inordinately fond of thunder."

Gwendolyn stared at him, speechless, her eyes filled with tears. No warning could protect him from Robert's newly acquired invincibility. Nor could she tell him in these final moments that she loved him, for fear that Robert might take pleasure in torturing MacDunn to further torment her.

"What a pleasant surprise, MacDunn," sneered Robert. "For a moment I actually feared I was going to have to ride all the way back to your holding to kill you. This is far more convenient—although rest assured, I do intend to return and slaughter everyone in your clan, down to the last squalling babe."

"Good Lord, Robert," Alex sputtered, "whatever have you done to your hair?"

Robert's hand self-conciously flew to the ludicrously charred ends. "The witch did it," he snarled, glaring at Gwendolyn. "And she will pay for it handsomely."

Alex blinked. "But why would she cast a spell to make you look so thoroughly absurd?"

"She didn't do it with a spell!" snapped Robert. "She did it with a torch. Now if we could proceed with the matter at hand—"

"You burned his hair off with a torch?" interrupted Alex, looking incredulously at Gwendolyn.

She nodded.

"Next time, try a pair of scissors," he advised amiably. "I think you'll find the results are far more even."

"You may be interested to know, MacDunn, that I am now ruler of Scotland," Robert announced grandly.

Alex raised his brows. "How fascinating. Does King William know about this?"

"I expect he does," replied Robert, not sounding overly certain.

"Well, if you have become king, surely you must have defeated him in some great battle. I can't see how he would fail to notice a thing like that."

Robert's mouth curved in a thin smile. "All I did was use this stone." He held the precious gem between his thumb and forefinger. "It has made me the mightiest ruler in the land."

Alex cocked his head to one side. "Your pardon, Robert, but you don't look very mighty," he observed candidly. "If that stone can grant wishes, perhaps you should wish for your hair to grow back—and maybe for your face to be cleaned up a bit—"

"Enough!" Robert snarled, exasperated.

Alex shrugged. "Well, then, now that you're king, what are you going to do?"

Robert smiled and drew his sword from its sheath. "The first thing I'm going to do, you mad idiot, is kill you."

"No!" cried Gwendolyn. "Please, Robert, I beg you, do not do this. I will do whatever you say—just let him live!"

"You will do whatever I say regardless of what happens to him," he said harshly. "And now that the stone has given me this power, you are of no further use to me anyway." He waved his sword at Alex. "Come down off your horse, Mad MacDunn, and meet your death."

"Don't do it, MacDunn!" Gwendolyn cried, rushing toward him. Tears spilled down her cheeks as she clung to his heavily muscled leg, trying to hold him to his mount. "Ride away!" she pleaded softly. "You still have a chance if you just turn and ride away!"

Alex's expression remained a cross between amusement and bewilderment. "Really, m'lady, your lack of faith in me is almost insulting."

"You don't understand," said Gwendolyn desperately. "Robert cannot be defeated—the stone has given him that power! No matter how bravely you fight, you will die. You have a son who needs you and a clan who must have your protection." She pressed her forehead against his thigh and finished in a ragged whisper, "I beg you, Alex, do not sacrifice yourself for nothing."

Alex gently tipped her chin up with his fingers, forcing her to meet his gaze. No hint of madness clouded the piercing blue of his eyes, and even the insouciance he had affected but an instant earlier had vanished. "You are not nothing to me, Gwendolyn," he said, his voice achingly low and reverent. He tenderly caressed her tear-streaked cheek as he finished roughly, "You are *everything*."

Gwendolyn stared at him in wonder as she slowly absorbed the meaning of his words, his touch, the solemn, powerful intensity of his gaze. And then she shook her head and glared at him, fighting her emotions, knowing that if she opened her heart to him, they would both surely die.

"I cannot be everything to you," she informed him coldly. She shoved his hand away and stepped back. "I am a witch, and I need no one. Do you understand? Now stop being such a fool and ride away, before Robert hacks your mad head from your body!"

Alex regarded her a long moment. She was pretending indifference, but her gray eyes were glittering with fear and her hands were gripping her cloak so tightly her knuckles looked like tiny bleached pebbles beneath the taut skin.

"Come, MacDunn," Robert called out gleefully, waving his sword in the air. "I haven't got all night, you know."

A brilliant flash of lightning creased the sky.

"Trust me, Gwendolyn," Alex urged softly, ignoring Robert. "I vowed to protect you, and I will. Not because you belong to me," he added, seeing her about to protest. "But because without you, I am lost."

Tears dripped down her cheeks. "If you care at all about me, then you will turn and ride away before he kills you."

Alex swung himself down from his horse. "Just try to keep the rain off awhile longer," he said, unsheathing his sword. "I do dislike fighting in the rain." He winked at her, then turned and walked toward Robert.

"At last." Robert held his sword out before him.

"Really, Robert, I never knew you were so fond of fighting," said Alex, leaning casually against his own weapon. "Did you not receive enough attention as a lad?"

"Try to distract me if you wish," retorted Robert, slowly circling him. "It will not affect the outcome of this battle."

"Ah, yes, Gwendolyn has told me that you are now invincible. Seems to me that takes some of the amusement out of swordplay."

"Believe me, MacDunn, the fact that I know you are about to die does not mar the perfection of this moment in the slightest," Robert assured him, moving closer.

Alex meticulously adjusted one of the pleats in his plaid. "I'm delighted that you're enjoying yourself. Just let me know when you are ready to begin."

"We have already begun, you mad fool!" Robert snapped. "Prepare to die!" He charged toward him.

Alex made a final, minor modification to the drape of his mantle, then raised his sword just in time to deflect Robert's powerful blow.

The crash of steel filled the night, with silver sparks exploding into the air each time the sharp edges of their blades met. The two warriors were more than equally matched, for Alex met Robert's thrusts blow for blow, driving him back a few steps before Robert forced Alex to relinquish some ground. Lightning webbed the black cloak of sky around them, punctuating the clang of metal with a deafening crash and drowning the hard grunts the warriors made as each struggled to gain the advantage.

"You cannot win, MacDunn," Robert ground out, trying to wrest Alex's sword from him. "You might as well surrender and let me finish you off quickly."

"That's exceptionally gallant of you, Robert," observed Alex. "Forgive me if I seem ungrateful, but I do enjoy a good fight now and again."

"As you wish." Robert sliced down suddenly, raking the edge of his sword across Alex's chest.

Hot blood leaked down his torso and seeped into his shirt.

"You see?" said Robert, smiling as he surveyed the damage. "You cannot best me, MacDunn. I am unconquerable."

"So you keep saying," returned Alex, clenching his jaw as the pain burned through his chest. "But if that is so, Robert, why are you taking so long to kill me? Surely as ruler of Scotland you have far more urgent matters to attend to." He frowned. "Could it be that stone you're clutching is nothing but a pretty pendant?"

Robert roared with rage and charged toward him. Alex held his sword low, then raised it in a powerful arc at the last moment, propelling Robert's weapon to the side as Alex swiftly slashed at his upper arm. Robert howled with pain and staggered back, staring in confusion at the scarlet stream racing down toward his wrist.

"If you wish, we can stop and have Gwendolyn take a look at that for you," Alex offered graciously. "I think you'll find she's exceptionally handy with a needle and a few strands of hair."

"I'm going to kill you!"

"As you wish," said Alex, shrugging. "Let us continue."

Gwendolyn watched in mute horror as the two men raised their swords and began again, each hacking at the other with savage determination. Despite Alex's affected bravado, she could see that he was not impervious to the wound in his chest, for each time he lifted his sword he winced, and his shirt grew dark and heavy with blood. Still he crashed his sword against Robert's blade again and again, forcing his opponent to dance backward. Moonlight spilled in a pale aura over the two warriors, etching them in a ghostly light as they battled amid the ancient stones.

"You have fought well, MacDunn," Robert admitted, breathing heavily. "However, as you have pointed out, I have more important matters to attend to. The time has come for you to die."

Alex immediately lowered his sword and stepped back. "Very well, then, Robert. Do what you will."

Gripping his sword in both hands, Robert let out a triumphant roar and charged forward, his eyes afire with victory.

Please God, pleaded Gwendolyn, her heart shattering, *please God, don't let him die.*

Alex held his ground, waiting until the last second.

And then he suddenly spun aside and drove his own sword deep into Robert's gut.

"No," said Robert, staring in astonishment at the cold strip of silver disappearing into his belly. He raised his eyes to Alex. "It cannot be. I—I cannot be defeated. I am invincible."

"Forgive me, Robert," said Alex, "but you must have been mistaken about that." He yanked his sword from Robert's stomach, releasing a gush of scarlet onto the ground.

"You have not won, MacDunn," Robert said through gritted teeth. He raised his blood-drenched fingers to his mouth and managed a shrill whistle. "My men will enjoy hacking both of you to pieces," he spat, clutching his bleeding belly as he sank to his knees. "But first they will use you like a whore," he finished, casting a vicious smile at Gwendolyn.

She glanced fearfully at the crest of the hill, waiting for Robert's warriors to thunder into sight.

No one appeared.

Alex sighed. "Unfortunately, I believe your men are otherwise engaged," he said apologetically. "I hope you don't mind, but I asked my men to keep them entertained while I visited with you."

Undiluted rage contorted Robert's pain-clenched face. He gripped the jewel in his fist, as if trying to squeeze some last drop of strength from it.

Alex sheathed his bloodied sword and turned to face Gwendolyn.

"Come, Gwendolyn," he said gently, holding his hand out to her. "It is time to—"

"*No!*" she screamed, her eyes wide with terror.

Alex turned just in time to see Robert on his feet, slicing his raised sword toward Alex's head. He instinctively reached for his own weapon, knowing he could never liberate it before Robert cleaved his skull.

Fly, commanded Gwendolyn, locking her gaze on Robert's discarded dirk. *Fly into his back and kill him.*

Lightning lashed across the sky, and for one agonizing moment everything froze.

"My God," Robert murmured, his sword locked in mid-air. He stared at Gwendolyn a long moment, as if he had never really seen her before.

And then he collapsed onto the ground, the hilt of his dirk protruding from his back.

Gwendolyn raised her hand to her mouth as she stared in horror at Robert's lifeless body. She searched the darkness beyond, looking for the warrior who had found the dirk and hurled it through the air.

There was no one.

Horrified, she dropped her gaze to Robert once more. A dark stain was rapidly soaking the fabric of his shirt.

"I—I didn't mean to," she stammered.

"I know," Alex said quietly. He stooped and retrieved the stone from Robert's grasp.

She shook her head, struggling to understand what she had done. "He was going to kill you and . . . I couldn't bear it. I had to stop him." She began to tremble. "It was just a thought. I didn't think it would actually happen."

"You saved my life. And you needed to call upon your powers to do it."

"I don't have any powers, MacDunn!" she objected desperately. "I never have. I let you believe that I did because I was afraid you would send me back to the MacSweens if you knew the truth, but . . . I am not really a witch."

Alex wrapped his arms around her and pulled her close, heedless of the bloody wound in his chest. "You're wrong, my love," he murmured, grazing his fingers against her tear-stained cheek. "You have powers that you have inherited through the women of your line. Your mother did not have them, but you do. And that is why your mother entrusted you with this stone," he explained, placing the chain around her neck. "It does not grant wishes, as you and Robert believed. It is to keep the gifted girls of your line safe, until their powers have matured."

"No," she protested, shivering. "You're wrong."

"Think, Gwendolyn," he urged, gently stroking her hair. "You conjured up a storm the night I asked you to demonstrate your abilities to me . . ."

"That was just a coincidence—"

". . . and then you made it pour rain when Robert set the cottages afire . . ."

"That storm was coming anyway—I didn't start it—"

"Then how do you explain that dirk in Robert's back?" he demanded quietly.

"I don't know!" she cried, burying her head against his shoulder. "It just happened!"

"Hush, now," he soothed, tightening his hold on her as he caressed her back. "It's all right, my love. You're safe now."

Gwendolyn wept against him as he held her. All her life she had been accused of being a witch, but there had been a modicum of solace in knowing that these allegations were false, even if she was the only one who knew it. Yet she could not deny the powerful sensation that had swept through her as she commanded Robert's dirk to kill him.

She had made that dirk fly through the air with nothing but the force of her will.

MacDunn stiffened suddenly.

"What is it?" she asked, pulling away.

"We have company."

The ground began to rumble from the pounding of hooves. Gwendolyn looked up the hill to see a wave of riders pouring down the slope, many carrying torches. As they drew near, she could see that the MacDunn warriors were being led by Cameron, Brodick, and Ned.

"Good evening, Gwendolyn," Cameron called out jovially, reigning in his horse beside her. He raised his sword and drew a silvery circle in the air, signaling for the warriors to form a ring around Alex and Gwendolyn.

"We thought we would join you because you're about to have some visitors," Brodick explained, tilting his head toward the woods. He glanced at Robert's lifeless body. "I see you finally killed the bastard."

"Actually, Gwendolyn killed him," Alex said.

"MacSween won't like that," Ned predicted, moving protectively closer to her.

At that moment some fifty riders burst from the surrounding woods. They halted when they saw the MacDunn warriors positioned in a circle of fire around Alex and Gwendolyn, but their swords remained drawn and glinting in the torchlight.

"Good evening, MacDunn," said Laird MacSween, riding to the front of his men. His gaze swept over Gwendolyn, then fell to the limp, bleeding form of his brother. Regret shadowed his features.

"He had to die, MacSween," Alex said grimly. "He murdered Gwendolyn's father for his own selfish gain, then falsely accused her of the murder. And he further poisoned his accusations with lies about witchcraft and evil, so that instead of listening to Gwendolyn as you should have, you wrongly convicted her." His tone was heavy with condemnation.

MacSween's expression grew even more desolate. "I have long known that my brother was avaricious," he confessed quietly, "but I did not believe he would ever bring harm to a member of his own clan."

"She is of your clan no longer, MacSween," Alex said in a hard voice. "She is a MacDunn now. If you or any of your clan ever try to harm her again, I will kill you."

"And so will I," added Cameron, raising his sword. "Even if it should cost me my life."

"And I," said Brodick, also lifting his weapon.

"And I," vowed Ned.

"And I," added Munro.

Gwendolyn stared at the MacDunns in astonishment. The pledge spilled around the circle of warriors in a slow ripple as each man solemnly vowed to protect her. Every warrior lifted his sword or his torch as he made his pledge, until a magnificent ring of silver and gold gleamed against the roiling sky.

Overwhelmed with emotion, Gwendolyn blinked and

looked away, unable to comprehend why these brave men would be willing to sacrifice themselves for her.

"The men Robert brought with him to attack my holding are bound and waiting just over the crest of that hill," Alex told Laird MacSween. "If I have your assurance that you will let us return to our home in peace, MacSween, you may retrieve them. And you are also welcome to take Robert's body with you," he added, "so that he may have a decent burial."

MacSween nodded and gave the command for two of his men to fetch Robert's body and his horse. Once they had done so, he hesitated.

"Forgive me, MacDunn, but I must know—how does my Isabella fare?" The roughness of his tone suggested that he had suffered greatly in his concern for her.

His fatherly anguish prompted Gwendolyn to find her voice. "She is well, MacSween," she replied, anxious to put him at ease. "The MacDunns have treated her with honor and kindness, and no man has ever dishonored her."

His eyes lit with hope. "Do you think she will come home, then?"

"No," interjected Brodick, before Alex could tell MacSween that he would happily have her delivered back to her home within the week.

Everyone stared at him in surprise.

"Isabella is to be my wife," Brodick stated flatly. His voice was gruff as he added, "I'm certain it would please her, MacSween, if you were to give us your blessing."

MacSween studied him a moment, his expression puzzled. "Are you not the warrior who held a dirk to her throat and threatened to kill her while a guest at my home?"

"I am. My name is Brodick."

"My daughter had much to say about you. I'm surprised to see you are still alive and of sound body. Since you are, I commend you on your fortitude, and give you my blessing."

Brodick smiled. "I will bring Isabella to you for a visit, MacSween, once we are wed."

"I shall look forward to it," the laird assured him. "I bid you and your men a safe journey, MacDunn." He nodded a final time to Alex, then turned his horse and led his men up the hill to retrieve Robert's warriors.

"We'd best take to the woods and make camp for the night," said Cameron, studying the sky. "This storm is likely to break any moment."

"Maybe Gwendolyn could stop it from coming," suggested Brodick.

"She has had enough to deal with tonight without having to change the weather just to please you," objected Ned. "She just killed Robert, for God's sake."

"Aye, that's true," agreed Cameron. "The lass is tired."

"We don't mind a good storm, lass," added Munro cheerfully, "so don't ye worry about it."

"I've grown rather fond of them, actually," remarked Ewan, "ever since you conjured up that beast of a gale when Robert attacked."

"Now, *that* was a storm," reminisced Garrick enthusiastically. "Remember how she stood on the parapet with the wind blowing around her—"

" 'Twas almost as if she was floating in the air," interjected Quentin, "like something not of this world. . . ."

The warriors swiftly disappeared into the woods, still discussing the wonder of Gwendolyn's storm.

Gwendolyn stared after them a long moment. And when their voices had died and the last flicker of golden flames had faded amid the trees, she slowly raised her gaze to MacDunn.

He stood tall and powerful before her, etched against the darkness in a filmy veil of moonlight. His shirt was torn and drenched in blood, but he seemed utterly impervious to his injury as he gazed back at her. No hint of madness clouded the penetrating blue of his gaze, nor was the desire she had come to know so well heating his tender study of her.

"Why did you come after me?" she finally managed, her voice barely a whisper.

Alex reached out and gently traced the contour of her jaw. "For years now, I have waged a battle with myself I feared I could never win," he confessed quietly. "My battle raged the hardest in the first year after my wife died. I wanted to die as well, so I didn't give a damn about the instability of my mind. Eventually, however, I remembered that I had a son and a clan who needed me, and so I forced myself to control my fancies and rages, until I could generally appear sound in front of others. But it was a lie. I was drowning, and I lived in constant fear that one day I would no longer be able to fight the waves crashing over me." His voice grew rough with emotion as he added, "When David fell ill, I knew that day had come."

"But David is well now, MacDunn," Gwendolyn assured him. "For whatever reason, his body began to reject certain foods. But if he refrains from ever eating them, I believe he will continue to grow strong and well."

"I know. And as he healed, so did I, until I felt as if I were in control of myself again. But then you left," he said hoarsely, "and it was as if I had been torn apart." He grasped her hand and reverently kissed her palm, then pressed it firmly against his bleeding chest. "Marry me, Gwendolyn," he pleaded, fighting to keep his voice from breaking. "Marry me, and I swear I will love you and keep you safe until my dying breath. Not because you belong to me," he added, capturing with his finger the silver drop that was trickling down her cheek, "but because without you, I am lost."

"But I am a witch," Gwendolyn protested, her voice small and quivering.

"And I am a mad laird," he countered irreverently, shrugging. "We are a perfect match."

Gwendolyn swallowed and shook her head. "When your people learn of my powers, they will want to drive me away—"

"My people have always believed you had great powers," Alex interrupted, "including my son, who absolutely adores you. The only person for whom this is a revelation is you. As for your being driven away, it was Robena who tried so relentlessly to make you leave, and her motives were far more mundane than any noble desire to protect the clan. She will not touch you again."

His heart beat strong and steady against her palm as the blood from his wound wet her fingers. In that moment she could feel his love pouring into her, through flesh and muscle and bone, penetrating her being as it filled her with warmth and courage—the courage she needed to love, and to be loved in return. MacDunn had said that without her he was lost. He was wrong, she realized, feeling a wobbly, guarded joy begin to flood through her.

It was she who was lost without him.

With a tiny cry, she raised herself on her toes and wrapped her arms tightly around his massive shoulders. "Yes," she murmured, her lips barely a breath from his. "I will marry you, Mad MacDunn."

Alex hauled her up against him and crushed his mouth to hers. Something small and hard bit into his chest. Wincing slightly, he relaxed his hold on her.

"What is it?" asked Gwendolyn worriedly. "Does your wound pain you? Shall I stitch it now?"

"It is not the wound," he assured her. He grasped the pendant nestled at her breasts and raised it to the moonlight, enabling him to better study the glittering stone in its gold setting. Suddenly he began to laugh.

"What's so funny?"

"I was just thinking about what a time I am in for," he mused, pulling her close once more, "if we should have a daughter."

"Oh, no!" gasped Gwendolyn. "You don't think my pow-ers—"

"I am hoping, Gwendolyn," he told her, tenderly caressing the pale silk of her cheek. "When I think of the happiness just one witch has brought me, I find myself utterly enchanted by the possibility of having two."

He bent his head and kissed her deeply, sharing the healing power of his love. And then he tightened his embrace and laughed again, his mind whole and his heart sure as he led his beloved witch out of the garden of ancient stones and into the wonder of their new life.

ABOUT THE AUTHOR

KARYN MONK has been writing since she was a girl. In university she discovered a love for history. After several years working in the highly charged world of advertising, she turned to writing historical romance. She is married to a wonderfully romantic husband, Philip, whom she allows to believe is the model for her heroes.

"A REMARKABLE NEW VOICE IN HISTORICAL ROMANCE."
—*Nationally bestselling author Jane Feather*

Karyn Monk

Once a Warrior 🐍

A medieval Scottish tale of a Highland beauty desperate to save her clan, and a shattered hero fighting for redemption—and fighting for love. ___57422-1 $5.99/$7.99 Can.

The Witch and the Warrior 🐍

A tale of an unearthly beauty, wrongly condemned for witchcraft, and the fierce and handsome Highland warrior who saves her from death so that she may save his dying son. ___57760-3 $5.99/$7.99 Can.

Ask for these books at your local bookstore or use this page to order.

Please send me the books I have checked above. I am enclosing $____ (add $2.50 to cover postage and handling). Send check or money order, no cash or C.O.D.'s, please.

Name _____

Address _____

City/State/Zip _____

Send order to: Bantam Books, Dept. FN 13 , 2451 S. Wolf Rd., Des Plaines, IL 60018

Allow four to six weeks for delivery.

Prices and availability subject to change without notice.   FN 13 4/98